FIREFAX

A. M. VERGARA

FIREFAX

By A.M. Vergara

For Danger Girl.
I am happy to report it was worth it, after all.

PROLOGUE

February 19, 1781
Vermont Republic

"By God, what happened here?"

The voice was familiar, and full of horror, but it was a thousand, no—a million miles away from the young woman kneeling on the packed frozen earth of the pasture. She had been there for . . . she considered, finally deciding with a faint smile that she had always been there, since the dawn of time. She frowned, wrinkling her nose, noticing for the first time that her spectacles were gone. She considered lifting her head to look for them, but no, she could not do that. She could not see the blood all around her—so much blood. She could not see the carnage visited upon the snow-crusted, frozen dirt. She had only just reached that faraway place where everything that had happened was a dream, a hideous nightmare, but just a dream after all, and if she stayed where she was, then it would all go away forever, and very soon.

"There she is!" cried another voice, softer, warmer, full of relief, and she heard running footsteps crunching dully through the snow.

"Is she all right?"

"I don't . . . I don't know. Cara? Cara, are you all right? Can you talk to me?"

She frowned again but lifted her head a little, enough to see that there was nothing to see anymore. Everything was mercifully dark. There were vague, eerie shapes all around, black earth making grotesque silhouettes in twisted white patches of snow. There was someone crouched before her, a young man, squeezing her shoulder and holding a lantern up to illuminate her face. It was the faint warmth of the lantern that made her realize how cold she was. Cold through and through, as cold as death, as cold as the two lifeless corpses lying nearby in the dirt. The young man removed his coat and draped it over her, and, for the first time in hours, she shivered. It was Raf, she realized through the fog clouding her hypothermic mind. Dear, sweet Raf.

"Is Robert there?" Rafael asked. As he spoke, he took her hands, hanging forgotten at her sides, and gently rubbed them between his own, blowing upon them with warm, life-giving breaths. The warmth was surreal. So different from the cold that had become her all-consuming reality.

"Yes," said the other voice from the darkness, and there was a strange, heavy finality to that word. She blinked, still feeling that this was all a dream. Her brothers were not there. She had conjured them out of the horror to bring her comfort. Her stolid life-long companions, Henry and Rafael.

"Is he—"

"He's dead, Raf. He's dead."

She heard Rafael sigh, a long, slow sigh, and then felt him tucking her frigid hands under his armpits. He touched her face, bringing it toward him, and she did not fight his touch, but she did not look at him either. She continued staring straight ahead, quiet, unmoving, unthinking. She did not dare think.

"The horse?" asked Rafael.

"The mare's dead too," replied Henry, his voice soft, almost inaudible to his stunned sister. "That's where all the blood came from. It's not Robert's. It's awful."

"What happened?" asked Rafael. "Are there any signs that someone else was here? Signs of a fight?"

Henry appeared out of the darkness. His youthful, pudgy face, with its endearing smile creases, looked old and strained to Cara, so unlike the ever-cheerful, fatherly, encouraging older brother she knew. "No. I think the horse killed Robert. Just based on what I can make out in the dark. He's still tangled in the stirrups. And then . . ."

"And then she killed the horse." Rafael finished, and a strange, ominous change came into his voice.

Cara shuddered hard at that but did not speak or look up, her eyes still staring off into nothing. She was annoyed. Why did they bring this all up? Why were her brothers torturing her with these reminders of what had happened in that nightmare? How could they be so cruel? She had only done what she had been taught to do for as long as she could remember. There was a threat, a threat against her father, and she had neutralized that threat. She had done what her brothers and her father had always stopped her from doing before.

She winced as she saw again the vision, as real as the cool, penetrating mist surrounding the three siblings, as real as the ice beneath them. She could see the languid, graceful rise and fall of the horse's gait as she galloped. Beautiful. Such gorgeous, effortless motion, muscles rippling all across the fiery red mare's body. Then came the bucking. It was beautiful too, sinuous, dance-like motions, up and down, and up again, until the man she loved most in all the world fell, his head cracking backward, buckling unnaturally upon his neck the instant he hit the ground. But it was not the angle of his twisted neck or the dent in his skull that made her shudder. It was his eyes, his face that haunted her. She had seen his face in that last instant, before he hit the ground, before the light went out from his eyes. She had acted, yes, but she had acted too late. She shuddered again and then, as if she was finally unfrozen, she toppled forward into Rafael's arms.

"I've got her!" cried Rafael, and then he whispered into her ear, "I've got you." He hoisted her up in his arms, and she felt him struggling a little beneath her tall, gangly form. "It's too late to sort it all out now and she's . . . she's not well, Henry. We need to get her warmed up. We can figure out what to do with the bodies in the morning. We'll make more sense of it all in the light of day, anyway."

"Not long to wait for that. It'll be morning soon," replied Henry, and Cara saw the faint, dull yellow glow in the east.

Her brothers began their long trek back to the farmhouse, leaving the gore of the pasture and the two frozen bodies behind. Rafael, still cradling his sister's ice-cold form, whispered in her ear over and over again, "You're all right, Cara. You're all right. We'll get you warmed up and you'll see. You'll be just fine."

Cara shivered, feeling not horror, not pain, but the sense deep within her that Rafael was wrong. She would never be fine again. She had seen for the first time in her life that there was a killer within her, like the one inside her brothers, like the one that had been inside her father, but a killer much more cruel, more ruthless, and more deadly than any of them.

Chapter 1

A Matter Of
Vital Importance

1781 ⚔ Early March
New York City, New York

A young man with brilliant green eyes stood silent in the narrow room, his back to the door. The small, dusty office was largely empty, furnished only by a desk, behind which sat a chair nearly lost beneath the girth of a plump older man, and a few bookcases and closed chests lining the wood-paneled walls. Shafts of fading evening light streamed through two curtainless windows, and the creaking of carriage wheels and jingling of harnesses drifted faintly in from the streets beyond.

The plump man cracked his knuckles as he studied the green-eyed youth, each joint making a resounding pop in the quiet of the office. Parbleu had known the young man nearly all the boy's life. His proper name was Istäni, but in the network they called him Noaidi. Parbleu had known him since the day the agent they called Thrayder had brought him, tiny, silent, and studying, into the midst of their intelligence network.

"He's not my son," was all Thrayder had said in the way of providing background on the child. That much had been obvious; no one would mistake the beautiful child for the son of that hideous man. It was little wonder that Istäni had grown into such a strange, impenetrable adult, raised and trained as he had been by the mysterious Thrayder, the best agent they'd ever had, and the one that got away. Parbleu did not like that Thrayder's protégé had come calling today, dressed in his strange, archaic green tunic, sporting at least a rapier and a pistol, though probably that was only the tip of the arsenal concealed among the young man's garments. No, he did not like that the boy had come at all.

"My dear Noaidi," Parbleu finally gathered himself and tried unsuccessfully to exude confidence under the young man's unnerving, mesmerizing stare. "I am sensible of your plight, I really am. Who among us is not somewhat obsessed with our own personal struggles? However, you cannot be allowed to endanger another mission. I know it is your vision. You're the one who supplied the information and secured the funding, but I've been in council with some of the others, Lottie and even Silver, to name a few. It has been determined that you are not to lead another mission. Not until you've learned some self-control. Your personal grudges and ambitions cannot get in the way of our unified goals. *Bonum commune communitatis* and all that . . ." He trailed off as he spoke the last few words, swallowing nervously and reaching up to loosen his cravat.

Istäni's eyes suddenly seemed to catch fire, becoming somehow brighter as passion flooded across his face. Parbleu forced himself to look down.

"I did not ask for your permission, Parbleu. I've already secured funding for this project and I'm not passing it off to some incompetent sod." Istäni's voice, with its lilting, untraceable accent, held a faint hint of danger. "All I am telling you to do is to give me a list of the contacts in Boston."

"Indeed, yes," blustered Parbleu, swelling his chest out. "Yes, well, I don't believe the major would condone my giving you that information. I'm sorry, you will have to go to him yourself, and return with a signed order."

Istäni sneered, a twisted, condescending smile, almost pitying. "You misunderstand me, my dear old fellow. Perhaps it's my accent? I have been authorized and funded to find Lubrerum. You are obstructing me. What do you think the major would think of that?" Then, without another word, he slipped past the desk and tossed open one of the chests behind Parbleu, overflowing with heaps of papers, all painstakingly encoded.

"You can't!" cried Parbleu, turning excitedly from Istäni to the door and then back again, as if expecting someone else to appear and enforce his frantic orders. "What do you think you're doing? You can't look through those!"

Istäni continued rummaging among the dusty parchments, tossing them away in turn after a brief scan revealed they did not contain the information he sought. As he worked, he said, "What are you afraid of, Parbleu? Do you think I'm a traitor? If you consider me a threat, I wonder why you haven't had me killed. Yes, I know you've tried, three times now, but all rather half-hearted attempts, weren't they? Has the major not given you permission to kill off the best agent you have?"

At the casual accusation Parbleu let out a dismayed choking sound that faded into a low whine.

Hardly seeming to notice the older man's reaction, Istäni continued, "Last year, in Charlestown, you pitted me against Thrayder. I am surprised that your opinion of my skill is so low that you imagined it inferior to his. I would have killed him, had it not been for that meddling new boy of theirs.

Then I suppose Charlotte's lobster could be considered an attempt upon my life, though it was even clumsier than the first. Poison, isn't that a bit primitive? And the day Rounder shot at me was the third attempt, though you meant that to look like an accident. Actually, there were four attempts, weren't there?"

"No, no, there weren't," the older man squeaked, then gathered himself and deepened his tone. "I don't know what you're trying to say. There have been no attacks, no attempts of any kind. You're a respected, indeed, a crucial member of our network, Noaidi."

"Your fourth attempt was very recent. Your marksman did manage to rip my coat, but that is all that he achieved. Tell me, Parbleu, did you decide to have me killed when I first sent word that I was coming today, or was it not until you heard that I was wearing my hunting doublet?"

Istäni paused in shuffling through the papers and gently laid his hand upon the rapier hilt hanging at his left side. He was smiling, the pleasant, joyful creases making his eyes stand out even more, accentuated by the old-fashioned emerald tunic he wore. Noaidi never killed without his archaic green costume—everyone knew that, every agent in the network. The young man moved his hand to touch the new tear on his sleeve with tenderness, almost lovingly. The moment passed and Istäni went back to sifting through the documents in the chest, as Parbleu's breathing grew harsh behind him. The older man was mouth breathing in coarse, shaky gasps, the sound of ragged, unfiltered fear. Istäni could almost hear Parbleu's thoughts, could see without looking that the man was drawing the knife from his boot, the one he always carried there, and reaching for his pistol at the same time.

Istäni let one hand trail over his own pistol, stuffed in the center of his belt, but drew back, shifting instead to his right side and fondling the axe hanging there. It was a small, ancient-looking weapon, little more than a hatchet in size, with an exquisite whalebone handle, and intricate carvings that laced up the handle and into the dark metal of the blade, strange twisting, sinuous shapes and symbols. The axe would do, he decided. Parbleu did not deserve to die so sophisticated a death as the rapier would afford him. The pistol too was just a little too good for the conniving old weasel.

The axe slid from its loop easily, and he turned about to face Parbleu, who stood trembling with his back to the door, a knife in one hand, a pistol in the other. Parbleu was panting, wearing the crazed, horrified expression of a man without hope, facing his own mortality. Istäni was still grinning.

"What's the matter, old friend?" Istäni inquired, his voice gently mocking. "Have you not yet made peace with your maker? I have time, Parbleu; confess and commit your soul. I will wait."

"No! You fool, I have a gun, I could kill you. In a second. Without a thought. I could kill you now. Before you even get near me, with your blasted, barbaric axe. Don't try it, Mr. Seänkea. That's right, I know your proper name! Istäni Seänkea. Don't move . . . stay put. I said don't move!" Sweat dribbled from the plump man's face, and his eyes were rolling with fear, his pistol jerking violently. "Rounder missed you, but he was far away! I can't miss! Don't try it! I'm warning you, don't try it!"

Wordless, Istäni crossed the distance between them. A loud, shattering bang broke the tension in the room, but the old man trembled so severely that Istäni did not even need to dodge. Parbleu dropped the empty pistol, smoke pouring from its barrel, and took one step backward. He fell upon his knees, as if weak and powerless, utter despair inscribed across his sagging countenance, gazing up at his advancing doom. Istäni stopped before him and raised the axe high above his head. The young man had entered a shaft of light from the open window, which reflected off his eyes, making them seem for an instant almost as bright as the sun, as fearsome as the coming of the Lord's Judgment.

Parbleu let out a garbled cry and threw himself at the young man's knees, driving his knife deep into Istäni's thigh, through flesh, muscle, nerve, and blood vessels. Then he tore the blade out, ripping the wound wide. He was trembling too hard to hold on to the knife and it fell with a clatter to the floorboards. He shoved at the young man, trying to crawl past him, and Istäni lost his balance, falling backward but catching himself with one hand. Istäni twisted, pushing himself upward and swinging the axe down on Parbleu's head with fantastic strength. There was a sound of bone crunching, and an arc of scarlet raindrops, and then the pudgy old man lay still, his bald head a mass of blood, shattered fragments of bone, and the white, stewy liquid of brain.

In agony, Istäni grasped at the laceration on his thigh. Blood spurted rhythmically from the wound, cascading fountains of rich maroon. His handsome, tan face had become ghostly pale as he clutched at the cut. He undid his belt hurriedly and bound it above the wound. Then, taking the axe handle, he twisted it in the belt, tightening and tightening until at last the fountain of blood slowed and then trickled to a stop. He paused, securing the axe in place, panting. Then, rallying his strength, he peered at the bloody wound, looking for the severed artery.

He pulled out the whalebone needle habitually stashed in his cuff and tore a string of thread from his jacket. He sewed quickly, without grimace or groan of pain, deft movements in the still-oozing wound, sweat dripping down his face as he worked. Finally finished repairing the vessels and skin, he released the axe, letting the blood flow return to his leg. The spurting did not start anew, just a gentle ooze from the expertly sewn laceration. He closed his eyes, leaning back again on the gory wooden floor. A new smile, a weary, triumphant smile, spread across his gray, clammy face.

He waited, listening to the faint sounds from the street outside, for any noise that might indicate someone looking for the source of Parbleu's shot. But one pistol shot was not enough to concern anyone in that enormous, bustling new-world city. Satisfied with the undisturbed traffic outside, Istäni struggled to his feet, wiping the blood from his hands onto his equally bloody breeches. "*Bonum commune communitatis*, and all that, Mr. Parbleu," he said, with a nod toward the still form on the floor and then turned back to the chests against the wall.

1781 ⚔ MID-MARCH
BOSTON, MASSACHUSETTS

Though it was early in the evening, the tavern tables were already packed. It was cold outside and the ale warmed the grubby men gathering to their tankards. Nestled in the corner of the crowded room, a lanky man sprawled lazily in his chair, speaking to no one, listening idly to the low chatter around him. His clothing was dirty and disheveled. Though he still kept his jacket on, half the buttons of his waistcoat and shirt were undone to make allowance for the relative heat of the crowded alehouse. On his neck, a jagged white scar traced along his trachea, past his protruding Adam's apple, then cut abruptly toward his left shoulder, disappearing under his shirt. His long arms draped over the back of his chair and his legs stretched out before him, his muddy boots resting on a chair on the other side of the narrow table. His face was mostly concealed beneath the shadow of a drooping chapeau, but the tip of his sharp nose projected from beneath the brim, and in the dark space between the hat and nose, two eyes, so dark brown they appeared black, gleamed dully with drink and amusement. He nestled his angular body deeper into his jacket and let his gaze drift back to the gazette open on his lap.

A short, shifty man entered the tavern. He was nearly lost in an enormous wool coat, a warm cap pulled low over his ears, his collar turned up to hide his face. He scanned the crowd for a while, finally catching sight of the tall, thin man lounging so carelessly in the corner. He shoved his way through the smelly farmers, darting anxious glances around him. Intermittently he shrugged his left shoulder, tilting his head as he did so in an awkward manner. He plopped himself down beside the tall man, clumsily dropping a small scrap of paper onto the gazette.

The tall man studied the paper fragment briefly, quickly deciphering the few encoded lines scrawled upon it. He slid it back to his new companion, shrugged and then spoke in a hoarse, rasping voice. "Is this supposed to mean something to me?"

"Do you need the cipher key?" asked the smaller man, misinterpreting the question.

The tall man shook his head with a patronizing smile. "I invented this cipher, Lefty." It was not lost on him that if the message had been written in this particular code, the author had probably expected it to fall into his hands. Noaidi was issuing his challenge.

"Oh, well, yes. Of course. I mean—" Lefty took a deep breath and blew it out forcefully. He began speaking in what he imagined was a more authoritative tone. "Listen here, Mr. Thrayder, I do everything I can to protect you."

"Because I'm valuable to you."

"Aye, certainly. I'll give you that. But, I mean, nevertheless, I protect your identity."

"You don't know my identity."

"But I protect . . . listen here, show a little respect. I haven't told anyone about where the information you bring me comes from. Nothing, nothing at all. I am asking for your help because you are . . . well traveled, and know a great many things, and I thought of anyone you would know what this message means. I don't want to miss something of vital importance, something we should be involved in countervailing, if you take my meaning."

"It's not of vital importance."

"Then you do know what it refers to?"

"A myth. It refers to a myth. If General Clinton has extra money to throw away chasing fairy tales, then you should be happy. Less funds devoted to the war and feeding his soldiers."

"But what is it, this Lubrerum? What does it mean? Is it worth something? Is it a place? A person? A weapon? Why so much money? It would have to be worth a great deal for Clinton to authorize such a sum in pursuing it."

"Because they are getting desperate. Ever since Cowpens. They are becoming more willing to risk pursuing the ravings of lunatics like Noaidi."

"You're not helping me. You obviously know more than you are letting on. Things are happening. You've heard about Parbleu, haven't you? Someone snabbled him, but not one of ours, one of theirs. Unrest and a change in leadership could mean something very dangerous is happening. I need to know if I should approach the Committee about this. If we need to track down Noaidi and ascertain his designs."

"I wouldn't, if I were you," answered Thrayder, a glib warning in his voice.

"Why not?"

Thrayder paused, staring at the newspaper in his lap for a long moment. Then, quite unexpectedly, he stood up, his head pressing into the beams of the low roof. "Some things are better left alone. Lubrerum is no concern of yours, or of the Committee's, or of your almighty General's, trust me. But if you really are insistent, why don't you find Noaidi and ask him yourself? Your last interaction was so pleasant, after all." With that he swatted Lefty's empty right sleeve with his newspaper, then thrust the gazette deep into his jacket pocket.

"Where are you going?" asked Lefty indignantly.

"I'm going to need a bit of furlough. I have personal affairs I need to see to. You understand, I'm sure."

"Personal affairs? There are no personal affairs in this business, sir, let me remind you. There's a war on!" A few others in the tavern looked around in alarm when Lefty's shrill voice began to rise, and he stifled his outrage. Without looking back, Thrayder slid through the throngs of farmers and merchants crowding into the tavern to trade rumors of the war over tankards of ale and vanished into the gathering night outside.

※ ※ ※

1781 ⚔ Late March
Vermont Republic

The noise of men's voices, loud, inappropriately loud in a house still in mourning, wafted into the room that had once belonged to Cara's father. The room was tiny and cluttered, full of drifting dust and cobwebs, a shabby structure jury-rigged to the back of the main residence. Nothing had been moved since Robert's death. A book had been sitting open on his desk for a month, along with a quill resting in dried and fissured ink, a candle burned to a stub, and a piece of parchment with nothing written on it save the date: *'February 18, 1781'*. His bed was made as he had left it, covered by an old, stained quilt, folded back at the top corner. It was a bed Cara had always thought too small to fit her lanky father. The room still smelled like him: of dirt, gunpowder, and tobacco.

Cara sat at his little desk. She was hunched in a chair with uneven legs that perpetually rocked with any movement, even a breath. As she sat, she wondered if perhaps it wasn't the chair, perhaps the floor itself was uneven. It didn't matter. The room was nothing without its former occupant. The last book Robert had ever read lay open before her, the words written in the archaic language the Firefax children learned as toddlers. A useless tongue, spoken by no known nation or tribe in the world. A shaft of light from a crack in the shingles illuminated the words inscribed painstakingly in the heavy tome.

The voices were getting louder. Cara closed her eyes, willing the noise to fade. Once she had pushed the sounds away, she opened her eyes again and smoothed her plain brown polonaise gown, the seams straining around her broad, angular shoulders. She adjusted her spectacles, tucked her dark, straight hair behind her ears, and focused on the book before her, tracing her finger along the opening line.

'*Com res grum tops scuim, praun vo tei plac aet sturvant, mo a aet vo la.*'

The words came back to her slowly, so long had it been since she read in the tongue. 'Behold this mystery, we all shall not sleep, but all of us will vary.' No. That wasn't right. 'Be changed.' A faint glimmer of triumph stole across Cara's face as she decoded the verse. 'We shall not all sleep, but we shall all be changed.'

The door opened and closed quietly on well-oiled hinges. She did not look up; the footsteps were unmistakable.

"There you are," Rafael said softly, plopping himself onto Robert's bed. He stared at her with that same worried look of trepidation that everyone had been giving her since the day their father died.

"These bloody farmers, all coming after Robert's debts. And him hardly cold in his grave," Rafael continued, blowing out a breath and shaking his head. "Halstead says Robert owed him a whole cow. You know what Robert would say to that, right? *Udder* nonsense."

She gave him the slightest upward tilt of one corner of her thin lips.

Rafael beamed at this meager sign of life. "What have you got there? The versebook in Erlandagar?"

Cara nodded.

"One of the many pointless things Robert taught us. Are you going to teach it to Henry's younger ones?"

She shrugged.

"Come on, I know you're not talking to anyone else, but we've always talked, Cara, always. Before you talked to anyone else, we talked, remember?" She remained quiet, and after a moment he went on, "I don't know. You can teach it to them if you like. It's tradition, after all. Useful for ciphers. The older ones already learned it anyway. But what really is the point?"

"Mother said they speak it in Lubrerum," Cara said, startled by her own voice. She had not spoken to anyone since the day her father died. She sounded hoarse, raspy, her voice a strained, sharp gasp, like metal scraping against metal.

"Yes." As Rafael spoke, his warm brown eyes lit up with joy. "That she did. And that Ali Baba discovered the secret magical caves of a network of thieves, full to overflowing with unimaginable wealth. Mother told us a lot of fairy tales, Cara."

"Was Murdoch also a fairy tale?"

"I don't know. I would think so if not for those clothes he left behind, the ones you wear sometimes."

She always went hunting in the cast-off garments of their oldest brother, Murdoch, the only one of her brothers whose clothes she could still fit into with her ridiculous dimensions. Wearing his clothes made her feel a strange kinship with the man who had vanished from the farm long before she was born.

Rafael flipped through the pages of the Erlandagar verse-book, nearly to the end. "Have you ever read this one? It's quite a beautiful poem in English."

Cara peered at it through her spectacles and shook her head. "The handwriting is different."

"It's Mother's. She wrote this one."

"She did?"

"Of course. Don't you recognize your own mother's script? This is why I do all the forging. Look at these *e*'s—the loop is incredibly tiny. They all look like *c*'s. She had such a peculiar way of writing. I can't quite remember how it starts, something about everything being blue and turning it red . . ."

He trailed off as the voices outside the room crescendoed in the negotiations over how much Robert had owed Mr. Halstead.

"I wish they would leave off, really," Rafael continued. "I know it's been a month, but it still feels too soon. And we haven't the money right now. One more contract and we can settle them all and have a great deal left over."

"That last contract," said Cara. "You remember?"

"The last contract that Henry and I did without you, or you mean the one before?"

"The last one I did, in Paris, with you and Father."

"Of course I do, yes."

"I had him, I had that target. But Father knocked me over and killed the man himself."

"Did he? I wondered about that one. He said you did it, but . . ."

"He shouted 'Murdoch, wait! Don't do it!' and pushed me over and stabbed the man. Why would he do that? I'm not Murdoch."

Rafael bit his lower lip. "I . . . I don't know, Cara."

"Yes, you do. You all know. You all keep taking my targets. What are you afraid would happen if I killed someone?"

"Nothing. We just . . . it's instinct, you know. Protect your little sister. Protect your daughter. It's natural."

"I'm almost as tall as you are now, and better at every weapon and hand-to-hand combat than you. I'm not your little sister in any way that counts, Raf. So what are you afraid of?"

"Well, what are you afraid would happen? If you really wanted to kill a target, you could. You're good enough to stop us from taking them. Good enough by far."

Cara's frown deepened. "I'm afraid that I would . . . I don't know." She turned back to the book, her gut twisting. The vision of the mare running thundered into her mind again. The rise and fall of her perfect gallop, the hooves drumming, punctuated by the thuds of her father's head upon the frozen earth, like the beats of some dark destiny relentlessly bearing down on her.

Rafael rose. "Anyway, I think Henry might need reinforcements out there. I'm glad you're talking again."

"I'm not," Cara said quickly, looking up at her brother with an earnest, pleading expression. "I'm not talking to them yet. I'm not ready, Raf. I still see Father dying every time I close my eyes. I still see that horse . . . and what I did . . . I'm just not talking yet."

Rafael nodded, and for a moment his face saddened, but then he smiled again, encouragingly. "That's fine, Cara. Your secret's safe with me."

Then her brother slipped out of the shabby little room, leaving her alone in the dim light, staring at the old book written in the dead language of a fairy-tale place.

CHAPTER 2

A DANGEROUS FAMILY

March 30, 1781

My dear, honorable Mr. Seänkea,

I was surprised, and indeed delighted to receive your inquiry into the curious case of the Firefax family. You will forgive my assertions in the following pages, some of which may be speculation alone, but some of which I know to be true from my own personal acquaintance with the matters and the persons involved. I have the immense honor of being related to the family, in a manner of speaking; my half brother having married Helga Marchworth, whose mother's cousin was briefly married to India Kent's second cousin. I consider myself really an uncle to the young Firefaxes, and fancy they return the sentiment.

There was a time when the Firefaxes were the most talked-of family east of the Green Mountains, if you believe it. Now finding information about them is like looking for a needle in a haystack, as, it seems, you've discovered. Their forefather, Isaac, arrived to the colonies sometime in the 1690s, I believe. He and his wife, Hannah, set their claim to a plot of land near what is now called Draper or Wilmington—I can scarcely keep up with all these changing names in our New World. I believe they may have been the first settlers in that region, and, out of fear or respect, no one else has ever attempted to push them off their land or claim it in any charter. No one knows where they came from. Hannah never learned to speak a word of English, and hers was not a language known to anyone in those parts.

They cleared their land, built their home, and kept to themselves; not difficult, for at that time there weren't any other settlers really close enough to properly associate with as neighbors. Some say that from the time they first arrived, strange visitors began to appear in that part of the New Hampshire Grants, coming and going from abroad. But the small family was nearly forgotten, until someone sent an invitation to their residence for a wedding in Deerfield in the year 1715, I believe it was. Imagine the surprise it caused when, rather than Isaac and Hannah responding to the invitation, their son, whom no one knew they had, appeared at this party, a full-grown man, claiming that his parents had died two years before.

Henry Firefax, the first, I should say, for there have been two more since then, took control of Isaac's estate, hiring hordes of workers to run the farm, which he called Maralah, while he traveled, meeting with people from all over the world and disappearing for months at a time, doing God alone knows what. When home, he was an amiable, if a bit hot-blooded, social creature, and went to every outing he could. He managed to get himself into a number of scrapes, duels, and feuds over the years. Henry eventually married the lovely India Kent, whose family was pleased to see her matched with someone so wealthy. The couple had one son together, Robert, and, a few years later, ill with smallpox, India died.

No sooner was she gone than Henry sent Robert away to a boarding school in New York, seeming to forget the boy had ever existed. I have heard from folk that worked at Maralah in those days that the boy's letters went unanswered and even unopened.

Henry took to making even more journeys abroad, away for weeks, months, even years at a time, until one day he stopped coming home altogether. That was about the same time that young Robert Firefax returned home, with his own sweetheart, the lady Elizabeth Loxley. I do not know if the father and son met together before Henry left, but I do know that Henry never returned. There are rumors that a pirate ship, called the India, wreaked havoc upon the coastal towns lining the Gulf of Guinea, the Caribbean, and South America as far as Cape Horn in those years, and some say that Henry Firefax captained that vessel. Robert, meanwhile, was a respectable man, and a welcome replacement to his fiery, unpredictable father. He kept to normal social engagements, getting himself into less trouble, though still disappearing like his father and grandfather before him, and still entertaining guests from all over the world at their then lush and prosperous estate.

From here on, the accounts are things I heard from witnesses themselves, for it was not so long ago, and the family was better known, for a while, as more people moved to the Draper area. Elizabeth, especially, was beloved in all the social circles of her day. Many people remember her well and still talk of her fondly. She gave to Robert two sons. The first, Murdoch, was . . . well, I do not wish to speculate on a man I have never met. The rumors are that from earliest childhood he was like a demon; he was evil, hateful, cruel, uncaring, except in regard to his younger brother, Henry II, and his mother, Elizabeth. Every Firefax before him wore a veneer of congeniality, at least. Even the elder Henry I was pleasant in society. But not Murdoch—he was malice in human form, or so the stories go.

Murdoch was still a boy when his mother died, leaving him and his brother bereft, and, to all appearances, Robert was heartbroken as well. However, later that same year, a beautiful woman came from abroad, Katerina Yurtaev, and Robert married her practically the day she arrived, they say. She had a son, about five months after the marriage, Louis Firefax. Now mind you, from the beginning, Louis was beautiful, angelic, unlike his brothers or his father in his perfection, and the people living in Draper did not believe him to be Robert's son—understandable, given the time from his mother's arrival to his birth. They called him with his lovely golden curls "Katerina's indiscretion." A few years after Louis' birth, the boy fell sick. It was clear that he was dying, and about that same time, Murdoch, after yet another feud with his father and Katerina, whom he hated, left Maralah. The story is that Henry II tried to stop him, and Murdoch crushed the other boy's hand so badly that it was thought he would never use it again. The community was happy to see Murdoch leave, and, by all accounts, Robert Firefax was as well. Some people are not fit to live in polite society.

Murdoch has not been heard from since. Who can say if he grew to full, hateful manhood, or died soon after he set out on his own? For years the people thought that there would be no more Firefaxes, and Henry and Robert continued disappearing wherever it is that Firefaxes go. At last, Rafael was born, and then his sister Cara, shortly after. They were barely a year apart, as close as twins. Henry II wedded Halsey Marsh, from a local established family, and they have had a number of children of their own now. As of this writing, the Firefaxes are well-liked, keeping mostly to themselves, and Maralah itself is a difficult place to find, nestled under the shadow of one of the Green Mountains, only able to be discovered by the markings on trees and vague footpaths through that entangling wilderness. They are not complete recluses, though; I have heard that Henry and Robert made an excellent accounting of themselves in the Battle of Bennington.

Now, Mr. Seänkea, I know you may have no interest in speculation, but the Firefaxes invite it with their strange ways. I have heard many rumors, and shadows of rumors, each somehow more absurd than the one before. I will spare you most

*of these wild theories. Indulge me, however, in sharing one specu-
lation that I have heard. It is not quite so poorly founded as
others. I have in my acquaintance a very fine lady, Esperanza
Vidal. You may have heard of her; a very accomplished soprano,
and a beautiful woman. She has the honor of being close in
connection with one of this current generation of Firefaxes, and
she has told me, in confidence, that the family has been hired to
dispose of political enemies, quietly, surreptitiously, for centuries.
Not lowborn targets, but great nobles. They are hired to kill
them, and to hide every trace that they did it. I don't know if it
is true—indeed, I feel foolish writing it, but you had asked for
all that I know of them, so here I have bared it all, and couldn't
leave this last speculation out and call my accounting complete. I
would advise you, young man, to take care around anyone with
the surname Firefax. I know not if the rumors be true that they
be king killers, but they are, without any doubt, a dangerous
family.*

*With my sincerest wishes for success in your quest for infor-
mation, and safety in your journeys,*
Julius Clemont Augustine

CHAPTER 3

THE PRODIGAL

1781 ✗ MID-APRIL
VERMONT REPUBLIC

The man called Thrayder came in the early weeks of the spring of 1781, long legs striding resolutely, eating up broad stretches of earth with each confident step along the overgrown path running northwest from Wilmington. He was a gaunt, gangly form, like a scarecrow from the fields come to life. Despite the chill that remained in the spring air, he had his sleeves rolled up, revealing lean, sinewed arms. His hat still concealed much of his face as it had in the tavern, but every few moments he would glance up and the sun would illuminate a craggy set of structures; a long, pointed nose, skin stretched taut from his sharp cheekbones to his clean-shaven, angular jaw, lips so thin that they were almost nonexistent, drawn tight over tobacco-stained teeth. Sunk deep in the caverns above his cheekbones gleamed two coal-black eyes. His every feature was piercing and sharp, one body part jutting into another, jagged and grotesque. There was, however, a certain grace to his walk, the easy confidence of a man who knew his place and purpose in the world.

The terrain north and west of Wilmington became gradually more hilly, and he could make out the shapes of low, rolling mountains in the distance; brown tufts jutting into the cloud-studded blue sky. The land was barren, the trees devoid of leaves, and he was alone in the encircling wilderness, save for the occasional deer, squirrel, or rabbit, and the twittering of infernal cardinals and warblers from the bare branches above him. The path dwindled, sometimes fading completely into the early-spring trilliums, mayapples, green shoots of poison ivy, and thick bracken that coated the forest floor, but Thrayder's feet remembered the way without the help of a clear trail. Occasionally he passed a confirmatory carving in the bark of an apple tree: the image of a dagger pointing him on, toward Maralah.

The narrow path wound across tiny streams that bubbled from woodland springs, past outcroppings of gnarled, twisted sandstone, appearing as if from nowhere in the thick surrounding forest. His steps began to slope upward, the terrain forcing his jaunty clip to a slow, dogged rhythm, proceeding up the steep rise of a low dome-shaped mountain. He found at last the overlook he remembered, the trees parting to reveal domesticated, spreading farmland below.

Scattered clouds had gathered above, gliding slowly past, casting their dark shadows over the partially plowed fields. There were three visible pastures, surrounded by crumbling fences. Within one pasture, two thin cows grazed morosely; a cadaverous carthorse stood sleeping in another. A few chickens and goats ambled just outside the house, searching the muddy yard for any scrap of nourishment. A pond stood east and north of the main farmyard, surrounded by barren magnolias, sycamores, and shrubs. The farmhouse itself was a large, gray, boxlike structure, windows lining the upper and lower stories, with one central door, and a ramshackle room cobbled to the back. There were two chimneys; the one on the far eastern side of the house sat quiet, while the other, in the center of the house, was busily spewing smoke.

Little had changed, he reflected, aside from the barn, which had lost a few boards and shingles, and the addition of a few extra outhouses. There was a stump where the enormous walnut tree that he had climbed hundreds of times had once sat. The fields, half plowed already into meandering, crooked furrows, wrapped around the side of the mountain, out of his view. He paused for a long time there, taking in the peacefulness of it, watching as a herd of small children spilled out into the yard and played, intermittently bickering and wrestling in the mud.

He heard the faint cry of a female voice, calling angrily from the door, and the children ran for the house all at once, nearly trampling each other, never noticing the distant form watching them from the mountainside. His brow wrinkled and the thin set of his lips grew thinner still as he started down the mountain toward the farmyard waiting nescient below.

Standing at the door of the house, Cara, as tall, thin, and strangely stretched and ugly as the man far above on the mountainside, held the door open while the last mud-covered child scampered through. She scanned the mountain briefly, sensing something, but seeing no one. It was just paranoia, the restless wariness of her perturbed mind, she reflected despondently as she let the door swing shut. She followed the children, passing through the chaos of the dim kitchen, where the handsome dark-haired Halsey, mother of the six squirming, shrieking youngsters, worked ceaselessly on their dinner, peeling an enormous pile of gnarled little potatoes, some of the last remnants of their winter stores. Halsey paused in her work and smiled in a kind, but pitying way, wiping the black tangles of her hair back behind her ears.

"You're a saint, Cara," she said. "I'm sorry. If you like I can take over their studies for the afternoon."

Cara shook her head. "No, no. You know I burn everything I cook."

"True, and I only know about three Latin phrases, none of them appropriate," replied Halsey wryly. "The offer remains, nonetheless, should they begin to drive you mad."

"Don't fret, Halsey. They are, in truth, the only things keeping me sane."

Halsey balked and the pity in her expression deepened. Cara flushed and quickly moved into the larger room on the west side of the house that served as a space for both family dining and the children's studies. She shuddered at a brief unsolicited vision of a horse running and a mangled corpse dragging behind it. The image faded, much to her relief, as the first eager questions greeted her, something about the pluperfect active conjugation of *prosum*. Adjusting her spectacles, she set to work.

For hours Cara devotedly taught her nieces and nephews, until, at last, as the golden afternoon waned toward its end, she set her prisoners free and they fled from their books, sending parchment and quills flying in all directions. She let out a weary sigh as she began gathering up the papers and books and putting them into some semblance of order. The room was absurdly quiet after all the shouting, bickering and ceaseless kicking of feet on the table legs. She heard Halsey outside, rapidly assigning evening chores to the children before they could escape into the forest. The house smelled so strongly of chicken stew and fresh cornbread that Cara's mouth watered as she finished cleaning up.

Left behind, Amos, the second smallest of the children, waddled from the parlor, through the kitchen and into the dining room, catching hold of her leg. She hoisted him into her arms. He spoke only a little yet, and poorly. He was holding something in his hand, playing with it and occasionally popping it into his mouth. She caught his chubby hand and pulled it back, startling at the golden ring he was holding, imprinted with one word: *Patcretei*. It looked like the ring her father had worn. She stared at it, waiting again for the surge of hideous memories to abate.

"Where did you get that? Is your father home already?"

The toddler, his eyes round and solemn, shook his head and pointed behind her, toward the parlor. Thinking the ring must have fallen from the mantlepiece, she set Amos down and he stumbled off, heading outside to catch up with his siblings. Picking up a stack of books, she made her way through the empty kitchen and entered the parlor through the narrow, leaning door frame.

The parlor was the most comfortable room in the farmhouse. Two south-facing windows maintained a little light in the dim chamber, illuminating the stone hearth and a ring of chairs and stools lining the walls, piled with blankets. Bookshelves flanked the windows, heaped with dusty manuscripts and ledgers. In the center of the wooden floor was a dingy, threadbare rug with no discernible color or pattern, and upon that rug stood a beautiful polished mahogany piano, the red-tinged wood glowing in the sepia rays of sunlight streaming through the windows.

Cara jerked to a halt, startling so violently that she dropped all the books. A man stretched carelessly in her brother Henry's fine rocking chair, his long legs propped on the piano. He seemed apathetic of the mud actively transposing from his tall boots to the instrument. His clothing hung in loose, weathered folds about a thin frame. He had two pistols tucked in his belt, and against the hearthstones leaned a sheathed rapier that Cara did not recognize. The man did not even lift his hat from his eyes to acknowledge her presence but lay heedlessly as she had found him while she knelt to gather the books she had dropped.

"I'm sorry," she said, flustered. "Are you . . . is there something I can do for you?"

"I'm waiting for Mr. Firefax," replied the man, his voice a harsh sound, tearing from his throat like the rasping of steel on steel. He wore a stained cravat around his neck, but Cara could see a jagged scar extending up his throat and along his collarbone where it became obscured by his shirt.

"Oh," she said and paused for a moment, biting her lip. There had been only one client since word had gotten out of her father's death; indeed, there had been few enough before that. "Mr. Firefax, you mean Henry? You know that Robert is . . ."

"Deceased? Yes. Yes, I know."

"Well, very well, then. You are . . . acquainted with my brother?"

The man nodded but did not speak another word, settling still further into the confines of his jacket and hat.

"Unfortunately both my brothers are working in the fields. Since supper has been finished for some time, Mrs. Firefax has gone to fetch them. I'm sure they won't be long now. Is there anything I can offer while you wait? Water? Port?" She trailed off, about to offer more options but suddenly noticing the open decanter and crystal sitting on the piano. She frowned, pushing her spectacles further up her nose, and seated herself on a chair across from the man, annoyed at him for making himself so comfortable in their home, annoyed at the mud on the piano, another gift from her father. A less ill-fated gift than his final one, she reflected sorrowfully. She resented this strange, easy man, lying so relaxed in their parlor, without a worry in the world, acting as if he owned the building. She resolved not to speak again, or offer him anything else. The silence weighed heavily in the room, and, despite her anger, Cara felt her curiosity growing. The man's face remained obscured under his hat and he stayed silent, almost statuesque, his only movement the rise and fall of his narrow chest.

The sobbing, shrieking cries of Obadiah, her youngest nephew, as he awoke from his nap in the loft, jerked Cara from her resentment of the stranger draped over her father's gift. She leaped to her feet, darting from the parlor and bounding up the stairs to collect the infant and comfort him.

Despite his apparent disinterest, from beneath his hat Thrayder had watched the young woman while she stewed. She was an ugly woman. She could have been his twin if she were older. She had the same jagged frame, coal-black eyes set deep in a sharp, angular face, against a backdrop of straight black hair that glinted with threads of fiery mahogany in the light from the windows. Her pair of wire-rimmed spectacles completed her unseemly appearance. She had a pensive, lost look about her, as a woman searching for something. She would be Katerina's daughter, he thought, though she looked little enough like her handsome mother. When she leaped to her feet and ran from the parlor, he flitted his gaze back to the window, and a loud cardinal calling for a mate just outside, perched in the branches of a maple sapling. Gradually the sun set, and then clattering and shouting filled the house as the remainder of the family returned. The sobs of the infant had eventually faded, but the young woman had not returned.

Someone lit a few candles in the dining room and chattering voices, along with the clanking of platters and spoons, echoed through the kitchen and into the parlor. Thrayder could hear Halsey struggling to keep her children seated, one after the other leaping up to run to the kitchen and grab something that they had forgotten, knocking over plates, bowls, cups, and chairs with every mad dash. Sitting up, the man listened closer, finally picking out a familiar voice, little changed, he thought, since the last time he had heard it, despite the many years that had passed. It was deeper and more mellow, perhaps, but still with the same cheerfulness, the same friendly, lighthearted warmth.

"Elihu! You've gone and guzzled the last bit of cornbread! Blazes. Your son, Halsey!"

The woman's voice rippled with laughter when she responded, "My son? Only when he displeases you do you forget your part in his existence."

"I never forget that," Henry replied, chuckling. "And what is Cara to eat? Wherever is Cara? Has anyone seen her? There won't be a scrap left at the rate these rascals are going after the soup."

"I saved some out for her. I haven't seen her since I went looking for you."

"I can go find her," offered a third adult voice, male, and richer even than Henry's, but younger.

"No, no, I'll go look for her. I . . ." Henry trailed off, but there was something changed in his tone, and the man in the parlor knew that Henry felt something, some hint of his presence. A moment later Thrayder heard Henry moving through the kitchen and he stood, melting back into the shadows behind the piano as the younger man appeared at the leaning door frame, peering into the darkness that had swallowed the parlor.

"Cara? Are you in here?" Henry called, then, still seeming to sense the other man's presence, he called again, "Hello?"

Thrayder recognized the soft oval face, slightly too pudgy, the autumn-brown curls thinned a little, the lips still just a tad too full for a male. Henry had grown into a tolerably good looking man, and his wife was obviously keeping him well fed, as evidenced by the small paunch overhanging his belt. As

Thrayder watched from the shadows, Henry reached down with his left hand to clasp and stroke his right hand, opening and closing his fist, its misshapen form noticeable even in the dark.

"Did it not heal?" asked Thrayder, stepping from behind the piano, staring at Henry's hand.

Henry drew back, his face paling, mouth gaping, as if a ghost had emerged from the recesses of the parlor. "It can't be," he whispered, then he reeled backward, unsteady on his feet and the tall man darted forward to catch him, overturning the decanter on the piano, which fell, shattering loudly.

The chatter in the dining room abruptly changed to scraping chairs and footsteps rushing toward the parlor. The tall man did not flinch, steadying Henry, who stared at him with disbelief, and something more; the glow of hope in his gentle brown eyes. A moment later the scene was illuminated by several flickering candles and the two men were surrounded by children, and a young man, similar in appearance to Henry, a rifle gripped in his hands. Halsey was there too, dark-haired, comely, and bright-eyed with charming dimples in her cheeks. Finally Cara appeared, holding the baby she had gone to comfort, who was just starting to awaken again in her arms.

"Oh!" cried Cara, breaking the tense silence in the room. "I'm sorry. I quite forgot. He was waiting for you, Henry. I don't know who he is, or his business with you."

Henry was still pale, but a broad grin nearly split his face as he spoke. "It did heal. Works just as well as the other, if you believe that, though every bone in it was broken. That's what the doctor said, anyway. I just . . . it hurt, for a moment, just then. It's fine now."

His family stared at him in confusion, unsure what he was alluding to, as he reached out with his misshapen right hand and grasped the shoulder of the taller man, turning him to face the others. "Cara, Rafael, Halsey, all my children, it is with great joy, and a certain amount of incredulity, I confess, that I must introduce you to your brother, and uncle, Murdoch Firefax."

CHAPTER 4

MARALAH

urdoch Firefax scanned the faces around him as Henry rattled off introductions. Rafael, his younger half brother, the one who looked like Henry, bore an expression of wonder and curiosity. Halsey's lips were pursed in trepidation, though her bright eyes glowed with delight, for she likely knew better than anyone else how much her husband adored and missed his older brother. The children gazed up at him in absolute awe, as if some monster from their fairy tales had come to life. Last he lingered on Cara, Katerina's daughter, amused by how she shrank back in horror and disgust at the revelation of their connection.

"How . . . ?" began Rafael, but trailed off.

Murdoch rustled in his waistcoat pocket and produced a worn shred of paper, the printing just barely still visible. It was an advertisement torn from a Boston gazette. He handed the paper to Rafael, who raised his candle and read.

"'If this ad should come into the hands of M., my eldest brother, let it serve as notice that your father, R., has died, and we have need of your presence at M. With hope, H.'" Rafael turned toward Henry, who shrugged.

"I didn't have much hope, really, but I thought it was worth it. I put it in a few papers, actually. If I'd had an address I would have sent word a little more directly."

"Yes," said Halsey, turning back to Murdoch, her eyes narrowing. "The next time you disappear for twenty years, sir, do us the honor of leaving a new address."

"Twenty-two years," corrected Henry. "I can hardly credit it has been so long. It seems only yesterday that you and I were the terrors of all the surrounding villages. The trouble we caused. Regular hellions, I tell you. Perhaps you've heard from the Halsteads about us? Murdoch, do you remember the time—"

Murdoch glanced down at the seven children surrounding him, including the startled infant in Cara's arms. "Perhaps not the time for reminiscing, Henry. You've been busy during those twenty-two years, I see."

Henry burst into a peel of laughter, the kind of laugh that invites anyone within hearing distance to join the gaiety. "You haven't changed a bit, brother," he proclaimed, and Henry's happiness and adoration of the strange, tall man was so intense that everyone in the room felt themselves warming toward him as well. "But come on. I'm being quite rude. We must feed our prodigal, Halsey. Surely there's something left?"

"He can have mine," Cara offered. "I know Halsey always sets some aside, but I'm not hungry."

"Come now, Cara, you need your nourishment," Henry chided her.

"I do not. I can assure you it shall not be eaten, and will go completely to waste, unless you give it to him."

Eventually Halsey agreed to share some of Cara's food with Murdoch, but only on the condition that Cara ate a portion of it as well. They all returned to the table to watch Murdoch, leaving his cap rudely in place, shovel the food appreciatively in his mouth. There was no talk at the table, all eyes staring at the strange specter from the past, little more than a legend at Maralah and in the surrounding villages and farms. All the stories they had heard came racing back as they watched their silent guest eat. The food at last devoured, Murdoch pushed his chair back and smoothed his waistcoat, turning his piercing dark eyes toward Henry.

"Well, are you going to tell me what happened to Robert?"

Henry glanced uneasily at Cara. "I, well, yes, but not here, Murdoch. Sometime later, in private."

"He was my father, too. Haven't I the right to hear how he died?"

"Of course you do," Cara murmured, and then, standing abruptly, she darted across the room and into the kitchen, taking the stairs to the second floor.

"Robert . . . well, he doted on Cara—she was his everything, as youngest daughters often are to fathers that have had only sons," Henry explained. "She's taken his loss hard. Very hard. But, really, Murdoch, I would rather tell you about it in private."

Murdoch raised his eyebrows but then nodded curtly, and did not pursue his questioning further.

"Perhaps . . . perhaps Uncle Murdoch could tell us a story?" asked Henry III, the second-oldest of Henry's boys, and the bravest. All the children nodded eagerly at this, their eyes wide.

"I'm not here to serve as your entertainment. For that you should try the theater," Murdoch snapped and the children shrank from him.

"Oh, my apologies, dear brother, they are inquisitive, and quite rude, I'm afraid," said Henry, with a disapproving glance at his children. "My darlings, your uncle is weary from travel and you must be going to bed anyway. Run on up and get ready for sleep. Cara can help you, no doubt."

"I'll get them ready," said Halsey. "Elihu, Abigail, wash the dishes this evening, please?" The two eldest of Henry's brood set to work immediately gathering all the platters and cutlery as their mother herded the smaller children from the dining room, leaving only Henry, Rafael, and Murdoch seated at the broad oak table.

"Well, since everyone of the more sensitive sex and age has departed, perhaps you would be so kind as to tell me how my father died. Or is that too emotional a tale for you too, Rafael?"

"You don't know what Cara went through that day," rebuked the young man sharply. "But, in answer to your question, I can hear the tale again, if, indeed, it must be told."

Henry glanced uneasily toward the kitchen, listening to the chaotic bustle upstairs and the clanking of Abigail and Elihu reluctantly heading outside to the pond to wash the dinner dishes. He lowered his voice and leaned close to Murdoch. "It's not what you might think. No one did him in. Even getting older as he was, he was still more than a match for any one of us. He had many enemies. Indeed, someone for years had been poaching contracts from us, if you can believe that. But, no, no one came after him like that. His clients wouldn't have come after him—they respected him, us, our business."

"Is that what the families of your targets think? That it's just business, nothing personal?" asked Murdoch, a flicker of amusement dancing in his dark eyes.

"Of course not, but our targets don't know who we are, or what we do. Only those who pay for our services know. We've not been so careless as to start letting that information slip. At least, well, anyone who did find out was quickly sent to their maker, as has always been our policy."

"Glad to hear the entire family business hasn't gone to rubble while I've been away."

"Of course it hasn't. It's the only thing keeping us in

stockings and candles. Robert was no farmer, though he wanted to be."

"So, it was a farming accident, then? His beloved Maralah fields did him in?"

"Shrewd as ever, brother," replied Henry. "It was Cara's birthday, and Robert loved her more than he loved any of us, as I said, or at least he loved her differently, I suppose, than he loved any of us."

"First I've heard that Robert loved any of his offspring."

Henry ignored this remark. "He doted on her, Murdoch. She is seventeen years old and still hasn't made her first kill, because Robert wouldn't let her. He sheltered her, trained her, yes, took her out for contracts like the rest of us, but he kept her from the ugliest parts of our work. Seventeen, without a kill, and the last name Firefax, can you imagine?"

"That's not fair," Rafael interrupted. "First of all, it wasn't just Robert that sheltered her—you've taken a few of her kills yourself. For another thing, you know she took out that target in Tripoli, two years back."

"She most certainly did not. It's stupid of you to keep taking her targets and pretending she did the work. You're only hurting yourself in the end. With you giving your kills to Cara and the sparsity of work we've had of late, and with that interloper stealing our contracts from under our noses, you'll be an old man before you make it to Oxford. How many more do you need before you'll have enough saved up?"

"Only three more, at the current going rate for contracts, anyway," replied Rafael, brightening.

"What are you going to study?" asked Murdoch with a bland expression, only mildly interested.

"To be a minister. Of course."

Murdoch let out an uncharacteristic startled guffaw, an alarming noise given his hoarse, terrible voice, as frightening and off-putting as Henry's laugh was inviting. "Indeed? What flavor of clergyman?"

"Methodist."

"Oh, a follower of the great Reverend Wesley? Going to be the first minister to fund their seminary education with money earned from assassinations?"

"David was a man of the sword, but also a great man of God. Once I have enough saved up I plan on putting up my sword and pistol permanently."

"Whatever happened to '*thou shalt not kill*'? Has that been struck from the Commandments since the last time I read them?" asked Murdoch, still shaking with barely contained mirth.

"I'm surprised you've read them at all," Rafael countered. "But, we all find atonement in our own ways, brother."

"Those of us that need it. Aren't you a little old to be going to seminary?"

"I'm only just eighteen, not that you would know that since you've been gone so long. Anyway, many Firefaxes leave the family work eventually, to do other things. We only need one sibling in a generation to carry on the business. Do you want to continue laughing at me, or would you like to hear the rest of the story?"

"Easy, little Reverend. So testy," Murdoch replied in a mock soothing tone.

Henry waited until Rafael's face had returned to his usual sanguine expression and some of the tension at the table melted. The candle flames flickered back and forth, illuminating the brothers. Abigail and Elihu had returned from the pond and Henry knew the two youngsters were hiding near the door to the dining room to listen. He licked his lips and continued, "At any rate, Robert took it into his head to purchase her something special for her seventeenth birthday. He took a great deal of money, much more than anyone would have advised him to spend on something so frivolous, and bought her a beautiful horse, an import from England, a real thoroughbred. That was something they both shared, a love and skill at riding that far surpassed the rest of us. You should have seen that mare, Murdoch, even you would have been astounded. She was really something to behold; she was tall, fine-boned, a coat of fiery red, and a spirit just as fiery, I would say."

"I take it that the option to see the mare is no longer available?"

Henry sighed, his face grim. "I don't know what happened out there. Robert took Cara to meet the horse. He had been keeping her in a separate pasture, a few miles from here. He kept her out there so he could surprise Cara. I believe he demonstrated the paces of the animal for her. You know as well as I do that man had a seat like tar. He could hang on until the end of time. But somehow, and, as I said, I don't know how it happened—Cara hasn't told us anything since that awful day—the horse threw him, snapped his neck and cracked his head open. But his foot was still caught in the stirrup and that horse ran on, dragging our poor dead father across the pasture, thumping and bumping along, while Cara watched.

"It was very late, well past nightfall when we set out to look for them. What we eventually found out there would make the hardest-hearted man weep. Cara was kneeling in the pasture, staring, unwilling to speak, not even looking at us. She was nearly frozen. Robert's head was split open, hanging off his neck at a terrible angle. He was all battered and crushed from being dragged. The horse . . . Cara had killed it with a pitchfork. There was blood everywhere. It was like the worst contract you've been on."

"No. It wasn't," replied Murdoch. "Is the girl—"

"She's fine," said Rafael quickly. "She only did what she was trained to do."

Henry gave Murdoch a brief, significant look, and Murdoch asked no further questions in regard to Cara. The prodigal leaned back in his chair, lacing his thumbs into his waistcoat, staring into the flame of the candle, which had burned nearly to its end. "All those years, all the work he did, all the dangers he faced . . . to die from falling off a horse, on a little farm in the middle of nowhere. It's absurd, really."

"Well, how did Grandfather die?" asked Rafael.

"What makes you think I would know the answer to that question?"

"Where have you been all these years if not with him? Everyone knows you went off to sea with him."

"Everyone also believed me dead. Little brother, I owe you no explanation of what I have been doing for the last twenty-two years."

"Perhaps you'll tell us what you plan to do here, then?"

"Maybe I mean to retire and become a farmer, like my father, and his father before him, and his father before him. Haven't I earned some respite after all these years?"

Henry laughed. "Murdoch Firefax, a farmer? That'll be the day."

"Then Robert didn't leave Maralah to me?"

"No, no, that he certainly did," replied Henry, sobering. "Though what he imagined you would do with it I don't know. Much as he hated you all these years, I don't know why he never took the time to alter his will. But he didn't, and Maralah is legally yours."

The three brothers stayed up late into the night, Rafael and Henry reminiscing over contracts they had fulfilled with the legendary Robert Firefax. Murdoch listened quietly, adding nothing to the conversations save the few times Henry invited him to comment on some aspect of their late father's mannerisms. Eventually even Abigail and Elihu grew tired and abandoned their eavesdropping in the kitchen. As they talked, Murdoch studied the youth, Rafael. The boy was earnest, devout, and kind. He would make a good clergyman, Murdoch decided. He was a sincere soul, and the multiple displays of anger he had shown seemed quite uncharacteristic. The candles were only tiny sputtering puddles of wax when Rafael finally rose, yawning and stretching.

"It's to be an early morning tomorrow, if we're going to get the last part of the northeast section tilled. Murdoch, I'm sorry if I was short with you. It is a gift to meet you, after believing my whole life that you were dead. I look forward to becoming better acquainted with my eldest brother, should you choose to stay a while."

The two sons of Elizabeth remained at the table, silent, as the candle burned out completely, dwindling away to nothing. The air in the room filled with a faint smoky odor as the light dissipated.

"It feels good, Murdoch, to have you home. I thought . . ." Henry's voice caught in his throat, and he paused for a second before continuing, "I thought I would never see you again."

Murdoch did not answer but waited for Henry to compose himself. Finally he asked, "Is the girl disturbed?"

"No. I mean, no more than the rest of us," replied Henry with a chuckle. "They were born less than a year apart, she and Rafael. They've been close, very close. When they were little they had their own language that they jabbered to each other. It was the sweetest thing. Rafael learned to speak, but she didn't start talking properly until she was . . . I don't know, maybe five. Very serious child, solemn, careful, studious. Then one day she began conversing in full sentences, damnedest thing you've ever seen. The more children I have, the more strange and rare I find her development was. What I'm trying to say is, she's an odd woman. She always has been. After she saw Robert die and killed that horse, she wouldn't speak, she didn't eat, she just lay in bed, or wandered aimlessly. I despaired of her, honestly. I thought we had lost Robert and Cara that day. She only just started speaking again about a week ago. The children really pulled her out of it. They would not stop pestering her. They're good at that."

"Seven children. You went and had seven children."

"Eight."

Murdoch raised an eyebrow.

"One on the way!" Even in the darkness, Murdoch knew his brother was grinning proudly.

"How many are you going to have?"

"I don't know. Whatever it is that makes them keeps happening," said Henry, tittering childishly at his own jest.

Murdoch shook his head. "Cara looks—"

Wiping tears from his eyes, still heaving from repressed gales of laughter, Henry yawned and stood, scraping his chair against the floor as he rose. "Like you? I know. A veritable human facsimile. She fights like you too, Murdoch. You should see it. You wouldn't believe it. She's a regular Robin Hood with a pistol or a rifle. Where she really shines, though, is in stealth. She is soundless when she moves. You never know she's there, even when she's right beside you. Sometimes I thought Robert saw her as you reborn—his chance to do things right."

"He might have done things right in the first place and avoided any repetition."

"True enough. But you know, he tried. I think. The more children I have, the less I fault him for his mistakes."

Murdoch let out a soft chuckle at that.

"It's hard with the first one, I think," continued Henry. "I'm still waiting for the day my Abigail takes a gun and a cutlass and disappears in a righteous rage. But, Murdoch, I say Cara fights like you and looks like you reborn, but she's not like you. She's a good woman. She's kind and loving. She spends her time caring for our children, helping neighbors in need, attending births. She's . . . she's just not like you."

"Perhaps not. Or perhaps she's never been given the chance to show what she really is."

Henry took a last look at his brother's silhouette, as if assuring himself that he was really, truly there. "Maybe so. Maybe so. I keep thinking this is all a dream, Murdoch. I know I've already said this, but I'm glad you're back. Maralah is yours, and you can stay however long you like. Hell, I hope you stay forever. You can sleep in Robert's room—it's attached to the kitchen, that door behind the stairs." He clapped his long-lost brother on the back before retreating from the dining room, his footsteps gradually fading up the stairs.

Murdoch waited in the darkness until the house became quiet, Henry's faint snores the only sound from the upper rooms. Then he rose and slipped outside, making his way to the enormous walnut stump a few yards behind the residence. For some reason Robert had cut down the tree where Murdoch had spent countless hours sitting in his childhood, perhaps to spite the memory of his eldest son, who had left without a word, without a trace save Henry's crippled hand. He settled on the stump, folding his long legs beneath him, and removed his pipe from his coat pocket, lighting it with his flint. The blazing coal soon reflected back in his black eyes as he sat pondering, a flood of memories, distant and devoid of sensibilities, rushing back to his mind. As the night wore on, he turned his gaze toward the mountain, and the tiny path that led back toward Wilmington.

It was nearing morning when Cara woke with a start, covered in sweat. She slid off the mattress she shared with Henry's daughters. She had slept little since her father died. Her dreams, when she had them, were haunted by the memories of the horse's screams, of her father's body flopping on the hard frozen earth of the paddock. She made her way to the window and moved the curtains back, letting the cool, cleansing air wash over her, the scent of late-spring frost sticking in her nose. Then her breath caught as she saw the shape of a tall, silent man seated on the walnut stump, puffing on his pipe, staring toward the mountain, as if waiting.

In the weeks that followed his arrival, the Firefaxes became accustomed to the silent man's ways, his constant watching of the road, his sleeplessness, his taciturnity, the sense of foreboding and fear that he brought with him everywhere. The children, normally curious of newcomers, gave him a wide berth, sensing his dislike of them. The only times they dared approach was when he was practicing his swordsmanship or marksmanship; then they gathered to watch in awe. Robert had, of course, begun the work of teaching his grandchildren the skills they would need to succeed in their familial line of work, though the bulk of their training fell to Henry, Rafael, and Cara. But still, the children had never seen the kind of frenetic, yet effective skill Murdoch exhibited with a blade. He allowed Henry's offspring to challenge him, and his brothers at times as well, but it was useless. His long arms and legs and flailing movements were bewilderingly swift, unpredictable, and he outfought them all.

During the days, Murdoch worked the fields alongside Rafael and Henry, making no allusions to his past, or his future. In the afternoons, he drilled with his sword and pistol like a madman, as if preparing for some impending battle. Then, every single night, Cara would look outside to see him perched on the remnant of the walnut tree, staring down the path away from Maralah, and she dreaded to learn what or who he was waiting for.

Word spread quickly to Wilmington, Brattleborough, and even as far as Bennington that Robert's prodigal son had returned, and visits to Maralah increased that spring. Curious people from neighboring farms and villages made excuses to come to see Halsey, or Cara, all eager to catch a glimpse of the legendary Murdoch Firefax, who had, for more than twenty years, been nothing but a bedtime story to frighten children. Some of the young females in the region thought instantly that he would be an excellent marital prospect, in a region depleted of eligible bachelors by the war. Not only was Murdoch the heir of a prominent family that was believed to have a great deal of wealth, but he also possessed an intriguing, mysterious past, the kind of thing that any young frontier woman, raised her whole life in the same small social circles, might find enticing. However, the few local women who managed to catch a glimpse of him were immediately persuaded against making any romantic connection with such a hideous, menacing person.

Six weeks after his arrival, Cara found him in the parlor, poring over a thick ledger. He was covered in sweat and dirt from the fields but paid no attention to the trail of mud he had left behind him. Her forehead wrinkled as she took in the mess he had made.

"It's almost time for dinner. What's that you're reading?" she asked.

"Robert's account book."

"Oh. I thought I recognized it. He spent a lot of time with that one, especially the last few years. I think it was making him old."

"It should have. He was practically in the almshouse. Any more debt and he would have lost Maralah entirely."

"Yes, someone was stealing contracts from us. He talked

about that a great deal, but not so much to me. He never talked much about the business with me."

"Thought it was too much for your fragile, feminine mind?"

The furrows in her forehead deepened. "I was the youngest. He didn't want to worry me."

"I'm not judging," Murdoch replied with the hint of a mocking smile dancing across his thin lips.

"Why did you leave?" asked Cara suddenly.

Murdoch grinned broadly at that, a hideous, leering expression. He flipped back through the pages of the old account book, encrypted in the strange archaic language called Erlandagar. It contained only information about the money made from contracts. Robert had kept other accountings, for farming and neighborly transactions, in a separate ledger. Murdoch stopped at last on one page and passed it across to Cara.

She peered at the faded lines, written twenty-two years before. One line, '*1758—Josef I—Lisbon*', an enormous sum, and then a line drawn through it.

"That was you?" she asked. "That was a breached contract."

"Indeed it was."

"Father said he lost two friends in the attempt."

"Yes, yes, he did. He did not believe that I could handle the contract on my own, so he sent his two friends with me. Two blundering buffoons. And they nearly got us all killed. But that stupid, hateful man blamed me for their deaths and blamed me for the breached contract. He is the one that cost us that contract and all the lives lost over it."

"I'm . . . sorry. I think he would have forgiven you, eventually, if you had stayed, or if you had come back before he died."

"Interesting theory, little sister. Are we talking about the same man? At any rate, I do not care if he ever forgave me. He was a stupid man, Cara, and I was delighted to learn that he had died."

She stared at him for a moment, wrestling with a surge of hatred rising within her, a loathing for her brother, but also, by extension, for herself. She could not hate him without hating herself, for they were similar in ways that terrified her. "You took those contracts from him, didn't you?"

Murdoch smirked again, reaching down to touch the gold ring on his finger with the word *Patcretei* carved into it. "They don't give contracts like those to someone who isn't a Firefax. I hope he knew it, and I hope it drove him mad."

"You're an evil, hateful person."

"It takes one to know one, Cara," replied Murdoch, and flipped the book back to where he had been reading when she had entered the parlor.

CHAPTER 5

LIGHTFOOT

During Murdoch's arrival to Maralah, the New England forest had still been sparse. Only the evergreens had been full, lining the narrow path east along the dome-shaped mountain. The buds of the maple, oak, elm, ash, and walnut trees had just been appearing, the ground barely covered in sprouting plants. A few weeks later, as May advanced, the mountain was covered in a lush green carpet and the thick foliage of the canopy was punctuated with clusters of delicate white and pink flowers on the scattered apple, dogwood, and cherry trees. Each day since returning, Murdoch had patrolled the woods before taking his nightly post on the walnut stump.

He was getting ever more restless on the isolated farm deep in the Vermont forest. It had been long enough that the lack of activity was making him uneasy. It was not possible that Lefty would simply let him slip away and disappear in peace, nor that Istäni would give up looking for Lubrerum so easily. Not the boy he had raised. He did not like the waiting, the endless preparation without even a single scout sent to flush him out.

He was filled with these brooding thoughts on his late-afternoon stroll through the forest. The woodlands were peaceful, undisturbed by the sound of man, his own footsteps soundless in the grass. Then he paused, hearing hoofbeats moving at a steady clip, trotting, then walking in a rhythmic fashion. He almost didn't believe it as he stood for a while listening to the thumping of hooves on soft earth. Convinced at last that his ears were not playing tricks on him, Murdoch felt a wild thrill of joy at the prospect of action. He began moving quickly, making his way toward the overgrown trail to his right. When at last he caught sight of the rider through the tree branches, the eager expression on his face gave way to one of annoyance.

The rider was a young man, perhaps twenty-five or so, and to say he was beautiful would have been a criminal understatement. The young man was painfully handsome. He had absurdly milk-pale skin, devoid of scar, acne, or freckle. He had a strong, clean-shaven jaw, and a proportionately large, but becoming nose like Michaelangelo's David, framed by blond brows overhanging vibrant blue eyes. Waves of curling, almost white-blond hair flowed around his face like a halo of shimmering gold. He was broad-shouldered and trim-waisted and sat his horse as if he had been born there. The sight of the youth trotting on his fine gray horse, carefree, no attention to his whereabouts, no attention to anything, filled Murdoch with a surging, overwhelming hatred. Of all the useless, stupid agents that Lefty could have sent, he had to send Lightfoot.

At Lightfoot's side hung a rapier, but Murdoch saw no other weapons, and no firearms, giving himself a slight advantage if he wished to end things quickly. But he did not. He wanted to interrogate the boy, to find out what was known, what remained unknown, and how many more were coming. Lightfoot was a talker, and Murdoch knew he could get information out of him. Murdoch swung himself into a tall maple, sliding out along a limb overhanging the path. The horse startled first and the rider reached down to calm him, before glancing up to see what was bothering the animal. When Lightfoot did look up, it was only just in time to see the wraithlike form of Murdoch dropping on him like an avenging demon.

The two men tumbled to the ground while the horse bolted a few yards, before slowing and turning back to watch the battle on the trail. Lightfoot had his breath knocked from him by the assault, and Murdoch landed on top of him and grasped his throat, squeezing with satisfaction while his stunned enemy struggled to break free and regain his breath. Gathering himself, Lightfoot drew his feet up and shoved them into Murdoch's abdomen, kicking him away. The younger man leaped up, rubbing his neck with his left hand while drawing his rapier with his right. In the fall from the horse, Lightfoot had twisted his ankle, and he limped as he took a few steps back, putting on a bold, arrogant smile.

"I thought they would send someone," said Murdoch, standing slowly and drawing his blade. "But I am disappointed that they picked you, Lightfoot. Of all the inept fools on their payroll."

"Perhaps I am a fool, but at least I'm not a madman who jumps out of trees onto unsuspecting passersby," retorted Lightfoot.

Murdoch did not answer, attacking instead. He was a vehement, fierce fencer, absurd in his movements. His great strength was his ability to use both hands equally well, easily tossing his rapier from left to right. His adversary countered Murdoch's relatively wild, flailing attacks with a graceful, fluid style, just as deadly as Murdoch's. Back and forth they bounded, Murdoch like a cobra, striking, falling back, then striking again. There was no rhythm to him, making it nearly impossible for Lightfoot to anticipate his movements. The divergence between the two men's styles was of two highly trained combatants, one with an overabundance of natural talent, the other with dedication and detached ferocity, combined with far greater experience and years of ceaseless practice. Natural gifting versus fanatical zeal.

"Dear God, Thrayder, you really should see a doctor," Lightfoot said as he parried. "Do you often have these fits? Attacking random people in the forest without provocation?"

"You play stupid very well. I've often wondered if it is play or simply your natural state," replied Murdoch, catching a thrust by Lightfoot and turning it away.

"Oh ho! Sharp are the daggers of Thrayder's wit!" Lightfoot grinned as he spoke, pressing forward hard, pushing Murdoch back into the trees.

"Upon reflection, I'm glad they sent you," continued Murdoch between parries and thrusts. "I will be happy to rid the world of your simpering soul."

"I could say the same thing to you. Out of all of them, you are certainly the one I've most wanted to challenge. You're so arrogant, so sure no one could ever match you for skill. Well, you've met your match today."

"The haughty do loathe competition."

"But you picked a poor moment to snap, honestly," continued Lightfoot. "I'm not really in the mood for blood."

"If it makes you feel any better, I plan on killing you, so your afternoon won't be spoiled at all," replied Murdoch as Lightfoot again pushed him back.

"Empty threats. You can't kill me, Thrayder. Out of curiosity, though, have you really lost your mind? Or are you acting under orders? Or have you split to the other side again?"

"You already know why I attacked you. You were sent to spy on my whereabouts. You found me, but I'm certainly not letting you escape alive to report to Lefty."

"I think there must be some misunderstanding. I'm not following anyone today, least of all you. Such vanity! You're becoming paranoid in your old age."

Murdoch had started a vicious forward advance, driving the limping younger man back onto the trail, toward his horse, who balked as the men approached and then bolted before their clanging blades. As Lightfoot backed away, his foot caught in a root and he tripped, landing on his back, his sword raised. Rather than taking advantage of his adversary's fall, Murdoch, quite unexpectedly, stopped and sheathed his blade.

"I let you live. Consider us even from Charlestown last year. But you need to leave, Lightfoot. Go back to Boston or wherever it is you're posted these days. If you leave and tell no one you saw me here, I won't kill you. But if you do tell anyone, rest assured I will find you and kill you wherever you may be."

"Why should I? This isn't your forest. I've just as much right to it as anyone else. I'm going on. I have business up ahead. A personal affair."

"There are no personal affairs in our work. I'm surprised Lefty didn't tell you that when he recruited you."

"Oh, there bloody well are, and you bloody well know it! You, of all people, nearly two months you've been playing truant. Don't tell me it isn't for some private matter of your own. I won't tell the blighters where I saw you and you won't tell them where you saw me, and there's an end to it. I'm going on, anyway, and you can go to hell. Now, where the blazes has my horse gotten to?"

Quiet, consumed with his own thoughts, Murdoch watched as Lightfoot limped up the little path, whistling to the animal he had lost. The expression on the older man's face gradually shifted from thoughtful pondering to absolute cynicism, a faint memory returning unwelcome to his mind. He turned away twice, but then, finally, letting out an exasperated sigh, he spun about and headed down the narrow trail after the younger man. With his long legs it took him but a few minutes to overtake the limping Lightfoot.

"What, again?" exclaimed Lightfoot, reaching to redraw his rapier. "Don't you ever give up?"

"I am going with you, back to Maralah, Louis Firefax. That is if you have no objections?" replied Murdoch, ignoring the half-drawn sword and striding past the younger man.

There was nothing Lightfoot, or Louis, as Murdoch had rightfully called him, could say. He stood frozen and gaped at the back of the lanky older man. He sputtered a few times, but there were no discernible words among his mutterings. He sounded rather like a frog choking.

"Take care not to strain your mind, little brother," Murdoch called back, almost gaily.

"Murdoch!" cried Louis, sagging. Then, his twisted ankle forgotten, he raced after the tall man ahead. "You cannot possibly be . . . there is some mistake, you are trying to trick me. Murdoch is dead. It's nonsense. Impossible. You're playing some stupid, childish prank on me."

"As I said, don't strain yourself. It is a bit much for a weak mind to take in all at once. Even *I* didn't believe it at first."

The insulting intimation about the weakness of his mind snapped Louis from his shocked babbling. He glared, though the expression only enhanced his lovely features. It was gross, Murdoch thought, such a depraved lack of physical fault. Yet there it was, in all its glory, absolute human perfection. It did not matter what expression scrunched and maligned Louis' countenance—it never changed from archetypal beauty. Murdoch wanted very much to mutilate the lovely face glowering at him, to cut off the ringlets of platinum gold, put out the brilliant blue eyes, knock out a few of the snow-white teeth, but he repressed his murderous urges.

"I sincerely hope this is a nightmare," said Louis, and broke into a wild, nervous laugh.

He had a beautiful laugh, Murdoch noted with disgust, similar to Henry's, but not so free and sincere.

"Of course, though," Louis continued. "How could two people hate one another so viscerally and not be related? I did notice you looked similar to Robert. If you were just twenty years older and maybe five stone heavier, you might have been brothers. Were you here before he died? Did you kill him?"

Murdoch shook his head. "I regret that I did not have that satisfaction. I was not here, and I am leaving soon."

"What, for good? Isn't Maralah yours now, with Robert dead?"

"I'm selling it to Henry."

"Oh, well, then, I guess that's settled. Selling it, though? Really Thrayder—er, Murdoch? The family is in dire straits as it is. They'll be in the almshouse soon, Maralah or no Maralah. Can't get a contract to save their lives. But I suppose you don't really care."

"Correct," answered Murdoch, striding on ahead of Louis, who had finally caught sight of his spooked horse, grazing under the trees.

Murdoch arrived back to Maralah before Louis, who had to calm and collect his gray gelding. Henry was standing by the door, reprimanding Elihu for not putting the chickens in the night before and costing the family one of their best laying hens to a marauding fox. They both turned at the sight of the tall, scarecrow-like figure stalking with all the fury of an avenging angel toward the house.

"Whatever's the matter?" asked Henry.

"Nothing is the matter. Only that you neglected to tell me that Louis survived."

Henry's eyes widened and Elihu, his shame forgotten, began leaping up and down, calling the other children to the yard. "Uncle Losi's coming! Uncle Losi!" he shouted and raced away toward the forest, leaving Henry and Murdoch alone.

"Oh," said Henry. "I forgot he was sick when you left. Though, mind you, Father never did. Hated you all the more for choosing to run off while your brother was, to all appearances, dying. Thought he was going to be left with just me, the pudgy, inept disappointment. It's been twenty-two years, Murdoch! You can't expect me to remember everything that was happening when you left. I just assumed you knew Louis was still alive."

"Well, I do now. And he is a delight, really." As Murdoch said this, Louis entered the yard on his gray, still spooked gelding, the animal balking from the throngs of children that raced toward him.

"He's insufferable," said Henry with a chuckle, then winced. "You two are really not going to get along."

"Truer words were never spoken!" called Louis, having gotten close enough to hear the discussion his older brothers were having. Murdoch shot a warning glance at him. Their handsome half brother dismounted, handing the reins of his steed to the eager Elihu. Cara and Rafael, hearing the hubbub had come outside and Louis embraced them both. He offered Henry a more formal handshake, but his older brother crushed him into a warm hug instead. The five offspring of Robert Firefax stood back in a wide circle, staring at one another, with joy on their faces, except Murdoch, whose lip curled in disgust.

"Can you imagine, Cara, all these years Murdoch didn't even know Louis was alive?" said Henry. "What a surprise it must have been to meet each other for the first time on the road. Louis, what happened to your neck? And why are you limping?"

The pale young man had the type of skin that showed any

injury immediately, and the marks of fingers on his neck were unmistakable.

"Nothing, nothing at all," replied Louis, glancing toward Murdoch. "Well, I fell off my horse, if you must know. He's young and a bit reactive."

Henry frowned, not buying the explanation, well aware of his younger brother's skill at riding, but he shrugged after a moment. "So you received my letter, then?"

"Yes, I did. I was in port, in Boston, two weeks back and ran into Julius. He had a whole passel of letters for me. I've been abroad for the last few months, so it took me quite a while to get through the whole pile. It broke my heart to learn of Father's death."

Murdoch snorted at that, and again the two men exchanged a furtive glance. Cara had been the first to notice these silent exchanges, pregnant with some secret understanding, but she could see that the looks were not lost on Rafael either.

"Well, come inside, brother," continued Henry. "We can get you some refreshments. I'm sure the children would welcome a break from their afternoon lessons to hear tales from faraway places."

"And I have years' worth of adventures to regale them with!" cried Louis, joyful at the prospect of a full audience to boast to. The Firefaxes retired inside to listen to the effusive stories in which Louis invariably played the hero.

CHAPTER 6

ISTÄNI

The lush greenness of spring was fast yellowing into the broiling heat of summer days. Several weeks had passed since Louis' arrival and life at Maralah had settled into the monotonous rhythm of weeding, fixing fences, milking, gathering eggs, cooking, cleaning, and mending. Cara and Rafael worked side by side in the long rows of chest-high corn, hacking at weeds with old, rusted hoes, pausing every few minutes to wipe curtains of sweat from their faces. They were on the far northern field, near the forest, their view of the house obscured by the edge of the mountain.

"What do you think Murdoch and Louis are hiding from us?" asked Cara, swinging the long shaft of the hoe into the dirt as she spoke.

"That question's been vexing you for weeks, hasn't it?" replied Rafael with a grin, then his brow wrinkled. "I don't know. I've been heckling Losi, but he won't give me anything."

"It must be something awful if even Losi won't talk about it."

"Maybe they've become Tories."

"Is that the worst you can think of?"

Rafael laughed and said, "No, I suppose I could imagine worse things."

"Murdoch watches the road every night, and scouts in the forests for someone or something, every single day."

"I've noticed. And I've a feeling whoever he's expecting is not going to be anyone we want to become acquainted with."

Cara frowned. "I wish he would leave, Raf. I hate him."

"He's your brother, Cara."

"I know, but he's . . . he's . . ."

"Evil?"

Cara nodded without speaking.

Their conversation was interrupted by a flash of movement in the forest, and Cara raised a hand, silencing Rafael. They both glanced at the wood, trying to be surreptitious. There was another glimpse of brown cloth, moving among the foliage, unmistakably a waistcoat and a jacket. The siblings exchanged a quick series of movements with their hands, signals without words. Then Rafael continued to swing his hoe, working his way toward the trees. Cara, keeping her head below the corn, circled wide through the rows. She made for the flintlock fowler leaning against a maple at the edge of the forest, a weapon they habitually brought to work in the fields, though for game, not for defense.

The person watching them had melted into the brush, but Rafael could still see the fabric of his jacket. Then, just as Cara reached the gun by the woods, the man broke into a run. Cara abandoned the weapon and took off at a sprint after the man. Rafael had barely reached the outskirts of the forest when he heard the struggle: twigs snapping, and the grunts of two people wrestling on the forest floor.

Cara and the man were fighting for control of the stranger's pistol. As Rafael reached them, the man twisted the pistol free of Cara's grasp. But before he could aim it at Cara, Rafael swung the hoe, catching the man's wrist. The stranger yelped in pain, blood spurting from his arm. The pistol went flying and Rafael, dropping his hoe, lunged for it. The man yanked himself free of Cara, running for the gun as well, but Rafael snatched it up first, swinging the barrel toward the man, who froze, hands raised.

The small, whiskered man was breathing rapidly, his chest heaving and his eyes darting uneasily between Rafael with the pistol and the unarmed Cara. He brought his hands down slowly, clamping his left hand over his bleeding right wrist.

"Who are you?" asked Rafael. "And what are you doing here?"

The man's shoulders relaxed, and he smiled, as if to set the two young people at ease. "No one, no one really. Just . . . I'm looking for a man called Thrayder—perhaps you know him?"

"There's no one called Thrayder here," replied Cara.

"Are you sure? Tall, gangly man, hideous, long nose, black eyes, looks like a scarecrow come to life?"

"And what would you want with that man, if he were here?" asked Cara.

"I just want to talk to him."

"Talk about what?" prompted Rafael.

"That's between myself and Thrayder."

"You're an armed man skulking on our property, during a war, sir. You've made your business with this Thrayder fellow our business. So perhaps you'd like to offer some further clarification? If not, I'm sure the captain of our local militia would be interested in your clandestine activities."

The man grinned disarmingly and then lunged at Rafael, trying to duck beneath the pistol. A shot rang out and the stranger dropped to the ground before Cara could even react to his desperate attack. The siblings stood over the body, their eyes wide as wisps of smoke spewed from the pistol in Rafael's hand.

"Well, maybe all Murdoch has been waiting for is this bastard," said Rafael after a moment. "Either way, he owes us an explanation now."

"He owed us an explanation before."

"What do you think, drag the body back toward the house and confront our dear elder brother?"

Cara nodded and the two siblings gathered the man in their arms, Cara taking his legs while Rafael grasped him under his armpits. They awkwardly carried him back across the field but hadn't made it within sight of the house before they met Louis, Henry, and Murdoch coming toward them. They laid the body down when their brothers reached them.

"We heard a shot," Louis explained. "Thought perhaps you'd just killed a turkey or something, but Henry's an old housewife and insisted we come out and check."

"And it looks like I was right," interjected Henry. "Who's this you've killed?"

"Don't know," said Rafael. "But he was looking for Murdoch. Or a man he described that looked like Murdoch, a man he called Thrayder. So perhaps Murdoch can tell us who he is?"

Murdoch's lip curled up in a hideous, amused grin. He shared a long look with Louis and then said, "He's probably a client that our paranoid little brother has put to bed with a shovel. No wonder the business is in shambles."

"He wasn't a client!" cried Cara.

Louis frowned. "Murdoch, I think . . . I think we should probably tell them."

Murdoch sneered. "Is that what you think, Louis? Perhaps you should leave thinking to people with brains."

Louis took a slow, calming breath and continued, "They're family. They deserve an explanation if these bastards are coming here now."

"They're *my* family, yes, but didn't they used to call you 'Katerina's indiscretion'?" Murdoch taunted.

Before any of the others could react, Louis' rapier was out and pressed against Murdoch's neck, the sharp blade held directly against the white scar that ran along his older brother's throat. Then the other three siblings leaped forward, Cara and Rafael drawing Louis back while Henry pressed himself between Murdoch and Louis' blade. For a moment Louis resisted, but then he allowed Cara and Rafael to yank him away, still seething. Murdoch's mocking, laughing expression hadn't changed.

"Blazes, Losi! Are you going to kill your own brother?" exclaimed Henry, his brown eyes wide.

"And why shouldn't I? Do you think he would hesitate to kill any one of us if it benefited him in the slightest?"

"What the devil is wrong with you?" replied Henry. "You've been sulking around the house and fields ever since you arrived. The only time you ever show spirit is when there's a girl around. And I do not understand at all this animosity toward Murdoch. It's exasperating, and, quite frankly, exhausting."

"Don't understand this animosity!" cried Louis, shaking Cara and Rafael's hands away. "I, the man who saved his bloody life not a year ago, and have had nothing but grief and insults and ridicule—" He stopped abruptly, fuming.

Murdoch's smile flattened, a warning in his eyes, though he did not speak. Louis sheathed his rapier and spun around, leaving in a huff back toward the farmyard.

After a moment, Rafael turned to Murdoch. "We could certainly pretend that didn't happen, but it did. It's time for you to give us some answers. Especially now that we've got people coming onto the property trying to kill us. Louis and you are obviously well acquainted, even if, somehow, you didn't know you were brothers. Perhaps you would share with the rest of your siblings what the nature of your association is?"

"No," replied Murdoch simply.

"Do you deny that you two knew each other before you met on the path to Maralah?" asked Rafael.

"I do not."

"Then why continue to hide things from us?" Cara demanded.

"I don't need justification, little sister."

"Just because you've gotten along fine without a family for twenty-two years doesn't mean that you can continue to pretend we don't exist, or that we are so foolish and trivial that we don't deserve to know what's going on. You watch the trails like a fugitive. You've set everything here at Maralah in order and we can all see you're getting restless, ready to move on, and likely you'll be gone another twenty-two years, or never return. But this man was spying on us in the forest, looking for a man called Thrayder that he described exactly as you look. Whoever it is you watch those roads for knows you came here. We deserve to know what sort of danger you've put us in."

"Don't fret yourselves. If I have indeed put you in danger, then I'll see you through it."

"If you've put us in danger, we ought to know the manner of the threat before we come face-to-face with it," said Rafael.

Cara, her face flushed with anger, added, "We have no reason to trust that you'll see us through anything. You don't care about us at all."

"Well, why don't you run after your precious little Losi, then, and have him tell you what trouble you have to look forward to? He seems only too eager to share."

"I will if he's still at Maralah when we get back. But he's likely gone, and that leaves you to tell us, as you should have when you first arrived," insisted Cara.

"Then you'll have to wait until he has nursed his pride back to health sucking the tits of loose women in Wilmington or Brattleborough, or wherever he ends up tonight. It's not my habit to send children to bed with nightmares. You have known a little danger, Cara, but only a little."

"You're impossible!" cried Cara. She felt the anger boiling up within her, threatening to spill over.

"So my reserved little sister has some spirit after all?" Murdoch's eyes gleamed with amusement as he spoke.

"You've not seen anything of me yet."

"I don't doubt it. You're a Firefax, after all. Or so they tell me."

"I could defeat you at fencing or at pistols."

Murdoch chuckled and said, "I've been far beyond your skill level since before you were born."

"If you're not going to help us, then just leave, Murdoch. No one asked you to return to Maralah."

"I believe Henry did, actually."

"Well, I did, but I didn't know—" Henry began, but Cara interrupted him.

"He didn't know what he was asking for. He didn't know that you would only bring danger to our home. I'm asking you to leave before your presence costs us something we cannot pay. Leave now, if you love us."

"If I love you," echoed Murdoch with such mocking in his tone that Cara shuddered.

"Cara, and all of us, just want to know what danger is coming," Rafael said slowly, carefully.

"Yes, because I care about my family, unlike you," said Cara, still staring boldly at Murdoch..

"You think we are so different, then?" Murdoch was taunting again.

"I'm nothing like you."

"No? You killed a horse for revenge. A poor, dumb animal."

"That's enough, Murdoch—" Rafael began.

"I just did what I was trained to do," said Cara, tears beginning to burn at the back of her lids.

"Indeed. And what did you feel the moment you saw your father die, Cara Firefax?"

Cara blinked hard. "Rage, and despair, and . . ."

"Perhaps a little thrill of excitement?"

Cara's eyes widened, but her reply caught in her throat, and she felt an awful sensation, as if some monstrous thing was clawing at her chest.

"That's enough. More than enough, by far," said Henry, his voice sad but also firm. He stepped forward, putting his arm around Cara's shoulder. "I think you should leave, Murdoch. At least for the night. Let everyone cool off a bit."

Murdoch studied his siblings for a moment, eyes twinkling with mirth. Then he nodded his head. "Very well. I'll leave. But you don't want to face what's coming here without my help." Then he turned and followed Louis' path back toward the house.

Rafael stared at the body lying in the field, then back at their eldest brother's vanishing form. "Can't say I'm sorry to see him go. Though I should have liked some answers first." He turned his gaze toward Cara, noting the distant expression in her eyes, reminiscent of the state she had been in the night Henry and he found her after the death of their father. "Why don't you take Cara back to Maralah? I'll bury the body, over under the trees. Maybe send Elihu and little Henry out to give me a hand?"

Henry nodded, equally aware of his sister's traumatized state.

As they walked, Henry wrapped an arm comfortingly around his sister's shoulder. Cara drew in a slow, shaky breath, staring straight ahead. Finally she spoke, her voice so low that even though he was right beside her, Henry had to strain to catch her words.

"I am just like him."

"Is that it? Is that what torments you? Cara, don't be a fool. You may share an uncanny physical resemblance with Murdoch, but otherwise you and he could not be more dissimilar. You are good, and caring. I have watched you tend the sick, the injured, the helpless, my own children, my wife, even myself. You are all goodness, Cara, all goodness—there is not an ounce of evil in you. Murdoch is not that. Murdoch was never that."

"I hope he's leaving forever tonight."

"I think he is. Yesterday he signed the deed of Maralah over to me."

Cara breathed out a long sigh of relief. Then she stopped and turned toward Henry, wrapping her arms around her brother's neck and pressing her head into his shoulder. "I'm sorry. I know you love him," she whispered.

"But it's all right. It's better for us and for him that he moves on. Nothing to fear now, little Cara. Let's get you inside for a good, long rest tonight."

For the first time since her father died, Cara slept the entire night, a dreamless, perfect sleep, awakening refreshed and full of optimism. The next morning was the sabbath, and the entire family piled into the wagon or jogged along beside it to the small town of Wilmington, where they participated in a packed Sunday service, spilling outside onto the dirt street. When they arrived home, there was still no sign of Murdoch, nor Louis, and everyone scattered, enjoying the peace of a Sunday afternoon. Most of the children went to the woods or down to the pond. Cara and Halsey brought their cooking onto the lawn, plucking a hen that Rafael had executed. The sun was pouring down, warm but not uncomfortable, and the sound of Henry playing variations on "My Lady Greensleeves" at the piano inside carried across the lawn, punctuated by the happy cries of the children, shrieking and laughing as they reenacted what they knew of the Battle of Bennington. The heaviness that had hung over Maralah as long as Murdoch had lived there seemed, at last, to have lifted.

Rafael joined the ladies, dutifully peeling potatoes, the very last the root cellar had to offer; poor, shriveled affairs. He heard the sound first and glanced up. "Is that a horse coming up the trail?" he asked, at which the two women turned their heads and listened.

"Maybe it's Louis returning?" suggested Halsey.

Assuming that to be the case, no one moved to tidy themselves, continuing with their dinner preparations. Gradually the clattering of hooves grew louder, until at last there burst from the trees a horse, ridden by a tall young man with dark hair, tanned skin, and vibrant green eyes. He scanned the yard, a faint smirk on his face, before dismounting and leading his horse toward them. He wore an old-fashioned green tunic, somewhat torn and weathered, embroidered with strange figures and symbols. His once-white gloves were stained with the grime of travel and upon his dark brown hair sat a dusty black tricorn hat. He removed the hat and bowed graciously as Halsey rose to greet him, wiping her hands on her apron and blushing. The sound of the piano, which had drifted into a haunting orchestral suite by Bach, halted abruptly and Henry stepped out of the house.

The stranger rose from his bow, a playful, kindly smile on his face, and turned to address Henry. "You must be the master of this fine abode?" He had a strange accent, but spoke English perfectly.

"I am Henry Firefax, yes," replied Henry, scanning the stranger for any sign of recognition. But the man was too young to have been a client of Robert's. He was an unknown.

Unexpectedly the stranger took a few strides forward and grasped Henry's hand, shaking it vigorously. "I am Istäni Seänkea, and honored to meet you, and your lovely family. Let me try to guess who is who here." He turned back to the others, grinning at Rafael. "This must be the wise Rafael, and here, the lady Halsey, your esteemed wife, and you,"—he paused in his review of the family, his bright face becoming somehow even more joyful—"you must be the beautiful lady Cara, Robert's princess, no?"

Cara snorted and adjusted her spectacles. No one had ever called her beautiful. But there was no mockery in the stranger's eyes, and she smiled and bobbed her head, allowing him the honor of taking her hand and kissing it.

Henry spoke up again. "You seem to know us quite well, Mr. Sinkiah, er, Seänkea? Sorry. But we do not know your name at all. You are surely not from these parts?"

Istäni laughed and said, "Is my accent so noticeable? If you had heard of me, you would have been told I came from Lapland, from the northern tribal people there, though that is not entirely correct. I am honored to meet the Firefax family, having heard only rumors and hints that you existed. Your family is truly the stuff of legend and secrecy. But, alas, I see the man I am seeking is not here. Is Murdoch Firefax not home at present?"

A cold thrill ran down Cara's spine and she stiffened, scanning the youth again, looking for any hint that he was the danger Murdoch had watched for so patiently on the walnut stump each night. But this young man was nothing but charm, kindness, openness—there seemed nothing dangerous about him. Even his weapons had been left attached to the saddle save a strange, ornamental-looking hatchet at his waist.

"He is not here, no," replied Rafael.

"Oh, how foolish of me to forget what manner of man Murdoch is, keeping his own counsel and schedule. I assumed he would be home on the sabbath. Foolish of me to imagine he would do the predictable thing."

"Perhaps you would like to wait for him?" asked Cara unexpectedly, and all the others glanced at her.

"You are too kind. Such hospitality. Exactly the generosity I would have anticipated from the incomparable Cara, a true gem among women. If it is acceptable to the proprietors of your fine residence, I will certainly wait. Though, a great lot of good it will do me. One never knows when to expect Murdoch, and when he is most wanted he is least there. Of course, in contrast to that, when he is most needed he always manages to be present—have you ever noticed? I'm sorry, perhaps I talk too much. Where may I rest my horse? It looks as if rain is coming."

"I'll take him for you," Rafael offered, rising and dusting off the potato peels.

"My thanks to you," replied Istäni, graciously. "If it is agreeable to you fine ladies, perhaps I can assist with the potatoes while Rafael so kindly cares for my steed?" He drew up the stool Rafael had abandoned and set to peeling potatoes with an almost surgical precision.

"You'll pardon our curiosity," said Cara, emboldened by the stranger's flattery of her. "But, how long have you known our brother, and how did you come to make his acquaintance?"

"When have I not known your brother? And how did I come to know him? Why, I was born, I suppose. I have known your brother since nearly as far back as my recollection goes. The man practically raised me, you know. Surely he's mentioned me?" Istäni noted the bemused faces around him and chuckled. "Of course he didn't. How obtuse of me to imagine that. What has he told you about his past?"

"Apparently less than he told you about his family," said Henry, eyeing the stranger with a dubious expression.

Istäni laughed heartily, a pleasant, musical sound, as disarming as everything else about him—his odd accent, his quaint garb, his ready grin, and his riveting, mesmerizing green eyes. He was still laughing when Rafael returned from the barn. Finally the laughter of the stranger subsided and he looked up brightly at the men and women around him. "The man you know as Murdoch I have called Thrayder for my whole life, until now. Only recently have I learned his true identity and who his family might be. If you know who to ask, you can learn about the Firefaxes and what they do."

Halsey's face blanched ever so slightly at the reminder of what she had married into. She rose and took the plucked chicken inside. Rafael followed his sister-in-law with the pot of potatoes and returned a few moments later to squat on the ground near Istäni, who rose and offered the younger man his stool again. The stranger paced briefly, a frown marring his handsome face. Finally his expression cleared and he began to speak again.

"I first met your brother aboard the *India*, sailing with the original Henry Firefax. Henry I."

The three Firefaxes startled at once, exchanging glances of surprise.

"You sailed with Grandfather?" asked Henry.

"Yes, with your inestimable grandfather, a truly great man, as ruthless and irresistible as the sea he sailed on. I was the son of his quartermaster, Killinger, by an island lady. I was a child, however, a small child, and Murdoch was a young man at the time. Henry and Murdoch used different appellations and hid their connection to each other. If I were older I think I would have realized they had some relation. They looked like one another, but, you know, there are plenty of hideous people in the world. They aren't all necessarily of the same blood. I'm sorry, have I said something amiss? You all look so astonished."

"*I* never even met my grandfather," said Henry. "To hear

such a young man claim to have sailed aboard his vessel with him is difficult to credit, Mr. Seänkea."

"I was little more than a toddler when I came aboard, maybe six or seven years of age. Many of my earliest memories are aboard that vessel. It was ostensibly a privateer for King George, though I don't believe Henry possessed a real letter of marque, so I suppose we were, in actuality, pirates."

"I'm sure he did have a letter of marque. A Firefax can get any letter they desire from leaders of state. It is the nature of our business, as you seem to know already," explained Henry. "What happened to Grandfather? No one knows to this day what became of the *India*. There are only rumors that she sank in the West Indies."

Istäni smiled. "Forgive me, I had not realized that you knew nothing. Perhaps you would indulge me in a proper storytelling?"

"You have all our attention. It's about time we learned some of the things our oldest brother has been hiding from us," said Rafael, and they all drew their stools closer to the stranger, to listen to his tale.

CHAPTER 7

THE "INDIA"

1765 ⚔ LATE AUGUST
SOMEWHERE IN THE ATLANTIC

It was four bells into the first watch on a moonless night. The only light came from the cold, feeble glow of a million stars bespeckling the black sky. The *India* moved gracefully over the ocean surface, a dreamy, gliding movement, little breezes fluttering her cloudlike sails. The stars reflected into the dark ocean waters, just as black as the sky above, making it appear as though the sky and sea had merged into one mass of darkness, glistening with scattered fragments of diamond light.

The larboard division, finished with most of their duties, were seated idle in the prow. They pretended to busy themselves with splicing rope as the officer of the watch passed by. Once the officer was out of earshot, one of the sailors leaned toward a chiseled old gunner.

"What's this, then, Olly?" he asked. "An island, you say?"

"That's what I heard. I don't know if it be true, but that's what they're telling me."

"Stands to reason, really, if you think about it," piped up one of the other men. "What in the name of Heaven are we doing out here? We ought to be back in the colonies by now—that's where nigh on half the crew is from. Where's he taking us? There's nothing in these waters. Not a damn thing."

"And they're all closed as stones—Killinger, Kent, that bloody boy Kent's so attached to," another sailor interjected. "But there ain't no island in these waters, that's what I don't understand. There's nothin' on the map."

"This island ain't on no map," replied Olly, touching his finger to his nose. "It's a place, they say, where there's treasure hoarded, more money than you could imagine, more than the King of England has in all his coffers. I heard there's more money there than all the wealth of all the courts of Europe."

"What's it doin' there? And how did that much money get on an island in the middle of bloody nowhere?"

"They say it all belongs to a family, and Kent hisself is one of 'em. That's how he knows where 'tis."

"There's folk on this island?"

"That's what they say, strange folk. They live there and never leave, though they could if they wanted."

"If I had all the wealth of Europe on one island where folks let me be, I don't reckon I'd leave neither," said Vincent, an older seaman, without a single tooth in his mouth. "Are we goin' there to take the treasure? We're already loaded from those raids in the South Atlantic. I reckon we take on any more loot and the *India*'ll sink."

"No, no, no," replied Olly solemnly. "They're going to unload all the money, store it there like the rest of it. That's what Kent's about, if it's true he's of that family."

"What about our share? My share's enough to move me family to the Ohio Country and stake out me own piece of land," said one of the other sailors with a scowl, casting a glance across the ship, toward a tall, silent form standing on the quarterdeck.

"I don't rightly know. Mayhap he's only takin' his share there and lettin' us have the rest."

"That's a fool thing to do. Once we know where this here island is, we'll all be coming back to get more o' that loot."

"I don't rightly know the thinkin' behind it all. Kent's a closed bastard, you know that, always has been. But, anyhow, that's what I heard," Olly finished.

The men fell silent, all of them now looking toward a black shape on the quarterdeck, standing tall against the sky behind him. The lapping of the waves and creaking of the rigging provided a soft, soothing background noise to their discussion, calming their outrage a little. In truth, they had been talking of similar things for weeks, but the information about the island was new to the men in the larboard watch and added to their disgust at their present state, sitting in the middle of nowhere, with no destination, and no prizes for weeks.

"Who told you all this?" asked one of the men suddenly, breaking the pregnant silence.

Olly shrugged. "I don't recollect. Folks been talkin' about it belowdecks the last few nights."

"Anyway, say 'tis true, an' ole Henry means to make off with all our loot—what are we going to do about it?"

"I'll tell you what we're going to do about it," said a steely-eyed man who had remained silent throughout the duration of the conversation. He had been Henry's navigator, before they had taken aboard the young man standing silent on the quarterdeck, nearly eight months before. "It's like we've been saying for the last week. We slit their throats an' take this ship and all the loot on it, and any more prizes we find. Make our fortunes."

"Slit whose throats?"

"Henry Kent, Harvey Killinger, that bloody Thrayder, who fancies hisself a navigator now. And anyone else that wants to side with 'em—the old mute, the officers, that eerie, phantom child—"

The gunner shushed the speaker quite suddenly, gripping his arm and nodding further aft. There was a humming sound, faint and wordless. Once the men were silent, the only noise that disturbed the night was that soft humming. Even the waves seemed briefly to still, the rolling of the ship lessened, and a hush fell upon the ocean. The eerie, phantom child padded softly across the deck, his gaze fixed on the foresail, looking neither left nor right. The boy could almost feel the anger of the sailors as he passed them, their eyes fixed on him. While he pretended to be unaware, he had keen ears and little of their preceding conversation had been lost upon him.

The men watched the boy pass, then, once he reached the furthest place forward that he could, they continued speaking in hushed tones. The child scooted his way out onto the bowsprit easily, fingers grasping the smooth wood, legs dangling toward the water far below.

"I think even Killinger would turn agin' him, after today," said Vincent, out of the side of his mouth, so quiet the boy could barely make out the words.

"We don't bloody need Killinger. Forty crew against a doddering old man, six officers, a boy, and Killinger?" the deposed navigator said, his eyes blazing with hatred.

"Aye, but as long as Killinger still sides with him, some of the men are bound to stay on his side. The men don't care about Henry, one way or the other, 'cept the money he brings 'em, but they're loyal to Killinger. He's always been a good quartermaster to 'em. Fair."

"That was one hell of a brawl they had, shouting at each

other in the open air like that. Not a man among us would have been sorry to take that little sloop. Easy pickings. Would have done us some good after all these months of nothing but staring at treasures that we can't do nothin' with."

"I don't know what we're waitin' for. We've enough men on our side. Why not tonight?"

"Keep it down!" warned Olly, glancing again toward the child, staring serenely out at the sea, still humming.

"The little brat don't speak English, and even Killinger can't understand the tongue he do speak. Them quaint folk up in those northern parts of Lapland, they don't talk like other Finns. No danger of that one squawking."

"I don't think he's a Laplander at all. Never seen eyes like that in a Finn. I'll grant you he don't talk, but he seems to understand when you ask him to do somethin'."

"Just 'cause of the context. He don't know nothin'. I called his father every curse word under the sun right in front of him a few days back, took a good lickin' for that too. The boy didn't bat a lid. He's a simpleton."

"Still, I'd feel safer if someone cut his little windpipe. Always creeping around, staring dumbly, like he's a spirit. Killinger should have left him with his mother, wherever he came from. Anyway, it can't be tonight. Tomorrow night, probably, or the night after, but the men are tired—they won't rouse tonight."

"It has to be tomorrow night, then," said the deposed navigator grimly. "We can't wait."

The men moved away slowly as the fifth bell sounded. Easing himself back along the bowsprit, the child dropped onto the deck and padded behind them. No one stopped him, or even glanced at him, accustomed to the strange child moving in their midst. He ascended the stairs to the quarter-deck and stopped before the tall, gangly form of Thrayder standing at the wheel.

Thrayder, seeing the boy and recognizing a look of urgency in his wide eyes, crouched down beside him. "The men talking again?"

The boy nodded.

"When?"

The boy mimed the sun rising and setting and held up one finger.

"Nothing new there, then, that's when we expected it," said Thrayder. He fished in his pocket, finding a candied pecan, which he handed to the boy, who crunched it gratefully. "Don't fret, Noaidi, you stick close to me and Killinger, and you'll be fine. I doubt most of them would stoop to cutting a child's throat. They're not assassins. They've little ones of their own at home."

The child pointed at Thrayder and then down, indicating Killinger's cabin beneath them. He shook his head as he pointed, eyes growing still wider.

"Don't fret, I know your father would like to slip a knife between my ribs, but he won't. I'm more useful alive, for now. If we cross swords with the crew, he, the captain, and all the other officers won't survive without me."

For eight years Harvey Killinger had been Henry Kent's second-in-command; there had been no question of his loyalty, indeed, his devotion to Henry. He was unquestionably the man who would take over the ship if ever the aged but still capable captain were unable to perform his duties. All that had changed the day Thrayder came, as if from nowhere, boarding in Jacmel and, despite his youth, quickly becoming a close and treasured confidant to Henry. The first quarrel between the captain and the quartermaster had been over Killinger's opposition to Thrayder joining the crew at all. But Henry had insisted, claiming to see himself in the wiry, hideous, and cunning young man. Ever since then, nearly everything had become a point of contention between the two officers, particularly any suggestions made by the young man called Thrayder. However wise and well thought out his ideas were, Killinger always took a stand against them.

The greatest conflict had occurred the day before that starry, moonless night, when a ship had been sighted in the distance, flying strange colors, not hailing them, nor fleeing from the *India*, but sitting quiet, easy prey, only a few miles away. Killinger had instantly advocated for taking the prize, but Thrayder had opposed the move. They were already heavily laden with spoils and had no need for more prize money. Killinger had argued loudly for taking the little sloop, but Henry had dismissed him. It was this altercation that the sailors referred to as the moment when they felt at last that the quartermaster would side with them in a mutiny.

The day after the boy's warning to Thrayder, the *India* reached a new level of tension as the strange sloop was again sighted, near dusk, closer than before, her sails hanging slack, a flag, impossible to make out, dangling from her mast. Again Henry made his way to the quarterdeck, the wizened, tall old man standing against the railing, undisturbed, staring at the ship, the faintest hint of a smile on his craggy face, while Killinger spoke to him in a rising voice.

"We fire one shot across their bow and I guarantee they'll surrender," he hissed. "Easiest prize we'll ever have had."

Henry shook his head slowly, still grinning. "No need, Harvey, my old friend. No need. We've enough now. More than enough."

"Perhaps enough for you! You've no need of it anymore. You're closer to the grave than anyone else aboard this vessel. But what about the rest of us? What about our spoils?"

"You, and all the sailors, have enough for your needs as well, old friend."

Killinger drew himself up, but the quartermaster could not come close to Henry Kent's height, even stooped as he was in his old age. Killinger pawed at the sword sheathed at his side, until the long shadow of Thrayder fell across him and he backed away. The crew, hearing the altercation, drew near, fondling their own cutlasses and knives, ready at a moment's notice to enact the mutiny that had been brewing for weeks. But Killinger, still trembling with rage, turned and stormed away from the captain, disappearing below decks. The child followed him noiselessly, watching as Killinger paced in his small cabin, his arms trembling from repressed rage. Sensing movement behind him, he whirled, drawing his sword, but, upon seeing the child, he relaxed again.

"Oh, it's you," he said. "You startled me, Istäni. What are you playing at?"

Istäni did not speak, staring up at Killinger with those enormous green eyes.

Killinger squatted down, tousling the boy's dark hair. "You look like your mother, you know? Not like me at all. Lucky for you, really. The men think I'll turn against him, but I've sailed with Henry for too long. I'm the only person alive, aside from him, who knows everything. Everything, I tell you! Me alone, in all the world, and him, of course. I love the man, in truth, I love him dearly. It's that boy he's taken on that I hate. I'd like to see his insides spilled on the deck."

The child stared without speaking.

"Things are going to get hot tonight, my boy," said Killinger. "When they do, I'm standing beside Henry, just as I always have, but . . ." He leaned in, his voice a whisper. "I plan to do Thrayder in at the end of it all. I think Henry's leaving. He's halfway gone already. I don't know how he's going to make his exit, but he's leaving. We're close now, you know, very close. Someone's got to carry his secret afterward, and take care of this ship, and that'll be me, Istäni, as Henry would want it. That upstart Thrayder gets a knife in his heart." He paused and chuckled. "If he has a heart, ha! We'll find out one way or another tonight. Eight years I've been with Henry, and that boy not even a year and yet he's getting special favors and attention. Henry's listening to his counsel, as if that boy could know anything, at his age."

Istäni pointed toward himself, raising his eyebrows.

"You'll be with me, my boy, always. And before I die, I'll pass the secret to you, and you to your son, or daughter, it don't matter to me—I'll be dead by then. Here, my boy, in case things get warm even for children tonight." He passed a small hatchet secured in a leather sheath to the boy, who ran his fingers over the intricately carved whalebone handle. "Your mother would've wanted you to have that anyway. Now, run along. It's getting late—we've got a murderous crew to battle this evening."

The distant, unknown sloop had reappeared briefly the following day, causing another scene on deck. Then it had vanished again as night was just beginning to fall, the last rays of sun spreading across the ocean, fingers of light creeping into the crevices between oak, iron, and tar, before darkness swallowed the wooden hull entirely. The boy moved swiftly across the darkened deck, coming to a halt just before the captain's cabin, his hands on the axe inside his jacket. Through the cracks in the door he could see two tall, gangly forms, talking in quiet, muffled voices, their conversation barely audible above the creaks and groans of the rigging and boards.

"You'll have to defeat Harvey if you want this vessel, and he's a wily man, and a canny fighter."

The boy saw Thrayder shrug his thin shoulders, wearing a twisted, easy smile on his sharp features.

"You're arrogant. So sure of your ability to handle him," said Henry, with a hint of admiration in his voice.

"Should I not be?" whispered Thrayder, his voice harsh and croaking, though it was not yet as grating as it became in the years that followed.

"Harvey Killinger shouldn't have escaped, but he found his way into the right woman's heart and boudoir. Fortunately for him, he's not a confident man. He trusts no one, and that's a useful thing aboard a privateer, so I've let him be all these years. Anyway, I didn't know if there would be anyone else to carry on the secret, until you came."

"So the only people that know are myself, and Killinger?"

"Aye."

"Soon only myself."

"As you say."

Killinger appeared, scurrying across the deck with a smattering of officers and crew behind him. He burst through the door of the cabin, shoving Istäni in front of him as he entered. Thrayder and Henry both looked up at the panting quartermaster but showed no sign of alarm.

"They're coming!" cried Killinger. "I brought the boatswain, the carpenter, six other officers, and two seamen still loyal to you, Captain."

The captain turned and peered out the door behind the defenders as the first cries of rage sounded on the deck outside, and the first pistol shot rang out, echoing across the empty ocean. They barricaded the door quickly with Henry's sparse furnishings. Istäni, keeping low to the floor, found a knothole in the wall and peered through, taking in the angry crew gathering outside, a few brandishing torches, all of them waving guns and cutlasses. He pulled back as a bullet passed through the wall near his head, and turned, panting to stare up at the officers. Thrayder drew his two pistols, and Istäni noted the young man's sword, and the row of knives sheathed in a long belt across his narrow chest, along with a pack of powder and bullets hanging from his belt. He was a walking arsenal. Thrayder lay down on the ground by the hole where Istäni crouched.

"Reload my pistols?" he asked, his voice calm and even.

Istäni nodded and took the satchel of powder and shot. Thrayder raised one pistol, aimed it through the hole, and squeezed the trigger. There was a resounding bang, and then Thrayder handed the pistol to the boy, who dutifully reloaded it. When the first shots from the besieged cabin rang out, the crew fell back, hiding behind barrels, cannons, and heavy crates. Istäni watched in awe as every shot Thrayder fired hit its target, sometimes nothing more than the ear of a sailor exposed for an instant from behind a barrel. But even that was enough. The lanky young man did not miss once. Istäni shivered as bullets ricocheted off the walls, some shattering through the wooden planks, narrowly missing the silent, deadly young man. But Thrayder never flinched.

"That's enough!" cried Killinger at last. "They ain't got more bullets out there. Come on! We'll run the blaggards into the bulwarks and split them open head to toe!"

Without waiting to see if anyone agreed with his plan, Killinger, bristling with rage and impatience, slid a heavy chest away from the door and burst through, roaring as he ran toward the seamen, who scattered before him. Istäni had just exchanged pistols again with Thrayder and watched as the youth sighted down along the barrel. Istäni's eyes grew enormous as he saw Thrayder's aim adjust from the fleeing crew to Killinger's back. Thrayder drew back the cock with a resounding click and his finger hovered over the trigger.

"Thrayder," came a soft voice from behind them, and instantly the young man lowered his gun, releasing the cock and rising. The sound of hand-to-hand combat on deck drifted back to the cabin, empty save for Thrayder, Istäni, and Henry Kent.

"Get on with it, boy. Give your father a hand," said Thrayder, giving Istäni a shove out the door, before turning back to the captain. Istäni diligently took a few running strides, but, at the last instant he stopped and turned around. To his surprise, Henry was disappearing over the windowsill of the great cabin. The old man paused, one hand on the sill, the other on a rope that trailed over the vessel's stern. The little boy strained his ears to catch the last snatches of conversation between the two men.

"And you've nothing, no word or letter for me to take back to your son?" asked Thrayder.

Henry laughed and replied, "What would I ever have to share with him? I'd be surprised if you ever see him again yourself."

"As would I."

"Well, boy, the ship is yours if you can handle Killinger. If not, . . . sorry," said the old man with a wry grin and a shrug.

"I can handle him," replied Thrayder as the spry old man disappeared over the window ledge.

Thrayder spun his gangly body, darting from the cabin toward the fight. Istäni whirled about, trying to appear intent on chasing after Killinger, afraid to give the impression that he had witnessed the last exchange of the mysterious Thrayder and old Henry Kent. Thrayder paid the boy no mind, practically stepping on him in his haste to engage in the battle. There were about fifteen mutineers who had not yet been wounded or killed, nor had they yet laid down their weapons or slunk off below decks to pretend they had not been involved in the mutiny at all. The child, largely ignored by the fighters, kept to the side, watching the brutal battle around him.

Thrayder, panting from effort, his dark eyes shining with

glee, drove the deposed navigator backward. Neatly tripping him onto his back, the young man viciously skewered his adversary through the trachea. The man cried out, gurgling and reaching up as if to stem the air and blood flowing from his windpipe. Thrayder withdrew his weapon and stepped on the man's bleeding neck, crushing it inward, a wicked smile on his face. Turning suddenly from his kill, Thrayder made as if to run at the remaining sailors, but they all backed away from him, uneasily eyeing the deposed navigator as he thrashed, struggling, breathless, blood spurting from his neck like a fountain. Finally the man's thrashing movements stilled and his eyes glazed over in death. Even Killinger drew back in horror.

"Kent is gone," said Thrayder. "He left the ship in my command. Unless you would like to challenge that?" With his black eyes, he scanned the few petrified men that remained on deck.

"Gone where?" cried Killinger. "We're in the middle of the ocean—where can he have gone? I'm the quartermaster, duly elected by this crew. Why would he have left the ship to you? Did you kill the captain, you spawn of Satan?"

"Oh, that was his caveat, wasn't it," said Thrayder, smiling as if remembering something of minor importance that he had carelessly forgotten. "That the ship would be mine if I could handle you."

"So the ship was left to me, then!" Killinger triumphantly lunged forward, his cutlass striking Thrayder's rapier with a loud ringing clash. The two men battled across the deck, Killinger always attacking, using his weight and brute strength against his tall, rail-thin opponent, pushing Thrayder ever backward. The younger man showed no sign of fear, dancing over the obstacles on the deck with graceless, ungainly ease. Thrayder was toying with the angry quartermaster, Istäni thought as he watched in admiration.

Several times Killinger managed to wedge Thrayder against the railing or into a tight corner, and Istäni thought for certain the young man would die. But each time the younger man dodged beneath the flashing cutlass, managing to get himself out of every scrape by a hairsbreadth. Finally Killinger had him up against the captain's cabin and, with a masterful twist, managed to disarm the younger man. He caught hold of Thrayder's neck, drawing back his cutlass for the killing blow, crushing Thrayder's throat in his enormous hand.

"Not so amusing when it's you who can't breathe, is it?" he hissed, his face inches from Thrayder's.

The black-eyed youth was still smirking as Killinger relentlessly squeezed his throat. Killinger swung his cutlass toward his pinned, helpless adversary and Thrayder glanced toward Istäni. The child thought for an instant that he was seeing the last, haughty expression of a dying, unrepentant man. But what happened next was so swift that Istäni, years later, could hardly credit it. Thrayder had been trying to pry Killinger's hands from his neck, then, suddenly, he relaxed as Killinger swung his weapon, becoming for a moment a dead weight. It was surprising enough to loosen Killinger's grasp. As Killinger groped to keep hold of the younger man, Thrayder twisted free, catching Killinger's cutlass-wielding arm, though not in time to prevent the weapon from piercing his neck. A thick, dark stream of blood started down Thrayder's shirt, but he ignored it, kicking a long leg into Killinger's gut. As Killinger fell backward, dropping his cutlass, Thrayder was on him like a panther, and when he stood again, two knife handles protruded from Killinger's unmoving chest.

Thrayder turned toward the crew, who wilted before his menacing presence. The officers herded the sailors away, issuing orders to clear the chaos of the deck. There was blood bubbling from Thrayder's wound, and a high-pitched whistling sound emanating from his neck with each breath.

Thrayder reached directly into the wound with one finger, pressing hard, and the high-pitched sound stopped. He scanned the bodies, noting, with some disappointment, the man who had served as ship's surgeon, lying dead on the deck.

Istäni caught hold of Thrayder's pant leg, pointing at the wound and making a motion like a needle and thread.

When Thrayder spoke, his voice was horrible, strained and harsh, like the cawing of a raven. "You can fix it?"

Istäni nodded emphatically, then turned and padded away, toward the sick bay. Thrayder hesitated, but, despite his finger plugging the hole, he could still feel the air flowing out of his trachea, and there were growing crinkling pockets of subcutaneous emphysema, all along his neck and chest wall. He followed the silent child.

<hr>

Henry Firefax II stared, mouth agape, at the young man as he finished his tale. "But where did Grandfather go? And are you telling me that Murdoch then just quietly raised you after killing your father?"

"It does seem that way, doesn't it?" said Istäni. "Thrayder raised me until I could take care of myself, yes. There wasn't anything like love or affection in those actions, you understand. Of course there wouldn't be. Not with him. But he raised me nonetheless. And your grandfather . . . where did he go? That is the question, isn't it? Where could he have gone? We were in the middle of nowhere. Of course, I was only a child, with little idea of navigation or time. But I believe it took nearly a month to get back to shore after the mutiny. Your brother sold the ship. He divided the spoils between the remaining crew, keeping a good deal for himself, obviously, and that was the last time I knew him to go to sea, other than as a passenger."

"Surprising, if he was indeed trained to be a navigator," Rafael commented. "That's a skilled position. Highly sought after."

"He didn't have much to learn," said Henry. "Did I ever tell you how he wouldn't leave the navigator's side on our voyages with Robert when we were young? Well, except to sit with me in the cabin while I vomited my very soul out, getting me a fresh bucket every hour. He spent all his time aboard ship doing one or the other of those two things."

Istäni turned toward Henry, and a strange look crossed his face, a mingling of realization and gleeful triumph.

"So you know all the things he has been up to these last twenty-two years?" asked Cara hopefully.

Istäni let out a soft chuckle, shaking his head. "I know little more than you do. I was there for a few of his escapades, of course, but he kept his own counsel and was given to disappearing and leaving me with strangers for months at a time. As I said, until only a few months ago I did not realize he was Henry's grandson, and a Firefax himself. But I am looking for him now and took it upon myself to do some research into the identity of my benefactor, which is how I come to be upon your lovely estate. But, alas, he has not come, and I have things I need to be getting done in the next few days. With your permission, I must take my leave."

Halsey had just emerged from the house and began ringing the iron farm bell, calling the children back for dinner.

"Won't you stay to eat with us?" asked Cara.

"No, no, unfortunately not. Perhaps another time, my lady. My apologies for the abruptness of my leavetaking, but I hope to have the pleasure of your company again, very soon," said Istäni, and, bowing to all those assembled, he started toward the barn to get his horse.

For a moment everyone sat as if frozen, except for the seven children, who thundered toward the house in a torrent of chatter, bickering about a turtle they had found in the pond that Henry III insisted they should keep in the house. The yard descended into domestic chaos, Halsey insisting that the children wash their hands before they were allowed through the door. Someone stepped on little Hannah's foot and she began screaming loudly. Cara suddenly leaped to her feet, lifted her skirts, and took off at an ungainly sprint to the barn, almost crashing into Istäni as he exited the building, leading his horse.

"You know more than you say," she gasped, breathless from her mad dash to the stables.

"More about what, in particular?" asked Istäni, soothing his horse, which had been alarmed by the sudden appearance of the young woman in its path.

"About Murdoch. Why he came back, what he wants, what this game is that he's playing. You know the danger that he is watching for at night. You know what he has been doing and what kind of people he has been associated with these last two decades."

"You overestimate my knowledge, Cara, or you underestimate your brother's opacity. I do not know why Murdoch came back. I can only guarantee it was not for love of his family."

"I just . . . I want to know if my family will be all right, when all this is over. When he's gone."

Istäni swung into the saddle, holding his horse back as he replied, "You won't be. None of you will be. The day Murdoch came into your life, it changed, forever. He is pure, unadulterated evil. The kind of evil that even your saintly Rafael couldn't usher into God's grace."

"I—" Cara stopped herself.

"You are afraid because you think yourself like him, as alike as two peas, is that the expression?" asked Istäni. She startled, surprised at the stranger's ability to read her very mind.

"Don't worry about that now. Your focus should rather be on survival, for yourself, and for your family. Where Murdoch goes, chaos and death follow close behind, as they always have. As he likes it."

With that the handsome young man kicked his heels into his horse's flanks and trotted from the yard, and, as suddenly and strangely as he had come, the green-eyed man was gone.

CHAPTER 8

THE GOLDEN APPLE

The ominous words of the stranger quickly faded from Cara's mind as the Firefaxes continued the endless stream of work that kept Maralah functioning. The first cutting of hay had ripened to tall, waving fronds of yellowish-green, ready for harvest. Soon all the members of the household older than little Obadiah were spending their days ceaselessly scything the stalks to dry in the sun.

After a particularly long day of sweaty, backbreaking work, the family, covered in stinging scratches from the unforgiving timothy and tassel, trooped home from the fields in an exhausted daze. They ate the cold beans and boiled corn that Cara and Halsey had prepared the night before and then everyone went to bed, most of them not bothering to change into nightclothes. Everyone, that is, except Cara, who found herself still restless. She took her spectacles, most useful for reading and close work, and a spare candle, part of a little stock she kept aside for nights of reading, and made her way to the parlor with a heavy tome under her arm. Louis had brought back the last in the set of Raynal's *Histoire des deux Indes* for her, and she was eager to sink her teeth into it. She set the leather-bound volume on the piano bench to light the candle. After a few strikes with the flint, the room took shape around her dimly, and then she let out a scream and launched herself toward the hearth, snatching up a metal poker.

"Get ahold of yourself," said the harsh voice she had learned to hate so much in the past few months. She set the poker back, recognizing the long legs of her eldest brother, strewn between two chairs that sagged under his gangly, awkward form.

Footsteps sounded behind her and Halsey, Henry, and Rafael burst through the door, weapons in hand. Henry grinned upon seeing his older brother. "My God, Cara, I thought we were under attack from the redcoats!"

"She's a bit excitable for a Firefax," said Murdoch, tilting his hat back. He drew his pipe from his jacket pocket and began to empty the ashes onto the floor, picking at the bowl with a thin stick.

"Excitable?" replied Cara, her anger rising. "Tell me you would not have been startled if someone snuck into your house in the dark and made themselves at home in your parlor?"

"I wouldn't, Cara, because no one would sneak into my house without my knowing."

"Oh, I say, Murdoch, glad you've come back, actually," said Henry. "You didn't leave a new address or anything this time either. And imagine, just after you left, you had a visitor!"

Murdoch stopped digging in his pipe and sat bolt upright. It was the first time that any of his siblings had seen him look alert. "Who?"

"A Mr. Sincla, Sinkea—what was it, Cara?"

"Seänkea," Murdoch finished before Cara could respond. "When was he here?"

"Four days ago," whispered Cara, remembering the young

man fondly, his sinister warning, and his kind, flattering manner toward her.

"Well, well," said Murdoch cryptically and stood up, dusting off his jacket, his abrupt alertness gone as quickly as it had appeared. "Rafael, perhaps you would like to get the cart ready? The game's already afoot."

"Ready the cart? For what?" asked Rafael, bemused. "It's late—you can't be thinking of going out?"

"I'm not *thinking* of going out, Rafael. We're all going out."

"Where to?" asked Henry.

"To find Louis, of course."

"And then?" Rafael dared to question a little further.

"Get the cart ready."

Rafael glanced at Cara and then slipped away, sliding his shoes and jacket on and lighting a lantern before tromping to the barn in annoyance.

Halsey studied her husband's face as he began gathering his weapons. After a moment she snatched a shawl from one of the parlor chairs and raced after Rafael. She found him in the barn, fitting the old mare with her harness by the faint light of the dirty lantern set above the horse's stall.

"I know I have to stay," she said.

Rafael finished tightening the belly band and turned to his sister-in-law, taking her shoulders in his hands. She was shivering, though it was warm that evening and humid. The air was slick with moisture, as if a summer storm was brewing. In Halsey's dark eyes, there was an unmistakable look of dread.

"Halsey," he said softly. "Sister, you know we believe you capable of everything. But there are things that a Firefax does that are . . . not safe, and the children will need you here. You have to understand."

"I do understand. I've always understood. I understood when I married Henry. I've understood all the other times he's left. I didn't come out here to mourn the fact that I must stay behind while you and your siblings rush off into some unknown danger again. It is the one part of this family that I do not mourn my being kept from, and that I fear my children growing into."

"It is a true sign of how great your love for Henry is, that you chose to marry him, knowing what he was."

"He is not his profession, Raf. You know that. Henry is so much more than . . ." Halsey paused and licked her lips, unable to say the word. She gathered herself, taking a deep breath, and continued, her voice a little shaky. "But I did come out here to ask something of you. Every time Henry leaves, he comes back battered and maimed. Every single time. He is prone to accident. He's not . . . good at this work, Rafael, not as good, anyway, as the rest of you. And he cares about all of you so much, he would give his life for any one of his siblings without a second's hesitation—that's part of why he always gets hurt. Robert protected him. That was our agreement, our understanding. But Robert is gone, and still Henry rides into danger. I must ask you—no, beg you, to take care of him, to protect him."

"You only ask me to do the same thing that I always have, ever since I was a boy. It was not Father that protected Henry. He is just as safe now as he was before Robert died."

Halsey nodded, staring into Rafael's soft brown eyes, her own brimming with unshed tears. Finally, just as Rafael began to turn back to his task, she spoke again. "Why do you do it? You don't have to do this work. We can survive on the money from farming. We don't need this. You are too good to keep going out there. To keep killing."

"I would've quit long ago if not for my love of my brothers and sister and the need to protect them. That, and I need the money if I'm ever to go to Oxford. I promise you, Halsey, I will protect your husband, as I always have. And, if anything, you can take comfort in knowing that this time we go with Murdoch as well. He'll protect Henry better than any of us."

"I don't think Murdoch will protect anyone but himself if you get into trouble."

"He may be a hard man, Halsey, but Murdoch cares about Henry deeply. I can feel it."

"You're too charitable to people who don't deserve it, Raf. Stay safe yourself out there." Then Halsey embraced her brother-in-law before slipping back inside to bid farewell to her husband and Cara.

Less than half an hour later, the four Firefaxes climbed into the little wagon and set off, creaking and bouncing along the narrow forest track toward Wilmington. Henry held the reins while Murdoch sat beside him sharpening one of the knives he nearly always wore belted across his chest, and occasionally inspecting and then reinspecting his pistols. Rafael squinted into the open Bible in his lap, taking advantage of the occasional shaft of moonlight that appeared from behind the looming clouds. Cara spaced herself as far from her eldest brother as she could, near the back of the wagon, brooding. Her mind danced over images of the handsome young man who had ridden into their farmyard, his mesmerizing green eyes, and the insights, mysteries, and riddles he had woven.

"I do hope Louis is all right," said Henry after a long time, unable to stand the silence in the cart any longer. "If this Seänkea is an unsavory character, then he may be in danger."

"I'm sure he's fine," said Rafael, putting a finger in the Bible to hold his page. "He probably found a particularly engrossing specimen of femininity and hasn't come up from her fish pond for air since."

"I don't like that kind of talk, Rafael. Some minister you'll make with that mouth."

"A clergyman lives in this world, Henry. He works to give visions of another, but he lives in this one."

"Anyway, it doesn't work like that with Louis, you know that. Women fall all over themselves for him, but he has never once found a female that could keep his attention."

"Maybe he's found the exception to that rule, and that's why he hasn't returned."

Henry chuckled at that, then said, "I suppose there's a first time for everything. Anyway, what of you, Murdoch? You know what that lad, that Seänkea boy told us? He told us a grand tale of you sailing aboard the *India* with Grandfather, and Grandfather disappearing off the ship in the middle of—well, I don't know where, the middle of some ocean."

"The Atlantic," Murdoch offered.

"Very specific location. It's a big bloody ocean. So you don't deny his story?"

"Istäni is many things, Henry. He is not a liar."

"Then you knew Grandfather! Why didn't you just tell us that when we asked?"

"Not really any of your business."

"You're impossible, you know that?"

"I am what I am."

"St. Paul!" cried Rafael. "You're surprisingly well versed in the scriptures, Murdoch."

Murdoch raised an eyebrow. "Well versed, really? You're worse with puns than Robert was. As I recall, even the Devil knew the scriptures well, and used them to tempt Jesus in the wilderness."

"True enough," replied Rafael. "Knowing the scripture does not mean one honors it. Still, it surprises me that you know so much of the Word."

"I think it more surprising that you believe so firmly in all that nonsense. You are a murderer by trade, Rafael."

"By trade, yes, because I was born into the profession, but not by choice, and, might I add, not for much longer."

Their conversation trailed off. Having traveled for some

hours along twisted woodland paths, they were nearing Wilmington. The tavern they thought Louis most likely to be at was about two miles outside the village itself. Henry pointed it out along the cart track ahead of them, a tall, dark building, with new siding, built in a clumsy attempt at the new, classical style of building that was becoming vogue. It sat across from the little Presbyterian church where the Firefaxes most commonly worshiped. Above the tavern hung a weatherbeaten sign, the paint worn away but the carved letters still visible—*The Golden Apple*.

"That's the whorehouse?" asked Murdoch. "They can whore and then go straight to confession afterward? Real American efficiency. Who runs it?"

"Old man Borden," said Henry. "If you can believe that."

"I can."

While Rafael watered the carthorse and hitched her to the post outside the tavern, Murdoch went to the door, rapping on it loudly.

"I've said it before and I'll say it again, a tavern is no place to be at night. Vile, uncouth, dangerous places," muttered Henry as they waited.

For a long time nothing stirred, and Murdoch knocked twice more, before taking a step back into the street to survey the windows, as if looking for a way to break in. Then a faint rattling sounded, and the door opened an inch, not more; just enough to see the wavering of a candle flame within. After a moment the door opened wide to reveal a rotund old man, with wobbling jowls, dressed in a nightshirt tucked hastily into unsecured breeches.

"Oh, Henry? It's you. And Rafael? Is that Cara, too? I thought you might come," he said, and then he raised his candle to illuminate the man in the street behind them. "Murdoch? You here too? I heard rumors, but I can't say I gave them much credit."

"Charles Borden, I see you haven't changed."

"You've come for Louis?"

"Don't ask stupid questions, Borden," replied Murdoch. "We didn't come here to diddle your assortment of old milk-maids. Where is he?"

"You've not become more pleasant with age, Murdoch, if you don't mind me saying. Come on, then, follow me," sighed the bleary-eyed old man, and he led them into the pitch black of the empty tavern. He tripped and stumbled his way back among empty chairs and tables, while the Firefaxes, with catlike stealth, avoided the obstacles even in the darkness. Borden kept talking as he walked, the stairs creaking, his hands trembling, making the light ahead of them flicker, illuminating the stained walls in a mad, erratic manner.

"Always trouble when you have a passel of Firefaxes together. Even one of them spells trouble, that's why I didn't want Louis to stay. But he has money, good money, and what was I to do? The women need feeding, you know. They don't provide their services for nothing."

"Just close to nothing?" asked Rafael glibly.

"What? Oh." Borden paused and peered down at him. "Sorry, young master. Didn't realize I was talking aloud."

The old man stopped at a room on the northwest end of the dingy hall on the second floor. There was no window in the hall, and the air was stifling and dank. Borden quietly tapped on the wood. When nothing happened, Murdoch pushed him aside and tried the handle. Finding the door bolted, he pounded an earth-shattering knock.

"Who is it?" called Louis' unmistakable voice. "If it's you again, Silver, then I swear to God I will blow you to hell right through that door."

"It's not Silver," replied Murdoch.

They heard fumbling and the bolt drew back. Louis, holding his pistol before him, opened the door, eyeing them all uncertainly. He sighed and let the door swing wide, allowing his siblings to slide past him into the cramped little room. A bed stood by the wall, just big enough for two, the blankets tousled. Louis' few belongings lay strewn about the floor. Louis was half-dressed, and when Borden raised the candle, Cara noted fresh bruises littering his chest, arms, neck, and face.

"Are you all right?" asked Cara.

"Of course," Louis retorted brusquely. "Though you might have shown up yesterday evening. I could have used the help."

"Fought with Silver and didn't think to warn your family that he was here?" asked Murdoch.

"Silver doesn't know who I am. No danger to them."

"A few questions around town and he would know."

"Oh bugger off, old man. Silver isn't going to harm you lot. I made sure of that. I'd be surprised if he can even walk today after that pounding last night. You're all most welcome."

Murdoch went to the room's corner window and opened it, peering out into the dark forest beyond. "No one's thanking you, Lightfoot, nor should they be. Noaidi is here."

Louis drew in a sharp breath. "Here? How could he be? If they're both here, then . . ."

"Then there's more, and this is no ordinary little intelligence operation."

"Will you two stop speaking in riddles and tell us what in blazes is going on?" Henry demanded. "What are we up against here?"

"Dangerous men," replied Murdoch. "I suspect Silver only attacked you because you recognized him. You would be dead if he weren't under strict orders not to kill you."

"Strict orders? That's absurd. I would be dead if I weren't the better fighter of the two of us, as I always have been. This from the man whose life I saved from Noaidi himself, only a year ago in Charlestown."

Murdoch chuckled, a dry, hideous sound.

"Your petty squabbling is not particularly enlightening," said Rafael, frowning.

"Step out of the room, Borden," Louis ordered. The old man grudgingly obliged. Louis paused for some time after the man left, then, with another sigh, he explained, "I cannot speak to everything Murdoch has been doing the last two decades, but I can tell you that we are both members of a network of spies, a group known as the Argonauts, by the few who do know of them. We work for General Washington, though indirectly, of course, very indirectly. It's a motley assortment of work—information gathering, sabotage, even the occasional assassination. To their credit, they're no amateur group of yeoman farmers. On the other side, another ring has been our nemesis throughout this war—they're called the Myrmidons. They're a relatively small ring of British intelligence agents. They are older, and well established. I do believe Murdoch used to work for them, actually, during the French and Indian War. Noaidi is currently their best agent."

"Noaidi the rest of you know better as Istäni Seänkea," Murdoch interjected.

"Yes, your protégé, from what we understand—" Rafael began, but was interrupted as a shot rang out, followed by blood-chilling cries ringing from the forest, whooping and hollering, a cacophony of strident battle screams. Borden howled in alarm and opened the door again, lunging across the room to slam the window where Murdoch stood.

"Is this place defensible?" asked Louis.

"Defensible?" Borden repeated, incredulous. "This is a tavern, not a fortress. There's a whole war band of Indians outside, by the sound of it!"

"You have two options, Borden," said Murdoch. "Get

your girls out of here, go hide in the church, or you're more than welcome to shelter here, under fire alongside us."

Borden whimpered and scampered down the hall, collecting a small assortment of wide-eyed women of all ages and sizes, terrified into wakefulness by the noises from the forest. A few half-clothed men scuttled from the rooms as well. Murdoch had already knocked out a few strategic boards in the wall of Louis' room, and Cara calmly readied her pistol, making sure her rapier was loose in its sheath.

"Borden will send someone to try to rouse the militia. That will take a few hours, at least," said Henry.

"Istäni will be long gone by then," replied Murdoch.

"Istäni? Were those not Indian war cries?" asked Cara.

"Smoke and mirrors," answered Louis, who was still dressing and arming himself with the scattered weapons around his room. "The Myrmidons are good at that. But really, Murdoch, what on earth would prompt such a large operation?"

Murdoch scanned his siblings—Louis' fair, haughty countenance, Cara's offended expression, Rafael's grave face—and finally his gaze settled on Henry, who fairly glowed with excitement at the prospect of a battle.

"Me, of course," said Murdoch, as if it was a foregone conclusion, then he turned back to the hole he had made in the wall. "I can take this room, if you want to disperse to the other corners of the building. We have five. Someone ought to take the top of the stairs."

"I will!" Louis volunteered. "That's where the blighters will be coming up. They won't get past me."

The siblings dispersed silently to separate rooms in the four corners of the building and Louis to the top of the stairs, his rapier drawn. There were a few more whoops and hollers, but once the taverngoers, Borden, and his women had vanished into the church, the sounds died away, and an ominous silence fell. Cara, who had taken the northeast corner of the building, squinted, making out faint movements in the darkness. There were multiple figures—more flickering shadows than real, flesh-and-blood human forms—and they were closing in. The Myrmidons were advancing slowly and cautiously, taking cover behind anything they could find as they edged their way forward.

After the first few shots there was no more gunfire from the forest, only from the Firefaxes themselves, aiming at anything that moved. A faint wind had picked up outside, and more than once Cara felt she was firing at a waving branch or a shrub, not a human at all. Her breathing was rapid, but she felt calm, and her hands did not shake. This was what she had trained her whole life for, and certainly not her first action. But usually she and her family were the aggressors, descending unseen upon their victims' homes after weeks of careful reconnaissance, taking the intended target's life with brutal efficiency, and vanishing into the night with never a trace that they had been there.

Cara startled when, for a brief second, she thought she saw a flash of silver from the trees, but it was gone when she looked again. She blinked and rubbed her eyes and then heard the sound of metal against metal in the dark behind her, near the stairwell. The Myrmidons were in the tavern and had encountered Louis' ready blade at the top of the stairs.

"Do you need help, Losi?" she called toward the hall.

"Certainly not. Keep to your post. They can't fit more than one at a time up these stairs," Louis shouted back. He continued, but now addressing his adversaries, "What do you cads even want? All this fuss over that bastard Thrayder?"

Cara, adjusting her spectacles, relaxed slightly, turning back to her window just as a large man with gleaming silver hair came flying through it, slamming into her, sending her pistol and rapier clattering across the floor. In the brief moment that she had looked back toward the hall and Louis, her assailant had managed to climb an ash tree just below the window. She had little time to reprove herself for her inattention, however, needing all her strength and focus to combat her much larger adversary in a desperate wrestling match.

She rolled over, twisting and contorting her wiry body, using her relatively smaller size to an advantage, wriggling free from the man's holds like a snake. As she evaded him, she saw another flash of movement in the darkness. The silver-haired man was not the only one who had made it through the window. She maneuvered on top of the man, sitting hard on his chest, her knees driving his arms into the floor, reaching for the knife belted to her back. A set of strong arms grasped her from behind, pinning her arms to her side. The man beneath her grabbed her neck so roughly she thought he would break it. The person behind her twisted her arms until she yelped in pain.

"Oh! It's a girl," said a deep, but feminine voice near her ear, sounding surprised. There was a rising, rounded accent, an island accent, to the woman's rich voice. Cara felt strong, inescapable hands binding her wrists tightly behind her with a piece of rope, the hemp fibers cutting into her as she struggled.

"Aye, Lottie, that's the youngest of the brood there," replied the man, who Cara rightly guessed to be the one Louis had called Silver. "Though she's ugly enough to be a lad, and fights like a man too." Then, drawing back his hand, he struck Cara so hard across the face that she saw stars bursting in her vision, and for an instant everything went dim and quiet. Shaking her head to clear it, she yanked at her arms, lunging at the man who had struck her, but a blade pressed against her throat from behind and she stilled.

"I don't care if you're a girl, I'll cut your head clean off if you keep fightin' me," hissed the woman Silver had called Lottie.

Silver lit a lantern, and Lottie began walking, pushing Cara bodily before her toward the hall. She smelled of lilac, Cara thought, a jarring, alluring scent in the middle of the chaos. Cara's mind raced, dashing through every maneuver she might use to escape from her two captors. She could hear her brothers fighting, steel ringing against steel and the thud of fists sounding from multiple corners of the house. Apparently the enemy had breached more windows than just hers.

"Hold it, Lightfoot! Hold it!" called Silver. He had a deep, commanding voice that echoed over the noise of battle. "Let my men up the stairs or Lottie'll kill your sister." As he spoke, he raised the lantern to illuminate the truth of his threat.

"Let her go!" cried Henry, emerging almost immediately from his room on hearing the danger Cara was in. He leaped toward them, but Lottie drew back, pressing her knife so tightly to Cara's neck that she cut her skin, a line of blood seeping down into the collar of her shirt. Cara stared at her brother, lips pursed, eyes urgent, and he stepped back and dropped his weapons, raising his hands.

Louis obligingly drew away from the stairwell and the men coming up the stairs pinned him against the wall, multiple swords and pistols held against him. Two men took his arms as he dropped his weapons with a clatter, an insolent smirk on his face. Rafael had come out of his corner of the building as well and set his weapons on the floor, but he appeared calm, almost serene, keeping constant eye contact with Cara. Murdoch did not materialize, and the room he had been in was perfectly silent. In the low glow from Silver's lantern, Cara counted quickly. Fifteen—there were fifteen Myrmidons crowded in the narrow hall; it would not be too many. She could see her brothers running the same calculations in their heads.

"Where is he?" asked Silver.

"Who?" retorted Louis, receiving a blow across his face for his feigned ignorance.

"Thrayder. Where is Thrayder?"

"He's not here. You've come to the wrong place if you're looking for Thrayder."

The other siblings attempted to disguise their expressions of surprise, more at Louis sticking his neck out for Murdoch than at the denial itself.

"Don't be stupid, Lightfoot. We saw him go in," said Lottie.

"I don't know who you saw go into the tavern, but it certainly wasn't Thrayder."

"And here I thought you were an honest man, Louis," came a new, cheerful voice from the stairwell, the tone wildly dissonant with everything else happening in the dark tavern. A moment later Istäni, dressed in the same archaic emerald doublet he had worn when he visited Maralah, emerged from the lower floor. He was carrying his own lantern and raised it, surveying his captives one by one. Cara glanced toward the door of the far room, wondering where Murdoch had gone, and when he would reappear. Or perhaps, she mused bitterly, he had merely escaped and left his siblings there to die in his stead.

Istäni paced past each of his prisoners, studying their faces. He stopped finally at Henry, who stood restrained beside Louis. Reaching out, Istäni ran his fingers along Henry's cheek, tenderly, almost sensuously. "You're a very special man, Henry Firefax. Do you know why?"

"I make the most delicious sourdough this side of the Green Mountains?"

Istäni laughed and said, "Perhaps I have underestimated you—I did not take your baking skills into my accountings. No, no, dear Henry. You are a special man because you are the one person, the only person in the entire world, who Murdoch Firefax loves."

The woman holding Cara tightened her grip noticeably, and Louis snorted aloud at that statement, causing Istäni to turn toward him. "Jealous, Louis?"

"Of course not. Don't be absurd. But it's ridiculous that you think Murdoch Firefax capable of loving anyone, whether Henry or anyone else in the world."

"Everyone has a weakness, somewhere. Even godlike Achilles had his mortal heel. It took me a very long time to find Murdoch's. But I am sure now that he loves Henry and would do anything for him. That is why I came here." Then Istäni drew the ancient axe from its sheath attached to his belt. The lantern light reflected off a thick, dark, gleaming substance smeared over the blade.

"What do you want from Murdoch?" asked Henry, drawing back as Istäni brought the axe toward him, tracing the blade gently over Henry's chest, toying with him.

"What do I want? Isn't that obvious? I want Lubrerum, Henry, and, with your help, Murdoch is going to give it to me." As he spoke, Istäni raised the axe to swing at Henry.

Gradually the smell of smoke had been tickling Cara's nostrils, and it suddenly became overpowering, a dark cloud billowing from the room at the end of the hall where Murdoch had been. Cara allowed her body to relax and felt Lottie's grip slacken in response. The woman was engrossed in the drama between Henry and Istäni. It was enough. With her fingertips Cara could feel the handle of the small knife sheathed at her back, just above her left buttock. She twisted forcefully and ducked, burning pain igniting along the side of her neck where Lottie's knife sliced into her skin as she slammed herself backward, wrapping her leg around the other woman to unbalance her. In an instant Lottie was on the ground and Cara was moving away, lungeing awkwardly toward Henry and Istäni while struggling with her bound hands to flip her knife and cut the ropes around her wrists.

Rafael was moving just as quickly to get to Henry. He had managed to wrestle free of the men holding him and, with a deft movement of his foot, he kicked his rapier into his hand. In a series of swift thrusts, he dispatched two of the men guarding him before vaulting toward his brother. Henry, hardly helpless, hurled himself backward and kicked out as the poisoned weapon arced toward him. Istäni just missed his mark, partly from Henry's movements and partly from Louis, who had managed to break free from his captors with a wild leap, catching Istäni's hand. Rafael cut down one of the men still trying to keep hold of Henry, while Henry, free at last, spun, grabbing his other captor around the neck with both hands. Behind them Louis and Istäni grappled at the top of the stairs for possession of the poisoned axe, just as flames began to roar forth from the far room, casting tall, distorted shadows from the forms struggling desperately in the hall.

"My orders still stand!" called Istäni over the melee. "Don't kill them! I need the Firefaxes alive."

Cara, her arms clumsily freed with her knife, found herself nearly overpowered again by Lottie. The woman, skin dark as midnight, was stronger, larger, and much more experienced than Cara. Cara managed to scramble on top of her adversary, slamming her hand into Lottie's face and reaching with her long fingers for the woman's gleaming eyes, but Lottie caught hold of her neck and began to choke the very life out of her, twisting her face to keep her eyes from Cara's pawing fingers. Just as Cara's vision began to dim, another pair of hands grabbed her about the waist, tearing her away from Lottie and hurling her into Rafael's arms as he rushed toward her. She turned and saw Murdoch behind her, standing back as Lottie leaped to her feet.

For a moment Murdoch and Lottie stood, regarding each

other in the flickering light of the fire, as Istäni's Myrmidons and the Firefaxes battled all around them. Cara, taking a rapier that Rafael shoved into her hands, hardly had time to notice, but in that brief stand off, she saw a curious change come over Lottie's face, a look of . . . something . . . longing, perhaps. Cara shrugged it off quickly; it was her imagination and she had a battle to fight. She turned all her concentration back to the duel at hand as one of the Myrmidon's closed with her. Then, before she had a chance to look again at Murdoch and the woman, shots rang out from the forest and the fighting slowed.

"That'll be the Argonauts, no doubt, killing the sentries you had outside," said Murdoch, his harsh voice rising just above the din of battle.

"To the forest!" cried Silver.

"Not without the Firefaxes!" shouted Istäni.

"Fuck you, Noaidi," Silver replied. "I'm getting my men out of this tavern alive."

The northwest end of the hall was fully engulfed in flames, and they were all sweating from the heat of the fire, and coughing from the suffocating, acrid smoke filling the air. Silver was still shouting orders at his men and Lottie as they tumbled after him down the stairs, leaving behind five dead Myrmidons, the five Firefaxes, and Istäni in the hall. Appearing oblivious to the new developments, Louis and Istäni, who had each managed to gain their rapiers, were battling back and forth in the hall; evenly matched, masterful swordsmen.

"Look at him," remarked Henry, surveying Istäni with open admiration. He turned and grinned at Murdoch. "He could be one of us."

"You should get out of here," answered Murdoch, looking pointedly at Henry before swinging his gaze to the other two. "All of you."

"I'm staying here. I'm not a child anymore, Murdoch. But, you two, do as he says," said Henry, becoming serious as he glanced at Rafael and Cara. "Outside, now, and hide—don't engage with Istäni's men or the blasted Ark O' Knots or whatever these other blighters are called."

"You should come with us," said Rafael, remembering Halsey's exhortation.

"It's fine. We've only one enemy left here, no real danger. One single man against three adult Firefaxes. Nothing to worry about. I'll be right behind you. Protect your sister, Raf."

Rafael nodded wearily and grabbed Cara's wrist, bleeding from where she had accidentally sliced it when trying to cut her bonds. They ran together down the stairs. Keenly aware that they might be followed, Cara and Rafael dropped to the floor and kept low, slinking soundlessly among the tables and chairs, making for the kitchen and a back exit. The clanging of Louis' and Istäni's swords still rang out above them, but muffled by the crackling of the flames and the sound of groaning timbers as the fire weakened the structure.

Outside the wind had picked up, and a faint spattering of raindrops had started. Rafael and Cara crept slowly around to the front of the tavern. They found to their surprise their wagon and horse undisturbed there, though the animal was pulling at her lead rope, distraught from the smell of smoke and the clamor of battle. Taking the lead rope and gently soothing the animal, Rafael led her away from the fire, tying her at the front of the small church across the street. Silver's men had vanished into the darkness, but the noises of battle between the Myrmidons and the unseen Argonauts still sounded around them in the forest—pistol shots, thuds of fists, and the clang of steel. But even with the light from the tavern's blaze, they could see none of these struggles, which sounded as if they were getting further away every minute. The two siblings finally rested against the wall of the church, keeping to the shadows, staring back at the tavern, engulfed in flames, waiting for their brothers to emerge.

Cara, panting, allowed Rafael to dab at her bleeding neck and wrist with his handkerchief. She was the first to speak. "Lubrerum's not real, is it?" she half gasped, half whispered.

"I . . . I don't know. But the idea of it is enough for men to kill each other, so I suppose it doesn't have to be real." Rafael stared at the burning building, a look of deep fear and consternation on his face. The noise of fighting in the forest had faded, and the only sounds were the faint whine of the wind rustling the trees, spattering rain, and the roar of the flames. He wrapped the handkerchief gently around Cara's neck and stood. "I should go back."

Cara grabbed his arm to stop him, staring wide-eyed at the building as a loud groaning sound echoed through the night. The building heaved, lurching awkwardly as the flames enveloped the entire second floor. Louis stumbled out the front door, illuminated by the fire behind him. He raced across the street, looking neither to the left, nor the right, dashing toward the church. Rafael waved at him, and in a moment he slid hard into the grass beside them. Louis was panting, wiping sweat and grime from his brow as he lay on his back, letting the raindrops cool him.

He turned his head toward them. "You blighters might have given a man a hand in there," he gasped out in annoyance. Then he noticed Cara's bleeding neck and asked, "You're all right?"

"Yes, yes, we're fine," replied Cara. "You? Henry?"

"I—" But whatever Louis was going to say was cut short by the crack of four pistol shots from within what remained of the burning tavern. The shots were so close together they nearly coalesced into one sound. The three siblings leaped forward, staring at each other and then back at the building as the top floor yawed, groaning as it began to collapse into the lower story. Forgetting the danger from Istäni's agents, they each took a few running steps toward the rapidly collapsing building. With a roar the entire upper story of The Golden Apple fell thunderously into the lower section and they froze in horror.

Silhouetted against the impressive conflagration, a tall, thin man with jerking, uneven steps approached them. In his arms he carried another man, his form limp. He did not stop to look at them but strode past, going to their wagon, where he laid his terrible burden down. Murdoch was gentle with the body, almost tender. Approaching in horrified silence, the remaining Firefaxes gazed down at the pale, still figure, his jolly face unmoving, eyes closed, his skin shining from the rain pattering on his unheeding form. If he had not been so still, Cara would have thought he was merely sleeping. There was only a little blood around the hole in his jacket. It hardly seemed a serious enough thing to kill a man so filled with life as Henry had been. She felt as if someone had shot a hole in her own heart, and then came the surge of rage, killing rage, and she glanced back toward the burning building.

"Istäni?" asked Louis, as if reading her mind. His voice was a faint murmur as he sagged against the wagon's side. Cara glanced at him, thinking for a moment it was grief that made him require the support of the cart. Then she noticed for the first time that there was blood staining his shirt red and dripping on the ground below him.

"I shot him," said Murdoch.

CHAPTER 9

THE ARGONAUTS

The day after Henry died was a hellish blur for Cara as she struggled to wrap her mind around what had happened. There was nothing left but an empty space where her laughing, vivacious older brother had once been, and even the possibility of vengeance had been stolen by Murdoch's pistol. Murdoch vanished almost immediately, leaving his younger siblings to bring the body of their brother back to his widow, who stood waiting at the door to Maralah in the gray predawn light.

Halsey Firefax wore a devastated, pale, but determined look, the expression of someone who knew of her loss long before the mournful cart appeared at the edge of the farmyard. She awoke her bewildered, sobbing children to say goodbye to their fallen father.

Louis washed and sewed his own wound, not allowing Rafael or Cara to even see it. He recovered quickly and stayed nearly a week, helping with the funeral arrangements, and the never-ending farmwork, though he was sullen and withdrawn even more than he had been in the presence of Murdoch. On the sixth day after Henry died, a letter came for him. After reading it, Louis left without explanation, and Maralah fell quiet and dark.

After long days in the fields, Cara and Rafael dueled for hours, well into the night. Each evening Henry's children would lie awake listening to the clanking of steel on steel echoing through the darkness outside. The air grew steadily more sweltering as June advanced. One night both siblings were drenched in unrelenting sweat as Cara backed Rafael into the shrubs lining the pond. They were both quite lost in the match, but Cara especially; these were the moments she could forget the aching hole Henry's loss had torn within her soul; a soul already shattered by the loss of her father. Rafael continued backing away from her, her attacks taking all his concentration to counter, and she kept pushing, desperately, maniacally, as if Rafael's defeat would bring Henry back, or Robert back, or that poor stupid mare back. She saw something stir to her right and cursed herself for her distraction. She spun instantly, rapier outstretched, and it rang out as it clashed against another raised blade.

"Easy, lady, I only drew to protect myself." said the stranger, a faint gleam of moonlight illuminating his face, shiny with sweat under a poorly fitted wig.

"Who are you?" Cara demanded, letting her blade lower slightly but remaining en garde.

The man did not advance. "I would be pleased to answer your questions—at least, as many as I am able to while maintaining discretion—in exchange for some answers to my own queries." As he spoke, he lifted his left shoulder mechanically and bent his head, bringing his ear down to it, then relaxing and shrugging his shoulder back in place. His right sleeve lay empty and unmoving. He smiled at them, sheathing his sword and spreading his one arm wide. "Most people call me Lefty."

Rafael had come to stand beside his sister, keeping his own sword leveled. The two siblings exchanged a glance, both panting and perspiring. Rafael sheathed his sword and held out his hand.

"Forgive us, Mr. Lefty, we've recently suffered the tragic loss of our brother, by murder. We are a little on edge."

Lefty's grin widened, the smile of a man who thinks himself more clever than the people he addresses, and he took the younger man's hand. Rafael had counted three others hidden around the pond since Lefty began speaking, and he wagered there were more.

"Quite, quite, I do know about your brother. It is for this reason that I've waited a few weeks to approach you. I knew it would be difficult to ask anything from a family so deeply in mourning. I understand your father was only recently lost as well. My condolences to yourselves and your brother's widow, of course."

"Much appreciated," replied Rafael. "You're well informed on our family's tragedies."

Cara said nothing, staring at the man with dark, fierce eyes that seemed almost to bore through him. The man shifted again, twitching his shoulder nervously under the young woman's unrelenting gaze. "Perhaps we should repair indoors for a more comfortable discussion?" Lefty suggested.

"You're not coming inside our house," replied Cara, her voice low and menacing. "We don't even know who you are."

"My sister isn't wrong. As well, your henchmen in the trees hardly reassure us that your intentions here are benign."

Lefty mopped at his brow with a handkerchief, glancing nervously from side to side. The faint croaking of a bullfrog grew louder against the constant background of chorusing peeping frogs, the thrilling of katydids, and the chirping of crickets. "Listen here, young sir, I'm a very important man, very important to General Washington himself, you see. I owe it to this fledgling country to take every precaution necessary."

"You're one of the Argonauts," said Cara.

"I am the leader, or, I suppose I should say, one of the leaders of the Argonauts, and I am Thrayder's, or rather, Murdoch Firefax's minder or, one could say, his handler, if you will." As he spoke Lefty puffed out his chest indignantly.

Unexpectedly the cold, stern Cara broke into a tittering, childish giggle. The man's chest deflated as he stared at her. It took a few minutes before Cara regained her composure, though she was still grinning like a fool, a hideous, leering expression on her narrow, jagged face.

"His handler, yes, I'm sure you are," she said at last, wiping at the tears of mirth on her cheeks. "Well, Murdoch is not here, so if that's who you came for you're in the wrong place."

"No, no, I didn't come for him. I came specifically to talk to you both. I am trying to learn the significance of something called Lubrerum."

That statement wiped the smile completely from Cara's face, and Rafael drew in a breath sharply.

"Why would we tell you anything about Lubrerum?" Rafael asked. "We've already lost one brother to treasure hunters."

"So it is treasure?"

"You'll get no information from us," Rafael replied, his tone firm.

Lefty began pacing before them, pausing every few minutes for his habitual shoulder twitch. "Well, my dear young people, I wanted to keep things civil, your brother just freshly passed, your father only recently gone too, and you both so young. But, unfortunately, you force my hand." As he spoke, both Cara and Rafael raised their blades but Lefty did not draw his sword again. Instead he placed his fingers in his mouth and let out a high-pitched whistle.

Cara started forward but then stopped abruptly. Lefty had not backed away, but rather had turned toward the house, ignoring the threatening young woman. Two men stepped from behind Maralah with lit torches and began setting down a series of grimy rags around the base of the building. Realizing they were putting down cloths soaked in oil, and cursing herself even more for her inattention to their surroundings during her match with Rafael, Cara took a few steps toward the house, but the Argonauts around the pond rushed from their hiding places and blocked her path, their cutlasses and pistols raised.

"You'll tell me the information I want to know, or I'll burn Maralah."

"There are children inside!" Rafael protested, also finding himself surrounded by Lefty's men.

"All the more reason for you to be forthcoming."

Cara's eyes were blazing, and Rafael could see she was very close to erupting. There were seven men near them, three around her, four surrounding him. They had misjudged where the danger lay, he thought. Rafael's eyes darted between the men with torches standing by the house, and then back to Cara.

"Even if my men let you run in there to try to rescue them, and they won't, not everyone is getting out alive. One whistle and the rest of your family dies," said Lefty, and raised his fingers to his lips.

"Lubrerum is an island," Rafael said, and saw Cara deflating slightly.

Lefty grinned and then let out a twittering bird call. The men by the house stood back, though still ready with their torches. Everyone turned toward Rafael, who was breathing heavily, still staring at his sister.

"Yes, go on," Lefty encouraged.

"It may just be a tale for children. That's all it was to us coming up, a story our mother told us at bedtime."

"Well, tell us your mother's bedtime story, then."

"There's an island that was gifted to the Firefaxes,

hundreds, perhaps thousands of years ago. A sacred, secret place to store the money we've earned."

"Money you've earned doing what?"

"Services rendered to many kings, queens, lords, ladies, nobles all over the world. That's not important. There was an agreement that the island would remain secret, off the maps. No one was allowed there and no country could lay claim to it."

"How can you keep an entire island secret?" asked Lefty.

"Well, you didn't even know what Lubrerum was, so apparently it has worked so far," snapped Rafael, irritated. "Our mother said there are people on Lubrerum. They live inside a golden city, bedecked with jewels and precious metals and stones. Their leader is an abbot, who governs justly and wisely over his subjects, and they have their own defenses against outsiders. Our mother . . . well, she told us there was some spell upon the island, that if anyone who isn't a Firefax goes there, they die."

"Where is this fabled, cursed island?"

Rafael shook his head. "I don't know."

"Who knows?" asked Lefty, raising his fingers to his lips again as if to whistle.

"Only Murdoch," Cara said quickly. "The agent you say you handle is the only one who knows where Lubrerum is."

Lefty's eyes widened, then he turned to his men. "Well, perhaps with his little siblings as leverage he'll give us that information. Come quietly, my dears, or I promise I will burn that house and everyone in it to the ground."

"You fool!" cried Cara, lunging forward. Then, with a glance toward the men still menacing Maralah she allowed herself to be seized, disarmed, and her wrists bound behind her. As the Argonauts tied her, she continued speaking. "Murdoch doesn't care what happens to us! He doesn't care about anything! You've got the wrong leverage."

Lefty scanned her. "And what, pray tell, is the correct leverage, then, Miss Firefax?"

"Some handler you are—you don't even know what motivates him. The brother we had that isn't yet cold in his grave, Henry, he was the right leverage." Her voice broke a little as she spoke. Istäni had been right. With Henry's death, there was nothing on earth that would induce Murdoch to comply with anyone, of that she was certain. There was no one that he cared about, save himself. A wave of overwhelming, suffocating guilt flooded her. She was the one who had allowed herself to be overpowered in the tavern, the reason they had all five been in such a compromised position in the hall, the reason Henry had died.

"Don't undervalue yourself, Miss Firefax. If he cared so much for one brother, then I'm sure he'll care about you. Family is family, after all. And if he doesn't . . ." Lefty shrugged. "If he doesn't, well, what happens to the two of you makes little difference in the grand scheme of things."

Cara seethed as she and Rafael were marched in silence together through the dark forest. After the wave of guilt, she found herself filled with such choking hatred for the odious, simpering Lefty that she could hardly think. In her mind flickered pictures of murder, death, everything she wanted to do to her captor in grotesque, livid detail.

Every once in a while a cloud shifted, uncovering the silvery gleam of the moon, and she caught sight of Rafael, glancing toward her with his soft, somber gaze, his lips moving in his habitual prayers. It calmed her, but at the same time it made her more angry, seeing his arms twisted cruelly behind his back, seeing the men rushing him along, making him stumble without the balance of his arms. Then, quite suddenly, everyone stopped as Lefty snapped out orders in the darkness. The Argonauts split into two groups, four heading south with Cara, the others moving Rafael north.

"What are you doing?" cried Cara, struggling in her bonds. They pushed her forward, but she planted her feet. "I'm not leaving my brother. Where are you taking him?"

Above the sound of her own voice, she could hear Rafael struggling and shouting as well as he was hurried away. Then came the thuds of fists striking flesh and another sound, softer, in the back of her mind, the memory of hoofbeats drumming on the frozen earth. She contorted her shoulders, just like Robert had taught her, painfully, unnaturally, until she dislocated the right one, instantly loosening the ropes as agony surged through her. She ignored the pain in her need to get to Rafael and shook the ropes off her arms. Before the Argonauts could stop her, she was racing toward the other group, maneuvering her right arm with her left until it snapped back into place, sending another bolt of lightning pain through her body. "Hold on, Raf! I'm coming!" she cried.

A dark form slammed into her from the side, knocking her to the ground, and the next instant she was wrestling in a tangle of men, leaves, sticks, and dirt. She grinned broadly in the darkness. Now, at last, she would show them what she was made of; she would show them what Robert had trained her to be. Through the mass of arms and legs she caught a glimpse of Rafael similarly struggling, fighting to get to her from twenty paces away.

"Stop, stop!" cried Lefty shrilly. "If you don't stop, Cara Firefax, I will have my men break both your brother's legs! The same goes for you, boy. Hold still or I will cut your sister's hands off. Really I only need one of you, so if you don't stop fighting I may end the life of whichever one of you I please, and make the other watch."

Cara froze and allowed the men to hoist her to her feet, yanking her arms again hard behind her back, exacerbating the tearing pain in the shoulder she had dislocated and relocated so quickly. The wild, intoxicating thrill of rage was fading, but she stared directly at Lefty as the Argonauts bound her arms and looped ropes around her torso, almost cutting off her ability to breathe as they pulled tighter and tighter. Rafael, who had surrendered immediately when Cara was threatened, had already been resecured and the Argonauts were hustling him away. A cloud covered the moon again and her brother was invisible in the darkness.

"I'm not stupid, Cara," continued Lefty. "You two obviously care about each other. If you behave I won't hurt your brother. Same goes for your dear brother—if he behaves, none of my men will harm you. It's that simple. But if you try that again, I promise I will not only have my men break both his legs, I will make him walk on those broken legs all the way to Boston."

Cara drew herself up, her face blazing with anger and hatred. "You touch one hair of my brother's head and I'll peel every scrap of skin from your body, immerse your raw, bleeding flesh in a vat of whiskey and lemon juice, and then, when you've screamed until you can't anymore, I'll light you on fire."

Lefty drew back, frowning and speechless. A woman among the Argonauts broke into a wild cackle. She was short and appeared to be missing most of her teeth, but stout and strong. She was the only woman among them, and Cara rightly guessed she would be her attendant on their march to Boston. At least, she thought, she knew now where they were going. The woman, mid-cackle, yanked Cara's neck down to her level and slammed a soiled kerchief into her mouth, earning a bite for her efforts.

"There, Lefty, she won't threaten you no more," the woman said, still laughing as she sucked on the bleeding wound to her finger. "Said so matter o' fact like that. I guess she is Thrayder's sister, ain't she?"

"Fucking ugly cunt, that's what she is," muttered Lefty,

shifting his left shoulder up and down in rolling, rapid movements. "Well, that settles it—orders are orders. Any questions?"

The assembled Argonauts shook their heads, and thus began Cara's lonely forced march to Boston; every moment of every day, waking and sleeping, haunted by fear for Rafael. Cara was kept bound, with three men and the sparsely toothed woman assigned to guard her. Rather than inviting questions by traveling on the main roads, they kept to overgrown trails through the forests, sleeping under the cover of the trees, or in houses, sheds, and barns along the way where the Argonauts seemed to have arrangements with the owners. The few settlers they did encounter were told that Cara was a dangerous loyalist spy, not to be trusted, and not to be freed. People asked no further questions. Even her sex afforded her no sympathy, for, dressed in the dirty shirt, waistcoat, and breeches she had worn while sparring with Rafael, she appeared to be a man to any cursory observation.

The days of forced marching, punctuated with little scraps of food, brief breaks for the woman guard to help Cara relieve herself while remaining tied, and fitful sleep, blended together into a haze of misery. At last they arrived on the outskirts of Boston's surrounding villages late one June evening, well after dark, and knocked at the door of a crumbling shack. A woman emerged, spoke briefly with the men, eyed Cara warily, and then pointed out a cellar, the doors opened wide to the outside world. Cara, still tied, was tossed unceremoniously into the dank, mildewed blackness, landing hard on her face and her shoulder. She lay quiet in the darkness, struggling to maintain the rage she had felt since she and Rafael were captured outside Maralah.

The cellar doors above her grated closed and she heard the sound of a heavy bolt being lowered, and chains fastened. She was secure. There was no way out, and she was alone, for perhaps the first time since they had left Maralah. She closed her eyes and allowed pictures of her father, of Henry, of Rafael, to flit through her mind. She would get out. She would find a way. But not yet. She was bone-tired and she could barely feel her hands from the tightness of the ropes. She drifted off to sleep, without even adjusting herself to a more comfortable position.

Her eyes snapped open. She had been drooling, she found. Her spectacles, half off her face, were crusted with dirt and the slime of her saliva. The bent wires dug sharply into her cheek. Her body felt irretrievably stuck in her contorted position on the ground, as if any movement would cause terrible pain. She did not shift, or change her breathing, but waited, as her father had taught her, waiting and listening to understand what had awakened her.

There was nothing obviously changed; it was some hours past midnight, she guessed, and perfectly dark in the cellar. She could not feel her fingers, and she twitched them feebly, making sure they still moved. Then, with a start, she realized what it was. There was a new smell mingled with the mildew and dirt of the cellar—a fragrance, lilac, but incredibly faint, as though someone had doused in it days ago, and only the faintest lingering of the perfume persisted. It was delightful and strangely familiar. She frowned, searching her memory. Then, in a flash, it came back. She remembered the tall woman at The Golden Apple, the ample breasts pressing into her back, the knife blade at her throat, the whispered threats with that hint of an island accent. She felt the woman's presence again, and very close. The warmth of her breathing disturbed the chill of the cellar. Ignoring the pain of moving muscles that had been stuck in too awkward and contorted a position for hours, Cara rolled over. She twisted and lunged at the place the breathing was coming from, and was rewarded with a grunt of pain as she slammed her head into the unsuspecting woman's abdomen.

"Easy, easy, *tifi*!" whispered Lottie when she had regained her breath, scrambling to escape her bound adversary. Cara wrapped her legs around the other woman's and flipped her hard against the wall. Lottie was too stunned to speak for a few seconds. After regaining her breath, she said, "You'll wake the guards. Dere's one just outside."

"What do you want?" hissed Cara, stilling.

"Well, I didn't exactly expect thanks and praise for my efforts," said the other woman, chuckling. "But attacking your savior is a little much."

"Savior?"

"I came to free you. Let me see your hands."

Cara obediently rotated in the dirt, allowing the woman to slice through her bonds in a few deft movements. She brought her hands to her front and began frantically trying to rub the unfeeling fingers back to life. "My brother?"

There was a faint catch in Lottie's voice when she answered. "Which brudder?"

"Rafael. I have to get him out."

"Rounder is already gettin' him."

"Who the hell is Rounder? Is he competent?"

"As competent as I am. Come on. We can't talk here or we'll end up with our throats cut. Follow me . . . uh, tell me, are you afraid of tight places?"

Cara shook her head, though it was not entirely true. She snatched up her spectacles and wedged the bent frame onto her face. Seconds later she found herself crawling behind Lottie through a tunnel so narrow she was surprised that the broad-shouldered older woman did not become stuck ahead of her. She felt as if she could hardly breathe as she scrambled through the inky darkness. They emerged on the bank of a small creek, tumbling from the tunnel entrance down along the rocky earth, and landing with a splash in the water. Lottie held her finger to her lips, staring back toward the house.

Though it felt as if Cara had been traversing the narrow crevice for an eternity, the tunnel itself was only a few body lengths long. Cara lay in the cold water, enjoying the ability to freely expand her rib cage, letting the creek flow over her, cleansing away the dirt and grime of her captivity. She stared up at the tree branches hanging over them; the edges of the world were just beginning to turn gray as predawn began. She let her eyes slide shut.

"Come on, *tifi*, don't fall asleep in de river," said Lottie, urgency still present in her voice.

With a sigh, Cara rose, pausing only to wash her spectacles and bend the wire frames back into shape before following Lottie along the creek bed. As they walked, the two women kept their feet partially in the water to hide their tracks. Cara studied Lottie from behind. She was an extraordinarily handsome woman, soft, with rounded curves, and long, braided hair that fell in swooping waves from a bun at the back of her head. The men's clothes she wore did not hide any of her beauty. She glanced back from time to time with her arresting brown eyes and smiled, a dimple appearing in one ebony cheek.

"Did you dig that hole to the cellar in one night?" asked Cara.

"No, no," Lottie said, laughing a little. Her voice slipped deeper into her accent as she relaxed in the presence of the younger woman. "A badger did most o' de work, I jes extended her tunnel a bit. We've had an eye on dat house for a long time. First time we've known dem ta use de cellar for hiding prisoners. It'll likely be de last time after dis."

Before long the sunlight was streaming out from the eastern sky, quickly drying the dew around them with orange and gold needles of light. Cara could hear the murmurs of a city coming to life in the distance, and she could smell the first scents of food cooking in the houses they were passing. They journeyed swiftly and silently, keeping well into the forest, away from the clatter of the roads.

"I think we're far enough away from the Argonauts now for me to ask you why you rescued me," said Cara.

"Sure, and you're right," replied Lottie. "Istäni sent me."

Cara stopped abruptly, a strange mingling of feelings rising in her: the longing she felt when she thought of the handsome green-eyed man, along with nauseating revulsion and anger for the death of Henry. But most of all she felt guilt, guilt for the desire that Istäni aroused in her. Lottie paused and turned around, as if she knew there would be more questions.

"I thought Istäni was dead. Murdoch said he shot him."

"He's not dead, far from it. Murdoch . . ." Lottie did not finish her sentence.

"Do you know my oldest brother well?"

Lottie shook her head. "No one knows him well, I suppose. But I know him better dan . . . better dan most. You're very . . . very like him."

"Lottie, I like you, truly. But I swear I will strangle the next fool that makes that observation."

The woman chuckled and said, "Well, I suppose dere's differences. You're softer. More human."

Cara wasn't sure how to respond to that, so she let it hang in the air between them as they continued their walk. There was something deeply comforting, warm, and inviting about the woman who had almost killed her in the tavern weeks before. Lottie led her to a clearing where a crumbling stone house sat, the roof long since rotted away, one wall fallen in, leaving a wide, gaping maw to welcome them.

"Dat's where we'll wait for Rounder and your brudder."

Cara found a comfortable corner in the old stone building

and set her spectacles in a crevice in the wall, evicting a large brown spider as she did so. She lay down, watching half-mesmerized as a bee sucked the nectar from the thistle flowers that were actively reclaiming the dilapidated residence. She let the soreness of her muscles transpose into the lush earth beneath her, listening to the droning of the bee in the ever-growing heat, intermittently flicking her eyes toward the beautiful Lottie. The older woman sat perfectly still in the weeds, constantly alert, watching the forest around them. Gradually Cara drifted off to sleep, content, feeling strangely safe under the watchful eyes of the Myrmidon agent.

She opened her eyes to see the blurry face of Rafael peering at her. Even without her spectacles, she could see he was dirtier than her, pale, covered in bruises and scratches, but his expression was all of concern for her. She smiled at him, nodded to his queries about her well-being, and sat up. She put on her spectacles as Rafael continued pestering her about her welfare and scanning her up and down for injuries. A thin, weasel like figure of a man with a long rifle in his hand was talking hurriedly with Lottie in a hushed voice. He glanced at them and then disappeared into the forest along the track Cara and Lottie had come from.

"He's an expert marksman, he'll take care of any followers dat we might have," Lottie explained.

Once alone with Lottie, the reunited siblings half expected her to change course entirely. Now they would find out that Lottie's intentions were not at all benign and be caught back up in the struggle over Lubrerum, questioned, tortured, whatever it took to continue the vain attempts to break the impregnable vault that was Murdoch Firefax. Lottie stood up, and Rafael took an instinctive step in front of his sister.

"You'll need weapons," said Lottie. "Or, I should say, hopefully you won't need weapons, but better to have dem and not need dem dan to find yourself without dem against a wall." From a corner of the crumbling structure she produced two pistols, a belt of knives, and two long cutlasses, sheathed in leather harnesses. She then passed them a satchel full of clean garments, a tricorn hat for Rafael, and then, last of all, a small scrap of paper.

"What's this?" asked Rafael, scanning the document.

"A place where you'll be safe, for now."

Cara was surveying the rumpled gown and corset from the bag with distaste. But her own clothes were more dirt than fabric, so she began changing quickly in the corner of the building, facing toward the wall. She felt Lottie's brown eyes dart toward her as she removed her shirt. She turned and caught the expression of blatant appreciation in the other woman's gaze, drinking in the lean, muscular form of the younger woman's body. Cara's cheeks darkened a shade and Lottie looked down. The Myrmidon agent waited until both Firefaxes had changed, then they burned their old garments and the scrap of paper, which Rafael had quickly memorized.

"Watch out for Argonauts. Boston is crawling with Lefty's network. Don't trust anyone. De house you're looking for has a cherry-red door, you can't miss it. Tell dem Lottie sent you for Julius. Dey'll let you in."

"Thank you," said Cara as they stood at the maw of the crumbling structure. "We . . . we owe you."

"And I'll hold you to dat, *tifi*," replied Lottie with a wink and a last, appreciative scan of Cara's body before turning to follow the same path Rounder had taken. In a few moments, her graceful, curved form melted into the waving nettles, sweet honeysuckle blooms, and dense, clinging brambles.

CHAPTER 10

ESPERANZA

Rafael stopped to ask for directions for the third time as the tired, disheveled siblings wound their way through the maze of unmarked lanes that made up the village of Newton. Each time he stopped, Cara kept watch, and this time she was sure of it: the lean, tall man with the skewed gray wig was following them. He had stopped when they had, pretending to be interested in a farmer's wool stall selling on the street corner a few dozen yards away. In between assessing each skein, he would cast a furtive glance toward her brother.

She narrowed her eyes and pushed her spectacles down for better distance vision. She thought he might have been one of Rafael's captors outside Maralah. She couldn't be sure, however, as it had been difficult in the darkness to make out the particular features of Lefty's henchmen.

"We're only a few lanes away, almost there," said Rafael when he returned to her side. "What is it?"

She nodded toward the man. "He's been following us."

Rafael swung about, scanning the man, and let out a low

whistle. "He's one of Lefty's men. One of the men that brought me here."

"That's what I thought," she said. "He'll wait till we're away from people before he makes a move."

"Or he won't make a move, just follow us to see where we go."

"Shall we give him the slip? Split up?"

Rafael shook his head. "No splitting up, Cara. One of us will get caught. I'm in no rush to be back in the clutches of those bastards. Follow me."

The path Rafael took passed through several side streets and cut across multiple yards. It was convoluted enough that even Cara wasn't sure how they eventually reached their destination. Their follower had to trot to keep up, and he seemed to care less and less that they knew he was tailing them. As they rounded a corner into a quiet, empty lane, they heard their pursuer whistle, and three more men joined him, two of whom Cara recognized immediately as her former captors.

"I thought Lottie and that Rounder fellow were going to take care of any followers," hissed Cara.

"Apparently they missed a few," replied Rafael. "Come on, nothing for it now. We're almost there. Follow my lead."

Rafael darted through another yard, upsetting a maidservant who was hanging sheets behind her master's residence. She screamed and the family from the house spilled out the door just as the four pursuers appeared in the yard, creating a mad hullabaloo and delaying the Argonauts. Rafael and Cara broke into a dead run.

Ahead of her, Cara saw Rafael turn abruptly, leap over a low stone wall, and crash through rows of crowded vegetable plants and under treelike sunflowers. Rose bushes tore at his garments as he dashed through the yard. Cara briefly took in the brick residence, smoke spewing from one of the chimneys, before she sprinted to catch up with her brother, who was already pounding on the inviting, cherry-red door.

They heard a voice call from inside, something about not breaking down the house, and then the door slid open and they pushed their way through, knocking over a frizzle-haired girl in a mobcap. They were in a dim, narrow hall, at the base of a staircase.

"What in God's name?" the girl started to say, but Rafael knelt and clamped a hand over her lips and Cara slammed the door behind them.

"Lottie sent us, for Julius," said Rafael.

"Who's Lottie? For Julius? Oh! Yes, well, he's out right now. I don't know that I should be letting strangers in the house." The girl rose, dusting herself off and straightening her flour-covered garments, creating a cloud in the entryway.

A loud knock sounded on the door behind them.

"Do you have somewhere to hide?" asked Rafael.

"I—" The girl seemed highly taken aback, and her gaze swept up and down the two disheveled travelers, taking in the armory of weapons they wore. Then her blue eyes settled on Rafael's handsome face, and she nodded. "Yes. Come on, this way."

She led them down the hall, past a cluttered study, and shoved them into a guest room. The knock sounded again in the hall, louder this time. The girl winked at them both and called behind her, "Espy! Could you see who's calling?"

Then she shut the guest room's door behind her, plunging the three of them into pitch darkness. They waited, breathless, listening intently.

"Why should I get the door?" they heard an imperious, commanding voice call out from the stairs. "Where even are you? Where are the servants?" Then came the tromping of feet down the staircase, and the faint creak of hinges.

"Excuse me, miss, we're lookin' for a young man and a

lady he has with him. Nothing important, common thieves, naught more. We thought they may 'ave come in here," said a wheedling voice at the door.

"They certainly have not come in here, and I'll thank you to leave," retorted the woman. "You can bring by payment later for the flowers and vegetables you've destroyed stomping about in our yard. Get out."

The entire house seemed to shudder as the door slammed. The Firefaxes saw the white teeth of the young woman who had sheltered them as she grinned and then ushered them back into the hall.

"What in heaven's name are you doing in the guest room, Haddy? Why couldn't you have opened the door? You have a boy stashed in there?" The fierce female voice stopped when Rafael and Cara appeared behind the girl she had called Haddy. "Who are you? The thieves those clowns were looking for? What are you doing in our house?"

"Lottie sent us, for Julius," replied Rafael.

The woman's shoulders relaxed when she heard Rafael's explanation, and she surveyed the rumpled siblings like a butcher admiring a cut of sirloin. She was a tall, dark-haired lady, handsome, with tan skin and an elegant set to her jaw, holding her head like a queen on her long neck. She wore a pale green, high-waisted levite gown with a silver ribbon tied about her middle, her garments a regal contrast to the simple, calico caraco and petticoat worn by Haddy.

"Did Lottie, now? And what are your names?"

"I am Rafael Firefax, and this is Cara, my sister."

The woman's eyes narrowed and they both felt themselves shrinking under the long, withering stare she gave them down her refined, perfect nose. "I suppose you've come to find Louis, then?"

"You know Louis?" replied Cara, brightening.

"We're getting ahead of ourselves," interrupted the other

young woman. "I'm Hadassah—Hadassah Marchworth, but most everyone calls me Haddy. This is my cousin, Esperanza Vidal, one of the finest opera singers this side of the Atlantic."

"Do they have an opera house in Boston?" asked Rafael.

"No, no, they do not," replied Esperanza coldly. "Not with these blasted Puritans running everything. And it's not Vidal anymore, Haddy, or have you forgotten?"

"Oh! Yes, I quite forgot. No, there's no opera house in Boston, not like in Charlestown, where we used to stay. But here they have recitals every few weeks, and Esperanza just performed last night. If only you had come earlier you might have heard her sing!"

"An enchanting experience, I'm sure," said Rafael.

"Don't flatter me," snapped Esperanza. "Haddy, why don't you get our guests some food?"

"Oh, yes, certainly. Absolutely," replied Haddy, spinning and scurrying off toward the kitchen at the back of the residence.

"That room you came from is the guest room, you can . . ." Esperanza scanned them up and down. "Well, you can doff all your weapons in there, anyway. No need to be carrying an entire armory around the house. Then why don't you wait in the parlor? I'm sure the refreshments won't be long." As the Firefaxes began to obligingly remove the weapons Lottie had supplied them, Esperanza turned on her heel and started back up the stairs.

"What of Louis?" asked Cara. "You said he was here."

"I did *not* say he was here," called Esperanza from above them. "You must be family. You have not only the same last name but the same lack of comprehension of spoken English as he does. I merely reflected aloud that you had likely come to see him. I said nothing of his whereabouts."

"And where are his whereabouts, if you'll pardon the directness of the question?" asked Rafael.

"Not here! How should I bloody know?" This last phrase was followed by the crash of a door shutting above them.

It took much longer than they had expected for Haddy to bring food out. Cara and Rafael settled in the parlor on the left side of the entryway. It was a comfortable room, furnished with a piano that made the Firefaxes' look like little more than a toy. Across from the piano sat a sumptuous embroidered sofa, and scattered oak chairs around a polished stone hearth took up the rest of the space. Until it began to get dark, Rafael and Cara constantly checked the windows, scrutinizing every passerby with unease.

As the evening light began to dim, one of the servants came and lit a lamp, setting it upon the piano. Rafael took a worn copy of the Bible from a shelf by the hall and began flipping through the pages.

"I'll lose my mind here, waiting," said Cara. "Why don't you read aloud?"

Rafael grinned. "Certainly. It's a passage that you'll recognize. Part of it's at the opening of the versebook in Erlandagar that we had to learn as children, just as lovely in English. Listen: 'There is one glory of the sun, and another glory of the moon, and another glory of the stars: for one star differeth from another star in glory. So also is the resurrection of the dead. It is sown in corruption; it is raised in incorruption: it is sown in dishonor; it is raised in glory: it is sown in weakness; it is raised in power: it is sown a natural body; it is raised a spiritual body, . . .

"Now this I say, brethren, that flesh and blood cannot inherit the kingdom of God; neither doth corruption inherit incorruption.'—here's the bit from the versebook: 'Behold, I shew you a mystery; We shall not all sleep, but we shall all be changed, in a moment, in the twinkling of an eye, at the last trump: for the trumpet shall sound, and the dead shall be raised incorruptible, and we shall be changed, . . . Death is swallowed up in victory. O death, where is thy sting? O grave, where is thy victory? . . .'"

Cara looked up to see Haddy standing at the doorway of the parlor, her eyes glowing with a strange enchantment, staring at Rafael as he read in his clear, riveting baritone, her mouth partly opened, a tray of food forgotten in her hands. She shook her head as if to clear it and bustled into the room, knocking over a chair with her skirt and nearly upsetting her entire tray as she instinctively grabbed at the fallen chair.

"You'll have to forgive Espy. It's most exciting, when a new opera opens," Haddy confided as they began digging into the steaming bread and stew she had brought. "She's still trembly and on edge from the difficulty and stress of it all, but she'll soon recover, you'll see."

"In truth, Miss Marchworth—" Rafael started to speak.

"Haddy, please, Mr. Firefax—just call me Haddy, everyone does."

"Very well, I will call you Haddy if you will do me the great honor of addressing me simply as Rafael. In truth, I must confess I find it difficult to credit that the lion of a woman we've just become acquainted with could be made to tremble by anything, let alone an opera where she triumphed in her performance. Even her speaking voice is irresistible."

"I know! Believe me, I know. Esperanza could command a man to cut off his own head and he would, without a moment's hesitation."

"Are you also an opera singer? Perhaps you could sing one of the arias for us. I haven't heard a proper opera since the last time we were in Europe. Cara and I both are accomplished enough at the piano. If you hum us the tune, I think we could play the piece for you as accompaniment."

Haddy burst into a gale of laughter. When she had contained her mirth, she answered, "I am not, Rafael. I some-times participate in the singing, providing some harmony, but

I can hardly carry a tune and the others at the recitals only permit me to try because I'm Espy's cousin, not for any merit of my own. In fact, when we used to live in Charlestown, before the British took it over, I broke not one but five of the other stage workers' legs through excessive clumsiness, and have also caused a number of other set accidents and injuries in my year with the recitals. I caused some very bad accidents before that too, back when Espy was training in Europe. I, unfortunately, have a voice that . . . Espy put it best, what was it? Oh, yes, she said it could be compared to the screeching of fingernails across a slate. They let me stay on in Charlestown and here with the recitals, helping with costumes and set changes, building the sets, selling tickets, anything really, because I am Espy's cousin. Believe me, if I were not, I would not be allowed through the door."

"Surely not! I can't imagine that someone with such a pleasing speaking voice could have an unpleasant singing voice," replied Rafael.

"Trust me on this, and if you don't trust me, just ask Espy when next you see her."

"You're being modest." Rafael, for a refreshing moment, had forgotten all the troubles of the last few months: the arrival of his cruel, mysterious eldest brother, the death of Henry, his and his sister's captivity, Istäni, and Lubrerum, the chase through the streets of Newton, all were as nothing in the presence of the sweet, glowing young woman before him.

"How did you come to be here?" asked Haddy.

"We were sent here by someone we met on the road," explained Cara. "The woman called Lottie—I thought you might know her, since you let us in. She said we would find . . . help here."

"Oh yes, Julius helps young people who need placing. That's his business, you know. He's been here for, I don't know, forty years at least. Families send him their youngsters when they don't know quite what to do with them. He uses his connections, finds them a place in the world, a proper livelihood, or a decent marriage, even posts in the military or navy. He absolutely knows everyone. That's how he manages to find homes for every wayward youth that comes here, except, I suppose, not me, so far at least. But there's still hope on that front. We were sent here by Espy's parents partly for that, partly to keep us safe after what happened in Charlestown. Did this Lottie send you here for placing?"

"I'm going to seminary," Rafael blurted out suddenly. "I don't really need placement, that's not why we're here—"

Cara gave her brother a warning glance and he stopped speaking. In the brief silence that followed, they heard a shuffling of feet on the stone path outside, and then soft footsteps entering the house as the door creaked open and shut in the hall. Both Cara and Rafael tensed, but Haddy, hardly noticing the sounds of the new arrival, continued chattering.

"Seminary? With all those weapons? A strong young man like you, with that many guns and knives and those swords, ought to be off fighting in the war, oughtn't he?"

"Haddy, is that you?" came a familiar voice from the hall, and both Cara and Rafael turned abruptly to see Louis standing in the door frame, staring back at them, his face mirroring their surprised expressions.

Their older brother was dressed in a thick overcoat with, it appeared, at least two more coats beneath, as though he were hiding under the heavy layers of fabric. He looked as handsome as ever, but, Cara noted, more weary than before and strangely hollow-cheeked, with dark caverns beneath his blue eyes. His hair was cropped and his face unshaven, with scattered golden stubble across his chin. Uncharacteristically, he bore no weapons that she could see. He did not look well; indeed, he looked the most unwell that Cara had ever seen her impervious, arrogant older brother.

"What in blazes are you doing here?" asked Louis, composing himself. "Did Thrayder bring you?"

"No, your bastard friend Lefty brought us to Boston, against our will," replied Cara angrily.

The siblings paused, Louis' eyebrows rising at Cara's accusatory statement. Then they all glanced toward Haddy. Awkwardly, Rafael stumbled forward and shook Louis' hand, and Cara embraced her older brother half-heartedly, keeping up the appearance of a proper, joyful reunion among family.

"You said Thrayder? Isn't that the hideous man that—" Haddy started to speak and then suddenly clamped her mouth shut as another voice interrupted their discussion.

"Louis, is that you?" called Esperanza, her voice beautiful as always, but also testy as it radiated down the stairs. They all turned as she glided into the parlor. She looked down her nose at the pale young man standing before her, ignoring everyone else in the room.

Louis bowed, letting out a faint sigh, and took her hand, giving it a gentle kiss before, never to be outdone in arrogance, he drew himself up to assume a posture of equal disdain and aloofness as that affected by the lady before him. "My fair lady, I presume you had a great triumph last night, as always?"

"It was sufficient," she replied stiffly. "But I rather thought you would be there to witness my 'triumph,' as you say, firsthand."

"Oh well, some of us cannot always indulge in entertainment, unfortunately. Really, I have things to do, business and work, Esperanza, and I cannot be present at all of your performances, riveting though they may be."

"Of course, my chivalrous Louis, I suppose, if it were not for the hard work of men like you, imbibing all the hateful liquors and spirits that might harm others, no one would have the leisure or the consciousness to watch recitals and operas at all."

The two younger Firefaxes' eyes widened, both of them startled by this display of naked animosity between the two beautiful people.

"That's my Esperanza. Always understanding," said Louis and turned back to the others with a grimacing smile. "You have probably been introduced already, however; you will not deny me a certain honor. Esperanza, this is my dear brother, Rafael, and my sister, Cara. Rafael, Cara, I would like you to meet my darling wife, Esperanza Firefax."

CHAPTER 11

DEVILS' BARGAIN

"I don't understand why this is so shocking to the two of you. Why should I not get married if I find a pleasing woman and wish to settle down?" Louis asked once the deluge of questions from his younger siblings had finally slowed.

"But . . . why now?" insisted Rafael. "Why would you just disappear after what happened to Henry and then just . . . get married? Without an announcement? Without any word?"

"There's a war on, which it seems the two of you are blissfully unaware of," Louis retorted. "There isn't enough time and money for lavish celebrations, and . . ." He trailed off. In truth, he had no desire for any celebration after Henry's death, for which, in part, he blamed himself as much as the other two blamed themselves. "I have just as much right to get married as anyone else, Rafael."

"No one's saying that you haven't!" cried Rafael. "But we would have liked to share in the joy of the union, and to have met Esperanza properly, under better circumstances, or have at least been introduced with the full knowledge that she was our sister-in-law. You could have sent a letter, or something!"

"I did send a letter. Not four days ago. I don't know why I'm defending myself to you. I'm married now. This is my beautiful, incomparable wife, and let that be an end to it."

"But when? How? Where? Why on such short notice?"

"I don't need to explain myself to you, little brother," replied Louis and cast himself wearily upon the sofa, running his hands through his hair and rubbing the deep caverns below his eyes.

Cara watched Louis carefully, studying his uncharacteristically drawn, almost pinched face. She might not have noticed a change if she had seen his form gradually shifting during the last few weeks, but to see him suddenly so altered from the last time she had set eyes on him was startling. To her knowledge he had not seen a doctor since he was wounded in the tavern, and his pallor and thinness spoke to perhaps a souring of the wound, to some infection, she suspected. There was a yellowish hue to his skin that she did not like, and she entertained the notion that the lady Esperanza was not merely being facetious when she accused him of drinking too heavily. But to have such a drastic change in such a short time she did not think could reasonably be attributed to drinking alone, unless Louis had not left the bottle since he rode away from Maralah.

"My apologies, lady Esperanza, sweet sister, I should say," said Rafael, turning back to the imposing beauty before him. "Our incredulity is doubtless making a poor impression on you. It is just that . . . our brother has been known to pull our legs before. He has chosen a most handsome woman as his wife and we are so pleased to have you in our family! I sincerely hope that you two shall be very happy together, for many, many years to come."

"Till death do us part," muttered Louis and exchanged a brief glance with Esperanza, a glance devoid of amorosity.

A clipped knock sounded on the door. Haddy looked

about in alarm and said, "It's quite late. Are you expecting anyone, Louis?"

"Probably another of his slewed friends from the tavern, too ashamed to go home tonight," snapped Esperanza.

Haddy went to the entryway with Rafael following behind her. The door creaked open to reveal the last man Rafael had expected standing on the front step. Istäni Seänkea took a step back and removed his tricorn cap, smiling. Rafael reached straight to his belt but found no knife, or sword, or pistol. He snatched up a parasol that Esperanza had left hanging in the hall and leaped through the door swinging it. Istäni caught the parasol in one hand, and a moment later the two men were wrestling in the garden, rolling over tomatoes and crushing flowers. The others, hearing the tumult, raced to the door.

It was Louis who tore Rafael off Istäni, much to both his younger siblings' surprise.

"What are you doing? Have you lost your mind? He killed Henry!" cried Rafael as he struggled against Louis.

Istäni rose slowly, dusting off his jacket. "Now, now, my dear Rafael, is that any way to greet a friend? To threaten me in front of ladies?"

"You're not our friend. Cara, get the pistols," said Rafael, still restrained by Louis. "You dared come here alone, after what you did? Let me go, Louis! I'll kill him with my bare hands."

Cara made no movement to get the pistols, her curiosity outweighing her hatred. Louis would not defend Istäni unless there was something else going on. Istäni's saving them from Lefty and the change that had come over Louis were new mysteries, and there would be time enough to tear Istäni limb from limb when they had answers. Istäni's playful, amused gaze passed slowly over those assembled at the door, one by one, lingering last and longest upon Esperanza. Finally he turned back to Rafael.

"Really, Rafael, I would think you would be at least grateful. If not for me both yourself and your lovely sister would be in captivity yet. Lady Cara, you look like an angel from heaven, as ever. Louis . . . I'm sorry to say you look like you've been dragged through the sewage gutters by a team of percherons."

"Still more than a match for you and fifteen of your best men," returned Louis coldly, still struggling to hold Rafael back. "What brings you here? The old man is out. This is not a safe town for traitors to the revolution."

"I didn't come to speak to the old man, nor am I afraid of the indomitable spirit of the Bostonian patriots. I came to speak to Thrayder."

"He's not here," replied Cara. "And just how do you come to be alive? Did Murdoch not shoot you in the tavern?"

"Indeed, indeed he did. But it was a glancing wound to the arm. I am much recovered now, thank you for asking after my welfare. You're sure that he is not here?"

"Of course we're sure!" retorted Rafael, prying himself free of Louis at last, who still blocked his access to Istäni. In exasperation he turned back to the house. "I'm getting the bloody pistols. Apparently both of you have already forgotten our brother, but I haven't." With that he darted down the hall to the guest room, where he and Cara had unloaded their weapons.

Overwhelmingly annoyed and taxed with the entire interaction, Louis had followed his brother inside and turned left toward the parlor with an exaggerated sigh. Then he stopped abruptly at the door of the parlor and called, "Raf . . ."

When Rafael reached his brother's side, half expecting some new danger, he froze. Stretched out upon the sofa where Louis had most recently lounged was a tall, thin man, with a long, crooked nose protruding from beneath the brim of his floppy chapeau and plumes of smoke rising from the pipe clamped in his teeth. The man pushed his hat back revealing amused black eyes.

"Was the caller for me, by chance?" Murdoch asked.

Rafael turned about and went back to the front door, which had begun to slide shut, throwing it wide again. Istäni grinned and bowed as he entered the house. He doffed his coat on a stand by the door but kept his dusty boots on. He went straight to the parlor, where he sat at the piano bench. The others gathered around the room, which had begun to feel alarmingly close.

"This is family business. I don't believe we'll require the ladies to be present," said Murdoch. "Esperanza, Hadassah, you may go."

Haddy began to protest. "But what about Cara? She's also a—"

"She's not like you. Now go," hissed Murdoch.

While Haddy scurried away in fear, Esperanza's gaze met Istäni's from across the piano. She drew herself up tall and said, "I am exceedingly weary. Much as I would like to spend the whole night listening to a group of such fascinating conversationalists as yourselves, I really must rest my vocal cords. Excuse me, all of you, and goodnight." With that she turned and vanished up the stairs.

"You both had the pleasure of meeting Lefty, Murdoch and Louis' associate," said Istäni, turning toward Cara and Rafael.

"Yes. Yes, we did," Rafael confirmed, still bristling with his desire for vengeance.

"And still no thanks to your rescuer? Your brothers didn't set you free, after all."

"As Rafael said," Cara answered. "You are either very brave or very stupid, to come here alone and unarmed into a nest of Firefaxes after murdering one of them. Why would you risk it?"

"All business, then, Miss Cara? No time to waste on pleasantries? Yours is an easy question to answer, however. I told you once before. Lubrerum. I want Lubrerum."

Murdoch shrugged. "That is also an easy question to answer, Istäni. No."

"Yes, for you it's so easy, especially now that the one piece of leverage I had over you is dead. Makes things quite simple. However, for your siblings, things are already in motion that cannot be undone, unless, perhaps, you take me to Lubrerum."

"What do you mean?" asked Cara, her throat tightening, as if she already knew what Istäni was referring to.

"Speak plainly, Istäni, we grow tired of your riddles and games," Rafael interjected.

"Very well, I will speak quite plainly—though, the two elder brothers already know what I am referring to, I believe, or they would have killed me already. Years ago, among my father's possessions, I found a bottle that contained a curious liquid substance. Among his papers I learned the mystery of what the substance was. It was a poison called simply *morsus dei*, found only upon the island of Lubrerum. It's a slow poison. Depending on the constitution of the person who imbibes it, it takes anywhere from one month to perhaps three, at the most, to kill its victim. This is the secret to how Lubrerum has remained unknown for so long. Anyone that comes to the island ingests the poison, and they are dead when they reach land, or too sick to walk or speak, unless they have taken the antidote, which can only be found on Lubrerum itself. *Morsus dei* seeps through the body, making the victim waste away in an agonizing, insidious manner. A victim would not know they had been poisoned at all. It just seems another cruel illness—cancer, plague, consumption, another consequence of the curse in the Garden of Eden, nothing more.

"When I learned of Murdoch's weakness at last, after

wondering for many years if he had one, I planned to poison Henry. If Henry was poisoned and the only thing that would save him was on that island, then Murdoch would take me to Lubrerum. He would do anything for Henry, anything. Not the least clever scheme that I have ever hatched, if you'll allow me to give myself some credit. However, that obviously didn't work, and Henry is dead, and someone else entirely took the wound of the poisoned axe and is now dying slowly of it." With these words Istäni turned toward Louis, seated on a rocking chair near the front window. The lamps had burned so low that it was difficult to see him, but Cara drew in a breath sharply, finally making sense of the change that had come over her invincible older brother.

"There, you hear that, Murdoch? The girl gasps. She loves him, though you may not, and so does your sweet little brother, Rafael. Will you take from them another brother? Will you let Louis die, the man who risked his own life in a vain effort to save your beloved Henry?"

For a long time Murdoch did not speak, and no one else dared interject their own thoughts, processing the information that Istäni had shared. Finally, Murdoch removed the pipe from between his thin lips, tossed his head back, and broke into a croaking laugh. He laughed until tears of mirth dripped from his eyes and he dashed them away with his sleeves. Finally, pausing to catch his breath, he shook his head slowly.

"You really are incredible, Istäni. I'm ashamed of my part in bringing you to adulthood. In the most spectacular failure that I have ever witnessed, you have not only completely bungled giving me any motivation to help you, but you have, in fact, given me a strong incentive not to. There is nothing I would like more than to watch Louis Firefax die with agonizing slowness, wasting away to a mewling, helpless creature, with someone else fulfilling his every physiological need, wiping his ass, cleaning his piss, rolling him to prevent oozing sores that come regardless, festering and weeping as his body rots alive. Nothing, and I mean this, nothing would give me more pleasure than to see this slow, ignoble death play out. Why, in God's name, would I take you to Lubrerum now? Let him die."

With that, Murdoch rose to his feet, and, in a moment, he was gone, the faint sound of his feet on the path outside quickly fading. After a moment of silence Istäni shrugged, turning to Cara. "If you see him again and can convince him to change his mind, please do let me know. I'm never far from here. In fact, I shall keep a guard posted outside this house, waiting for him to return."

Then, as quickly as he had come, Istäni too departed, while the oil lamps fizzled and died, leaving the last three Firefaxes in perfect darkness, the smoky haze and wafting odor from the exhausted lamps filling the air around them.

"You knew this already, didn't you?" asked Cara, directing her question at Louis.

"Yes. I knew what Istäni stabbed me with in the tavern, obviously," replied Louis.

"And you knew about the poison on the island?"

Louis nodded, but, realizing the others could not see him, he answered aloud, "Yes, yes, I knew. But it's like everything else we've been told about that island: fanciful, absurd, magical. A silly fable for children. The sailors who visit the island all die by the time they reach shore, save those who receive the antidote before they leave the island, which has always only been the Firefaxes. That is how the secret of the island has stayed secret for so long."

"Only it's not a fanciful, made-up story for children, is it?"

"No. I don't believe so. Based on how I've been feeling, I think at least the poison is real," replied Louis, his voice faint, then strengthening as he continued, "At any rate, it doesn't bloody matter. I'm not going to be some pawn in the game of those two devils."

"What are you going to do?" asked Rafael.

"I'm leaving. I'll die on my own fucking terms, not Istäni's, and not with that hateful monster of a brother of ours gloating over me, either." Louis began moving quickly and soundlessly about the room, peering through the windows to discern the location of Istäni's guards. He darted up the stairs, and his siblings could hear him rustling about, returning a few minutes later with a pack, a pistol, and a rapier, which he belted about his waist. Then he began to pile his layers of coats on as he continued, "Istäni's posted them out front, and nearly all around the house. But there is no one on the northeast corner. Likely they think no one could make it through those bushes without making a racket, but there's another way out of the house. I suspect it's how Murdoch got in. Are you coming with me?"

"To where?" asked Cara, her voice rising in pitch. "We leave here, we run away from Istäni and Murdoch, and there will be no hope of you surviving the poison."

"Listen," said Rafael. "Why don't we go find Murdoch ourselves? If he is the only one who knows the way and he won't take Istäni there, perhaps he'll agree to take us there. Just the four of us. We're family, after all. The island is ours."

"And you plan to charter a voyage on a vessel with what money?" asked Louis. "Has Murdoch shared his wealth with you? Did Father leave you thousands of pounds?"

"We can . . . we can use the money I've saved for Oxford."

They could see the curve of Louis' white teeth in the darkness as he grinned. "That's the kindest thing anyone has ever offered me, Rafael, to be sure. But I can't accept. Murdoch isn't on our side, or Istäni's side. He's not working for the good of the Continental Army, or for the British. He's not with the Myrmidons, or the Argonauts. He's on his own side, and I don't know what his final aim is, but he's not going to agree to take his siblings to Lubrerum, that much is clear, with or without Istäni. And if you think I'm going to beg Murdoch for my life, then you're more stupid than I thought. I won't give him the satisfaction. There isn't time to waste. We need to be well away from here by sunup."

"What of your wife?" asked Rafael. "Won't she worry when she wakes to find you gone?"

Louis threw back his head and let out a loud, bitter laugh, stifling it after a moment so as not to arouse anyone else in the house. "No, she'll rejoice at it, Rafael. She despises me, and I her. Now, that's enough chatter—let's get out of here before Istäni weaves his web too thick. Follow me."

Rafael and Cara took their weapons from the guest room and followed Louis into Julius' cluttered study to a tall wardrobe standing against the wall. There were only a few coats hanging in it, and for a moment Cara thought that Louis was going to put on another layer, but then he knelt and began lifting the boards from the floor. The wardrobe had a false bottom, and through it they could see a ladder leading down into a cellar. Louis had his siblings go first, passing their weapons down to them as they stood in the narrow tunnel below. A moment later he joined them, pausing to put the boards back in place above them.

"Is this where Julius keeps all his tea?" asked Rafael, wrinkling his nose as an herbal scent assailed his nostrils.

"His tea, his sugar, his rum, all his contraband, really. He keeps a great many things down here," answered Louis. "But it's a long cellar and there's an exit beyond his yard. It's usually a little wet and muddy to get out, and it's quite small. Keep your heads down."

The only way Cara knew which way to go in the blackness was the noise of Rafael shuffling ahead of her, and occasionally the splash of one of her brothers stepping in a puddle. She edged her way along the ever-tightening tunnel, feeling dirt from the walls crumble onto her skirt and jacket, and cobwebs clinging to her hair and face. At one point she stepped on something that scuttled away, squeaking in distress. She heard answering squeaks of outrage in the darkness behind her. The walls pressed in closer about her, crushing her head down, pressing into her shoulders, forcing her to wedge herself sideways to slide along the dirt walls, and a sense of panic rose inside her. The path was too tight; her brothers could not have fit, she reasoned, not if she was having so much trouble. Somehow she must have lost them. She considered twisting herself around or backing out, but then she felt the air stir. There was a faint draft ahead of her. Gulping in the fresh air she pushed forward, until, abruptly, she found herself looking up at the black sky overhead, dappled with pale white stars.

"Come on," whispered Rafael, and reaching down he took her hands and hoisted her from the cellar. They were under a set of close bushes. Louis lay stretched out on his belly a few feet from them, peering out at the streets. Rafael rolled a wooden cover, disguised with dirt and grass, over the opening to the cellar.

'Where are we?' Cara signed to Rafael, rather than speaking.

'Two houses down,' he signed in return.

Louis waved them over. He pointed out the guards, one standing behind a house across the street, watching Julius' residence, the other pacing along the road itself, slowly and methodically. They could see the faint glimmer of steel near the two men's waists. They were carrying swords, at least, and likely pistols as well. Louis began to gather himself to run, but Rafael stopped him, pointing instead at Cara, who, understanding her brother's intimation, grinned.

With a nod from Louis, Cara, waiting until the pacing soldier had turned away, darted from the cover of the bushes and vaulted over the stone fence that enclosed the yard. She scurried noiseless and swift, low to the ground, until she came to hide behind another house, a little way up the lane. She pressed herself against the wall, panting. She felt free, like a shadow in the night, completely invisible. She searched for the guards. The one against the neighboring house was obscured from her view; the other guard slowly completed his walk and turned his back on the place where her brothers crouched. She made a faint, trilling call, the cry of a chorus frog, twice, and then was silent. A few moments later Rafael pressed himself against the wall beside her, gasping, his eyes wide with alarm.

"What happened?" she whispered.

He nodded further down the lane. "Another one. Didn't see him until almost too late."

"Did he see you?" Cara felt panic rising inside her. She had not noticed a third watcher in the lane, she had not even looked that way before she called for Rafael to join her. She cursed her inattention. She was becoming dangerously lax after her months away from working in the family business. Just then she heard the cry of a chorus frog, somewhere in the darkness.

Rafael startled, turning back at a thud behind them in the street. He glanced at Cara, who had already half-drawn her rapier. Then Louis reached them, glaring and shaking his head.

"Why did you call if the lane wasn't clear?" he asked, his voice hissing with vehemence.

"I didn't call," replied Rafael. "Nor did Cara. What happened?"

"Well, you killed that blaggard and left him blocking the lane. I didn't realize it until I tripped over him."

They could hear the other two guards conversing. They had also heard the thud in the street, and began moving along the lane slowly with their swords drawn.

"I didn't kill anyone," said Rafael. "I saw a man coming up the lane and I took off. Not sure if he saw me."

"Then I guess he just had a sudden apoplexy and died in the middle of the street, conveniently, after he sighted you," replied Louis scornfully. "At any rate, we must get on, before those two oafs find the body. I lead this time."

Moving with his habitual grace and speed, Louis set off ahead of his siblings, keeping to the shadows. The city was quiet at that hour, but Cara was sure she could hear the sound of feet running somewhere in the distance. She kept her head constantly swiveling to examine every shadow.

Ahead of her, Louis was not so paranoid as his sister, but his lungs were burning, and a strange sense of nausea was rising in his gut. He was moving as quickly as he ever had, but it was not easy, as it should have been, as it had always been before. He longed to rest, just for a few moments, but he pushed on. His heart raced, and strange, stabbing pains wracked his chest and abdomen. Occasionally he glanced back at his siblings, as they followed him without difficulty. They were fit, and young, and had unconscious smiles on their faces from the exhilaration of the escape.

Louis had not decided where he would go, but his plan, insofar as it was formed, had been to join Washington's forces, find his way into battle or into some dark plot of subterfuge, as usual, and get himself killed. It would be a noble, heroic death, not what he considered the other option to be, the passage of an invalid in a sickbed, as the poison slowly worked its way through his organs. He felt already like half the man he had been before the wound.

They had been running for several hours when a wave of undeniable nausea hit Louis. Cara and Rafael had just come abreast of him and he shoved them into the shadow of a door frame, and then dropped into the nearby bushes on his hands and knees, retching uncontrollably until there was nothing left and he was simply heaving while the world around him spun.

As he rose gingerly, Cara touched his back; a tender, almost loving touch that made the hair on his neck stand up. He shoved her away, forcing himself to stand steady. "No time to waste," he said softly, hating the smell and taste of vomit that burned his nostrils and filled his throat. "Let's push on." He saw that Rafael had closed his eyes, but his lips were moving faintly. "Do you ever stop praying?" he spat out in disgust, before stumbling forward. He made it only a few steps before his feet gave out and he dropped to the ground again. The hedges, buildings, and his siblings were all swirling in his darkening vision. His siblings stayed back this time, warned away by his reactions to their concern before. Finally the world was still again and Louis hauled himself up once more, standing tall and holding his head at a haughty angle, though his hands were trembling. As he began walking again, Cara and Rafael followed a safe distance behind, exchanging obnoxious looks of concern that he felt rather than saw.

They did not run after that but walked at a brisk pace. The night was beginning to wane, though as yet there was no sign of the sun rising. The first calls of mourning doves echoed in the quiet, along with the faint hoots of owls, wending their way home from a night of hunting. The Firefaxes stayed alert to the sounds, knowing that any noise might be a signal between their enemies, working to encircle them. They had entered a more commercial area of town, empty shops lining the silent streets. A clatter of running footsteps behind them broke the quiet and they wedged themselves against the side of the nearest building.

Rafael and Louis exchanged a brief look, and Rafael raised three fingers, then cocked his head, listening closer, and brought down the third finger. The brothers grinned. They scanned the two figures as they passed at a quick trot, noting their weapons. Rafael was certain he recognized one of them as a Myrmidon that had been at the tavern the night Henry had died. Louis and Rafael dashed forward and, in a matter of seconds, their pursuers lay dead on the ground. They pushed on, Cara following behind.

Rafael took the lead, a fact the youngest Firefax brother did not like, for it meant that Louis was getting weaker. He found himself whispering prayers again, two for the souls of the dead men they left in their wake, one for the three of them in their mad dash to find safety somewhere in Boston, and one for the healing of his brother.

An enormous oak, out of place in the city streets, stretched its thick green canopy out over a wide square ahead of them, and Rafael saw movement by the trunk. He stopped immediately with his arms outstretched to warn his siblings, who halted beside him.

"Four, I think," he whispered.

Louis shrugged. "Shouldn't be a problem."

"They cut us off. How did they know we would come this way? Do they know where we are going? Do *you* know where we are going?" asked Cara.

"For your information, little sister, I do know where we are going and it will be quite safe, if we dispatch these four men, at any rate."

"But do *they* also know where you're leading us? How did they know to block us here?"

"It won't really matter when they're dead, will it?" Louis sneered in reply.

They continued, slowing their pace to a relaxed amble, pretending to be unaware of the men ahead of them. Rather than waiting for them to pass and ambushing them, the four men stepped out from the cover of the oak to block their path, rapiers and cutlasses drawn.

"Well, well, don't these bastards have some spunk?" remarked Louis, grinning as he drew his own blade.

Glancing at her brother, Cara saw the dreadful, sickening smile of a man seeking death—a man desperate for a swift end to his suffering. There was just enough light in the air to appreciate that he looked worse than he had the evening before, perhaps from the lack of rest, or the strain of flight, or perhaps it was only her imagination. She shuddered, trying to suppress the fear that she was about to see another brother die, and drew her sword. Istäni's men did not have any firearms; they were trying to take the Firefaxes alive. They would be of no use as leverage against Murdoch if they were dead. Louis broke into a run and Cara, with no more time for reflection, raced to follow him.

They met with a clash of steel in the center of the square. As she parried and then attacked her chosen adversary, a young man, little more than a boy, and no match for her in skill, Cara noted the salty scent of sea air wafting around them. They had come all the way from the western side of Newton, nearly to the wharves during the night. They had reached the harbor of Boston. The cries of a few gulls confirmed her suspicions. She continued to back the young man away with her relentless assaults, the movements of the duel like a second nature to her, instinctive and sure. Out of the corner of her eye she could see Louis battling two men, making it look like child's play, and Rafael fighting his one adversary with similar ease. Rafael was the first to down his opponent and, leaving the man exsanguinating in the street, he turned to assist Louis.

Switching her attention back to her opponent, Cara found the boy attacking her with renewed ferocity. She ducked and spun, pushing her back toward him and catching his sword arm. Still holding his arm, she twisted and bent over hard and fast, throwing the young man over her shoulder with his own momentum and wrenching his sword away as he hit the ground with a thud. He had struck his head hard on the stones and lay stunned for a moment, just enough time for her to pounce on his chest, toss both swords to the side, and press her knife blade to his throat. He stared up at her, his pupils wide and his breaths coming in short, shallow gasps.

"Roll over, slowly, and put your hands behind your back," she hissed.

Slowly, uncertainly, he rolled and brought his hands behind his back, while she kept her knife pressed tight to his throat. She yanked his wrists hard, pushing her knee into his back as she straddled him. In a few swift motions, she sheathed her knife and bound the youth with his own sword belt.

"Defeated by a girl," lamented the young man, and Cara smiled at that, but a familiar, cheerful voice interrupted her brief triumph.

"Now, now, Icarus, don't be dismayed. She's no ordinary girl, after all. Not like this one."

She whirled, snatching the knife from its sheath, and then froze. Istäni, along with Silver, was standing in the street behind her. Silver bent to pick up her sword and that of her disarmed adversary. Istäni, meanwhile, had his arm around Esperanza, who was bound and gagged. He held one arm just under her breasts, clutching her almost tenderly against him, while with his other hand he held a pistol, the barrel pressed to the side of her head. Behind the two men a half dozen of Istäni's men stood, swords and pistols drawn.

"Losi! Raf! You have to stop!" cried Cara. "You have to stop, now."

Rafael glanced toward his sister and almost immediately raised his hands, stepping back and letting his sword drop with a clatter to the stones. Louis continued to fight, even after he saw the danger menacing his wife. Three men to each of the two surrendering Firefaxes leaped forward, binding Rafael and Cara's hands behind their backs. The dull glow was strengthening in the east, but still Louis battled on, sweat dripping from his pale, faintly jaundiced skin, his exertion clearly taxing him to the point of exhaustion.

"Louis, Louis, Louis," said Istäni soothingly, keeping his gun trained on Esperanza's head. "They are not going to kill you, brother. They have their orders, and they know the penalty for disobedience. Give it up, Louis."

Still Louis fought, darting back and forth, his sword clinking against his two opponents' blades. He was still a match for any swordsman in the world, Cara thought, with a sense of pride. But her pride gave way to dread as she watched Istäni push the barrel of his gun deeper into Esperanza's black tresses, pushing her head awkwardly to the side. A click sounded as Istäni cocked the pistol, and Esperanza's flashing brown eyes grew wide, not with fear, thought Cara, but with blazing anger, directed toward her husband.

"Louis, I will only say this one more time. Surrender now, or your wife and your child perish," said Istäni, his voice calm, and low, but with a dangerous edge that made everyone listen sharply.

Louis turned immediately toward Istäni and Esperanza, staring in shock. "My . . . my what?"

"Your child, dear Louis. Do you think Esperanza agreed to wed you because of your good looks and winning way with words? Your excellent skills at wooing? No, she sent for you and agreed to marry you because she is carrying your child."

As Istäni spoke, his remaining men, including Silver, pounced on the stunned Louis, striking his face, his stomach, and his chest with their fists. For once Louis did not fight back; in fact, he did not even take a defensive posture, leaving himself open to their every blow, and Cara thought again that he was still seeking a quick end to his suffering. She winced and struggled against her own bonds as the men pummeled her brother repeatedly.

"Enough, enough!" called Istäni. "I will shoot the next man that strikes him. Or kicks him." Silver had drawn his leg back as Louis lay on the ground, but he let it fall at Istäni's threat. Istäni's men rolled Louis over and tied his hands behind him roughly. Louis kept his face pressed into the cobblestones and Cara could not tell if it was because he was insensate, or was simply in despair. He lay motionless except for the comforting rise and fall of his chest. Even with Louis subdued, Istäni kept his pistol pinned to the side of Esperanza's head as he moved forward to stand over his adversary.

"Louis, dear Louis, I had thought to treat you as a gentleman prisoner. I wanted to trust you, to allow you liberty —especially given your death sentence—to still have free rein to walk about the city, perhaps with an escort, but not requiring the indignity of physical bonds to keep you subdued. Alas, you make me look like a cad now, trussing a man in the street like a pig. All for what? For your pride? Louis Firefax is too good to die the ignoble death of a yeoman, wasting away quietly like so many millions of ordinary people do every year?"

Louis still did not stir, but Cara saw the blue flash of his eyes opening, and an expression of obstinance settled on his face. She had the distinct sense that he was steeling himself for something more, something that only he and Istäni knew was coming. Her nose wrinkled suddenly, assailed by a familiar, noxious odor, and she turned toward Rafael and saw that he too had caught the scent. For a moment they thought rescue was upon them, heralded by the unmistakable pungent odor of Murdoch's tobacco, but then they recalled who their brother was as he stepped from the shadow of a tall brick building. He came to stand a few feet from Louis and Istäni, staring not at his brother on the ground but directly into the eyes of Esperanza, until at last, cowed by those cold, dark orbs, she cast her gaze down. Still he looked at her, as though his vision could tunnel straight through her mind.

"I will still kill her, and with her, the child she carries, if you do not beg your brother to save your life by taking us to Lubrerum," said Istäni, addressing the prostrate man on the ground.

Louis did not move, but Cara noticed his jaw tightening. The hatred emanating from him was almost palpable. Istäni moved his arm from below Esperanza's breast, sliding it down over her softly rounded abdomen, obscured before by the looseness and thickness of her skirts and petticoats. He held her by the pelvis, stretching the fabric taut over her swollen abdomen as he moved the pistol from her head to point it directly at her womb.

"You know I don't lie, Louis." At that Esperanza jerked her head up, anger scrawled across her face, and for the first time, a flash of fear as she glanced toward Istäni.

Slowly and awkwardly without the use of his arms for balance, Louis struggled from his sprawled position to his knees. He was taking slow, deliberate gulps of air, as if to ready himself for the next step in his humiliation. Scooting forward on his knees, biting his lip so hard that it bled, he dropped onto Murdoch's boots and pressed his forehead into the muddy leather.

"Please," he said softly, and then nothing.

"Please what?" prompted Istäni, obviously enjoying the show.

Murdoch, curiously, had still hardly glanced at his brother and continued looking at Esperanza. Louis said nothing, and Istäni pressed the barrel of the gun so hard into Esperanza's abdomen that she let out an involuntary cry.

"Please, Murdoch," whispered Louis. "I beg you . . . take him to Lubrerum. Please . . . save my wife, my child . . . save me."

"Kiss his boots," Istäni instructed, still gleeful.

With a look of complete hatred darted at Istäni, Louis obliged, kissing the tall filthy boots that Murdoch wore. The first morning rooster crowing in the distance was the only noise that disturbed that strange scene in the square near the Boston Harbor. Cara shifted uncomfortably in the stillness, hating the pathetic obeisance foisted on Louis by his conqueror. Rafael had closed his eyes, and she could see his lips moving, murmuring quiet prayers. It was just barely light enough that they could make out the ship masts swaying in the harbor, only a few hundred feet away.

"I want half of what you take off the island," said Murdoch in his harsh, croaking voice, startling everyone.

"Half? Certainly not. Fifteen percent is my best offer," countered Istäni.

"Half. Half or you can forget the whole damn thing."

"Twenty percent."

Murdoch's eyes flashed. "You can kill everyone in this bloody square, Istäni, and Lightfoot can wash my boots with his tongue for the rest of his miserable life, it's not going to change my price."

For a moment Istäni said nothing. Then, as the first rays of morning light pierced the hazy gray sky, illuminating at last the Boston Harbor and the group of men and women standing under the ancient oak tree in the square, Istäni lifted his gun, releasing the cock back into place, and thrust Esperanza toward Silver. He stepped forward and held his hand out to Murdoch.

"Half," he said simply, and the two men shook hands over the prostrate form of Louis.

CHAPTER 12

PREPARATIONS

Rafael watched his brother with concern as Istäni's men shoved them to the docks. The Myrmidons were anxious to clear up the scene before Boston awakened; already the first few merchants and shopkeepers were beginning to appear on the streets. Istäni dropped a few shining coins into a constable's outstretched hands and moments later Louis and Rafael were being rowed away from Cara and Esperanza. None of the brief discussions on the dock appeared to have registered with his brother. Which, Rafael reflected, was just as well; Louis would have been enraged if he had heard Istäni's hasty arrangements. Esperanza would come with them on their voyage to Lubrerum, as insurance for Louis' good behavior. For tonight she would be locked up in a comfortable house that Istäni was letting near the harbor, with Lottie as her guard. Cara had insisted that she go on the voyage as well; that Louis would need an attendant as his health declined. Istäni agreed and also enlisted Cara to return to Julius' house with him, to gather the things Esperanza would need on the voyage. As for Murdoch . . . even Rafael, who was keenly alert during the short march to the dock, did not know where Murdoch went. After the two hateful men shook hands, his wraithlike oldest brother had melted into the background, and the next time Rafael had scanned the group, Murdoch was gone.

Rafael seethed as he sat in the cutter, half-heartedly yanking at the ropes binding his wrists, as Istäni's men rowed steadily toward a lithe vessel in the far reaches of the harbor. He toyed with the idea of making a daring escape, taking Louis and jumping over the side, trying to swim their way back to shore. Once in the water he could maneuver around to untie Louis' hands, and Louis could do the same for him. But, taking note again of the vacant, soulless expression on his brother's face, Rafael let the idea go. Louis was not well. In fact, he was very unwell, in more ways than one, and after the long run through the night, the battle in the square, and the beating he had taken, both physically and mentally, he was in no state for a long swim back to shore and another desperate rescue attempt of the women. He barely seemed present at all, staring into nothing, not moving or reacting as welts and bruises gradually darkened on the exposed bits of his unnaturally pale skin.

They were hoisted aboard the ship, a spritely little frigate with the word *Mariposa* scribed across its hull. The Myrmidons bundled them down a hatchway and tossed them unceremoniously facefirst into the brig. Rafael sputtered and shook his head as they landed in a startlingly cold pool of foul bilge water. Louis barely seemed to register the indignity, and lay still in the filthy puddle with his head turned to the side. His blue eyes dimmed and closed, slowly, as if he was falling asleep. Istäni's men slammed the iron grille behind the brothers, locking it and then thundering back up the stairs, joking among themselves about how they had successfully beaten the fabled Lightfoot of the Argonauts. Rafael rolled onto his back, twisting to get his arms out from under him, and sat up, resting his back against the iron bars of their cage. He stared at the motionless form of his brother, ensuring that Louis' mouth and nose were enough above the puddle of brackish water to let him breathe without drowning.

"Louis, are you all right?"

Louis let out a long, slow breath, a pent-up sigh. "I'm alive, aren't I?"

"Yes, but I mean, are you all right? You took quite a beating."

"Did I? Funny," said Louis, opening one eye and casting his gaze around their small cell before letting it drift closed again. "I don't feel a thing."

"Well, that's better than the alternative, I suppose," replied his brother, adjusting himself a little further. He waited in silence, but Louis spoke no more. Finally Rafael continued, his voice taking on a glib tone, "I guess congratulations are in order again? My elder brother, the unconquerable bachelor. Not only did you get spliced but you knocked the girl up as well? I'm not a medical man, but based on the size of her abdomen when Istäni held her like that, she's rather advanced in the pregnancy."

"You're no fool, little brother," replied Louis wearily. He opened his eyes, and despite his comment that he felt nothing, his face twisted with pain as he laboriously hoisted himself out of the pool of water and leaned against the metal grating of the brig beside his brother.

"What, then, is the truth about the relationship between you and the lady Esperanza? Is the child actually yours?"

"Oh, it's most certainly mine. Without a doubt. Esperanza could bed any man in Massachusetts. But she's not easy, she has very . . . high standards, impossible standards. I managed to win my way into her bed with my charming mannerisms, my rare good looks, and my voice, if you must know. But I don't believe she's been with anyone since me. Don't look dubious. I'm a bit jealous, honestly. I asked around. That Haddy is a great talker too—she would have known if anyone else had been with Esperanza. I first met Esperanza in Charlestown, doing a job for the Argonauts. We didn't start our real tryst until some five or six months ago, though. January, maybe February. A really pleasurable experience . . ." He trailed off, envisioning with longing the incomparable beauty of Esperanza's naked body, as he had seen it during their month together: her elegant tall form, with smooth, curving edges, her perfect set of breasts, and her flawless tan skin, complementing her beautiful brown eyes and the long dark tresses that fell like a curtain over her exquisite callipygian backside.

"Louis?"

"What?"

"You hadn't talked in a few minutes—I thought you'd fallen asleep."

"Oh, sorry, yes. Sex, Rafael, the kind of sex you could only dream of. You wouldn't have believed it. I conquered the most beautiful woman in Boston, maybe the most beautiful woman in all the colonies, and we had such glorious gallivants in the garden, if you know what I mean."

Rafael laughed and shook his head. "No, I don't. No one knows what that means. Nor do I think that I want to."

"Really, Rafael, I've been with a number of women over the years, but none even come close to what I had with her. Indeed, I've been unsatisfied since, thinking about her and her perfect lips, her glorious tulip-shaped—"

"That's fine, Louis, I don't really need an annotated description of the intercourse you had with Esperanza."

"Oh, right. Sorry. I just . . . a man could die happy between those breasts, you know."

"Listen, you keep talking about Esperanza like that and I shall ask our captors to put me in a different cell."

"Very well, as you wish, celibate, grumpy old prude. Where was I? Oh, yes, I was enraptured and utterly captivated by her. I asked her to marry me, Rafael, the first woman I've ever asked to marry me. She declined, and I heard nothing else from her until she sent a letter to me, just after . . . well, just after Henry died, requesting that I come to speak to her. Naturally, I wasn't about to say no."

"Really? Our brother had just been murdered and all you could think about was putting your member into some loose Boston strumpet?"

"Rafael! She's not a strumpet! She's many things, but you can't call her that. I could think of lots of other things at the time, and I was not really in the mood for her and her games, but . . . I knew about the axe, Rafael, I knew about the poison and I . . . I thought perhaps it would be a good thing to have a child, or at least to seed one, before I passed. So I went to her, and she agreed to marry me this time, under certain conditions."

"Conditions?"

"Namely that at any time, if she so chose, the marriage could be annulled, with or without cause. I agreed. I was dying, Raf. You can't begrudge a man wanting a bit of happiness."

"But you seemed as surprised as any of us to learn she was pregnant."

"Indeed. She has been wearing a different sort of fashion than what she sported in the winter, and she looks just as beautiful as before, maybe a touch plumper about the face and arms, her breasts are bigger too, I've certainly noticed that. But, Rafael, she hasn't allowed me back into her bed. There's been no consummation. So when Istäni held her the way he did, I confess it was the first I saw the silhouette of her abdomen since I've been back in Boston. She hasn't even let me touch her, really. She let me give her a chaste kiss during the little ceremony, but other than that I was just . . . waiting, pathetically, stupidly, thinking eventually she would give me the chance and I would impregnate her before the end. Turns out I already have." He chuckled ruefully at that and then fell silent again.

"Well, that would be a pretty easy union to nullify, if what you say is true."

"Yes, but I don't want it annulled, Rafael, now especially."

Rafael's expression softened. "I . . . I'm sorry, Louis, about all of this."

"It's all right," whispered Louis, leaning heavily to the side. He was grimacing again; Rafael could just make out the lines of his face in the darkness of the hold. Louis opened one startling blue eye again, so unlike the eyes of any of his siblings. "Perhaps you can practice your preaching, if we're going to be locked in this cage together the whole voyage. I reckon if you can save my miserable soul before I die, you can bring anyone to redemption."

"You're not going to die, Louis. That's the whole bloody point of this voyage, to get you to Lubrerum and get you that antidote."

Louis smiled again, a mournful, pained smile. "Right. Of course. That's the whole point. That's why Murdoch agreed, because he wanted to save his beloved baby brother." He laughed, the sound fading into a soft groan. "Bastard was following us to the wharf. He's the one who killed that blaggard I tripped over and called me out into the lane. Games, it's all games to him. Now he has all the power, all of it, over all our lives, and he despises me, Rafael, and I him, truly. If he does take us to Lubrerum, and that is a big if in itself, he will take this ship there so slowly that I will be nothing but a memory by the time you reach those shores."

"That's very pessimistic, brother. You have as powerful a reason to live now as anyone in the world."

"No, no, I've given up on that. I won't meet the child. It's fine, Raf, it's fine. I just, I would appreciate it if you could . . . after everything, help keep my child and Esperanza safe. I know it's a great deal to ask. I know I probably have no right to ask it of you. But . . . the child won't have a father, and Esperanza won't have a husband."

Rafael bit his lip, feeling as if a cord was tightening around his chest, squeezing his breath away, as he recalled the last time he had been asked to look after someone's spouse. He nodded, finally, letting his gaze drop to the curved, filthy floor of the ship.

"Thank you, brother, that will make the prospect of death a little more bearable," said Louis. "As I said, I am your captive audience, for a few more days at least. Feel free to sermonize, preach, or sing a few hymns if you like. I'm not saying it's going to help me, but it certainly can't hurt me now."

With this last, bitter reflection, Louis fell asleep, leaving Rafael alone in the brig, listening to the movements on deck and the dripping of water down the walls of the hold, adding slowly to the foul pool in which the brothers sat. He listened to the drips for some time, finally adjusting himself so he could just reach the knots binding Louis' wrists. He struggled to undo them, resting frequently as his own bonds tore at him with each twisting, awkward movement. He kept at it, doggedly, until at last his brother lay free beside him. Then he began to hum, first softly, but finally breaking into a meditative rendition of Wesley's "And Can It Be That I Should Gain", his lovely baritone voice strengthening as he continued, and finally rising through the floor above them and into the crew's sleeping quarters.

Cara, her arms untied once Rafael and Louis had been rowed away, walked quickly behind Istäni, wanting nothing more than to get back to her brothers. She wanted to examine Louis' bruises and scrapes and to make sure he was all right. The picture of Istäni's Myrmidons beating him ruthlessly in the square blended with another hideous image in her mind, the flashing vision of her father thumping on the ground over and over and over again, in a sickening, lifeless rhythm, a dead, flopping weight, attached to the panicked, bolting mare. Cara shuddered. Shaking herself from her reverie, she looked up and leaped suddenly to the side, her foot swallowed by a puddle of filth from an emptied chamber pot as she narrowly avoided a careening carriage.

"You won't be much help to your brother if you're splattered on the streets of Boston," remarked Istäni wryly, turning back to watch her as she lifted her sullied skirts and raced to catch up to him.

"It doesn't sound like I'll be much help to my brother either way. How long before your poison finishes its work? Did you see him? He's already half the man I knew before, and it's been less than a month."

"I saw him, and I'm not disagreeing with you. It's a bit of a gamble, really—most people ingest it, and the dose was probably higher than it should have been. But, he's a strong young man, he'll probably be fine. Depending on how long Murdoch takes to get us there."

"For your sake I hope you're right."

"Is that a threat? From Cara? Cara Firefax who has never killed a man?"

"I could kill you right now if I wanted."

"Why don't you, then?"

"I would if we didn't need you and your bloody ship to get us to Lubrerum to save my brother."

"Because Murdoch would never take you to the island without me?"

Cara frowned at this and bit her lip, searching for an appropriate snappy response, but none came. She continued to clench her jaw during the rest of the walk. Istäni kept his eyes ever roaming the streets around them for any followers, and Cara thought a few times she saw the cloaked form of the man called Rounder watching over them protectively from the alleys. It took several hours to return to Newton. Cara had not realized in the mad rush during the night how far they had gone.

It was Haddy who opened the cherry red-door when Cara knocked. Istäni moved deftly to the side, pushing himself against the bricks, out of sight of the girl in the doorway. Haddy, her apron covered in flour, the white powder also dusting her stray curls, gazed up at Cara with a mix of curiosity and something touching fear. Neither woman said anything for a long, awkward moment. To Cara's left, just outside of Haddy's vision, Istäni raised his eyebrows, prompting Cara to speak.

"I've come to collect Esperanza's things. Whatever she might need for a voyage."

"A voyage? How long of a voyage? Where are we going?"

"*We* are not going anywhere. Esperanza is going—with Louis, of course. He surprised her. A trip to Spain, can you imagine?"

Haddy's eyes widened. "She loathes him, you know. But I think it's cruel. He's so dashing and romantic, whatever she might say. Taking her back to Spain? She was born there, did you know that? But on such short notice! In the middle of a war? That'll be risky, don't you think? Where is she? She won't want to go without my help. I attend her, I always do, always have, since we were little, back when we lived in St.

Augustine with Espy's parents. Even when she was training in Europe, I was always by her side."

"She won't be needing you. This is an intimate voyage, with her husband."

But Haddy was suspicious, scanning the street behind Cara and frowning. "Can I bring her the belongings? At least see her off? This would be the longest we've been separated if she's really going all the way to Spain. How long will they be there? You're sure she doesn't want me to come along?"

"Miss Hadassah Marchworth," said Istäni suddenly, stepping forward to stand directly before the short young lady with her frizzled, flour-dusted hair. She drew back as if she had been bitten by a snake, and Cara could not mistake the look of terror on the girl's face. "The lady Esperanza Firefax does not wish you to accompany her on this voyage. Is that quite clear? Now, gather what you think she will need for . . . oh, say two months?"

Haddy's gaze shot between the two people outside the door. For a moment she hesitated, her lip trembling, then she turned and darted up the stairs, leaving the door open behind her. Cara and Istäni, taking this as an invitation, entered the parlor, listening to the rummaging and thumping above them. Cara sat stiff as a board on a chair near the hearth while Istäni settled comfortably on the piano bench. After a few moments he began to press his fingers along the ivory keys, and Cara straightened still more, recognizing the mournful orchestral suite that Henry had been playing the day Istäni first arrived at Maralah. She turned to stare at him, her eyes blazing with hatred, the rising sense of murderous rage almost choking her. He lingered over a chord and finally turned toward her as if he sensed her glare.

"Not even the dulcet strains of Johann Sebastian Bach can soften the hard soul of Robert's daughter?"

"You killed my brother."

"Did I? You think I killed Henry? Or are you referring to Louis' delicate state of health? He's not dead yet, you know, so you can hardly accuse me of murder."

"Who else could have—" She stopped abruptly and clamped her mouth shut.

"Who else indeed?" answered Istäni, his green eyes alive with merriment. "You are so certain that I killed Henry. Why, in God's name, would I kill Henry Firefax? He was my ticket to Lubrerum. He was the one thing I had been looking for, hopelessly, for years, the one thing that could get me to that island."

"You're playing games, trying to divide my family, to give yourself more power over us."

"Trying to divide the Firefaxes? As if your family needed any help with that! Is it such an absurd thing to suggest? If Achilles could have removed his heel to be truly immortal, don't you think he would have?"

Cara gripped the mahogany armrests of her chair so tight that her knuckles turned white. "Stop it. You're trying to turn us against each other. Haven't you done enough? Isn't it enough that one Firefax is dead and another is dying?"

"Oh my, the Firefaxes are the victims now? How grievous and painful for your precious family! After centuries of carrying on your murderous family business, heaven forbid that vengeance and persecution come after *you* for once. Before I began looking into your family, trying to find out who Thrayder was and what he knew of Lubrerum, I had no idea what kind of evil your forefathers had perpetrated in secret for so many centuries. But once I began to search, the litany of dead was unending. There were not only all those your family had personally murdered—and their servants, their families, anyone who witnessed what happened—but the wars you started, and the countless dead, and maimed, and famine-starved, as nations were thrown into turmoil. All that while you amassed the wealth of half the world on your phantom island. How am I the villain in this story?"

"And that's all it's for? Our wealth? You're just coming after us for our money?"

Istäni laughed and then said, "Are you disappointed that I'm not coming after the Firefaxes for the hand of their daughter? I've been granted a ship, a crew, and the funds for a voyage to find Lubrerum, so that the treasure your family hoards can stop this current war. Seems rather just, doesn't it?"

"And the colonies can be subdued under Britain again?"

"Now Cara Firefax is taking sides?"

"All this, killing Henry, hurting Louis, just for money?" She could feel her voice straining, as if choking back a sob. She wanted Henry back, and if he had to be gone, then she wished that he had died for something else. Not for money. Not to pad the pockets of rich men a thousand miles away.

"Isn't mammon why your family murders people?"

"I have never killed anyone for money."

"You have never killed anyone at all."

"True. But I would never kill just for money."

"Really? Then what, pray tell, would induce Cara Firefax to murder?"

"Damn it, Istäni!" exclaimed Cara vehemently. "If Louis dies you will be the first to know what would induce me to murder!"

"I can't really promise you that Louis will survive. In fact, there is only one thing that I can promise you on this voyage."

"What's that?"

"'We shall not all sleep, but we shall all be changed,'" he replied with a mischievous grin and a wink.

Cara's eyes widened, but before she could reply, Haddy interrupted them, calling from the hall above, "I have two chests ready. You will need to hire a coach to get them out of here, though. I can't bring them down the stairs by myself."

"Don't trouble yourself, Miss Haddy, we've a carriage coming." Istäni darted a glance out the window, and, in a lower voice to the still-bewildered Cara, he said, "Hopefully Icarus will be here soon. His instructions were quite clear. I wish to have everything and everyone aboard the ship before dark."

"Afraid of Lefty?"

"Afraid of him?" Istäni scoffed. "Afraid for him more like. Poor fool only has one arm left to lose. But, nevertheless, I am surprised he hasn't made a move yet."

Several hours later, Icarus arrived with a tall black coach, pulled by one weary horse. The young Myrmidon stayed well away from Cara, but leaped to assist Haddy as the four of them worked together to load the heavy luggage. After they had hoisted both enormous chests onto the carriage, while the men worked to secure them, Cara noticed Haddy biting her lip repeatedly, turning it red and raw. The young woman fidgeted, drawing in the dirt with her feet. Then, taking a deep breath, just as Istäni hopped into the carriage, she snatched hold of Cara's arm and drew her back.

"He's not a good man."

"Don't you think I know that?"

"Is Espy in danger, Cara? I know she's prickly, but . . . she's always looked out for me. And she's—"

"I know she's expecting, Haddy," said Cara, resting a hand gently upon Haddy's arm. "I'll watch out for her. She won't be the first woman I've attended giving birth, if it comes to that."

"But you don't understand her, Cara. You don't even like her! Though, I suppose, how could you, seeing the way she treats your brother—"

"Cara, are you coming?" Istäni called from inside the carriage.

"I'll be with her and take care of her, every step of the way,

Haddy. I've helped my other sister-in-law with the births of four of her children. She'll be in good hands. Try not to worry." With that, she vaulted into the carriage as the shadows of evening stretched out from the tall stalks of Julius' sunflowers.

Haddy caught the door as Cara reached to close it, thrusting a leather-bound book into her hands. "For Rafael, please."

Cara smiled faintly and closed the door. She flipped open the copy of the Bible, scanning the inscription Haddy had hastily scrawled on the blank first page.

"They've met but once, and the girl is so fond of him already?" asked Istäni.

"You should have seen them. Love at first sight. It was grotesque." Cara realized she was grinning. She frowned, averting her gaze suddenly, hating how easy it came to talk to the young man across from her.

Istäni smiled back at her but said nothing more, eventually turning his attention to the streets outside as they trotted toward the wharf. The walk that had taken her and Istäni hours took their horse only a little more than an hour. Despite herself, Cara found the rocking motion of the carriage soothing. She drifted into a fitful sleep, to flickering images in her mind of her brothers fighting in the square beneath the oak tree.

She shifted, lifting her head, feeling a sharp pain in the side of her neck from lying at such an awkward angle. The carriage had stopped, the door was open, and Istäni was gone. She sat bolt upright, nearly losing her spectacles, afraid suddenly that Istäni had taken her brothers to sea without her. She scrambled out of the carriage to see Istäni arguing with a constable at the edge of the wharf. Turning, she peered out at the dark vessels beyond. It was late, fully dark. The only light came from a few oil lanterns, casting dim rays of hazy yellow on the cobbled streets. The harbor was quiet and deserted. She had slept through the unloading of Esperanza's chests, which now sat on the edge of the dock.

"These be dangerous times, laddy, fair dangerous," the constable puttered suspiciously. "I dinnae think I can let ye go out, not in the night. Oye, that's a lassie ye have there too, is it? What would she be doin' aboard a privateer, tell me that naew?"

Istäni glanced back at Cara and said softly, "She's more qualified to be aboard a privateer than any sailor in this city, sir." Then, so quick Cara almost didn't see it, he drew the axe hanging at the side of his green doublet, and in two swift strokes the constable lay dead, his head half-severed from his neck. Istäni caught the constable's lantern as his limp body dropped to the ground. He raised it, covering and uncovering the glow of light with his tricorn hat in a rapid series of signals. "Icarus, help me dump him in the harbor. And where's Lottie with Esperanza?"

"Probably showing her a good time, if I know Lottie," called Icarus from somewhere in the darkness, out of view of the lamps or Istäni's lantern.

"I don't think so," replied Istäni. "Lottie's back to pining for Thrayder like a lovestruck goat. Man's like a barnacle. Once he latches on, you can't get him off."

"What do you mean—" Cara never finished her question. A look of urgency came into Istäni's eyes, staring at something behind her. She spun to see shadowy, silent forms materializing out of the night.

"Cara!" Istäni called her name as he backed away from other men that had encircled him, deftly countering their assaults with his rapier. "There's a cutlass under the driver's seat!"

But Cara didn't need the cutlass concealed in the carriage; she had already relieved her first opponent of his rapier. A blur of motion, she drove one of her adversaries back into the man behind him, and then scrambled atop the carriage roof and, in the brief respite that this height earned her, turned to make sure that the green-eyed man was all right. She needn't have worried. Istäni was gleefully skewering Argonauts with the ease and joy of a child hitting croquet balls.

Cara swiveled and kicked out one long leg, dislodging a man that was climbing the side of the carriage. Kneeling, she thrust her hands into the darkness under the driver's seat to find the cutlass. She rose with both weapons as two men sprang onto the carriage again, coming from either side. Cara knocked the first man off the carriage and heard him land hard on the stone pavement of the wharf. She whirled to face the other, who she recognized as one of the very guards who had marched her across Massachusetts.

With a cruel, leering smile, Cara stepped back, letting the man advance, giving him the taste of victory. Eagerly he lunged, and she evaded, stepping out of his way so quickly that he had to catch himself to keep from falling off the coach's roof, which bowed beneath their combined weight. The horse jerked forward, letting out a shrill neigh of alarm, and the man stumbled as he charged. Cara dodged him, this time bringing her cutlass down on his back as he passed her, rewarding herself with the scent of blood. Her leering grin broadened as she almost tasted that heady, metallic, intoxicating odor. She let him recover, and then for a few moments they battled fiercely, darting back and forth, giving and taking in an erratic dance.

The man she had knocked from the carriage before was halfway up it again. As she blocked yet another blow from the man atop the carriage, she spun and sliced an ear off the climber. He fell with a scream of pain, clutching his bloody face. A third, bigger man began climbing and Cara felt the box leaning. She pushed her adversary back toward the big man and the carriage began to unbalance, yawing to the left. At the critical moment, she leaped forward, adding her weight to that of the two men on the leaning side of the carriage. The wooden structure pitched and tumbled over with a crash, yanking the horse as the tongue twisted. The box landed atop the man that had been climbing it, crushing him, while Cara jumped clear, hitting the ground in a crouching position, both her swords raised.

The man beneath the carriage cried out and struggled. There were shouts of alarm from the buildings nearest the wharf. Cara could see the gleam of a lantern on the water, a cutter approaching, rowed swiftly toward the embattled group on the dock. With a shout of anger, her former Argonaut guard stumbled to his feet. She stabbed the rapier into one of his shoulders while parrying his blade with her cutlass. The man roared in pain, falling back, expecting a killing blow, but none came. Instead Cara waited, letting him come after her again. Crouching low, she lunged forward, catching the man's blade with her rapier while stabbing her cutlass into his leg. The man screamed as she attacked and then flitted away. He whirled about and brought his sword down hard on the cobblestones where Cara had been a second before.

Then, before Cara could attack her hapless adversary again, a pistol shot thundered in the night and the man fell in a lifeless heap. Cara turned to see Murdoch rush past her and cut the lines tethering the floundering horse to the fallen coach. He turned and fired his other pistol directly at her. For a second Cara thought Murdoch had shot her, then, glancing down to find no blood on her gown, she turned to see another Argonaut lying dead on the pavement behind her. Before she could say anything to her brother, Silver called for them as the *Mariposa*'s cutter reached the end of the dock.

"Why do you play? Just kill them," hissed Murdoch to Cara as he caught her arm, pushing her forward. She tore away from him, seeing the Bible Haddy had given her lying on the cobblestones. She snatched it up as Murdoch grabbed her roughly again and shoved her hard toward the dock.

Istäni was still battling as they passed him, and Murdoch did not even try to help. But Cara felt a rush of relief when a mad, dark blur of motion signaled the arrival of Lottie to aid the green-eyed man. Istäni and Lottie dispatched the remaining Argonauts quickly and raced after Cara and Murdoch, Lottie hustling the cloaked form of Esperanza before her. They assisted the pregnant opera singer into the boat, settling her beside Cara in the stern, both women surrounded by rowers. The sailors had already loaded one of Esperanza's heavy chests.

"No time for the other, the hue and cry has been raised," said Istäni, snatching the mooring line from Lottie, who still stood on the dock.

"Are you not coming with us?" Cara called to Lottie, feeling for a second that she wanted nothing more in all the world than for the comforting older woman to be aboard that ship with her.

The woman grinned at her, then darted a faint look of apprehension at Murdoch, who had taken the rudder. "No, *tifi*, I don't sail."

They heard the clatter of shoes upon wood and turned to see Icarus running down the dock toward them. He was racing just ahead of a crowd of men and women, spilling from nearby houses to find the cause of all the commotion on the wharf. Istäni, standing in the prow of the cutter, raised his pistol and shot the sprinting Icarus dead. Lottie turned toward her leader in surprise.

"One less traitor to worry about," said Istäni, by way of explanation, as the cutter began to move swiftly out into the harbor. "Try to keep the whole bloody organization from going to seed while I'm gone, Lottie."

"I'll do my best, sir," she replied.

The wharf behind her was swarming with a mob of bewildered, groggy Bostonians, checking the bodies scattered on the stones, talking in excitement and confusion. The rowers in the cutter began pumping rapidly, putting distance between themselves and the shore, and Cara watched with a strange feeling of longing as Lottie quietly melted into the crowd.

CHAPTER 13

A WOMAN SCORNED

The days in the hold passed fitfully, a blur of monotonous darkness with no way of measuring time save the ringing of the distant bells above. But Rafael had never been much for seafaring and didn't know the significance of the bells, and Louis, who had been as high in rank as a first lieutenant in the Royal Navy before the revolution, slept more than he was awake. The only break in the two brothers' rhythm of sleeping and being sick, was the changing of their chamber pot and the dirty, weevil-infested food thrown to them through the bars. The intestinal infection that settled upon them within a few days of their incarceration was devastating, but more so for Louis, in his already weakened state. While Rafael gradually recovered, Louis still burned with fever and kept no food or, at last, even water down. It was this, finally, that prompted Istäni to allow Cara to visit her brothers. She had been insisting since they weighed anchor, but Istäni always refused, and the guards would not allow her to pass. When a guard reported to Istäni that Louis had not woken that day at all and had drunk no water in two days, Cara was near enough to overhear.

"I came aboard as his nurse, did I not? He'll die down there, and then what reason will Murdoch have to take you to your bloody island?"

Istäni grinned cheekily. "I'm not sure, perhaps the untold millions of gold, silver, and jewels waiting for him there?"

"What if he was your brother?"

Istäni reflected on this for a few minutes. He was seated idly on the quarterdeck with his legs dangling over the bulkhead, kicking absently at the captain's cabin wall like a child. Finally he said, "If Louis Firefax was my brother I would let the arrogant bastard die."

"Well, he's not your brother! He's mine and I need him to survive. You've already taken one brother from me. At least give me the chance to save him, if I can."

Istäni studied Cara's face, then he nodded his head toward the guard. "I cannot resist you, Cara. For better or worse. Holmstead, Cooper, take this lovely lady to the prisoners, and follow her orders on how to care for them. If they must come up, they must come up."

Moments later, hearing his sister's voice in the dank foulness of the hold, Rafael startled upright, thinking that he had drifted off and was dreaming. But Cara's bespectacled visage was unmistakable, looming in the darkness on the other side of the bars.

"How is he?" she asked, nodding toward the still figure of their older brother lying on the ever-rocking floor.

"Not well," said Rafael. Fear for his brother's worsening condition had been tormenting him, a fear he tried to allay with prayers, to little avail. Every time he fitfully drifted off to sleep he expected to wake up to a cold, lifeless Louis. "I don't think it's so much the poison, though. We've both been dreadfully sick with vomiting and diarrhea, fevers. It's been awful. But I've gotten better, and he has . . . well, he just keeps getting worse. I can't get him to drink anything today, Cara. He won't even open his eyes."

Cara stared through the bars with a drawn, worried expression. "We have to get him out of here. I think I can nurse him back a bit, to at least close to what he was before we left Boston."

"Boston seems so long ago," remarked Rafael as the guards, following their master's orders to obey the girl, opened the bars of the brig and hoisted the inert Louis out. Cara assisted the weakened Rafael behind them.

"It's been nearly two weeks. Two weeks I've been trying to convince that monster to let me come and see you. I hate him so much, Rafael. I . . ." She trailed off, casting a worried look after Louis as the sailors lifted him through the hatch.

They settled Louis in what had served as the women's cabin, a simple affair near the stern of the vessel in the berth deck, separated from the crew by a thick curtain. To make room for him, they shifted Esperanza to the captain's cabin, as Istäni graciously offered to stay in one of the tiny closets that served as officers' quarters. The next week Cara spent working tirelessly to help Louis regain his strength, using all her knowledge of medicine and nearly every tincture they had on the ship, along with nourishing porridge and water, endless water. In truth she held out little hope of him rallying, despite her optimistic words to Rafael in the brig. Thus it was with joyful surprise that she saw him strengthen, and finally, by the end of their third week at sea, he was able to rise and amble, though unsteadily, to the deck.

As surprised as Cara was at her brother, wasted and weak, finally rallying, it was nothing compared to the astonishment of everyone else aboard ship when his transformed, ghostlike form emerged from their quarters, shakily ascended the stairs, and stood by the railing on the main deck, gripping the wood as if it were the only thing holding him in the mortal world.

He was gaunt, nearly skeletal, but his eyes, if anything, were brighter and more striking than they had ever been before. Murdoch was the only person who did not seem surprised to see Louis. He didn't start or sit up but just watched from his sprawled position on the stairs to the quarterdeck, puffing silently on his pipe.

Even the off-duty sailors were tense and alert on deck that day. A sail had been sighted behind them, for the third time since they left Boston. Istäni had someone in the rigging watching daily from the time the sail was first sighted. It was clear to all the crew, even those who knew nothing of the ship's purpose, that they were being followed.

As Louis stared vacantly out at the endless blue expanse surrounding their ship, the faintest hints of color returned to his cheeks, the first color that had touched them since Cara retrieved him from the brig. He smiled cheerily as Rafael approached with wild enthusiasm. Rafael had been put to hard labor as a clumsy seaman since coming out of the brig, but still he had made time every day to visit his sick brother, always with a new hymn or a ready sermon.

"It's good to see you in the light of day!" Rafael cried, clapping Louis on the back. He was not sure if he had been too forceful or if his brother was more frail than he had guessed, for Louis nearly fell from the friendly blow. The sick Firefax managed to catch himself on the rigging and remain upright.

"It's good to be in the light of day," replied Louis. "I don't think I ever realized how sweet it is to breathe, brother, and to feel the spray of the ocean on my face."

"You look like death, Lightfoot," came another encouraging call, this time from the ever-chipper Istäni, who approached and similarly clapped Louis on the back. But this time Louis was ready and braced himself appropriately.

"Yes, I would have put a little more effort into my appearance, but, unfortunately, someone poisoned me, and I'm having a lot of trouble keeping weight on since then. I do hope you understand," replied Louis with something of his old spirit.

At that, Murdoch did sit upright, raising his hat to regard his brother with a gleam of something that touched upon respect.

"Has anyone told his wife that he's up and about?" the eldest Firefax asked nonchalantly.

"Esperanza?" Louis turned in bewilderment toward Istäni. He had not registered anything in the square after Murdoch and Istäni's bargain, and the news that Esperanza was aboard the vessel came as a complete shock. "Esperanza can't be here! Esperanza is with child and ought to be home in Boston, in comfort. She cannot be on this ship." He started toward Istäni, rage flashing in his eyes. He would have looked threatening if he did not appear so fragile. He lunged at Istäni, who had no difficulty holding him off and pushing him back against the railing, pinning his hands to his sides. Both Cara and Rafael moved forward to assist their brother but were instantly hemmed in by sailors with their cutlasses drawn.

"Easy, easy, Louis, don't exert yourself overmuch. You've only just become well enough to come on deck. I'd hate to see you give yourself another setback."

"Give myself a setback?" Louis cried, struggling weakly against the much stronger man.

"Yes, Louis, I'm here," came a sultry female voice.

Istäni released Louis' arms and he relaxed against the rail, staring at the majestic Esperanza, who had emerged from her cabin at the sounds of the struggle. Her abdomen had enlarged since he had last seen her, plainly visible as the wind whipped at her dress. She looked tired but still regal, imposing, and unapproachable.

"I'm here because you wouldn't cooperate, dear Louis. Because even when Istäni had a gun to your child, and my head, you wouldn't surrender. Your dear friend Istäni has seen fit to bring me along to ensure that you cooperate. What the devil he was thinking I'm sure I don't know, because you proved so clearly in Boston that you don't care what happens to me, or this child. So, here I am, dragged from my home, forced to endure the heat of the doldrums, the battering of storms, and every conceivable indignity, because of you. I wish you had died in the brig." Then, as suddenly as she had appeared she spun about, slamming the door of the captain's cabin hard behind her.

Her husband had deflated more with each word she spoke, and then, quite suddenly, he passed out. Before anyone could catch him he landed with a dull thud on the deck. Cara felt tears of outrage, of pent-up, impotent anger, burning the back of her eyelids as she dropped to her knees beside her brother. She fought back the tears and lifted Louis' head onto her lap.

"I must have lost my balance," Louis said softly. "I'm sorry, Cara, let me just get up. I think I've had enough fresh air for the day. What do you think?"

"I don't think it's the fresh air that disagrees with you, Losi," she whispered, her voice catching as she helped him climb slowly to his feet. There was so little of her dear, arrogant, stupid Losi left. As she took one of his arms over her shoulder and Rafael took the other, she glanced up and found Murdoch staring directly into her eyes. He made no move to assist them, and, after a moment, he pulled his hat down over his eyes again and settled himself in quiet repose upon the quarterdeck stairs. After his half siblings had disappeared down the hatch, Murdoch finally spoke, directing his words toward Istäni.

"Well, he's not going to make it."

"I wouldn't be so sure of that, Murdoch. For what it's worth, I think you may have underestimated your little brother."

Murdoch scoffed and then rose, emptying his pipe out on the deck and stalking to the helm to relieve the man holding it. He was still there, gripping the spokes and looking pointedly out to sea, a few hours later when Esperanza again emerged from Istäni's cabin. She often took a turn about the quarterdeck at that hour. He watched in silence as she paced. Finally, scorched by those coal-dark eyes, she turned to him.

"I suppose you think I was too harsh with him."

The corners of Murdoch's lips twitched upward, ever so slightly, but he said nothing, waiting for her to continue.

"Am I not wrong? He got me into this hellish situation. He's the one that got me with child, then married me, binding me to him, then he put me and his child in harm's way with his dealings with Istäni. Now I'm stuck out here because that devil with the green eyes insisted that I come. I'm going to have this baby in the middle of the ocean with no one to attend me, not even my stupid, worthless cousin. And because of his foolishness Louis will be dead by then. He won't even have to worry about any of this, about the difficult position he's put me in. I'm about to be a widow with a child to raise on my own. I ask you, is any of this fair?"

"Certainly not," replied Murdoch and then waited so long that Esperanza thought he would not speak again. But, just as she was turning to descend from the quarterdeck, he continued, "I don't think it's fair that you met with Istäni in May and told him all you knew of Louis and his family, and of how madly that boy had fallen in love with you. I don't think it's fair that under Istäni's direction you constructed a letter summoning Louis to you, just to try to draw Louis away while Istäni attempted to poison Henry. Because Istäni knew he wasn't a match for my little brother. He's already been tested against that mettle and found wanting. I don't think it's fair that when the letter came late, and Louis arrived back to Boston, already poisoned, you agreed to marry a desperate, dying man and then continued to plot with Istäni, scheming against your husband. All for what? Because when Louis is dead Istäni has promised to use the riches of Lubrerum to provide a life of luxury for you and your child? No, Esperanza, I don't think any of that is fair at all."

Her mouth dropped open, and the great soprano was rendered speechless, though only for a few moments. "You're defending him now? You who hated him more than anyone? Don't think I've forgotten that night in Charlestown at the opera, when I bandaged your wounds."

"I believe it was your worthless, stupid cousin that did most of the work in Charlestown," replied Murdoch with a sneer. "You wouldn't touch me. I was far too hideous a creature for you to stain your delicate hands upon. How long have you been supplying information to the Myrmidons under Julius' name, affecting to be him? He was once a great informant, but the man's mind is about as useful as a puff of cotton now."

"It's not hard to affect a doddering, senile old man. So what if I provide information to the Myrmidons? They pay good money. And the stupid, Puritan, fanatical colonists aren't going to win this war. You're clever enough to realize that. Not that I owe you any explanation, but I am an opera singer, Murdoch—and not some poor ballad warbler from New Orleans—I sing real *opera seria*. I trained under some of the finest sopranos of this century in Milan and Venice. Yet in half the colonies my form of art is barely tolerated, and even legislated against, because those grubby, boorish farmers that make up your fledgeling country's citizenry have no sense of taste and some warped idea of a God that doesn't abide the finer things in life. At least the British have some rudimentary appreciation for beauty. Anyway, why have you changed your tune so much in regard to your brother? Going soft and stupid in your old age, like Julius? During our mercifully brief interaction in Charlestown the only thing I remember you saying was how you would kill the man I had just witnessed saving your life."

Murdoch shrugged. "I've learned there are people more worth killing than Lightfoot. At any rate, he is already dying, thanks to your precious Istäni, so there's little left for me to do there. Do you know what else I've learned since the last time we met, Mrs. Firefax?"

She made no reply, waiting with an expression of annoyance.

"I've learned that there are people in the world more hideous than I am." He waved for the boatswain, who had just emerged onto the quarterdeck, and handed the helm off to him with a brief set of instructions.

Rather than retiring to his own cabin, Murdoch went to Cara and Louis' quarters. He stepped inside, barely making a sound, and surveyed the scene within. Cara was sleeping in a hammock beside her brother, but Louis was awake, his eyes open, staring at the ceiling as his hammock gently rocked back and forth. He turned his head toward Murdoch, but neither of them spoke for a long moment.

"Come to gloat?" Louis asked at last, through dry, cracked lips.

Murdoch did not answer. Instead he drew up a small stool at the edge of the cabin and settled upon it. He lit his pipe, and Cara's nose wrinkled in her sleep, but she did not waken.

"Why should I not come and sit with my convalescing brother?" asked Murdoch.

Louis snorted. He leaned back a little, closing his eyes. "She's a right lovely little vessel, sprightly, fast, but a bit old. The *Mariposa*, he calls her? I think you could turn her into a fifth-rate, if you were really motivated."

"She was a fifth-rate, once. She's the *India*, and many years ago, when Isaac Firefax first stole her, she was called the *Fancy*, and something else before that," replied Murdoch and, when Louis opened his eyes in surprise, he grinned. "Istäni's idea of a joke, I suppose."

They were both quiet after that, watching Cara sleep.

"She's not like you, you know," said Louis. "Not actually, not in fact."

"Remains to be seen, really. Apparently the whole bloody family was too afraid of what she might become if they let her kill someone."

"It was Mother, our mother, that put that in all our heads. She was convinced the moment Cara killed she would become as evil and hateful as you have always been. That she would love it. That she would be addicted to the thrill of killing. So we never let her. But I think Katerina was wrong. Poor girl's been working herself nearly to death caring for me. That's not something you would ever do for anyone. I don't deserve the devotion she's shown, the devotion she shows constantly, every minute of every day. And Rafael—I never noticed before, Murdoch, but he's an absolute treasure. I would have died in the brig if he hadn't been there, singing hymns, telling me tales from the Bible that I swear I've never heard before. Even now, when he's not on watch he guards that curtain there, keeping the sailors from Cara and me. I think he hasn't slept since they brought us out, and even while we were in the brig he barely slept. I suppose I've been away for too many years—I didn't know what the two of them had grown up to be."

"So humble and contrite you've become in your illness."

"Yes, well, better late than never, I suppose," replied Louis, with a distant look in his eyes. He snapped back to the present after a moment. "Esperanza shouldn't be here, Murdoch. I can't believe that monster brought her on this ship. I suppose . . . perhaps she's right, it's my fault. And in the square, the way I kept fighting, I don't know why I did it. I didn't want him to hurt her, or her to die, or anything. I just . . . I wanted to end it all. I didn't want this, Murdoch. And truthfully, I didn't think he would hurt her."

"Perhaps you were right."

"Well, I'm glad I didn't push it any further to see, anyway." Sitting up a little, Louis reached toward a mug that sat on a barrel in the cabin, his hand trembling. After a sip of water, he continued through lips still dry as ash, "Is there anything else I need to know about Lubrerum? About what's coming? Do you have some secret master plan here, brother, or are you really just going to try to get half the riches of the island and bolt?"

"Do you think that Istäni, once he knows where the island is, is going to let any of us live?" asked Murdoch, smirking.

"I suppose not. But you'll make it out all right. You always do. Rafael and Cara are both handy as well—I'm hoping they can protect my wife."

"Esperanza doesn't need protecting," replied Murdoch, and then he stood in his usual abrupt manner and disappeared through the curtain just as Cara stretched and opened her eyes.

CHAPTER 14

SQUALLS AND SOIREES

Three bells into the afternoon watch, Rafael, seated just outside the galley on a crate of fish, feet kicking against the wood, finished scrawling the letter he had been painstakingly composing for the last few hours. He read it over briefly and winced when he reached the end. 'Once, and it seems so long ago, I slept through each night like a newborn babe, but since I became aware of you, your enticing voice, arresting eyes, your alluring figure, I no longer pass the nights in peace, but lie awake until the gleam of dawn, thinking only of you, my fair Miss Marchworth.' He wrestled for a moment with the idea of striking it all out and rewriting it entirely. But, he considered, it would likely never be seen by Haddy anyway, so an awkward turn of phrase mattered little.

He glanced up, making sure that Esperanza was still undisturbed. She sat near the bowsprit, stitching quietly on one of her dresses, altering the garment to fit her ever-expanding body. Rafael had taken Louis' entreaty in the brig quite seriously, considering it a sacred duty to protect Esperanza from the brazen stares and lewd comments of Istäni's men. Her pregnant state had done nothing to dull her beauty, and the men had been at sea for nearly seven weeks. They watched her with hungry, lustful eyes.

"Sail off the port stern!" came a cry from the platform constructed high in the mainmast as a lookout point. Esperanza leaped up and joined the gathering crowd of sailors at the rail, peering out over the empty expanse of gray-green waters. Rafael quickly shoved his way to her side.

Istäni pushed his way through the crowd to take a stand beside Silver, his quartermaster. He snatched the telescope from the tall, silver-haired man and peered out at the distant vessel, barely visible to those without a glass. Rafael noted a faint smile creasing Istäni's face. Murdoch stood at the helm above them, motionless, never even casting a glance toward the ship in the distance.

"Your friend Lefty is quite tenacious," called Istäni, handing the glass back to Silver and addressing himself toward the silent figure on the quarterdeck. "What did you tell him about Lubrerum?"

The crew raised their eyebrows at that. A few of the Mariposas were Myrmidons, those in the network with sailing experience, but the remainder were sailors that Istäni had picked out and hired for a pittance, with no explanation of where they were sailing and why. The men assumed, given the relative sparsity of the crew and the ladies on board, that it was some sort of passage for wealthy loyalists to safety beyond the rebelling colonies. The few Myrmidons had largely kept what little they knew to themselves. Thus at the hint of a greater purpose for their voyage, everyone perked up.

"I told him to leave it alone," replied Murdoch.

"Well, he didn't take your advice. I'm not feeling particularly inclined toward action yet. Shall we press on more sail and see if we can lose him?"

"If you like," was Murdoch's simple response.

Silver called out the orders and the crowd of men by the

rail began a chaotic stampede into the rigging and across the deck. In the middle of the melee, Silver turned and let his hand graze over Esperanza's backside. She struck him across the face immediately, the resounding slap so loud that half the crew froze mid-climb and turned back toward the deck. Silver grabbed her wrist, gripping it cruelly, and practically lifted her off the deck in his rage.

Rafael, already a few feet off the deck in the ropes, leaped down and ran at the bigger man. "Let her go!" he cried, launching himself onto Silver's back.

A wild struggle broke out, the sailors clamoring to fight for their quartermaster. Esperanza, free of Silver, began striking out with wicked punches that the men were loath to return against a pregnant woman. Rafael, devoid of weapons, concentrated on grappling with Silver while the sailors tried to tear him off. A deafening shot split the air and the battle stopped. All eyes turned to Istäni, standing on the quarterdeck, holding his pistol high as smoke spewed from the barrel.

"Give me that pistol and I'll take care of this boy!" cried Silver, starting toward the quarterdeck as his men pinned Rafael back against the mast.

"Two pistols, one for him, one for me, and we'll settle this like gentlemen!" cried Rafael.

"Settle what like gentlemen? If I want to touch Lightfoot's whore—"

"Enough. There will be no bloody duels on my ship," interrupted Istäni as Rafael, hearing yet another insult aimed at his sister-in-law, surged against the men holding him. "Back to your work, the lot of you. No grog for a week. It'll be two weeks if you dally."

The men groaned but returned to the rigging, releasing Rafael, who, once free, ran to Esperanza to make sure she was all right. Silver glared fiery hatred at the younger man and stomped up to the quarterdeck to argue with Istäni.

Into this chaos, to the sound of Silver's deep, angry voice rising steadily as he addressed his impervious captain, Cara assisted Louis onto the deck. Esperanza stalked past them just as they emerged from the hatch. She went out of her way to brush Louis roughly with her shoulder as she passed and entered her cabin, slamming the door behind her.

"Hateful cunt," murmured Cara, glowering at the closed door.

"Cara! That is my wife. She has every right to be upset with me," said Louis. "Though I do wish, someday, to earn her forgiveness. I wonder what she could have been doing on deck so late. It's nearly dark. It's not safe. You know how sailors can be—"

He turned toward his sister and stopped speaking. She was looking up at him with the expression of someone who has just had a terrible revelation, her eyes wide, her mouth slightly agape. She blinked hard. "Oh, Losi," she whispered, her voice breathy and anguished.

For a moment he did not understand, and then he heard a loud clanging—one of the crew was striking the bell, one, two, three, four times, the loud knells echoing across the bustling deck. He licked his lips, eyeing Cara uneasily.

"What . . . what watch is it, Cara?"

"Afternoon," she replied, her voice little more than a whisper.

He shuddered, realizing what Cara had understood only a moment earlier. He dropped his head into his hands, feeling very weak. It was as if every thread of strength and life left in him had been swept away in an instant: the instant everything had become dark and overcast to his eyes, while for everyone else the sun still illuminated the world with the same brightness it always had. Cara, seeing him sway, grabbed his arm and steered him to the stairs of the quarterdeck, where he allowed her to seat him.

"I . . . I didn't know the poison would do that," she whispered, too horrified to offer any encouragement. "Did . . . did you know?"

He shook his head, keeping his face buried in his hands to hide the tears of despair that threatened to flow down his cheeks.

Louis hadn't cried, Cara knew that, not since he had been stabbed, not as his skin yellowed, as practically everything he ate came up in endless waves of nausea, as he wasted away, as his strength failed, as his breathing became a taxing chore, as his legs barely held him anymore. Never once had he cried. She could see him working hard to hold back the tears, but, despite his best attempts, one slipped out, burning a hot trail down his sunken cheek.

"Oh God," he whispered shakily and almost too quiet for Cara to discern the words, though the tone of utter despondency was quite clear. "It is too much, dear God, too much. I cannot bear it. It is too much."

His sister knelt beside him and clasped her long arms around his shoulders, bringing his head to her chest while his body shook briefly with muffled sobs. She clutched him, not daring to let go, afraid that if she did he would break even further, another organ would shut down, less of her Losi would exist. Biting her lip, Cara glanced around, looking for Istäni, she realized, wanting as never before to kill him for hurting her proud brother.

"Rafael's coming," she whispered.

Instantly Louis became a stone, dashing away the tears, raising his head proudly, and turning to face the ocean. His long golden hair, fluttering in the breeze, further obscured the remnants of sorrow on his face. Cara knew she should have trimmed those flowing golden locks, but somehow it seemed a desecration to shear them.

"I don't want him to know."

"Who?"

"Rafael. No. Not just him. I don't want anyone to know, Cara."

"Then they won't know," replied Cara firmly. "Just wait." Leaving him staring out toward the sea, she moved to block Rafael's approach.

"How's our fair brother today?" asked Rafael.

"Oh, he continues to die, slowly. What happened to you? Your lip is bleeding."

"Bit of a misunderstanding with Silver. Nothing to worry about."

"Good, glad it's nothing to worry about," Cara said and glanced up to see Silver. The enormous man stood on the quarterdeck, seeming to swell as he looked down at them, breathing in slow, deep gulps as if trying to restrain his murderous anger.

"Get to work with the rest of them, boy," snapped the quartermaster. "The longer you stand there, the more likely I am to kill you."

The ship was already picking up speed, another four knots added with the sail adjustments. As Rafael departed, Istäni joined them, coming to stand before Cara and Louis and bowing with a flourish.

There was a blur of red before Cara's eyes, the same red she had seen the day her father died. She launched herself at Istäni, slamming him against the wall of the captain's cabin, her hands grasping his wrists, her face inches from his. The pulsing of her blood in her ears mimicked the sound of hooves at a gallop. A grin spread across Istäni's face.

"There are more than fifty men on this ship, Cara, do you think you can take them all?" he asked.

Behind her the crew on deck were moving hurriedly toward them. Cara glanced up through the red mist to see

Murdoch on the quarterdeck, black eyes watching, his expression inscrutable.

"Cara, it's all right, let him go," whispered Louis gently at her side, taking hold of her shoulder. "Killing him isn't going to get me any closer to that cure."

After a moment she relaxed, letting Louis pull her back, releasing Istäni's arms.

"Don't misinterpret me," said Istäni, straightening his jacket and waving the crewmembers away. "I do most certainly want to be there the day Cara Firefax finally snaps. But your brother is right. If anything, killing me now would only seal Louis' coffin."

"What are you about today?" asked Cara, clenching her fists at her sides.

"I am about serving my noble passengers, as always."

"By passengers you mean prisoners?"

"Semantics, my dear, semantics. I was thinking, perhaps you would be interested in a bit of diversion in a week, a sort of entertainment—music, a special dinner by the chef, and dancing? For the officers, and the passengers, of course. Everyone seems a bit glum and I should like to cheer the *Mariposa* up a bit."

"You call that bastard who can't cook an egg properly a chef?" asked Louis.

Cara glanced at him sharply but saw that he had rallied, the wind had dried the tears away, and he was himself again, as much as he ever was anymore. She turned back to Istäni and said, "I'm not sure that dancing and cheese and wine are really going to make me feel better about my brother dying."

"Dying? Surely not. Each day we draw closer to his salvation, dear Cara. I was wondering if perhaps you would accept my request to be the first on your dance card?"

Cara glared. "You really think I'm going to dance at some macabre, poorly advised soiree?"

"Well, if you are going to dance, I should like the honor of being your partner."

"Before you start planning nuptials with my sister, Seänkea," Louis interjected. "Perhaps you ought to wait until she gets back to Boston and see if she still chooses you when other options become available besides what this sorry ship's company has to offer."

"Easy, Louis, I haven't decided yet if I want to invite any old married men."

"This old married man could dance circles around you at any ball."

"Consider your challenge accepted!" exclaimed Istäni. "I shall see you at the party, seven days from now."

With that Istäni slipped below deck, leaving Cara and Louis alone again. The moment of weakness had passed, and Louis' ghostly emaciated form stood proud again as they took their usual slow stroll about the deck. They did not speak again of the new horror that the poison was wreaking on Louis' tortured body. They paced in silent circles until Louis grew too tired to carry on. As her brother cautiously descended to the berth deck again, Cara glanced up, scanning the quarterdeck to find Murdoch's cold, unreadable eyes fixed on her.

B y seven days later Louis was nearly blind. He could make out blurry shapes, bright spots of light, movements, but all were variations of gray and black, blending into indistinct blobs, clear forms and colors lost entirely. Even to Cara he did not share how quickly his vision was deteriorating. She asked every day, but he told her it had hardly changed at all.

But Cara was no fool; she knew he could see almost nothing, and she could feel his strength waning rapidly. He could barely drink water without vomiting and had taken to sucking on wet rags for hydration. Sometimes she soaked the rags in sugar water, but it wasn't nearly enough. She had approached Murdoch to tell him they were running out of time, but he remained impassive as ever, not hinting at how far they were from their destination, ever standing at the helm, silent, smoking, watching, like a demon from some laconic hell. Cara was convinced that Murdoch was delaying their progress intentionally, waiting for Louis to stop breathing.

"You're sure you want to do this?" asked Cara, scanning Louis, who was wearing a suit Istäni had lent him, a suit that hung about his gaunt frame like a tent.

He smiled at the blur where her voice had come from and nodded. "I'm sure. Do . . . do you think she'll speak to me? Let me dance with her?"

"No, Louis, I don't think so. Rafael said she was refusing to come to the dance, but Istäni told her that if she didn't attend he would make her sleep in the crew quarters."

"But surely she has to forgive me . . . before . . ." He trailed off, then continued on a different tack, "How long can a person bear a grudge, anyway?"

"I think Esperanza is capable of carrying a grudge for eternity."

"You're supposed to encourage me, Cara! Some nurse you've turned out to be. Next time I'm dying of a poisoned wound I'll have someone else attend me, and please don't come looking for a reference for your next nursing position."

Cara smiled half-heartedly at the joke. Louis had become quite morbid since his poisoning, and while she appreciated his attempts to keep his spirits up, she hated the references he made to his imminent demise. Taking his arm, she led him to the stairs and helped him up to the deck for Istäni's party.

CHAPTER 15

THE STORM

Muffled thunder crackled in the distance, and occasional raindrops spattered threateningly on the spare sail strung up as an awning over a cleared area on the deck. Lanterns hung beneath the sail provided a dim light to the perfunctory festivities below. Three crewmen knew how to play instruments, and tolerably well at that, making a trio of flute, violin, and cello. It was to the mournful, rising strains of the rather obscure "Canon in D" by Pachelbel that Louis and Cara arrived on deck, walking with halting, careful steps to join the few men and one other woman scattered under the sail. Cara scanned the figures, all dressed in their finest clothes, though rumpled and worn from their two months at sea. No one looked particularly merry, Cara thought, save Istäni, who beamed at her when she arrived on deck.

"Where is she?" whispered Louis in her ear, and she tore her gaze from Istäni's to scan the motley gathering.

"She's over in the corner, ahead and to your right."

"How does she look? Can you . . . describe her?"

"She's wearing a blue satin dress. It fits her closely about the chest, but is loose around her abdomen, and she has it gathered with a white ribbon tied just below her breasts. She has a silver necklace with a mother-of-pearl pendant around her neck. Her hair is drawn up, but with a few black curls hanging about her face. She . . . well, she looks beautiful, ravishing, actually. I can almost understand why you married her."

"Careful, Cara, I am a jealous man, after all. Oh, I can just picture exactly how she would look. You'll think me stupid, but I . . . I feel giddy. Are there men attending to her? Even in her condition Esperanza would command the attention of every man on this ship, especially dressed as you say, with her hair just so . . ."

"They're all watching her like starving animals."

"Tell me, is Murdoch over there?" Louis jerked his head slightly to the left.

Cara looked around in surprise. "Why, yes. How did you know?"

"I can always tell when he's watching me. He knows, Cara, I'm sure he knows. Nothing gets past that bastard."

"Well, if he does, he's the only one." She bit her lip, not wanting to ask her next question, already sensing from the cold glance Esperanza had thrown in their direction that Louis was not welcome. "Do you want to go to her?"

"Not yet," said Louis, shaking his head. "Can you lead me to the orchestra?"

"I'd hardly call them an orchestra," Cara commented as she carefully led her brother to the musicians, who stopped playing at their approach.

Louis spoke to them in a hushed voice, then hummed for a few minutes, then stepped back so quickly he almost knocked Cara over, not knowing where she was behind him. The instrumentalists talked to each other for a few moments, then the flutist began to play out a slow, melancholy tune, which the violinist joined with wonderful ease. Then, to the surprise of everyone assembled, Louis began to sing in a beautiful, perfect tenor, rising over the noise of the waves and the pattering raindrops, as if all the strength he had left went into that song.

> *"O delle mie fatiche meta dolce e soave,*
> *porto caro amoroso, dovo corro al riposo."*

For a moment the violinist hovered, uncertain, while all eyes turned toward Esperanza, who had drawn herself up immediately upon recognizing the tune. After an instant of hesitation, her voice rose, breathtaking in its piercing beauty.

> *"Fermati, cavaliero, incantator o mago!*
> *Di tue finte sembianze io non m'appago."*

Back and forth the voices of the husband and wife cavorted, so much pathos poured into their duet that Cara felt her eyes misting. The musicians fumbled uncertainly with the tune, but they kept going, carried along by the devastating, soaring melody created by the two singers, until at last, the voices melded together as one in their final, rapid refrain. The last notes rose against the backdrop of rumbling thunder.

> *"Del piacer, del goder venuto è 'l dì.*
> *Sì, sì, vita, sì, sì core, sì, sì!"*

As the refrain faded, the couple stood, staring breathless at each other, as if seeing one another for the first time. Istäni leaped forward to clap Louis on the back, practically knocking him over.

"Your talents are wasted as an assassin, if I may say so," Istäni murmured in his prisoner's ear.

Louis laughed aloud at that. "Perhaps, Istäni. I'll keep that in mind. In my next life I shall endeavor to become a legendary opera singer. Cara, I should like to see my wife."

Cara winced at the word *see* but guided Louis to Esperanza's side. The singer seemed almost taller and more powerful after her duet. She nodded her head slightly to Louis when he reached her side. The musicians had switched back to a sprightly English dancing song and some of the men were already pairing up, given the shortage of female partners.

"Miss Firefax," said Istäni. "I believe you did not exactly decline my request for your first dance." He glanced up at the flapping canvas over them. "Not to worry, though, I think it shall not be long before we are all forced to retire to proper shelter."

The starboard watch was already intermittently barrelling through the revelers, trying to trim the sails adequately and batten down anything mobile as the wind rose in its own dirgelike aria and the canvas and ropes whipped rhythmically over the deck. The dance floor was quickly becoming treacherous and slippery. Cara looked at Louis with concern, but he nodded his head at her.

"It's all right. Go ahead. I'm fine here."

"Don't stand too long, you'll exhaust yourself," she replied, and then reluctantly took Istäni's outstretched hand and moved to join the other dancers.

Istäni had broken out his stores of wine for the occasion, and his officers were drinking with gusto—dangerous gusto, Cara thought. They kept darting increasingly hungry glances at the two young women, even her own jagged, unwomanlike form.

"Rafael tells me they've sighted that vessel again a few more times this week," she said as they began their promenade.

"Ah yes, small frigate, not even sure if she has any guns. Shouldn't be anything to worry about. Silver's managed to press on sail and with Murdoch's maneuvering we've lost her every time."

"You think it's the Argonauts?"

"I do, though only time will tell, I suppose. I wouldn't fret your pretty head about it, Miss Firefax, I have had these louts drilling at battle stations five times a day since we first sighted her. We're ready for anything."

"I don't fret for myself, Mr. Seänkea, but for you if they do manage to catch up to us."

Istäni grinned gleefully. "I wish they would. You've barely seen me in action yet."

Cara slipped as the ship lurched, but Istäni caught her by the waist, steadying her. She felt her heart quicken at his touch, the same way her heart had quickened when Lottie's eyes had drifted over her body in that confident, appreciative way outside Boston. She took in a slow, calming breath to steady herself, reorienting her feelings back to hatred of her dance partner.

"You think a bunch of drunken officers are going to be helpful if this turns into a proper gale?" asked Cara.

"I have great hopes that the wine will improve their ability to deal with the storm."

She snorted at that, despite herself, and would have replied, but something halted her. The musicians were still playing, huddled miserably together in the driest place under the canvas, when Cara froze in the middle of a diagonal, causing the entire dance to fall apart. The sprightly tune faded as the dancers stopped, and all turned to follow Cara's gaze. Louis was walking toward them, slowly but steadily, leading his wife to the dance floor.

"Losi!" Cara called, a rising dread building in her stomach. "Are you sure?"

Louis grinned in her general direction. "Are you suggesting I pass on my last chance to dance with my wife?"

"No. No, of course not."

The musicians murmured together, then one called out, "Perhaps the ladies and gentlemen would enjoy a maggot?"

Everyone else nodded eagerly, warmed by wine, but Cara interrupted the assent, looking with concern at her brother. "Perhaps something a little slower? I'm afraid I'm becoming weary already. My apologies."

"'Childgrove'?" suggested the violinist.

"Yes, yes, I think that would serve nicely," Louis agreed.

The first lilting, playful notes began, the violin leading the other two instruments, while the dancers bowed to each other and then began the slow, regular steps, each couple siding with their partner. Louis, with the practiced ease of a man who had been dancing all his life, handled the rounds and diagonals without a single fumble, staring at where his partner should be. Though he could see nothing there but a faint blur, in his mind he had created the vision of what she looked like, and it loomed whole and splendid.

"You are more beautiful than ever. Though your scowl is a little distasteful, I must say."

"Scowl, what scowl?" asked Esperanza, smiling fakely.

"Don't try to pretend with me, my dear. A blind man could see that scowl. It goes all the way through you."

"And what, pray tell, is wrong with a little frown? We cannot all be happy all the time. Even Jesus wept, or so I have heard it read by your dear little brother."

"True enough, but we cannot all be angry all the time either."

"I do not remember any verses that read 'Jesus laughed.'"

"What an excellent justification for a life of bitterness! I do not recall you being such an impressive scholar of the Word of God before, nor that you were a great emulator of the Savior.

Tell me, is there a verse that says 'Blessed are the proud, for they shall inherit the earth'? Or maybe I'm remembering that wrong." He was mocking her, though somehow managing to do it gently. But Esperanza was not one to be teased or coddled, especially not by the man she now despised so passionately.

"My dearest husband," began Esperanza. "I have had the pleasure of visits from your delightful little brother almost daily, reading to me from the holy book. I see him more often now than I see you. There is nothing else to do on this bloody boat except listen to that precious little clergyman make his endless sermons. And, might I add, you are the last person in the world who has the right to lecture me on bitterness or arrogance. You have shown quite plainly since the first day I met you, there is no one on earth more conceited and prideful than you."

"Perhaps you're right, Esperanza. I have been a beast. But I'm sorry for the cruel way I've treated you. I . . . only want to make up for my mistakes now, before it's too late."

"Oh, you poor thing. Don't we all feel so much pity for you. You've been the hapless victim in this whole story. An innocent babe, above any reproach, who's been poisoned through no fault of his own. Stop seeking my forgiveness! When we negotiated this marriage you said I would be free to end it at any time. The marriage is over. It's been over since the day you let Istäni threaten me and my child. If we ever return alive to Boston I do not want to see your face ever again."

Louis did not answer. His steps were slowing, almost dragging, and his chest was heaving a little. He tripped once but managed to regain his rhythm immediately, only a half beat behind the other dancers.

"I am not the monster here, after all," Esperanza continued. "I'm not the one who forces you to carry my child, while sailing across the world to who knows where, possibly to die. Look at what you've done to me!"

She stepped back as if to give him a full view, but Louis, not seeing this movement, continued forward in their expected diagonal, reaching for her hand. Seeing his hand stretched out toward her, she struck him across the face, sharp fingernails raking along his cheek, tearing his fragile, paperlike skin. Louis, completely caught off guard, lost his balance, toppled, and struck the back of his head on the slippery deck with a loud thwack. Letting out a cry of inexpressible rage, Esperanza turned and ran across the deck toward her cabin.

Cara knelt and touched Louis' shoulder gently. He lay so still on the deck that for an instant she feared him gone. The wind was growing still higher in pitch, and streams of water were blowing sideways under the canvas, dousing the lanterns. With the dance completely disrupted, all the cheese and wine consumed, and chaos growing on deck, Istäni gave the orders to clear the party. Crouched by Louis' side, Cara waited in fear for him to draw breath, or speak, or move. Lightning flashed, illuminating his face. He was trembling a little and obviously stunned, but still alive. He turned his head from side to side, seeking something, some light, some form, a shape, anything.

"It's gone, Cara, it's gone. What little I had left. It's gone now," he whispered, with an expression of such loss and despair that it took Cara's breath away.

He said nothing more as Cara and Rafael assisted him belowdecks, and removed the sopping borrowed suit. He curled up in his hammock, shivering, all his brief return of confidence on the dance floor gone. The call for "all hands" went up on deck as the ship jolted fitfully under the duress of the mad waves and lashing wind.

"I . . . I have to go. Will you be all right?" Rafael asked Cara.

"I'm fine," she replied, all her attention intent on Louis.

On deck, Rafael stumbled to the pumps. An hour later, his hands raw and bleeding, he stepped back, allowing a fresher sailor to take his place. Turning, he saw Silver shoving his way into the captain's cabin. It took the exhausted Rafael a moment to comprehend what he was seeing, then he darted across the deck just as the door slammed behind the quartermaster. Rafael struck his shoulder against the solid door, but to no avail; it was barred from the inside. He struggled up the stairs to the quarterdeck, fighting against the sheets of rain and tearing wind. He ran past the sodden Murdoch without a word and slid his legs over the side of the rail.

Murdoch turned toward him, calling out above the howling wind, "I thought you couldn't get into the kingdom of heaven if you committed suicide?"

"This is no time for jokes!" shouted Rafael. "Silver's in Esperanza's cabin, and drunk as a piper!" The ship lurched again and he had to cling on for dear life, dangling cautiously from the rail and scrambling with his feet for the window. Clinging to the edge of the deck, he kicked as hard as he could against the glass panes. It took three forceful thrusts before he broke through, splintering the glass, a warm rush of blood streaming down his legs. Hooking his foot inside the sill, he let go of the quarterdeck and dropped as the ship plunged again. He caught the window grille, slicing his hands on the broken panes of glass as he hauled himself through, toppling onto the floor of the cabin.

The first thing he noticed was an overpowering scent of alcohol; the second was the enormous silver-haired man struggling with Esperanza on the four-posted bed. Silver had pinned her down, but she kept tearing one or the other arm free and striking him while he planted his body on her pelvis, fumbling clumsily as she fought him. As Rafael rose to his feet, Silver struck Esperanza so hard across the face that she lay still, stunned.

"Get off her!" cried Rafael, launching himself across the cabin and knocking Silver off the bed. Esperanza struggled to her feet and lurched toward the broken window as the ship pitched fitfully.

Silver shook himself free of Rafael, throwing the smaller man hard against the barricaded cabin door. Seeing the flash of a cutlass flying toward him, Rafael dodged, but the blade caught his right shoulder, slicing deep, through sinew and muscle. Rafael gasped involuntarily and dropped to the floor, rolling away as Silver raised his blade again, lunging after him.

The ship yawed to port so forcefully that Silver lost his balance and all the chests, the desk, and bookcase in the room tumbled hard, falling with terrible crashes. Rafael, bleeding profusely from his shoulder, chose that moment to strike, hurling himself on Silver as the other man stumbled. He slammed the quartermaster to the floor and, catching the cutlass-wielding hand, tried to wrench the blade away. They grappled on the floor, rolling in and out of the rapidly accumulating seawater and rain flooding through the broken window, and through Rafael's own sticky pool of blood.

No matter how hard he yanked with both his hands, Rafael could feel himself losing his grip on the cutlass handle, his fingers slipping. Something was terribly wrong with his wounded shoulder; it was powerless. He redoubled his effort with his left arm, and allowed his right to fall to his side. Suddenly Silver jammed his hand directly into the bleeding laceration on Rafael's shoulder, stabbing his fingers forcefully into the severed muscles and ligaments, tearing them further asunder. Rafael let out an agonized scream and released his grip completely on the cutlass. As he hurled himself away, Silver caught hold of his right forearm for a few seconds and a resounding pop split the tense air of the cabin.

Silver lost his grip on Rafael as the ship lurched again, and Rafael stumbled, gasping, bright lights flashing before his dimming vision, feeling as if Silver had ripped his right arm clean off. It dangled useless at his side, bleeding profusely, nothing more than a dead weight. He backed steadily away from the other man. It took every bit of concentration and strength within him not to vomit or faint. His mind reeling, he eased toward the window, where Esperanza hid behind the curtains, wet tangles of dense fabric swirling around her in the wind. Silver stalked after him.

Then, in another flash of lightning that illuminated Silver's rage-filled, drunken visage, Rafael saw a rope dangling past the broken windowpanes from the quarterdeck above.

"Esperanza! Can you climb out?" he called, waving toward the window.

Esperanza lifted her head, catching sight of the rope, and then, rather than answering, she grasped hold of it, wrapping it beneath her armpits. In a moment she was gone, half climbing half being dragged up the stern of the ship. Rafael let out a sigh of relief as her feet disappeared above the window and then turned back to his adversary, who was running at him again, cutlass raised. Rafael snatched up one of the panes of glass from the broken window and crouched as the bigger man hurtled toward him. At the last possible second, Rafael dodged to the right, stabbing upward with the broken windowpane, directly into Silver's wrist, slicing lengthwise toward the elbow.

Spurts of blood jetted rhythmically into the air as Silver dropped his weapon, clutching at his bleeding arm, roaring in pain. Rafael turned and raced to the window, catching hold of the rope, which had just reappeared. In a few delirious moments he was hoisted up the *Mariposa*'s hull and onto the quarterdeck, the rope twisted around his one good wrist, almost dislocating his left arm as well. He rolled over the railing, landing with a thud on the sopping wood of the quarter-deck, as the ship pitched and rolled beneath him. He lay still, eyes closed, panting slowly and unevenly. He took his right wrist in his left hand, adjusting the shoulder ever so slightly, enough to make the pain bearable. Then, grimacing, he allowed the darkness to close around him in a warm, comforting envelope, losing all sensibility of the ice-cold rain, the screaming wind, the streaks of lightning, the chaos of the deck; losing all sensibility of everything.

He opened his eyes again to the flickering light of a dim lantern's glow. Cara was leaning over him, and he was lying on the floor in the berth deck, just outside her and Louis' quarters.

"Your shoulder's dislocated."

"Thank you, doctor, very astute observation. Nothing gets past you."

"Come on, Raf. What happened?"

"Good question. Last I knew I was on the quarterdeck."

"Murdoch carried you here. Esperanza is here too. What happened?"

"Silver tried to . . ." Rafael glanced toward Esperanza, who had a cold, unreadable expression on her face.

"Rafael was helping me," Esperanza offered vaguely.

Cara's gaze flitted between the two of them, finally settling back on Rafael. "Is Silver dead?"

"No, no. I didn't really have a weapon, you see."

"Didn't stop you in Tripoli."

"Come on! I did my best. He's bleeding out through his wrist. I severed the artery. Also he's barricaded in the captain's cabin and drunk and confused as hell. That ought to be good enough, at least for now. I'm a little out of practice, you know. Anyway, can we stop talking about this and can you help me get this shoulder back in?"

"Yes, but you're going to need a lot of stitches too—not

just in the shoulder either, you've a few deep cuts on your arms and legs."

"Fine, fine, that's fine. I just need the shoulder put back in and then we can talk about the technicalities of what you want to do with the lacerations. Please, Cara?"

She nodded, and Rafael sat straight upright, bright stars flashing again in his vision at the sudden movement. Trustingly, Rafael let Cara take his right arm, despite the agony, the muscles crying out against her firm grasp. He clenched his jaw, trying to relax as his sister pulled down and twisted his elbow.

"Jesus fucking Christ!" he cried as the shoulder snapped into place. He blinked back tears, sweat dripping down his gray face.

"Taking the Lord's name in vain? I thought you were going to be a minister," said Cara.

"If my bloody siblings ever stop trying to disqualify me for everything I do and say, I will be a minister, Cara, and a damn fine one at that."

But his sister was not listening anymore. She had torn off a thick strip of cloth from the hem of her skirt and quickly bound the relocated arm into a sling. Then, while Esperanza held the lantern up, she intently inspected the open wound on his shoulder, picking through the still-oozing layers of flesh with her fingers as he winced and tried not to pull away.

"Hold on, shouldn't you be with Louis?" asked Rafael, his breath finally easing as Cara stopped tinkering with the wound.

"Murdoch asked me to leave. He's sitting with him now."

"And what, putting a pillow over his face?"

"No . . ." Cara's expression shifted to one of doubt and alarm, her glance darting toward the silent curtain. "I don't think so. Why would he . . . ?"

"It's just a joke, Cara. I'm sure they're having a wonderful, soul-baring conversation and mending all the old wounds between them."

Cara still frowned, distracted from her intense scrutiny of her brother's wound.

"If you want to go back to him, I can just throw a bandage on this. I'm sure it will be fine."

"It won't be," said Cara, turning her attention back to the wound. "Esperanza, do you think you could run to the sick bay, get me some cat gut and instruments, maybe some clean water?"

"Here, I'll come with you," Rafael offered, heaving himself up to a standing position, not wanting Esperanza to go alone after what had happened in the captain's cabin.

Cara's eyes again darted nervously back and forth between Rafael and the curtain that hid her other two brothers. "No, you just wait. You've already bled enough, don't you think? I'll go with her. You'll be all right for a few minutes? Don't do anything stupid."

"Wouldn't dream of it," replied Rafael, and took another piece of Cara's skirt that she offered, pressing it hard into the right shoulder with his left hand.

The two women disappeared and Rafael considered lying down again. He felt drained, still trembling from the explosive excitement he had felt during his battle with Silver. He stared at the silent curtain and then down at the inviting boards of the floor, swaying and heaving beneath him. His curiosity overcame his enervation and he moved silently across the deck, coming to stand before the curtain and listening, breathless, to the silence beyond. At last, it came—a faint noise, barely perceptible above the roar of the storm outside.

"I know you're sitting there, Murdoch. Though you're incredibly quiet. Have you come to kill me at last?" It was Louis, but unlike the beautiful strong tenor that he had sung with before the storm, his voice was thin, wavering, like the whisper of a breeze through reeds.

"You should be so lucky," returned Murdoch's harsh, gravelly voice.

"True, I do . . . long for death. Why, then, dear brother, have you come?"

"Can't a man visit his brother's deathbed without suspicion of ulterior motives?"

"Not when that brother is Murdoch Firefax."

After this half-laughing statement, there was silence again, except for Louis' rasping, labored breathing.

"Do you know the story of Joseph?" asked Louis suddenly, and Rafael felt a strange twisting sensation in his gut.

"Joseph . . . you'll have to be more specific."

"The son of Jacob. Joseph. In the Bible."

"I'm familiar."

"Well, I've been thinking about this story a great deal. Raf read it to me a week ago, maybe longer—I've lost track of time out here. I've been thinking about it, and about you, and I wasn't sure . . . until now, I didn't know. But I . . . well, I'm getting ahead of myself. Joseph was Jacob's favorite son, born of his favorite wife, Rachel. His brothers were jealous of him, jealous of the way Jacob doted on him. They planned to kill him, but instead they sold him into slavery. Slavery, can you imagine? Your own brother."

"Half brother, to be fair."

"And so are we, and so were Henry and I, but I would never have sold Henry into slavery, or plotted to kill him. At any rate, many years later, things turn completely. Joseph is in a position of great power in Egypt, and his brothers come begging for help during a famine. He recognizes them, but they don't recognize him. Joseph has them, all eleven of his brothers, at his mercy. He could have killed them, enslaved them, beaten them, done whatever he pleased. Finally he could have had his revenge for all the years of suffering they caused. But you know what, Murdoch, he didn't. He forgave them."

"I know the story, Louis."

"Yes, of course you do. I've been thinking about it a long time—well, not so long, I guess, just since Rafael read it to me —thinking about what I would do if I finally had the chance to speak to you alone, during this voyage, before . . . the end. I didn't think I would do it, but I . . . I guess like the Apostle Paul I needed to be struck blind to finally see. You know that story too, I'm sure. Listen, just listen, I know I'm rambling. But the point I want to make is that I . . . I know you're not going to get us to the island before I die, but still I . . . I forgive you, Murdoch."

Rafael wasn't sure if he imagined it or if it really happened, but he thought he heard a faint intake of breath behind the curtain. Then, after a strained silence, Murdoch spoke again, his tone vehement and angry.

"How magnanimous you've become on your deathbed, little brother. It is unfortunate that you didn't spend your whole life being so kind and generous and waited until the very end to become such a saint. Perhaps you never would have been in the condition you are now."

"It's all right," whispered Louis. "I know. I have a great number of regrets, an impossible number of regrets, and I wish . . . more than anything I just wish I had the chance to atone for all the evil I've done. But there's no more time. The only person I can atone to is you, by forgiving you, and letting you know how sorry I am for all the wrongs I've done to you as well."

"Fool!" snapped Murdoch. "You think I trouble myself with sentiment? You think that I lie awake at night wishing for the forgiveness of all those I've killed? My profession is murder by stealth, Louis, and I'm the most skilled practitioner of that profession in the entire fucking world. You think I don't sleep well at night? I'm not encumbered by your imbecilic sensibilities, Louis, that's how I can do the work that I do, and do it so fucking well. It's because I'm better than you, better than all of you, and because I don't possess your pathetic mortal weakness of feelings and attachments. I don't need your fucking forgiveness."

"Whatever you have to tell yourself, Murdoch. I've said my piece. Now I really must sleep. I haven't any strength left. I hope that you and the others make it safe to Lubrerum."

Not wanting to be discovered eavesdropping, Rafael turned and crept about a dozen feet further into the empty crew quarters and sat down, resting his back against the heaving wall. He kept pressing the torn portion of Cara's skirt hard into his wound, reeling with a strange pride and horror at Louis' words. He heard the tumbling of Cara and Esperanza returning from the sick bay with their supplies. Turning his head, he watched as Murdoch emerged from Louis' quarters like a specter of evil.

Murdoch studied Rafael with those strange, dark, all-knowing eyes. He approached and peered at the shoulder wound as the two women arrived with their lantern.

"You're going to want Istäni to fix that," said Murdoch.

"I can do it," replied Cara. "I've been repairing my family's wounds since as soon as I could hold a needle and thread."

"If you close it, Cara, you'll turn your brother into a cripple, without the use of his dominant arm. Trust me. You're going to want Istäni to fix that."

With that he stalked past them and climbed the stairs into the howling wind, sloshing waves, and flashing lightning above.

Cara, after checking to make sure that Louis was still breathing, went back on deck to find Istäni emerging from the captain's cabin, his garments covered in blood. Dripping wet, his dark hair hanging slick around his face, he grinned at her with a strangely exultant glow in his green eyes.

"Can I help you, Miss Firefax?"

"Murdoch said you should look at Rafael's shoulder."

"Then I should. Take me to him."

Working nearly until daybreak, Istäni Seänkea cleansed and repaired Rafael's wounds, knitting the blood vessels, nerves, tendons, muscles, and ligaments back together. Cara watched in awe as he painstakingly sewed by the dim light of the flickering lantern, with a level of skill that touched on artistry. Finally she placed Rafael's arm back in the makeshift sling and helped him into a hammock, where he fell fast asleep within minutes.

"Where did you learn to sew tissue like that?" asked Cara.

"That's a story for another time," replied Istäni, a distant expression on his face. Then he shook his head as if returning to the present. "A word to the wise, Miss Firefax, I said what I could to placate Silver while I was repairing his wound earlier, but I would advise your brother to avoid the quartermaster at all costs for the remainder of the voyage."

The storm raged for more than two days, and in that time, Louis declined still more, as if his efforts at the soiree had used the last fragments of life he had left. He no longer spoke except faint, delirious murmurs, his breathing became more ragged and painful, and he did not eat, nor drink. He stopped urinating, becoming more sickly yellow, and finally a dusky, lifeless gray color. During those two days Murdoch never left the helm, a sopping, determined phantom, roaring commands to the exhausted crew.

On the morning of the third day after Istäni's party, Cara awakened to a quiet cabin and lurched up suddenly in alarm, practically falling as she stumbled to Louis' side. He lay deathly still. She crouched down, pressing her ear against his chest, holding her own breath, until she finally heard the faint, slow thudding of his heart. The wind had stopped, the waves had abated, the lightning and thunder no longer flashed and cracked overhead, the rain had died away, the entire ship had fallen expectantly silent. Cara took Louis' shriveled hand in hers and pressed it to her lips, tears building in the corners of her eyelids. Then the silence of the morning was broken by a shrill, piercing wail from above.

"Land ho! Island off the starboard bow! Land ho!"

CHAPTER 16

LUBRERUM

The central island was hemmed in by coral, enormous outcroppings of stone, and small satellites of land, making access with a large ship nearly impossible. The treacherous rocky shallows yielded to a narrow strip of smooth white sand, dotted with green palms, heavily laden with coconuts. On the east side of the island, where Murdoch made his approach, the beach gave way after only a few dozen yards to the jutting form of a gray-slate mountain, clothed in vibrant green. The cone-shaped pinnacle high above them opened to the sky like a chimney. Beyond the mountain a narrow peninsula, covered in dense viridescent forest, tapered away in the distance. The air felt stuffy and humid, promising a long, sticky day, and perhaps another storm ahead.

On deck Cara found the *Mariposas* had already laid anchor, unable to penetrate further through the perilous shallows. Istäni was watching impatiently while the men prepared a long boat. He was dressed in the same striking green tunic she had seen him wear in Boston and at Maralah, a richly embroidered doublet with a full skirt that hung to his midthighs.

"That's it?" she asked Rafael, who was standing by the rail.

"That's it. Looks like some sort of dormant volcano. I would assume any civilization would be inside the caldera itself. So far I've only spotted a few goats climbing the rocks, and some gulls. Is . . . how is Louis?"

"Near the end, Rafael. It'll be today."

"Oy, Istäni, you hear that?" called Rafael.

"I'm impressed he has lasted this long," replied Istäni. "But don't worry, my dear Firefaxes, I fully intend to honor my word. I couldn't have helped him before, you know. The cure is there, upon Lubrerum."

"You could have helped him by not poisoning him in the first place," Cara murmured, then in a louder voice she asked, "How many are you taking ashore?"

"Myself, Istäni, and Louis. No one else," said Murdoch, startling the others who had not noticed his approach.

Istäni nodded deferentially. "Of course, of course, as we agreed upon. And no weapons, as we agreed upon?"

Murdoch nodded.

"He's not going to walk up here," said Cara. "He . . . he's not conscious at all, anymore. He doesn't open his eyes."

Murdoch turned to the long boat and the crewmembers waiting at the lines. "Don't lower it yet," he commanded, and disappeared below deck. A few moments later he emerged with his ungainly, jerking strides, cradling the emaciated, unmoving form of his brother in his arms easily, as if the younger man weighed nothing. Tight, breathtaking anxiety surged in Cara's chest as the image of Murdoch coming out of the burning tavern with Henry leaped unbidden to her mind.

Murdoch laid Louis on the blankets and turned to Rafael, who stood solemnly by the edge of the boat, staring down at his older brother, as if not believing how fragile and lifeless he had become.

"Do you have your Bible?" asked Murdoch.

Rafael nodded and handed it to him.

Murdoch flipped through the pages, surreptitiously sliding a leaf of paper into the book. He found the passage he sought and tore a few leaflets from it. "I need it more than you do," he said by way of explanation as he handed the book back to his surprised brother.

"You'd best barricade yourself and the ladies in my cabin," Istäni advised Rafael. "I've had the men lay up a stock of food and water there. They have orders not to harm you, but I will be the first to tell you that I wouldn't trust any of them as far as I can throw them."

Rafael nodded without speaking and then took Cara's elbow, practically tearing her away from the rail. She had been watching intently as the longboat was lowered with its dying burden inside. Rafael pulled her with him into Istäni's cabin, where Esperanza waited.

Murdoch and Istäni, each carrying a satchel of belongings, descended into the boat. Istäni took the oars, while Murdoch handled the tiller and they began making their way toward the island's coastline. Istäni glanced over his shoulder, noting the faint increase in the wind and the distant gray clouds, barely visible on the horizon, where the sea and sky became one.

"Another storm coming, Mr. Silver," he called as they pulled away.

"I see it, sir. I see it."

"Have a care, then, don't let my ship get blown into the bloody rocks," his captain instructed, grinning cheerfully. He turned back to Murdoch. "Fine day for a float. And I must say, I'm quite glad to be away from that packed vessel and all those stinking men. Aren't you?"

"It's not really a holiday, Istäni."

"Maybe not for you, but for me it certainly is. The achievement of all I've worked for all these years. It feels like . . . like coming home."

"Just row."

"Always so sour. You know, you might find you enjoy life more if you take part in the pleasures it offers."

"I do. Especially the pleasure of silence; that is, by far, the most enjoyable of all the pleasures in life, I've found. I liked you better before you learned to speak."

Istäni laughed at that, continuing to row at his own steady, unhurried pace. They wound their way in and out of the towering rock formations jutting from the water. Istäni watched with amusement the little sea creatures that scuttled away from them to hide in the colorful lichen-covered rocks and waving corals of purple, orange, and pale cream beneath their boat. When they reached the shore, they were both dripping sweat from the baking heat of the tropical sun and the unrelenting humidity. Istäni leaped from the boat as they struck the sand, sloshing onto the shore, heaving the vessel in. He tied the dock line to a palm and, turning, was surprised to encounter Murdoch's fist, slammed forcefully into his face.

Istäni's head snapped back, but he recovered quickly and ducked beneath the rope, making an ungainly dash across the shifting sand, away from Murdoch's vengeful fists. Murdoch strode after him, a cold fire smoldering in his dark eyes.

"You could have killed me aboard the ship a hundred times. Why now?" asked Istäni, still strangely gleeful.

"Why not now? You and your ship have brought me to my birthright. You've served your purpose."

Murdoch kicked out with one of his long legs, and Istäni ducked but slipped in the caving sand and fell, landing on his back and elbows, half in the water. He struggled to get up, but Murdoch was on him, punching his face and stomach repeatedly. There was a flash of silver and ivory and Murdoch caught Istäni's wrist. Twisting brutally, he wrenched the axe from Istäni's involuntarily trembling hand.

"I thought we agreed on no weapons," Murdoch hissed,

tossing the axe across the sand, where it skittered to a stop under the bushes and trees. Then he backhanded Istäni across the face. The two stared at each other, chests heaving, Murdoch, hideous, without expression, dark eyes glittering, and the handsome Istäni, bleeding from his nose and lip, a contusion forming around one eye and a stream of blood drizzling down the side of his face from a laceration above his brow.

"Give me one reason why I shouldn't kill you."

"She's not going to fix him for you," Istäni gasped, still smiling like a battered pugilist yet holding the upper hand.

"Who's not going to fix who?" asked Murdoch, raising his fist again.

"The Abbess! She's not going to heal Louis for you, Murdoch, not for you."

Murdoch faltered, and a curious expression crossed his face, half doubt, half realization. Then his countenance hardened again and he struck Istäni once more in the face, nearly knocking the younger man unconscious. He wrapped his hands around Istäni's throat, squeezing relentlessly.

Istäni, coming back to his senses, took hold of Murdoch's hands and tried to free himself, squirming, gasping for the air that was so easily denied him. But Istäni could not breathe, and his attempts to escape Murdoch's grasp became steadily weaker. Murdoch tightened his grip even more and the desperate flailing of his enemy became faint, flopping movements, sloshing in the water feebly, then his struggles ceased altogether, head lolling back helpless and limp in Murdoch's vengeful grasp. Just as Istäni stilled, there was a whoosh of air by Murdoch's head and he dropped his victim into the water, staring in surprise at the thick wooden spear sticking straight up from the sand beside him.

Murdoch rose, turning toward the forest. Five men stood just inside the cover of the trees, all but one holding a long spear in their hands. They were tall, tan-skinned, with dark brown eyes and hair. The four that were still armed had their spears raised in a threatening manner. Their garb was much like Istäni's, heavily embroidered antique doublets of wool, as if they too had stepped from a sixteenth-century painting. There was a distant sound of roaring and moaning, as though a baying pack of hunting dogs were descending from the mountainside. A sixth man, taller than the others and wearing a breastplate and helmet with a plume of red feathers rising gaudily from it, emerged from the forest and stood a few yards from Murdoch, studying him with keen, intelligent eyes.

After a long, tense moment, the man with the feathers in his helmet called out a command in a strangely familiar tongue and pointed toward the men on the beach. The other five men descended toward Murdoch and Istäni, and the baying, yelping sounds grew louder. Murdoch drew the spear from the sand beside him and then stood still, watching. His eyes flitted to the right and the left, and then he began to move slowly toward the boat behind him, keeping the spear raised.

Istäni, rubbing his throat, slowly hauled himself to his feet, and raised his arms skyward, calling out, "*Com res grum tops scuim, praun vo tei plac aet sturvant!*"

The leader of the islanders lifted his hand and his men halted. Then he spoke a questioning, halting greeting in return: "*Mo a aet vo la.*" As he spoke, he knelt and picked up the intricately carved axe lying on the sand where Murdoch had tossed it. He switched to English, which he spoke well and clearly. "Tell me, fair stranger, how do you come to know our tongue? And how do you come to have this axe, inscribed with our most holy symbols?"

"How did you come to learn English?" replied Istäni, with his usual disarming grin. "Our answer is the same—it was taught to us, brother, was it not? And as for the axe, perhaps you ought to ask the Mother Superior herself how I came by it. May I have it back?"

The man flipped the weapon, offering it back to Istäni, handle first. Curiously the islanders gathered around the strangers. The baying hounds grew louder, until at last they burst from the trees, enormous gray dogs, wolflike, with long teeth, sharp like razors, and blazing yellow eyes. They were held back by men in gleaming metal breastplates, golden helmets with feathers attached—though not such fine plumery as that worn by the first officer that had appeared— and scarlet capes fixed to their shoulders. The dogs strained against their leashes, snarling and howling to be denied their prey at the end of a chase.

One of the islanders approached the boat and Murdoch darted suddenly forward, blocking him, still gripping the spear that had been thrown at him. The man raised his own spear, but the islanders' leader called out in their tongue and the man relaxed, lowering his weapon.

"They . . . they bring a dead man to our shores," said the man in halting English, peering into the boat with curiosity.

"He is not dead, yet. But he needs medicine, the medicine your people can provide," said Murdoch. "He is the grandson of your last Prophet, as am I."

"Why should we believe you?" asked the man.

Murdoch raised his left hand, displaying his flashing golden ring, imprinted with the word *Patcretei* and said, "Do I not appear the very image of Henry Firefax, made young again?"

The man studied Murdoch, then nodded. "You do, brother. But the Devil may deceive the undiscerning by putting on false guises and forms."

"Ha, fear not the Devil. The Devil is a mere housewife compared to this man," exclaimed Istäni. "Our Henry look-alike here speaks the truth. The young man in the boat, for he is a young man, believe it or not, has need of the medicine only Lubrerum can provide."

"He does not need our medicine. He needs a miracle, or rather, a quiet place to die," said the islander standing nearest the boat.

"Nevertheless, far be it from the Lubrerites to refuse a man in need, still less if that man be a descendant of the Prophets," said the leader of the islanders. He barked out orders and his men hurried to construct a litter from long pieces of driftwood and their own cloaks and capes. They worked swiftly and soon laid Louis upon it, attaching him to the structure with ropes and making loops about their shoulders to harness themselves to the litter. Then the group began their march into the dense forest surrounding the sheer mountainside that rose above them. The dog handlers went ahead, fighting the animals the whole way as they continued to lunge at Istäni and Murdoch, growling and barking.

Murdoch strode with his strange, jerking steps near the rear of the party, watched warily by two men behind him, brandishing their spears. They made their way through the forest, though there was no proper path, winding past dense mahogany, logwood, and cedars, scratched constantly by the clinging tendrils of laurels, tangled junipers, heathers, and acacias. They threaded their way around fallen boulders of granite stone and volcanic rock scattered in the dense forest. Then, so suddenly that Murdoch did not even see the opening until they were within it, the group entered a narrow, dark tunnel of stone, where twisting stairs led upward into the heart of the silent volcano.

Hours passed before they emerged into the light of day again, stepping from a dark cavern to stand blinking in the sun, looking out upon a completely different landscape. They were standing on a broad stone terrace, stairs hewn into the rock wall leading via countless switchbacks down for nearly half a mile to the earth below. Before them stretched domesticated and well-tended fields, pastures where horses and cows grazed peacefully in lush emerald grass. Winding, hedged roads stretched along the flat expanse, weaving through dark rich earth dotted with orchards, vineyards, and gardens. Above the fields and pastures towered the walls of the ancient sleeping volcano, rising to its gaping maw, opening to a blue sky studded with gathering storm clouds. Some miles away, near the far wall of the volcano, Murdoch saw the glittering of brilliant yellow light, shimmering from high towers and golden buildings, surrounded by an enormous gilt wall. Despite himself, his mouth dropped open. The city appeared to be made entirely of gold, rising like a gaudy bauble from the surrounding green.

"Behold Lubrerum. Here it has waited for your coming since Henry went to his rest," said the leader of the Lubrerites, turning toward Murdoch.

"He is dead, then?" murmured Murdoch, still staring in awe at the aureate spires in the distance.

"I'm afraid so. But his end was peaceful, surrounded by his people."

Murdoch laughed at that, at the incredible irony of it. The sound of his hoarse, cackling laughter, like the harsh cries of a crow, caused all the islanders to stare at him in horror. The leader edged away, coming up against Istäni, and turning to look at the younger man.

"He is—"

"He is like his grandfather, is he not?"

"Yes, I suppose. But Henry was a kind, peaceful man, who came to us like a true prophet, bearing the words of God."

"And so come I," proclaimed Murdoch, his keen ears missing nothing. He drew from his pocket the wadded pages that he had torn from Rafael's Bible.

The islanders drew back, bowing down and shielding their eyes.

"This you must take to the Ted. Even I am not permitted to look upon the words of God," said the leader of the group. "Perhaps I should have introduced myself before. I am Shemuel Spiogni, the second Thrateer to the Abbess."

"And I am Istäni, and this is Murdoch Firefax."

"Have you a surname, Mr. Istäni?"

"Killinger," replied Istäni softly, with an odd glance at Murdoch, whose eyes narrowed, but he kept his mouth shut.

"Well met. We knew a Killinger once, a dear friend of Henry Firefax, a favored one upon the island, he was."

"Yes, my father," replied Istäni.

"Well met indeed, son of Harvey Killinger. There are not many who come to this island, still fewer who are favored, so the names of the favored we always remember and always treasure," replied the second Thrateer. "Come, let me bring you to the city to speak to the Ted, the Tribunal, I think you would call them in English, and to lodge this unfortunate one in our hospital. Though I know not what even our most skilled healers can do for him."

As they walked, the men leading the slavering dogs eventually turned off, and Murdoch watched them disappear into an outbuilding a few miles from the city, surrounded by high trellised fences of silver. The caravan continued, traversing the last few miles of orchards, vineyards, and carefully tended gardens. They at last entered through the broad gate, standing wide and welcoming, into Fluic Praem, the city at the center of Lubrerum.

The city was laid out on a grid, wide streets of gold and silver brick leading past houses with enclosed courtyards, their gates left open like those at the entrance to the city, exposing trees laden with fruit of all kinds—mangoes, apples, soursop, and bananas. Delicate carved fountains bubbled with water, and children played marbles in the courtyards with what Murdoch was certain were precious jewels. Eventually they entered the insulae, past a bathhouse full of the chatter of men and women, and approached the towering spires of the central church. At the entrance of the church stood enormous pillars of hewn gold, carved with figures from biblical scenes, a tree with Adam and Eve looking up at it in naked shame, the figure of Mary kneeling before the angel Gabriel, Moses with his stone tablets upon a mountain. They came to a halt beneath the pillars, overlooking the forum and central gardens, where Lubrerites in their rich, archaic garb ambled slowly, pausing to stare at the outsiders with interest.

The second Thrateer issued a few orders, and the men carrying Louis moved away through the streets. When Murdoch looked sharply after them and for an instant appeared to grow taller and more menacing, Spiogni gently explained, "They will take him to our hospital, as you requested. As for you, wait here, please." And, removing his shoes, the second Thrateer entered the great church, leaving the guards waiting with Murdoch and Istäni in the atrium beneath the imposing golden columns.

"Is it what you thought it would be?" Istäni asked Murdoch, a mischievous gleam in his eyes.

"No. It's far beyond what I imagined," replied Murdoch, his voice uncharacteristically soft, drinking in the elaborate gilded streets, looking for anything made of simple stone or wood, but finding nothing.

A few minutes later Spiogni returned and bowed to them. "Murdoch, grandchild of the last Prophet, may enter, and Killinger's son as well. The Ted will see you."

The Ted consisted of seven men, all elderly, indeed, ancient to Murdoch's eye, seated on imposing golden thrones lined with velvet and set upon a dais in the center of the church. Scanning the row of decrepit figures, Murdoch noted with amusement that the last man in the line, who bore a crown of snow-white hair and a beard that nearly reached the floor, was fast asleep, a fly buzzing in and out of his gaping mouth as he snored.

"These men bring the Word to us, or so they say," said Spiogni, taking a deferential posture before the Tribunal. "They speak English, so I speak it before you, as a courtesy to these, our guests."

"We have had no fragments of the Word in nigh on twenty years, not since the final return of Henry, for his well-deserved rest," said the elder in the center of the seven thrones, leaning forward with interest to inspect the two men. "If indeed they have brought us the Word, it will need to be verified by the Abbess."

"We can bring it before the Abbess, even now," offered Istäni eagerly. "If you will permit us."

"We cannot permit that. The Word can be taken to her by the Thrateer. You cannot see the Abbess unless the Mother Superior calls for you herself."

"She will call for us."

"You are very confident, boy, bordering on insolent," said the elder gravely. "You have been granted an audience with the High Tribunal of Lubrerum, ought that not be enough for you?"

"Forgive my insolence, *Queb Rem,*" replied Istäni quickly and drew his axe from its sheath beneath the skirt of his doublet, holding it out flat on both hands. "If you will but humor me. I ask that you take this token of mine to the Mother Superior and tell her that the visitors from far off-lands would speak with her and bring her the Word of God from beyond Lubrerum's holy shores."

The elder stared at the axe for a long moment. Then he spoke in a voice sharp with rebuke. "Second Thrateer Spiogni, is it customary to allow guests to bring weapons into audiences with the Ted?"

"No, my lord, no, it is not. But this weapon . . . was of particular interest, and we left it in his possession, not knowing how such a man came by such a thing."

"He dresses like us as well, as if he were one of us," murmured the elder, more to himself than to anyone else, staring at Istäni. He scanned the young man from head to toe, lingering longest on Istäni's vibrant, mesmerizing green eyes.

"He speaks our tongue, my lord."

The elder stroked his chin for a long time, exchanging glances with the other members of the Tribunal before finally shaking his head. "I think you would do well to take this axe to Her Holiness and advise her of these outsiders in our land. Then she can determine what the best course would be. We were told there were three guests. Do your guards and knights not know how to count, second Thrateer?"

"Our third member is gravely ill, near death even now. He has been taken to the hospital," Istäni explained.

"You speak a great deal, Mr. Killinger, is it? What of your friend, the silent one who appears almost as the Prophet Henry reborn? Why does he not speak?"

"I have nothing to say," replied Murdoch. "I would repair to the hospital to hear the words of your physicians in regard to my brother's illness and his prospects for healing. I care not to see the Abbess."

"Very well, take them to the hospital. The boy's axe, second Thrateer, I trust you can send it to Her Holiness and tell her of these strangers in our midst? These strangers will be kept under close guard for now."

Istäni bowed low, as did everyone else present, save Murdoch, who remained standing, a look of open scorn and mockery on his face.

"One thing, however. The fragment of the Word—I

would have you give it to us for initial review, and we will bring it before the Abbess," said the elder.

"Over my dead body will you take this fragment of the Word from me," replied Murdoch, sneering. "Here are the words you seek: 'Woe unto you, scribes and Pharisees, hypocrites! Because ye build the tombs of the prophets, and garnish the sepulchers of the righteous, and say, If we had been in the days of our fathers, we would not have been partakers with them in the blood of the prophets. Wherefore ye be witnesses unto yourselves, that ye are the children of them which killed the prophets.'"

The elder drew back as if stung, and, for a moment, Istäni thought he would order Murdoch's head cut off. But instead the ancient man rose and raised a shriveled, trembling hand, pointing it at Murdoch.

"If you dare to speak the words of the Christ himself again to me, with your wicked and vile tongue, I will have it cut out, be you a Firefax or no. Now get out of my sight before I regret my mercy to you."

Murdoch turned, without bowing, and strode from the hall. The guards, astounded at the contempt he had shown so openly to the revered elders, rushed to catch up with him. They ushered Murdoch and Istäni to the tall building a block away that served as a hospital. The beds were largely empty, save for a few sick children and elderly. The physicians of Lubrerum were all crowded around Louis, who lay, unconscious, struggling to breathe, unchanged from the last time Murdoch had seen him, teetering on the edge of eternity but, by some strange miracle, not yet falling.

"These are the men that came with him. The black-haired one is his brother, he claims, at least," said a guard that had taken over when the second Thrateer had scurried away with Istäni's axe. "They speak English, so if one of you speaks it well, perhaps he can tell them what your examinations reveal."

One of the physicians stepped forward, a wizened middle-aged man wearing a pair of gold-rimmed spectacles. "It is not well, not well, I'm afraid. No, it is quite impossible. May I ask, has he eaten of the Fruit of Lubrerum, but without the Favor of God bestowed upon him?"

"He has tasted of the Fruit of Lubrerum, yes," replied Istäni.

"We have seen what can happen to these, to an extent, but never a case so advanced as this. It is too late, I'm afraid, much too late. It would be a waste of the water of life to try to save him now."

"A waste?" hissed Murdoch. "Give him the bloody water or you yourself will stop wasting life faster than you can say the Favor of God."

The physician blinked at Murdoch, adjusting his spectacles and scanning him. "I'm sorry, who is this uncouth, rough man?"

"I am the heir of this city and this island. I am the eldest grandson of Henry Firefax. That man you are allowing to die is also the grandson of the Prophet you claim to revere so highly."

"I see," said the physician. "Well . . . I am sorry, I cannot advise, nor even can I, in truth, allow the wasting of any of life's water on this man. This corpse, if I am speaking clinically. It is better to let him pass peacefully into whatever holy reward or punishment awaits him. Better to summon the priests to perform the holy rites over his body. If the Favor of God did anything for him, it would only prolong his suffering."

Murdoch stepped forward threateningly. Istäni looked at him in surprise, then reached out, blocking Murdoch with his arm.

"What about the Abbess? She could save him," said Istäni. "She has the skills, the tools, and the knowledge. If he were to go to the Holy of Holies, to the Fluic tei Fluiceist and be under her care there, he would live."

"How do you know of the Holy of Holies, outsider?" asked the physician sharply.

"That's not important. I'm not wrong, am I?"

The physician looked uncertainly between Istäni and Louis, then he shook his head. "She will not take him. She has taken no one to the Holy of Holies for treatment in the last decade, not since the passing of our last Prophet. She will agree with me that it is better to allow him to pass on into eternal judgment than to torment him with hopeless remedies."

"Well, let's just take him to her and see what she says," sneered Murdoch and moved forward again, towering over the physician, who backed away, pushing his spectacles higher on his nose and staring up at Murdoch in terror.

The guards stepped forward, physically blocking Murdoch. As they reached to restrain him, a barely perceptible grin twisted across his thin lips, a smile that Istäni recognized all too well.

"Don't do it, Murdoch, there are too many—" But Istäni was cut off by the breathless arrival of the second Thrateer, who, it seemed, had been running all the time since they had last seen him.

"She . . . she . . . Her Holiness . . . Her Holiness . . . the Mother Superior . . . she will see the outsiders!" he managed to gasp out, and then it was Istäni's turn to smile.

It was darker outside than when they had first arrived, a flurry of swirling, angry dark gray clouds obscuring the blue sky above. Thunder rumbled in the distance and the air was full of a humid crackling tension. Istäni, Murdoch, and the guards, carrying Louis upon his litter, followed Spiogni across the forums, winding their way to the western wall of the volcano, where they started up a narrow staircase cut into the rockface, switchbacks lancing back and forth, seeming to go on forever. The clouds finally broke as they ascended, and plump drops of rain began falling through the volcano's maw, dampening the secret civilization in the caldera.

It took several hours of arduous climbing before they approached the highest point of the volcano and at last entered a wide cavern in its wall. There were guards posted outside, stern men dressed like knights of old in armor and cloaks, some plain, some with tall plumes of colorful feathers in their helmets like those worn by the Thrateer, Spiogni. Murdoch noted a pulley rigged near the opening of the cavern; a bucket attached to the end of the coiled rope sat empty. This was how word had been sent so quickly to the Abbess of the strangers.

The guards, Thrateers, and servants all stood at attention as Spiogni entered the cavern, leading the long column behind him. Spiogni himself bowed low, almost sweeping the ground with his feathered helmet, before a tall, broad-shouldered man with long dark hair and a thick, curling mustache. This formidable figure nodded to the second Thrateer and turned to face the strangers.

"I am Immanuel Prost, the first Thrateer of the Abbess. You are blessed and close to the lady's favor, for she has not entertained outsiders since the final coming of Henry. Please, follow me."

They followed him through the winding, narrow caverns, delving ever deeper into the side of the mountain before finally emerging into a wide chamber that opened onto a broad balcony overlooking the narrow expanse of the island and the endless blue sea beyond. There were curious objects lining the walls, strange contraptions built of wood, silver, and brass, interspersed with shelves hewn into the rockface that were crowded with crumbling tomes and scrolls, alongside vials, vases, and jars of colorful liquids. A bubbling fountain of crystal-clear water stood near the center of the room, set with the silver figure of the Holy Mother Mary, her child clasped in her hands. Just beyond the fountain, a woman sat on an opulent carved settee, gazing out at the rain. She was brown-skinned, curved, and imposing, with long dark hair threaded with faint tendrils of silver. She wore a flowing green dress, a lace cap set upon her hair and a silver girdle about her hips. As they entered, Murdoch could see her clutching Istäni's axe on her lap, her long, elegant fingers tracing the arcane inscriptions. Upon hearing them behind her, Murdoch thought she tensed, though she did not turn.

"They may approach," she said, her voice deep and refreshing, like the breeze on a humid summer day.

Istäni, needing no further invitation, leaped forward, bounding to the woman's side before the guards or Thrateers could restrain him. She turned then, looking up at him, with blazing, sparkling green eyes, accentuated by her emerald gown. Her lips parted slightly, and her grip on the axe in her hand tightened so much that Murdoch thought she would break it. In the melee that erupted, the guards and Thrateers drawing their weapons and running to pull Istäni back from the woman, Murdoch heard the young man whisper, "Hello, Mother. I told you I'd come back."

CHAPTER 17

THE ESCAPE

Those within the caldera of Lubrerum were well protected from the storm; not so those left out upon the raging sea. The three people in the cramped cabin were quiet, each lost in their own reflections. They had moved the oak desk, half-eaten by woodworms, to block the door along with the water barrels and wooden crates of food that Istäni's men had stockpiled for them. Esperanza insisted on putting a makeshift curtain of sailcloth around the bed to give herself privacy from the Firefaxes. Cara was staring despondently out the broken window at the distant island. Rafael sat at the desk, absently toying with the Bible Haddy had given him. He felt a sense of relief as the ship began to pitch and he heard the orders to pull up anchor. Fighting the storm would distract Silver and the others if they had any notions of trying to harm the three people in the cabin. He flipped open the Bible and took out the slip of paper that Murdoch had placed in it.

"What is that?" Esperanza asked, peering out from behind her makeshift canopy.

"What? Oh, this? I don't know. Murdoch slipped it in the Bible while he was desecrating it."

For the first time since they had been banished to the captain's cabin, Cara stirred and looked away from the island, now shrouded in ominous gray clouds. She went to Rafael's side and studied the scrap of paper. It was a crude drawing of Lubrerum and the smaller islets around it without words, but with a few arrows. Around the southern side of the island, an arrow pointed to one of the smaller islets, drawn in more detail than the others, a dark spot seeming to indicate a cave on the southern side of the tiny landmass.

"I've been taking it out and looking at it for the last few hours. Just sitting here, staring at it, questioning it. I don't know why."

"Probably because you don't trust Murdoch," replied Cara.

"What's not to trust? That saint of a man has only led us into safety and prosperity thus far," said Esperanza.

"We'll need to get one of the cutters loose," Rafael continued, ignoring his sister-in-law's sarcastic comment. "And hope to God that little cave is actually there, and we can hide completely from view."

"Get the cutter loose?" asked Esperanza incredulously, still peering from behind her curtains. "How do you intend to do that?"

"Something like Bombay, I was thinking," replied Rafael, grinning at Cara.

"You're really pushing the limits of my memory, Rafael. I was quite small in Bombay."

"We both were, but I remember it exactly, every detail. It was the first time I realized how bloody clever Robert was." Rafael liked the more nuanced and technical parts of their family profession, the ins and outs of complicated heists, like the stealing of a vessel from under the nose of her crew.

"We would need a proper distraction."

"The storm should be enough. Especially in the dark."

"If this storm is anything like the last one, we're liable to tip over while trying to row to the island."

"Not game for it?" Rafael playfully taunted his sister.

Cara's dark eyes flickered. She had always been cautious, too cautious, but worse since the day Robert died. Her glance darted back and forth between her two fellow conspirators. Rafael still wore a sling, his dominant arm unreliable and full of freshly sewn stitches, and she had already decided that Esperanza was worse than useless. Their sister-in-law was a burden, more than anything, and an irritable, pompous burden at that. If they were to steal a cutter, most of the work would fall to Cara alone.

"No, I'm game," Cara glimpsed a leering eye peeping through a knothole near the floor and frowned. The crew had barely been under control when Istäni was aboard, and with him gone, Cara did not feel they were in any position to linger. They would have to get off the ship, one way or another, if they were going to survive. The ship lurched as it was struck by an enormous wave, and the eye at the knothole vanished.

"As soon as it's fully dark, then?" asked Rafael.

Cara, moving behind Esperanza's curtained bed, changed into a pair of breeches, and a shirt and waistcoat from Istäni's stores. The only hope they had as far as she could see was if the crew decided to clear the deck. It was not possible that the three of them could get the cutter into the water without someone noticing, and certainly not with Rafael's arm out of commission.

"Sail! Sail ho! Sail to port!" A cry went up from on deck and Cara startled, her heart speeding up. Stepping from behind the curtain, she glanced meaningfully at Rafael.

"It has to be Lefty and his blasted Argonauts."

"Probably," Rafael agreed. "The same ship that's been

tailing us all along. Unless the island isn't as secret as Murdoch thought."

The ship yawed to port and they all tumbled. Esperanza clung to the bed, barely avoiding falling to the floor. Silver was still shouting orders on deck, speaking so rapidly and with words so laced with profanities, that it was a wonder anyone could understand him. The boatswain's keening whistle trilled and a drum began to beat, calling the sailors to quarters.

"It's nearly dark. I could go on deck now and see what's happening," Cara offered.

"Certainly not!" cried Rafael. "There's about to be a battle. If anyone goes out it should be me."

Cara placed her hand on Rafael's shoulder with just enough pressure to remind him of his still-fresh wound. "You've protected me enough. I'll stay out of sight, Raf, you know I can be invisible if I want to be. Silver will kill you if he sees you on deck, no matter what else is going on around him."

After a moment Rafael nodded, biting his lip, his rich brown eyes full of anxiety. Cara slipped on a greatcoat and plopped one of Istäni's tricorn hats on her head, drawing it down over her face. There was a looking glass in the room, mounted on the wall, and, catching sight of her reflection there for an instant, she shuddered and glanced behind herself to make sure there was no one else in the cabin. But for her spectacles, it was as though Murdoch himself were looking back at her from the mirror. She scrambled through the rear window of the cabin, taking care to avoid the few shards of shattered glass still clinging to the frame.

Pausing on the sill, she sized up the arching hull above her and then began her climb. As the ship lurched, Cara glanced over her shoulder, and saw, in the dying remainder of evening light, the tall masts of a frigate drawing steadily closer, buffeted by white-tipped, raging waves.

It was dark and the helmsman was distracted enough that he did not notice her shadowy form clambering over the rail and slipping past him and down the stairs to the main deck. Someone shouted at her to help at the pumps, and she found herself thrust into the midst of the sodden, smelly sailors, pumping up and down until her hands bled and someone snatched her shoulder and screamed in her ear to go to the gun furthest aft. As she staggered toward the gun, a flash of lightning illuminated the rising and plunging ship beyond them, which had efficiently maneuvered to the windward side of the *Mariposa*.

"Battle stations, you lazy sons of whores!" cried Silver. "Clear the fucking deck, goddamn you!"

Cara turned from the gun and joined the men clearing the deck in a mad, inefficient whirl of activity, trying to look as if she belonged. She was inept with the drenched, slippery ropes, clearing lumber and clumsily securing lines and chains. She saw a few men working to swing the cutters over the side and raced to join them, holding the ropes and slowly lowering the small vessels to tow behind.

As soon as the deck was reasonably clear, the sailors returned to their guns on the starboard side, as the closing enemy sidled around at last, broadside facing them, not more than two pistol shots away. Cara saw the *Mariposas* struggling to load their guns, cloddish despite Istäni's frequent drilling. A flash of white light burst from the heaving frigate beyond as they fired their first scattered volley at the *Mariposa*.

Though a poor showing, without a single ball making its mark, it was the first time Cara had seen a broadside at sea, and she felt a thrill of fear mingled with excitement, her heart beating with strange, deliberate thuds, her skin clammy. The other vessel was visible only when the flashes of fitful lightning illuminated her curved lines, and Cara could see the seamen reloading for another volley.

"Fire away!" called Silver as the ship rolled upward on a cresting wave, and the boatswain's piercing whistle split the air.

The loud roar of cannon fire and the rumbling of the guns' ponderous wheels nearly deafened Cara. She leaped instinctively sideways to avoid the recoil of the nearest gun, landing in a jumble on the deck, entangled in her greatcoat, her tricorn hat lost, slick cropped hair plastered over her face, obscuring her vision. She wiped the hair from her glasses, peering through the smoke toward the other vessel, which had moved still closer. They had cracked a sizable gash in her hull, but all her guns appeared still serviceable. A flash of lightning split the air just as flames burst from the gleaming metal barrels. This time Cara dove for the cover of the stairs by the captain's cabin. All around, pieces of rail and splintered deck showered the crew. The enemy's second broadside had been better aimed. A man, struck through the chest by an enormous shaft of wood, lay gasping and moaning on the deck near her, the light in his eyes fading swiftly as he reached toward her, unable to speak, unable to breathe, blood dribbling from his lips. She drew back in fear and horror as he died.

Silver, cursing uproariously, was still screaming orders through a raw, strained gullet, and Cara could see the surviving sailors shakily preparing the *Mariposa* for another volley. She crouched, staying low, out of Silver's sight and found her way to the small knothole in the cabin wall where she had seen the eye of the peeper earlier.

"Raf!"

He appeared almost immediately. "Cara! What's happening out there? You've got to come back. I've got two bags packed, we're ready. But it's not safe out there."

"This ship has fully engaged with us! It's a proper battle."

"In the middle of this storm? They must be mad. Is it the Argonauts?"

"No idea. Too bloody dark out here to see anything. Hellish conditions for a battle! But, you wanted a distraction. And they cleared the deck! Both cutters are in the water."

"Now or never, then, eh? Here, I'll open the door. We can all go out the window," Rafael moved away and Cara heard the sound of him grunting as he attempted to slide the enormous oaken desk across the floor with his one good shoulder. Another volley of shots hit the deck, and the thick, smoke-filled air erupted with the cracking of wood, flying splinters, and two deafening explosions. Splinters grazed Cara's face and arm and she stumbled and fell. Someone grabbed her bleeding arm and wrenched her to her feet.

"Secure that gun, stupid boy!" She looked up to see the livid face of Silver. He was brandishing a cutlass, his eyes wild, hair strewn in all directions, gleaming white in the flashes of lightning that still split the black night air. He thrust her forward, almost tossing her across the deck, and called up to the helmsman. "Bring her about for boarding, Mr. Campbell!"

Cara stumbled awkwardly across the deck to join a gun crew struggling to secure one of the cannons. The helmsman swiveled the wheel hard to bring the *Mariposa* around, heaving ponderously toward the other vessel. The gun secured, Cara turned, her excitement changing to dismay as she saw Rafael standing at the entrance to the cabin, peering into the darkness in search of her. Silver had seen him too and was stalking toward her unsuspecting brother, the impending boarding quite forgotten in his bloodlust for the young man.

"Raf!" she screamed, her voice drowned out by the roaring of the other ship's guns.

A loud, ship-shuddering crack sounded and ropes, spars, and pulleys crashed to the deck. Cara looked up, her mouth dropping open, and then she ran, dodging to avoid the falling pieces of rigging. The last broadside had split the mainmast, and the upper portion began to bow, tilting slowly, sustained by a thousand ropes.

Silver reached Rafael first, stabbing at the young man with his cutlass. Rafael leaped out of the way and onto the deck, slamming the cabin door behind him. He snatched up the cutlass from the corpse by the stairs that Cara had watched expire only a few minutes before. Using his left arm, he engaged Silver, blade against blade. All around them sailors were running to cut the ropes and clear the debris from the fallen mast as the *Mariposa* continued to turn.

"Get Esperanza off the ship!" cried Rafael to Cara as she drew near. "I can handle him!"

Cara felt terror rising in her chest and throat as her brother slowly backed away from Silver's relentless onslaught of thrusts and blows. Rafael gave her a quick, reassuring grin, and for a moment she saw not Raf but Henry the last time she had seen him alive, joking that Istäni could be a Firefax. With an involuntary shudder, she snatched up a loose section of spar, brandishing it as a weapon, and ran back into the cabin, heaving a large chest against the door.

"We have to get out of here," she said.

"To where? I'm not going out that window, Cara Firefax, if that's what you think. I am a pregnant woman!" Esperanza exclaimed. "And what about all of my things?"

Cara struck Esperanza across the face. It was instinct more than a conscious decision, an instinct that came from the two months she had spent at sea with the arrogant, vindictive woman, who had so tormented her dying brother. It was over before Cara realized what she was doing, and Esperanza drew back in surprise, reaching up to touch her reddening cheek.

"You don't need your fucking baubles and trinkets, you monster!" hissed Cara. "You will jump out that window and swim to that bloody cutter, now, or I won't even leave you here for the sailors to ravish. I'll just rape you myself with this stick, right here, right now, until you scream for mercy."

Esperanza stared at her for a few seconds, then, without another word, she picked up one of the satchels that Rafael had packed and launched herself through the window into the roiling water. Cara watched for a moment as the other woman floundered to keep her head above the white-tipped waves, struggling toward the cutter. Then she snatched up the other satchel and dove in, the ice-cold water overwhelming her, jerking her back from her own half-stunned state. She began swimming toward the cutter, repeatedly buffeted and tossed by the waves, until at last she felt Esperanza grab her arm and yank her into the boat.

Cara coughed loudly and, with numb, trembling fingers, rifled through the bag Rafael had packed. Finding a small, dull knife, she began sawing at the taut rope attaching them to the *Mariposa*. As she sawed she stared up at the dark ship above them, but there was no sign of her brother. Another bolt of lightning illuminated how close the two vessels had become, half a pistol shot from each other, just as another broadside roared out from the *Mariposa*. This earsplitting sound was followed almost immediately by a loud crash—the cracking of timbers as the two ships struck each other—followed by the relatively faint noises of clattering swords and pistol shots. Cara could see boathooks launched, securing the two vessels together as they pitched violently in the fitful waves.

The rope attaching them to the *Mariposa* tore through and the cutter was suddenly loose, completely at the whim of the water, twirling in mad circles. Esperanza had fixed the oars while Cara was cutting the rope, but as the boat spun violently she almost lost one. Cara lunged forward and caught hold of the oar, steadying the little cutter as best she could.

"Should we put the mast up?" asked Esperanza when they

had at last stopped the nauseating spinning motion of the boat.

"I don't think so, not in this swell. We're just going to have to try to keep her from overturning, and wait for Rafael."

Aboard the *Mariposa*, Rafael was not having an easy time handling Silver. Not being the ambidextrous fiend that Murdoch was, he had been forced to switch to his injured right arm to have any chance of defeating the quartermaster. It was easier, but sickeningly painful, every parried blow sending a bolt of tearing pain through his shoulder. After the boarding began the deck devolved into hell. Pistol shots punctuated the rolling thunder above, and all around him men struggled, roaring and screaming. All he needed, he thought, was to make it over the side without getting stabbed or shot. It should not have been hard, but every time he neared the rail someone blocked him, more often than not the hulking form of Silver.

His heart thumping and his shoulder feeling as if it were being torn apart a second time, Rafael edged away from Silver, barely managing to block the repeated hammering blows of the bigger man's cutlass. He clambered awkwardly through the wreckage of the fallen main mast. The severed portion of the mast was still attached by dozens of ropes and dragged the entire vessel toward the water. The starboard side of the *Mariposa* was fixed precariously to the port side of her adversary, and the two ships rocked unsteadily in the madness of the storm. Rafael backed further out along the mast, edging past the rail. He turned to dive, but his foot caught in the rigging as the ship plummeted suddenly. His cutlass fell and he found himself dangling helplessly from the mast, the rope biting into him, his lower leg bent unnaturally over the wooden mast.

Silver grinned, a vicious, wolflike smile, as he moved in for the kill. Rafael flailed, trying desperately to free his leg so he could drop into the water that splashed all around him, making him choke and sputter.

"Silver! Fancy seeing your ugly face here, in the middle of the bloody ocean. It's a small world, isn't it?" a voice called, stopping Silver in his tracks. The quartermaster turned from his helpless adversary back toward the hull of the *Mariposa*.

Rafael swung himself around to see the plump, balding figure of Lefty approaching, his pistol aimed directly at Silver's chest. Lefty shrugged his shoulder and hitched his ear toward it, still somehow maintaining his left hand in a steady position.

"I should've known it was you out there," said Silver scornfully. "How many gentlemen on your precious committee did you have to suck off for them to give you a ship of your own?"

Lefty didn't reply, firing his pistol instead. He just missed Silver, who launched himself at the Argonaut leader. Lefty managed to draw his sword just in time and the two sparred back and forth across the slanting deck. Rafael was left hanging upside down, feeling as if his leg was being sawed in two. He twisted and struggled again, trying to drag his leg from under the loops of ever-tightening hemp. He felt the mast shift beneath him, sliding still further into the sea. Panting, he redoubled his efforts. At last, chest heaving, he gave up, still dangling helplessly toward the ocean. Turning his head, for an instant he thought he could see the cutter in the distance, with two dark figures seated inside.

He heard the unmistakable blast of another broadside, from somewhere beyond the two entangled vessels. Blinking, he lifted himself one more time. A streak of lightning illuminated a third vessel, not more than a hundred yards away. Another volley of cannon fire went out from the new ship, and then came a horrifying crack. Looking up, Rafael saw the

Mariposa's foremast toppling directly toward him. Then he felt as though his leg exploded, and he was plunged under the water, and everything was tangled rope, sail, wood, blood, and agonizing, excruciating pain, and then there was nothing.

———

The island of Lubrerum had one ship, *Eliposti*, or the *Apostle*. She was well cared for; an ancient, slim two-masted sloop. Occasionally she had been used to sink a ship that had come too close to the island. More often she had been used to ferry the wealth from a Firefax vessel back to Lubrerum. This was the ship that Rafael had seen before the ocean claimed him, and the ship that subdued the Argonauts, and brought all the sailors from Lefty's vessel back to Fluic Praem to stand before the Tribunal.

The storm had left the world refreshed on that perfect, calm, cloudless morning. There was a scentless, freshly washed glory to the air, the oppressive humidity at last broken. The forum in Fluic Praem was full of the tittering of canaries and chatter of budgerigars. The sun shone through the cone far above, bathing the caldera floor in reassuring warmth, a soft, beaming glow of favor from on high. Murdoch, officially recognized as the new Prophet of Lubrerum and dressed in black, stood beside the Abbess. The Abbess wore a full head covering, only her eyes visible as she surveyed the prisoners. Slowly Murdoch's dark eyes roved along the rows of captives, only a few recognizable as Argonauts; the others were unfortunate, unsuspecting sailors that Lefty had hired. The people of Lubrerum had gathered all around the square, watching quietly and calmly for the justice of God to be meted out by their Abbess.

"You have come to this, the holy, chosen place of the Lord, to rob it of riches that are not yours to take." She spoke precisely and clearly in perfect, formal English. "You have wrongly pursued Murdoch Firefax, God's blessed and chosen Prophet. You are men of the sword, and it is written, 'Then said Jesus unto him, "Put up again thy sword into his place, for all they that take the sword shall perish with the sword."' So it is, with great sorrow, that I must judge on behalf of God Most High, the great, the merciful, that you all be put to death by the sword in the arena, this very day. As you have chosen to live by it, so shall you die by it. May it comfort you that your bodies shall fertilize the crops of this holy place, and give life to our children. My priests will perform the last rites for all of you, and my knights will take you to the arena. May God grant you mercy in the eternal realms."

Turning away from the prisoners, she began to speak her judgment in Erlandagar, the language of Lubrerum, and the people nodded their heads, murmuring assent at their matriarch's wisdom and her mercy in allowing last rites for the doomed men in the forum. As the Lubrerite priests began to move among the men, some weeping and shivering despite the warmth of the sun, Murdoch made his way to the portly man with one arm, at the end of the long line of prisoners.

"You lied to me," Lefty said accusingly as Murdoch approached.

"Did I?"

"You said Lubrerum was a matter of no importance."

"And so it isn't."

"You call this of no importance? This entire city is made of gold, silver, and jewels. There is more wealth on this bloody little island than anywhere else in the world, Thrayder, in the whole damn world! With this we could really make something of a free America. We would have no trouble defeating the British. All those farmers that won't join the army would come running for this money. We could buy allies as far away as China. Think of the infrastructure we could build! We wouldn't need to defeat the Indians to claim the western lands —we could just buy them off and have more than enough money to spare." He shook his head bitterly, still reeling from what he had seen of Lubrerum, still shocked by Murdoch's lie. "You said it was a matter of no importance!"

Murdoch shrugged. "It doesn't matter now, does it?"

"All this time you were working for the British, then? You brought them here so they could take this money and fund their war efforts? You are a cowardly, black-hearted bastard, Thrayder, you know that? What did you do, just sell the information to the highest bidder?"

A broad, knowing smile spread across Murdoch's hideous features, and Lefty shuddered at the sight of it.

"The game's not over, yet."

"This is not a game, Thrayder. These mad islanders are going to kill us." As he said this, the first few prisoners were forced up and marched away, heading toward the arena just outside the city. Lefty watched them leave and licked his lips. "All right, what is your game, then? I'm going to die today, in the service of my country, though no one will ever know my sacrifice. You can tell me your secrets and I will take them to my grave. Let me at least die knowing why I'm dying, what you are, and what your bloody plan is."

Murdoch, still smiling, leaned down and said, "Perhaps I don't have a plan, Lefty. Perhaps I'm just rolling the dice."

Lefty, eyes wide, stared after him as he stalked away. A few hours later, the knights of Fluic Praem brought the leader of the Argonauts to the bloody chopping block in Lubrerum's arena, and then Lefty wondered no more at the strange, cruel man who had led him to the nightmare that was Lubrerum.

CHAPTER 18

IN THE HOLY OF HOLIES

It was Esperanza who saw Rafael floating in the sloshing water. He was unearthly pale in the darkness of the storm, as white as the foam tips of the waves splashing around him. The two women hoisted him into the small boat, almost flipping it with the effort of lifting his dead weight. Then, combining what little sea knowledge they had, they struck out in the direction they thought the island on Murdoch's map had been. Esperanza proved the most knowledgeable about the handling of the cutter—a result of a great deal of her upbringing having occurred in the coastal city of St. Augustine—and she took the rudder while Cara rowed.

Rafael lay in a stupor at the bottom of the boat, somewhat awake, but dazed, occasionally coughing up water. When a wave buffeted the little cutter he would scream in agony. His left leg was a mangled mess, slowly oozing blood, the shin bones clearly visible protruding through the flesh. When they finally reached a shore in the darkness, they did not even know if it was the right one. Dawn was just beginning to break, and in the distance they could see the rising, ominous shape of the volcano on Lubrerum, which reassured them at least that they were not on the mainland. The two women dragged the battered vessel, with Rafael still lying in the bottom, onto the shore and hid it in the cover of mangroves lining the beach. They decided to wait the night there, using the vessel as cover. Hauling the screaming Rafael out of the cutter almost tore Cara's heart in two. At last they laid him down and tipped the vessel over him, using an oar dug deep into the sand to keep the hull lifted enough to allow entrance and exit. Then they crawled under it, shivering and sopping wet, and fell asleep in a matter of moments, to the sound of rain pattering softly on the wood of their makeshift shelter.

It was well into the afternoon when Cara awoke with a start, to the unmistakable feeling that someone was watching her. She rolled onto her side, taking a brief sweep with her eyes across the little island before looking back at the other two. Rafael was staring at her.

"You shouldn't move. Your leg is broken," she said.

"I already did move."

"And?"

"Found your advice to be correct, if a little ill timed." He grinned, and then grimaced at another lancing bolt of pain in his leg. "I'd like to get the bones back in place and some sort of splint on it."

"I can help you."

"I know, I just . . . I'm just waiting, trying to make myself ready, you know."

"You have to stop getting hurt, Rafael. You'll never make it out of this alive if you keep at it this way."

"Yes, I'm starting to feel like Henry's bad luck has been passed on to me. I suppose it's only fair."

"What do you mean by that?"

A distant, regretful expression crossed Rafael's face, then he shrugged. "Nothing, Cara, nothing. I think I'm as ready as I'm ever going to be."

"I'll need someone to hold your thigh while I set the calf bones."

Rafael glanced at the other woman, fast asleep, her thick black hair matted and plastered with sand. "I'm sure Esperanza has the stomach for it."

While Cara awakened Esperanza, Rafael cast about with his fingers, finally coming up with an appropriately sized stick of hard driftwood. He placed it between his teeth and gave the two women kneeling by his feet a nod. Esperanza took hold of his leg just above the knee with both hands, her grip viselike, then Cara pulled and Rafael nearly bit through the stick before he mercifully passed out.

He returned to consciousness an instant later to see Cara splinting his leg with sticks and strips of cloth from Esperanza's skirt.

"Perhaps we should try to fish?" asked Rafael. "I'm powerful hungry."

"I don't know," answered Cara dubiously, studying the open wound, planning how she would close it. "It's daylight. If there are people on that island I suspect they'll have lookouts near the top of the volcano. In the meantime, we've some ship's biscuits and a bit of water from the cutter."

"If there are people on the island and we are Firefaxes, we ought to be fine there. Why don't we just go across and turn ourselves in?"

Cara shook her head. "There must be some reason Murdoch directed us to this island, and not to the mainland."

"Trusting Murdoch now, are we?" replied Rafael cheekily.

After cleaning and sewing Rafael's wound with the supplies he had packed while aboard the ship, Cara did manage to catch a few fish and found a small spring of clear, fresh water on the island. She also stumbled upon a cave on the south side, facing out to sea, away from Lubrerum, the final confirmation that they had indeed found the islet

Murdoch had indicated. That night the two women moved the cutter's provisions to the cave; a few packages of biscuits, some tools including a dull knife, a machete, a hatchet, a small barrel of water and one of grog, several canteens, and an extra sailcloth. They left only the injured Rafael and his soggy Bible under the overturned cutter. Cara made a small fire in the cave, just enough to cook the snappers she had caught. With the freshly cooked fish in hand, along with a makeshift torch, she crept back to Rafael, keeping to the tree cover.

"I think I can probably drag myself up there, tonight, really," said Rafael as he munched gratefully on the fish. "I've already managed to go a little way to relieve myself and do some foraging. And I had to set the Bible out in the sun while we had some left. It was drenched."

"No, no. You're not going to drag yourself up there. We'll need to carry you. I don't need you hurting that leg anymore. We'll make a litter. We can do it tonight if you'd like to move up there sooner. What's all this?" She pointed at the scattered sticks, sailcloth, and bits of rope that Rafael had assembled around him in the sand.

"Making a pair of crutches. No reason I shouldn't be able to get around if I keep most of my weight off the leg. Remember how fast Henry was up after he broke his leg in Damascus?"

"Too soon. Much too soon. I don't think it healed straight. And his was a closed fracture, you recall."

"Mine is closed too now, thanks to your expert sewing."

"Raf . . . you know what I mean. You're likely to get infected."

Rafael laughed and said, "Maybe. Maybe not. You worry too much, Cara. You'd best go back to Esperanza, you know."

"She's fine. I want to stay here. If I have to spend another hour with Esperanza I swear I'll kill her."

A quiet, ominous chuckle followed this threat and

Rafael snatched up the knife he had been whittling his crutch with, hefting himself up on his arm and pointing the weapon into the darkness surrounding them. He instinctively reached out to pull Cara behind him, but she evaded his grasp. Cara took one of Rafael's half-finished crutches as a weapon, and she too crouched defensively under the cutter.

The spiderlike form of Murdoch materialized out of the darkness, folding himself to slide under the boat. They did not relax much on recognizing him, both still deeply suspicious of their oldest brother.

"So you found the island. Perhaps you are Firefaxes after all," he said, then he nodded toward Rafael's leg. "That's going to take a while to heal."

"What are you doing here? Where is Louis? Is he . . ." Cara found she could not finish the question.

"He's alive, for now. And for now you are as well," replied Murdoch, studying her with his cold, contemptuous eyes.

"What do you mean 'for now'?"

"The poison, Cara, the poison, *morsus dei*, as Istäni called it—here they also call it the Fruit of Lubrerum. It's in the soil, it's in every plant that grows on the island, it's in the fish, it's all around this place. It stands to reason that it's on these little satellite islands as well." He looked pointedly at the fish bones on a leaf beside Rafael.

"What are we going to eat, then?" cried Cara, despondent at this new invisible threat. "There aren't enough biscuits in the stores from the cutter to keep us alive for as long as it takes for Rafael and Louis to be fit to travel again."

"If Louis is ever fit to travel again. Yes, you will have to eat what you can. The only way to survive is to eat something that will kill you, it seems."

"But Istäni said there was an antidote on the island."

"Maybe he was lying."

Cara licked her lips, frowning, and Murdoch grinned at her discomfiture.

"There is an antidote. But it is more heavily guarded than anything else on the island." Murdoch picked up a small twig and began drawing in the sand, deftly outlining the volcano, and a cave near the top of it. "There is a spring, called Satcrei. They've built a fountain around it, here, in the center of this cave, the cave where the Abbess herself stays. That particular cavern they call the Fluic tei Fluiceist, the Holy of Holies. If you drink of that spring you shall not die, as the verse goes, I believe."

"But have everlasting life?" asked Rafael.

"I don't know about everlasting. Perhaps you should ask Istäni about that. He knows more about the island than I do."

"What do you mean by that?"

"The Abbess is his mother."

"How . . ." Cara trailed off, her mind racing to put together the pieces.

"It's a long story. At any rate, you will have to steal into the cave and get the water from Satcrei if you want to survive. It's a long swim, but there are many rocks along the way to rest and catch your breath. The climb to enter the Holy of Holies from the outside of the volcano is the more challenging feat."

"Why don't you just bring us some of the water?" asked Rafael. "Have you already had it?"

"Of course I have."

"Then why didn't you bring us any?"

Murdoch shrugged. "You're going to have to participate in your own survival, little brother."

"But we have a child to think of here. Surely that should inspire some charity in you."

"I didn't put that child in Esperanza."

"So you bear no responsibility for its well-being?"

"Correct. I gave you the location of this island, though I

suggest you keep to the cave on the southern side and stay well hidden. If you're out during the day on this side they can see you from their lookout posts on the rim of the volcano. I've even shown you the location of the spring. The rest, I'm afraid, is up to you."

"Of course it is," Rafael replied in exasperation. "Christ, I hope Father broke the mold when he made you."

"Remains to be seen, really," replied Murdoch with a meaningful glance at Cara.

"Why can't we just go to the island? You can introduce us to your precious Abbess, she can give us the water. Everyone will be happy," Cara suggested.

"You have no idea what kind of mad cult you would be walking into, and Istäni is still there, with his mother's ear. They killed all the Argonauts, chopped their heads off while the Lubrerites watched the slaughter like it was a Sunday picnic."

"Oh no, Lefty and his Argonauts? Say it isn't so," Rafael interjected wryly. "I'm going to lose a lot of sleep over that."

A trace of a smile slipped across Murdoch's face at the interruption, then he continued, "Every few decades or so, a Firefax comes to them as a Prophet and brings them a little fragment of the Bible to add to their collection. But only their Tribunal elders, and the Abbess or Abbot are permitted to read those fragments, and, with this deranged collection of random passages interpreted by warped, deluded elders, they've created laws, laws that cannot be broken, under penalty of death or maiming. I've barely begun to peel back the layers of living insanity that comprise Lubrerum. You're welcome to walk in and turn yourself in, claim a relation to Grandfather and see if they believe you. I wouldn't recommend it, but you do whatever it is that makes you happy. It doesn't matter to me."

Cara frowned and did not speak for some time. Finally she

said, "Tomorrow, maybe, or the next night, I'll go, and bring back a canteen for Rafael and Esperanza."

"Come on, Cara, you can't go alone," said Rafael immediately.

"You can't come with me, Rafael. First it was your arm, now your leg is broken. What are you going to do, climb a mountain with the miserable excuses for crutches that you're making?"

Rafael bit his lip, then said, "Take Esperanza, then."

Cara laughed and shook her head. "You're joking, right? She's pregnant, and I hate her."

"I know, Cara, believe me, I know. But she can swim, and she's strong. She can be your lookout when you go into the cave. Please take her. I'll feel better if you're not alone."

After a moment Cara nodded, and they both turned back to where Murdoch had been, but there was nothing there. He had vanished as suddenly as he had appeared.

Cara waited nearly a week. She made sure the cave was stocked with fish, berries, coconuts, and sea turtles. It was enough food to last for several weeks—just in case she and Esperanza did not return. Rafael had already been gamely trying out his leg with his crutches, but Cara scolded him every time. On the sixth day she found Rafael surreptitiously rewrapping the leg wound and was horrified to discover the foul smell and thick, purulent discharge expelling from around the stitches she had placed. His leg was hot, swollen, and red, the skin tense and bulging around his wound.

"Why didn't you tell me?" she exclaimed, touching his forehead and cheek, finding them warm and distressingly clammy. "You're going to have to soak it every day, in warm water—clean, fresh water. We're going to need to get some type of poultice to draw out the pus, and I haven't seen any likely plants on this little island. Perhaps Lubrerum itself will have some mustard, or chamomile, or something."

Rafael tried to reassure her, but Cara had had enough. She knew it was her imagination, but she could almost feel the poison working within her, binding to her organs, slowly destroying her from the inside out as she had seen it destroy Louis. Every meal she ate tasted like ash, and she thought all three of them had a new yellowish tint to their skin. That evening, with the reluctant Esperanza in tow, she set out swimming for Lubrerum. Each woman carried a canteen from the cutter, and Cara brought an extra satchel for any herbs she might find.

The ocean felt warmer than it had during the storm and Esperanza, Cara was forced to admit, was a keen swimmer. They stayed close together, stopping to rest every few hundred feet, pacing themselves. It had only just become dark when they set out, and Cara watched the mountainside with trepidation, not knowing if they could be spotted even after dark for their unnatural movements in the water.

The two sopping young women wasted no time after they reached shore, beginning their laborious climb up the steep mountainside. Cara felt certain they could summit the volcano before dawn; she was less sure of making it back down again, and anticipated at least one day spent hiding on Lubrerum itself. They ran a rope about their waists, attaching themselves together as the ascent grew steadily more vertical and treacherous. It was little wonder the civilization on the island had not been discovered all these years, Cara thought. No one would want to make such a climb without knowing there was something worth finding on the other side. Not to mention the constant nagging bites of fire ants, mosquitoes, and gnats.

After climbing for hours, Cara found herself up against a sheer rock face, with only a narrow ledge to stand on, an impossible drop gaping below. She and Esperanza edged along the treacherously thin path for nearly a hundred feet before finding a barely perceptible track that went straight up, tiny crevices in the rock serving as foot- and handholds. Cara started up, Esperanza following. She had nearly made it to the next ledge, panting, when Esperanza lost her grip entirely and fell. Cara leaped forward, catching hold of a scrubby, thorny bush that tore at her hands as the rope around her middle nearly ripped her from the rock face.

"Get a hold of something!" she hissed through gritted teeth, clinging to the bush with all her strength.

Esperanza scrambled for a moment, each swinging movement nearly tearing Cara's wiry body in two. Then, at last, the rope slackened as Esperanza gained the wall again. Cara lurched forward, scrambling onto the next narrow ledge and hoisting for all she was worth until Esperanza joined her. They sat quietly, gasping for air, drenched in sweat. Esperanza's normally tan face was waxy and gray.

"Thank you," she whispered as though it was the most difficult thing she had ever said.

"You're going to have to do better, or I'll have to leave you behind. We've probably got at least another mile of goat terrain left, not to mention the trip back down," replied Cara, panting.

Esperanza leaned back against the wall, waiting for her heart rate to slow, sweat streaming down her body. She winced at an unexpected kick from the infant inside her. After a long time she began to chuckle.

Cara looked at her in confusion, wondering if the near-deadly fall had broken her sister-in-law's mind.

"Were you really going to do it?" asked Esperanza, finally containing her laughter.

"Do what?"

"Rape me with that bloody stick on the ship?"

Cara pondered for a moment. "Well . . . at the time, yes, I think I would have done it. In the state I was in."

"God, you're just like Murdoch. Just like him. You know we're sisters now, don't you? You can't rape your sister!"

Cara frowned. "Yes, but Losi didn't ask me before he married you. I don't owe you an ounce of kindness, Esperanza, and I think you're a monster."

"Well, then, we both have the same assessment of one another. Yet you saved me when I fell."

"Instinct, really. And I think Louis would be broken-hearted if I let you die. But mark my words, if you are ever cruel to my brother again I won't rape you with a stick, I'll kill you."

"You won't have to. He's probably dead already."

"He's not dead," replied Cara, black eyes blazing.

She guzzled from her canteen, which was nearly empty and ready to be refilled with the life-giving water in the Satcrei fountain. Then, taking a few more deep breaths to slow the pattering of her heart, she set off again in the lead. It was closer to dawn than she liked when at last, sliding their way along the last narrow ledge, they nearly tumbled into the Holy of Holies as the stone wall opened up before them.

They were standing in a wide, open space, and Cara could hear the chuckling of water, along with an odd dull, whooshing sound at regular intervals, strangely familiar. For a long time she held quite still and listened to that sound, trying to place it. At last she gave up. It was too perfectly rhythmic to be human, she decided. It had to be some sort of mechanical device. She removed the rope about her waist, eager to be free of Esperanza for a few minutes. Their eyes darting side to side in the blackness, they edged their way toward the burbling water of the fountain. Then Esperanza yelped, tripping over something with a loud crash. Cara, hearing human footsteps echoing down distant tunnels, leaped forward and submerged her canteen in the fountain.

"Hurry, fill your canteen! We have to go!" she hissed.

Esperanza quickly finished filling her canteen and darted from the cave, beginning the difficult scramble down the mountainside alone, but Cara, no longer bound to Esperanza, did not make it so far. She started to run, but something in the darkness, a faint, familiar presence, stopped her, and she turned, slowly, toward the place the mechanical whooshing sound was coming from. Cautiously, she edged her way forward. The sound of alarm coming from deeper within the system of caves had faded, and she was alone walking toward that strange rhythmic noise, which, at last, she recognized. It was the sound of a bellows, but pumped with slow, perfect regularity, at exactly the same rate that a person might breathe.

Then she felt that she had entered a dream, for there, before her in the blackness, was Louis, but not all of Louis, only his head, protruding from an enormous box, a cloth looped around his neck. He was perfectly still. She stepped up to the enormous box, the size of a person's body, the size of a coffin, and placed her hand gently on his face, feeling down to his neck with dread rising inside her. She waited with her hand at the corner of his jaw, and then, steady, present, and a little stronger than when she had last felt it, she palpated the unmistakable jets of her brother's pulse.

Something cold and hard pressed against her own neck. She felt a tall, powerful person wrap their arms around her, pushing her against the box, pushing her against the sharp knife held at her throat.

"Art thou a thief, come to steal, kill, and destroy?" whispered a rich, sonorous voice.

The steel of the knife blade was too cold for this to be a dream, Cara decided at last. Her reverie broken, she began to struggle against her captor's unrelenting grasp. The person holding her drew blood from the side of her neck, just where Lottie had once drawn it before. Cara stilled.

"You haven't answered my question. Did you come to

steal the Favor of God? Have you come to kill my patient? What do you want in the Holy of Holies?"

"He's my brother," said Cara.

The person released Cara almost instantly, and she stumbled forward, dropping to her knees, resting her face on Louis' and kissing his cheek. A moment later there was a flash of light, dimming quickly to a dull yellow glow. She turned her head, still keeping her forehead pressed against Louis' skin. The faint lantern light illuminated a tall, imposing woman, long dark hair streaked with gray, broad shoulders drawn back in her flowing white nightgown, flashing green eyes, familiar eyes, the kind that a person, once caught under their spell, could not easily escape.

A muffled voice at the door to the cavern spoke in a familiar tongue and the woman answered sharply. Then came the sound of retreating footsteps beyond the chamber.

"I can see that you are a Firefax. That is plain, though I am less and less convinced that he is."

"What do you mean?"

"Even in his present state it is clear your brother, as you call him, is beautiful. Unlike any Firefax I have ever seen," said the woman. "I am the Abbess Seänkea. Rebecca is my given name, though no one calls me that anymore. What is your name, child?"

"My mother was a very beautiful woman," said Cara, staring vacantly at Louis. "He takes after her. What have you done to him?"

"Done to him? I am trying to save him. Now, what is your name?"

"Cara. I am Cara Firefax. What is this contraption you've put him in?"

The Abbess smiled and raised the lantern, better illuminating the contraption in question. The box was constructed of ironwood and silver, and a series of closed portholes lined its sides. Then the light spread across a form at the foot of the device and Cara gasped. It was a woman, she thought, but her face was horribly deformed. She sat as still as death, save for movements of her hands pumping the bellows, her face cast down. Where her eyes had been there were only hideous scars. Her ears had long ago been severed; nothing but scarred stumps remained. She continually pumped the bellows, never changing her rhythm or rate.

"Don't worry, she can't hear you, or see you, nor can she speak. I suppose they do not have these things in the outside world, then? It is a way of helping him breathe. The bellows changes the pressure of the air around him inside the box so that his chest expands and deflates, and he draws air in and out of his chest. He was breathing poorly, and I have him on sedatives, which made his breathing still less effective. He was in immense pain, dying, Cara, really dying. We do not see people reach this point with the Fruit of Lubrerum. We allow them to eat of the fruit, and then they leave."

"Will he wake up?"

The Abbess stepped forward, inspecting two large bladders that hung from the ceiling above Louis. Cara thought the bladders were made of some animal material, leather, perhaps, like a wineskin. Each container had a thick, waterproof cloth sewed into a long tube that ran into a port on the top of the box.

"Remains to be seen. He is better today than he was yesterday. But that is no promise of recovery."

Cara turned, scanning the walls, where carved shelves were lined with colorful liquids in glass vials, all marked in a strange but familiar script. "These words, I know these words."

"Yes, Henry told me all the Firefax children were taught Erlandagar, the tongue of Lubrerum. He said you use it in your codes and ciphers."

The words, learned from that curious old book of songs,

rhymes, and Bible verses hidden among Maralah's tomes, words long unused and almost forgotten, tumbled back into Cara's mind as she scanned the vials. *Epiglei* to prevent something, pain—that's what it was. *Ociubiri*, to induce something, she did not know that one. *Epitiuplei*, to stop a cough. *Ociubscu*, to counter infection. *Epihus*, to prevent vomiting.

"What is this place?"

"The Holy of Holies, child. Here we make the broken well, but not only that, here we mete out the punishment of the Almighty as well." As she said this, the Abbess' gaze lingered on the blind woman slowly pumping the bellows. "Do you know my son?"

"Istäni? Yes, yes, I know him," replied Cara.

"Yes, he has spoken of you, Cara. And because he has spoken of you with such reverence, I feel that I can trust you, as he does. This is where Istäni was born, and here was he raised until the day I let Killinger take him away. Here he spent every moment of the first seven years of his life."

"But he must have gone out and played with other children sometimes."

"No, no, he couldn't. This woman, you see her?"

"Yes. Yes, I see her."

"That's more than she can say. She has no tongue, no teeth, no eyes, and her ears were not only cut out but pins were used to rupture the membranes inside as well. She is just a shell now, a captive inside, with no way of telling what goes on in her mind, cut off until the end of her life. Do you know what crime she committed, Cara Firefax?"

"I don't know."

"She lay with a man outside the bonds of matrimony. There were six witnesses against her. So she was brought here, and here I performed this merciful punishment. She ought to have been put to death, you know."

"What happened to the man she lay with?"

"Oh, he was put to death." The Abbess laughed a little at the memory.

"Then, were you married to Killinger?"

The Abbess chuckled. "I was not married to Killinger. But perhaps Istäni isn't Killinger's—perhaps the spirit of God came into me and made me pregnant, like Mary. But the people of Lubrerum would not have believed that. They are malleable, to a point, but there are those that covet my station enough that they would have turned all the people against me had they learned of Istäni—my beautiful, perfect Istäni. There are less of them alive now, but still. A woman in a place of authority will always have enemies. Istäni helped me with this one, you know. He helped me with quite a few of them. There was a rash of sexual intercourse outside of the holy bonds of marriage that year, as I recall."

"What do you mean that he helped you?" Cara was not sure she wanted to know the answer.

The Abbess walked to the shelves and selected a vial, bringing it down, the one marked *ociubiri*. She held it out. "Do you know what this one does?"

"I don't know the word *iri*."

"*Iri*, it means to paralyze. For many, many years we had to tie men and women down to perform the punishments. Sometimes we needed ten men here to hold them down. When I was a girl I saw not one soul take their punishment with grace and poise. But the Abbot before me made this box, and it changed everything. If I give the *ociubiri*, the prisoner is paralyzed, completely awake, completely aware, but unable to move. Frozen. They become a statue. This becomes a problem because they stop breathing. Hence the box. If someone pumps the bellows, they continue to breathe and they survive the procedure. I administer this medication, they become frozen, I place them in the box, and I have nearly an hour from each dose to work with, until it wears off. As soon as he could walk I began teaching Istäni to tie off vessels and how to cut with the instruments. He helped me in punishing this woman, and many others. What else was there for a child trapped in the Holy of Holies to do?"

Cara recoiled with such a look of horror that the Abbess laughed again.

"Oh, child, don't fear, I'm not going to do it to you. It is only for those who have been judged and sentenced. It is not for the children of the Prophets, as a general rule."

"He was little more than an infant. To make him cut people apart while they still lived . . ."

"It is never too early to begin doing the Lord's work, even the work of judgment, though it be a great burden. He was brave, and very good with his little hands."

"I cannot believe you would teach a child to perform such inhuman tortures!"

"This from the girl whose father began teaching her the skills she would need to kill practically the day she was born. Am I not right? I did not teach my Istäni to kill."

"You didn't have to. You laid the foundation and Murdoch finished his education. You taught a child to maim and torture!"

"I taught him to mete out justice, Cara. And, when the time was right, I sent him away. So he did not have to spend his entire life shut up in this cavern. Since then I have had only this woman, and the others like her, for company here, little better than mole rats. You take away the ability to communicate and to understand, and a person becomes less than a worm. But come, these medicines and this box are rarely used for those purposes. I use these things as the Holy Mothers and Holy Fathers used the medicines before me, to heal, to mend, and to restore."

"Why are you telling me all this?"

"Are you not the granddaughter of Henry? A child of the

Prophets, one of the Holy Family who brings us the Word from afar?"

"I am Henry's granddaughter, yes."

"Then this place is your birthright, child, and everything that is here."

"I don't want it. I don't want this horrible place as my birthright."

"But you will if I can heal your brother. What medicine in the world beyond Lubrerum can do that? Henry told me many things of the outside world. I know that the people out there spend all their energy killing and consuming, but here, here we devote ourselves to the improvement of life; to saving and healing. That is how we have created all these medicines, this box, these bladders that I can administer life-giving fluids and medicines through, directly into the blood of my patients, and so many other things that I can show you. We do not use these things for evil, though sometimes we use the knowledge God has given us to chastise those who rebel against him."

"Can you heal him?"

For a long time the Abbess did not respond, staring at Louis' still face. Finally she said, "I think I can, yes."

Cara again scanned the shelves behind the tall, imposing woman, wondering if there was something there that would animate her brother again. The Abbess stepped to the shelf and replaced the paralyzing potion, then, after pausing for a long time, she removed another bottle from the shelf and held it out to Cara.

"What's this one? Something to augment a person's pain while they're paralyzed and you're cutting their eyes out of their head and having a toddler sew up their gushing arteries?"

The Abbess let out a hearty laugh, shaking her head. "No, no, my child. This is a medicine that I made. *Nab bemiub tei*, I call it. It is a potion that can heal aggressively, many, many things. One dose can bind up the blood vessels from the inside. I have seen it save a person who had fallen from seventy feet up. It took time, of course, for them to fully heal; it isn't magic. But I have seen it save some of the most wretched, hopeless cases. It has a way of healing inside that even my skill with a knife, needle, and thread cannot come close to, working on the level of microscopy whereas I can only heal what I can see with my eyes and reach with my hands."

"Why don't you give him that, then? If he is indeed so hopeless, then what can be the harm?"

The Abbess held the glass decanter up to the lantern, rocking it gently, watching as the thick liquid swirled back and forth in mesmerizing eddies, casting strange, curving lights on the ceiling of the cave. "I have never given it and seen the person come back the same. I know not if it is something in the medicine itself, or the horror of their visit to the doorsteps of death. Some don't come back; for some even this is not enough. Some of them come back without the memory of how to speak, without knowing who they are, without being able to walk ever again. Some come back with seizures, horrible seizures that nothing I give can abate. If your brother continues to linger on the edge of eternity, it may be his only hope, but it is not without great risk."

Cara swallowed hard, staring at Louis' deathly still face, his long golden locks falling in waves from the table on which his head rested. Then she turned back to the Abbess. "I need something for an infection, Abbess. My other brother is badly injured, an open fracture to the leg. It's starting to fester. He's got another wound on his shoulder that Istäni repaired, and it's also looking more sour and red every day. He was febrile yesterday, I could tell."

The Abbess replaced the *nab beimub tei* and removed another vial from the shelf and handed it to her. "Three times a day he should drink a spoonful of this. I think it should be enough."

"Thank you, Abbess Seänkea. I must go. It will be dawn soon. I do not wish to be caught by your people. Not everyone in my party is a Firefax by blood."

"Yes, it is better to keep hidden. The Lubrerites have tasted blood recently and would be only too eager to taste it again. Your secret is safe with me, Cara, as long as mine is safe with you."

"I'm hardly in a position to tell anyone anything about you, Abbess Seänkea."

"True enough. Godspeed, then, child. I hope your pregnant friend has not broken her neck while we talked here."

Cara turned and darted toward the opening of the cave, then paused as the Abbess called her back. The Abbess handed her the canteen, which she had dropped in her brief struggle with the older woman. It was full to the brim with the Favor of God. When she reached to take it from the Abbess, the older woman gripped her hands, looking straight at her with those irresistible, familiar emerald eyes.

"If it comes to the point where your brother is dying and there is no other hope, Cara Firefax, would you wish me to give him the *nab bemiub tei*, knowing that his life may be saved, but it may not save the same person that you loved?"

Cara blinked back the tears in her eyes, then snatched the canteen from the older woman, darting a final look at her brother. "Of course I would want you to give it to him. I want you to do anything and everything in your power to save my brother, no matter what the cost." With that she turned and disappeared over the edge of the cave and down the mountainside after the long-vanished Esperanza.

CHAPTER 19

ENTIRE OF ITSELF

A cool breeze drifted through the open wall of the Holy of Holies, carrying on it the scent of the sea, with refreshing hints of jasmine and plumeria. The wind brought with it the harsh cries of gulls, and somewhere in the distance, a ship's bell rang. It was this sound, harkening back to his memories in the Royal Navy, that woke Louis. The book he had been reading had fallen onto his chest, and, glancing down, he noticed that he had drooled on the ancient pages. Sheepishly he wiped at his lip with his sleeve and then startled at the sound of footsteps in the tunnels beyond. He was lying on a low settee before the fountain in the Holy of Holies, Mary's silver face staring at him, almost accusingly. On the small table beside him he saw the half-scribbled letter he had been working on and stuffed it into the book's pages. He slammed the tome closed and tossed it on the table just as the Abbess swept into the room, attended by her first and second Thrateers. They were flanked by several knights in armor, Istäni, and, finally, the stalking form of Murdoch.

"Reading again?" asked the Abbess merrily. "Have we not

already gone over the rules of the island ad nauseum, Mr. Firefax? Your brother is the Prophet, not you."

Putting on a cherublike expression, cognizant of the disapproving look of Prost at the Abbess' side, Louis defended himself. "It would be hard to unteach myself to read, Mother Superior, and I, unfortunately, have little else to do."

"You've completed your exercises?"

"Yes, yes, of course. But I will run them again, if you like."

"Please do, if it will keep you from doing evil, my child."

Istäni picked up the book from the table, and Louis started forward to grab it away, but a warning glance from Murdoch stopped him. He settled back on the settee while Istäni idly flipped through the pages, glancing up after a moment at Louis with a gleam of amusement in his eyes. He snapped the book shut and placed it back on the table.

"What brings you to my sickbed, Istäni, besides snooping through the forbidden books?"

"My dear Louis, regretfully I am here today to bid farewell to this holy isle. For now, but not forever."

"It is difficult to express the visceral sorrow this news causes me," said Louis, feigning a sad expression. "It's going to be a great setback in my recovery, of course. But, I'm sure the Holy Mother will have some tincture of something that will dull the edges of my grief."

Istäni laughed and replied, "Indeed, you'll be pleased to know that I mean to return in six weeks, at the most, if the weather favors me. We're not going all the way back to Boston, just a quick unload and return, though if I were returning to Boston I wouldn't take such a meandering, circuitous route as your brother did on the way here."

"Six weeks is a little optimistic, don't you think? All your men have now eaten the Fruit of Lubrerum, and they're all going to die before or soon after you reach port. You'll have to take on a whole new crew."

"Fortunately there is no shortage of unemployed or under-employed men in the world," returned Istäni.

"It will take you a hundred years of voyaging back and forth to empty the wealth of this island."

"Would it? I suppose if you consider the wealth to be the gold, silver, and precious jewels here. But I think you know better than most, Louis, where the true wealth of Lubrerum lies. Anyway, I just came to bid farewell to my favorite Firefax. I didn't think you were quite up to seeing me off."

"Your favorite Firefax? Since when have I earned such a status? I thought your eyes were more to my sister."

"Ah, but they tell me she has certainly perished." And a knowing smile appeared across Istäni's face as his gaze drifted for an instant back to the closed book on the table. "There has been no sign of her these last three weeks. Not since the battle with the Argonauts, so I must choose a new favorite. You are much more agreeable than the only other Firefax left alive. You are also the only one that seems truly capable of reform, though it took you nearly dying. You've come through a terrible crucible, Louis. Even I, who never doubted your strength, thought you were lost when we arrived at Lubrerum."

"Am I supposed to be grateful for the suffering you inflicted upon me?"

"If you like. It seems to have made a better man of you. Now you can't say I never did anything for you. But I'm rambling and will lose this wind if I don't hurry. My lady, Abbess Seänkea, I look forward to seeing you upon my return. Murdoch . . . try to contain your murderous urges for a few months. I may even consider bringing you back to the outside world with me on my next voyage. Louis . . . try not to sail too close to the wind."

"Wouldn't dream of it."

Istäni bowed to everyone, lingering last with the Abbess,

whose hand he kissed. Then he was gone, escorted out by the second Thrateer. Murdoch regarded his younger brother, who was making a speedy recovery. His vision had returned, but his body was still gaunt and frail compared to what it had been, his pale cheeks still colorless. Yet the vigor of life lit up his piercing blue eyes again; indeed, they seemed almost more vibrant than before his illness. He had even begun sparring with Murdoch for close to an hour every day, showing the same dash and talent he had before, only lacking his old stamina.

There was a faint urgency in Louis' expression and, as everyone else was still looking after Istäni's retreating form, he signed, 'Another letter,' to Murdoch.

Murdoch shook his head.

'Please,' Louis signed.

Murdoch's eyes widened with exasperation. He turned abruptly and followed the Abbess and her party out. They repaired to the rim of the volcano, on the western side, where a broad, open area along the top served as a lookout point. The knights of Lubrerum set out a lunch there, and Murdoch found a comfortable place to sprawl, hat pulled low over his eyes, puffing at his tobacco pipe. There was tobacco on the island, but he found it did not answer well. It had a foul, almost brackish taste to it, unlike the rich, deep, earthy flavor of the leaves grown on the island of Hispaniola, which he favored most of all the tobacco he had sampled around the world.

A few hours later they watched Istäni, who had ridden one of the island horses, reach the small inlet where the *Eliposti* sat and set off in a longboat, pulling toward the repaired Argonaut vessel. The *Mariposa* had been unsalvageable, and they had towed her shattered form to the inlet on the far western side of the island that served as their harbor. Istäni's crew and the coopers and carpenters among the Lubrerites used bits and pieces of the *Mariposa* for repairs of the other two ships. The Argonauts' ship, *Penumbra*, had required extensive repairs, but she was seaworthy, at least, and any additional work would have to wait until she reached the mainland.

Murdoch did not stir when the Abbess approached and seated herself on a rock beside him. She let out a long, slow sigh, watching after the *Penumbra* as the sails fell, catching the wind and the vessel turned with a slow, measured grace into the northwest. The guards and Thrateers waited solemnly until the sun began to set, orange light spilling over the waves, turning the white foam tips of the waves a delicious gold. Gradually the gold gave way to pastel pinks and purples stretching across the horizon in a breathtaking brilliance before fading to deepening shades of blue. Then the Abbess dismissed her guards and Thrateers, broaching no argument though they looked at Murdoch with suspicion. After they left she sat in silence beside him until it was nearly dark.

"You're very like Henry, you know," she said at last. "But not like him at the same time. He was cruel, but not like you. He was passionate in his enjoyment of living. He liked to turn off the killer inside him, to pretend he was just a man, like any other. You don't ever turn off the killer within you, I think."

"Should I?"

"I suppose not, it's . . . who you are, more of who you are than it was for Henry, even."

"Well, you're not afraid of me, despite knowing what I am. You sent all your guards and fawning Thrateers away."

"Yes, because I also know what you are not, Murdoch. You are not the great power of Lubrerum. You are a figurehead, little more than a myth to the people that live here. The real power on this island is held by the Ted and myself, and always has been held by those in our positions. Your family is just a legend to frighten the people into submission. If you dared raise a hand against me, the citizens of Lubrerum would tear you limb from limb."

"Just as long as we both know where we stand, then," said Murdoch, his lips twitching into a faint grin beneath the brim of his hat.

The Abbess didn't speak again for a few moments, then she said, "I do owe you some thanks though, I find. Istäni told me that after Killinger's death, you were the one who raised him. So, for that, for your protection of my son, I am grateful, more grateful than you will ever know."

Murdoch slid his hat back and turned his glittering dark eyes on the Abbess. "Perhaps you can answer a question I have, as a token of your appreciation."

"Perhaps."

"Aboard the *India* there was a rumor. The sailors said that Killinger loved his little Istäni so much and took the child with him from Lapland, where they thought he was born, because the boy was something of a miracle. Killinger was a sailor in the Royal Navy in the forties and during an action in Cartagena they say he suffered an awful wound to the groin. He never could have children, though I did see him trying with gusto in many ports along our voyage. So, tell me, was it one of your magic potions that healed his loins?"

The Abbess was silent for a very long time. In the distance, the cries of monkeys drifted hauntingly across the island as the stars began to appear in the velvet night sky. Finally she said, "There is another way in which you resemble your grandfather, Murdoch. You're shrewd. Nothing slips by you."

"Well, then, who, pray tell, was Istäni's father?"

"You ask but you already know the answer, don't you?"

"A cruel but passionate man?"

"Your grandfather was an irresistible force, Murdoch, you should know that better than most people."

Murdoch chuckled. "Istäni doesn't know?"

"No. I have no plans to tell him."

"Then who is really the cruel one, Abbess?"

The Abbess dropped to her knees and knocked the pipe from Murdoch's hand, pressing her lips firmly against his, her fingers tracing their way sensuously along his chest, over his abdomen, and finally, tantalizingly resting upon his groin. Then, a moment later, she drew back with a look of surprise at her own forwardness.

"How long has it been since Henry died and deprived you of the joys of his company?" asked Murdoch.

"Ten years. All the medicine of Lubrerum couldn't keep him alive. When I saw you it was like he had appeared again, made young, but unmistakably the same hideous man that gave me such pleasure for so many years."

"It's lonely being the Holy Mother of such a strange, illiterate civilization, isn't it, Rebecca?" asked Murdoch, and, hoisting himself up from his lazed position, he took the Abbess in his lean, powerful arms and drew her down to the rocky earth beside him.

Sometime later Murdoch returned to the lamplit Holy of Holies. Louis was going through his exercises again, despite the late hour. He scrambled to his feet, wiping sweat from his brow and dusting his hands off as his brother approached. Murdoch paused, studying him intently. Louis was swaying a little and his hands were trembling. Attempting to appear casual, Louis sat down on the settee before he could fall.

"Oh, I'm glad you came back. I've got that letter for her. Are you going tonight?"

Murdoch sighed. "These letters are going to get you executed."

"Not if you don't get caught with them!"

"I wouldn't worry about me getting caught, brother. Give it to me."

"You're very bright-eyed tonight—happy to see the last of Istäni for a while?"

"Something like that," sneered Murdoch, snatching the letter from his brother and turning.

"Give them all my love!" Louis called as Murdoch disappeared down the corridor beyond.

It was late, well past midnight, and Cara, accustomed to being awake at night, felt certain Murdoch would not come. It was too late for him. She was sweeping the cave, an endless chore. The marooned trio had gradually been improving on their dwelling, building makeshift walls in the cave with sticks, palm leaves, and driftwood to give some semblance of privacy.

At the entrance to the cave she paused, sweeping repeatedly over a hard item on the floor; a log, she thought, that Esperanza must have dropped. Mechanically she swept at the object, staring out at the shimmering sea beyond the cave entrance. The sigh of the waves was like a lullaby, beckoning her. She watched, mesmerized as the waves rose and then dashed themselves to pieces. Their rhythmic suicide resonated in her. It was lovely and aching, as they were consumed over and over by the endless expanse of unheeding water. They had failed, but they would regroup, and as long as the sun rose in the sky they would continue their relentless washing of the sandy shore. To what end, she wondered. The more she stared, the more things faded around her, until she was staring out at nothing, and there was nothing around her, just herself, in a sea of nothingness. Her sweeping slowed. But something of her was still conscious, and she saw a movement in the corner of her vision. She turned her head and let out a horrified gasp, leaping backward, brandishing the broom like a sword as she struck her head against the low ceiling of the cave. Murdoch drew his one outstretched leg up and rose.

"Courageous little sister, was it a snake?" he asked with a grin.

"Yes, yes, it was," she said, annoyed partly at herself, but more so at her wraithlike older brother.

"I thought you really were going to sweep me out onto the beach for a while there. The opulence of your dwelling has increased since my last visit."

"Please," said Cara. "What do you want?"

"Just here to visit my darling little brother and my sisters. I brought you a few things." He dropped a drenched bundle on the ground.

Cara knelt and began emptying the contents of the bundle onto the floor, still frowning as she sorted through new clothes, soap, a comb, a new pot, and two jeweled cups.

"Where is Rafael?" asked Murdoch.

"I believe he's asleep. It's quite late. Did Istäni leave?"

"Yes, your beau left this evening, as planned."

"He's not my beau."

"Then why do you still wear his garments when I bring you the latest fashion from Fluic Praem?"

"You bring me antique garments that appear to have been passed down directly from Queen Elizabeth and don't fit me at all. That's why I'm still wearing Istäni's clothes. How is Louis?"

"Louis is thriving, better every day. He has sent another letter to the lady Esperanza. Longer this time, I think."

"Oh joy," said a voice from further in the cave.

They both turned to see the ragged, weary Esperanza, her abdomen more swollen than even a few days before, when Murdoch had last visited.

"Curb your enthusiasm, dear sister," said Murdoch.

"Have a seat. If Cara would be so kind as to light one of the candles I brought last time, I will read it aloud to you."

"Must you?"

"I would give it to you and let you read it yourself, but last time I did that you tore it up. So, here we are, unfortunately."

Esperanza plopped herself onto a large rock, a makeshift stool, folding her arms over her chest. Cara brought a candle and then moved further back into the cave to continue sorting through Murdoch's offerings. Murdoch stretched out on the floor of the cave, propping himself up on an elbow. He withdrew a glass vial from his wet jacket, popped the cork, and slid a dry scroll of paper out.

"'Fair Queen of my Heart—'"

Esperanza scoffed, and Murdoch gave her a hard look until her scornful smile faded, before continuing, "'I hope, at all times, that you are well, and that you are getting adequate rest and comfort in your refuge. I pray that the infant you carry is not causing an undue burden upon you.'" Again Murdoch was forced to pause for Esperanza's reaction to the sentiment. "'As I have stated before, I look forward to pampering you for the rest of our lives together, since my mortal end has been so graciously delayed. I will spend the rest of the life God has granted me serving my fair Esperanza, and doing everything in my power to make up for the horrific indignities you have suffered these last few months. Murdoch tells me that we will all be getting off the island together, just as soon as Rafael and I are recovered enough to travel. He has a plan, Esperanza, and much as I am loath to admit it, he is not a stupid man. I can think of no one else, under these circumstances, whose hands I would rather be in.

"'But, enough of dwelling upon dreams not yet realized. I have continued my study of the island people, reading through their edicts and laws, and pestering the Abbess with questions. What a strange and perturbing civilization. Every layer I peel back leads to yet another layer of this complicated matrix. The Mother Superior tells me that no one marries on this island without her permission, nor are animals bred without her say-so. Here, in her cloister, she keeps the most detailed genealogies you could imagine, not simply of the people, but of all the animals. The Firefaxes, when they come, sometimes supplement the stock of the island, bringing a few horses to mix in new blood, or greyhounds, or other creatures, cows, sheep, goats, even chickens and ducks. Similarly, over the years, a few of the sailors that came with the Firefaxes have stayed behind, mixing in the stock of Lubrerum's people. The Abbess must first check the lineage of a person, make certain that they have not been mixed in line too recently, before bestowing permission to wed. I tell you, fair Esperanza, the more I learn of the island, the more bizarre and complex I find it to be. It reminds me of a line from an old poem I read once, "No man is an island, entire of itself." I fancy, despite what the poet wrote, no island is entire of itself either.

"'That said, I think that any naturalist or philosopher would be hard-pressed to find a more unique place and people to study. But, I find I must break off this letter, for now. The Thrateers are coming, and if I am caught writing, a cardinal sin here, then I will likely answer with my life or some barbaric maiming. I shall have further interesting tales to tell of my research in my next letter, I'm sure. With all my ardent, passionate love, your devoted husband, Louis Firefax.'"

After a moment, Mudoch leaned forward. "I also brought paper, quill, and ink. What reply would you like to make to your husband?"

"What reply could I possibly have to make to that oafish fool and his ramblings? I haven't asked him to correspond with me. I owe him no answer."

Murdoch chuckled. "Esperanza, Esperanza, so bold and fierce, revered for your beauty and the beauty of your voice, now laid so low. You are ugly, Esperanza, and the more time you spend out here in this cave, scorning a man who loves you, the only man who ever truly loved you, the more hideous you become. It's as if your physical appearance is finally matching your inner form. How does it feel to be ugly, when you have been worshiped like a goddess for so long for your incomparable beauty?"

Esperanza drew herself up tall and stiff. "An interesting statement coming from the world's most hideous hired killer. I do have a reply, now that I think upon it. Tell Mr. Firefax to stop wasting his energy on writing me. Our marriage remains annulled and I continue to loathe him. Thank you." With a rustle of her grubby, ragged skirts, she rose and moved ponderously away, into the recesses of the cave.

Murdoch drew his pipe from his jacket and clenched it in his teeth, remaining in his lounging position. "Not dead yet, Rafael?" he asked without looking up.

Rafael chuckled, hobbling from his enclosure on his crutches. "Not yet, brother. Sorry, I didn't mean to eavesdrop. Actually, I . . . have something of an idea. I'd like to make a reply, in Esperanza's hand. She is being too cruel. Much too cruel."

"You can write in her hand?"

"Yes, yes, I can, and very prettily. I've seen a few samples on the ship when I would come and read to her."

"He's right, he can do it. None of the rest of us ever came close to Rafael's skill at forgery," Cara said, with a little reluctance. "But don't you think it would be even more cruel to send Losi false letters and give him false hope that she returns his affection? When we are all reunited again he will know at once that she hates him, and that may crush him even more, having held out hope because of a few forged letters."

"I won't be excessive," said Rafael. "Just cordial, polite. Not evil."

Murdoch obligingly produced the paper and quill. In less than an hour Rafael had dashed off a tolerable, brief note. It was cold and direct, but not hateful. Murdoch corked it in the vial and then stowed it inside his jacket.

"The vessel is as ready as it will ever be to sail, I think," said Cara.

"You mean the cutter? We're not leaving Lubrerum in that tiny thing," Murdoch replied.

"Then how are we getting away?"

"When Rafael and Louis have both pulled themselves together, we're taking the island's ship on the west side, hidden in their little inlet there, the *Apostle*."

"We're stealing their ship?" asked Rafael incredulously. "Is it not guarded?"

"A few lazy guards who've never fought before. Don't think you'll be up to the task?"

"Not right now, but I will be once this leg is mended."

"See that it mends quickly. The soonest Istäni could return would be six weeks. It would be better if we are no longer here when he comes back," said Murdoch, unfolding his long legs and standing. Then, with a curt nod to his siblings, he disappeared through the cave entrance.

"Steal the *Apostle*, from our own island?" exclaimed Rafael to Cara.

"It will certainly be a more comfortable journey home than aboard that tiny cutter," replied Cara. She frowned, her eyes sinking deeper beneath the shadow of her knitted black brows. "Six weeks will be about the time Esperanza is due. Raf?"

"Yes?"

"What was the passage of the Bible that Murdoch gave to the islanders?"

"Nothing of importance. I think it was a few chapters from *1 Kings*, about the war that King Ahab of Israel had with the King of Syria, perhaps a bit about Naboth, if I'm remembering correctly. I only glanced at it, honestly, before everything else that happened that night."

"Can you . . . can you tell me about that passage? Do you remember it?"

Surprised by his sister's sudden interest in the Word of God, Rafael flipped to the portion of the Bible where Murdoch had torn away several pages. Then, searching his memory, he began to tell Cara the story that was missing.

CHAPTER 20

———

CLOSE TO THE WIND

Over the next six weeks, while Murdoch grew ever more impatient, Rafael's leg and shoulder healed slowly and Louis continued to pore over the lore of the island. First he studied in the libraries of the Holy of Holies and then, when he was well enough to leave the Abbess' vigilant care, by interviewing the people of Fluic Praem. The Abbess was alarmed by the young man's unrepentant reading in the library, and still more by the voracious curiosity he exhibited interviewing the Lubrerites. She set guards to watch him and he was not permitted to leave the city. Her fears were not unfounded, for Louis was cautiously seeking out anyone that might be willing to flee Lubrerum and crew the *Apostle*.

In between his clandestine recruiting activities, Louis continued to send weekly letters to Esperanza, for Murdoch refused to go out to the islet more than once a week, and each week Murdoch brought back a message written by Rafael, each one slightly warmer and kinder than the proceeding letter. Louis studied these pages, reading and rereading them, memorizing them, clinging to every word.

Murdoch often spent his days stalking along the upper rim of the volcano, sometimes in the company of the Abbess, but more often alone, plying his spyglass to the distant waters, looking for Istäni's return. He watched with satisfaction as the carpenters disassembled what remained of the *Mariposa*, using her parts to supplement the older components of the ship he planned to steal.

Cara and Rafael took to sparring with sticks to pass the time, though with Rafael often in a seated position, or leaning on his crutch. Esperanza joined in occasionally and showed a certain aptitude for swordsmanship but was hampered by her protuberant abdomen. Murdoch brought them one sword and one of the Lubrerite spears. The people of Lubrerum did not have pistols or guns of any kind aside from the cannons aboard the *Apostle*. The few other firearms that had arrived on their shores over the years, typically among the accouterments of their Prophets, had invariably been destroyed.

The Abbess gave Murdoch and Louis an empty residence in the southeastern section of the city. It was an open structure with a few scattered walls, vine-covered lattices, and carved pillars holding up the shingled roof. The floor was a colorful mosaic that depicted Jesus on the cross and three women reaching toward him. The only fully enclosed rooms were the bedrooms, kitchen, and outhouse. A waist-high fence surrounded the courtyard, overgrown with tall tropical grasses, gardenias, and plumerias. When not exercising, secretly writing in his chamber, or out among the Lubrerites, Louis would habitually lie in a hammock in the lush garden, sometimes whittling or singing, more often just drinking in the sweet smell of plumeria and jasmine. Murdoch found him there on a relatively chilly day in October.

"Is that you, brother?" called Louis.

"You're very good at that."

"At what?"

"Sensing me coming."

"Perhaps if you bathed more frequently," replied Louis, glancing up.

Murdoch smiled, and there was a startling fondness in the smile, a look that Louis thought he had never seen before on the hideous man's face. The look of affection disappeared almost as quickly as it had materialized, replaced by his habitual mocking smirk.

Louis, trying to shake the strange moment, continued, "I've another one for you."

"Would you like to advertise it to the whole bloody city, or perhaps tell me in a room where your guards can't hear?"

"Right you are," replied Louis, sliding easily out of the hammock. They retired to his bedchamber and in a low whisper Louis described the twentieth potential deserter he had recruited.

"I don't think we can take any more, Louis. It takes time to convince them. And each addition increases the risk that one of them will blab. We need to leave soon, within the week."

"But Esperanza hasn't given birth yet. It would be dangerous to leave now, with her so close to her time."

"The risk of staying any longer, of Istäni returning and finding us still here, would seem to outweigh the risk of one unborn child's life."

"Would you say that if it was your child?"

"Yes, of course I would, idiot. You're not going to die anymore, so you can make as many children as you like when we get out of here. This one potential life isn't special."

Louis frowned. "I guess that's not how I feel, Murdoch. But this young lady, she's strong, she's a baker's apprentice, and she longs to escape, to see something of the world. I think she would make an excellent addition to our crew."

"What did you have to do to get her to admit to wanting

to leave? A little cataglottism? Perhaps with a side of cunnilingus?"

"I'm wounded that you would accuse me of such inconstancy, Murdoch. I'm a married man."

"Since when has that stopped anyone?"

"You're impossible. I didn't have to press or cajole her. She's desperate and was just looking for a listening ear."

"How do you know you can trust her?"

"So cynical! I am cautious, Murdoch, always have been. That's why they called me Lightfoot, you know. She's deeply unhappy, ready for a change, for an escape. She described the feeling so well, you know, the way we used to feel at Maralah, like captives, longing to be free."

"Curb your sentimentalism, for God's sake. You keep caving to every woebegone tale you hear and eventually you'll trust the wrong enchantress."

"Oh, come off it. It's getting dark, are you going tonight?"

"I am. Should be my last visit. I have to make sure they are ready to leave. You have a letter, I presume?"

"You presume correctly." Louis knelt and pried a slab of marble from beneath his hammock, revealing a hole beneath that was stuffed with papers. He took out one of the letters and kissed it before handing it to his brother. "The last letter before I see her again! I can hardly credit it, Murdoch, it's been an eternity. And she's warming to me, slowly, but surely. You can see it in those letters she sends. Give Rafael and Cara my love, as always."

Almost before Louis finished speaking, Murdoch had vanished into the growing gloom of that brisk autumn evening. He found Cara and Rafael sitting in the common area of the cave, looking anxiously at each other. Rafael was humming a hymn, as if to distract himself from what was happening in Esperanza's chamber. Murdoch could just see the top of Esperanza's hair protruding over her makeshift wall of driftwood as she paced back and forth. Occasionally she paused and her head disappeared as she crouched down for a moment of blistering agony, letting out grunts of pain.

"She's been at this all evening," explained Rafael solemnly. "It kicks up for a few hours, then she rests and it goes away. She keeps telling us the baby's not coming yet, but it has to be soon."

"About damn time," replied Murdoch.

"Is that the Devil out there or Murdoch Firefax?" called Esperanza.

"Just your dear sweet brother, come to call upon you," he returned glibly.

"You have—" She groaned and then began to pace again. "You have impeccable timing, Mr. Firefax."

"The letters of your loving husband cannot wait, unfortunately. Also I have come to encourage you in your labors. We're getting off this island soon, so you'll either need to have the little bastard in the next few days, or have it at sea."

"I'll take your recommendations under advisement. But please, today, more than ever before, I don't wish to hear from the blaggard who put me in this state."

Murdoch, without any pretense at decency, pushed his way around the wall and came to stand before her with the letter in hand. He seated himself on the ground, legs folded, and began reading aloud by the dim light of Esperanza's candle.

"'My darling Esperanza,

"'You will never know how much time I spend thinking about you every day. I've even taken to trying my clumsy hand at drawing you. You would laugh to see the shaky, obtuse images I've managed to create. But, even if I cannot ever recreate your gorgeous likeness by drawing, or sculpture, or poetry, know that the perfection of your form is forever locked in my mind. I trace it over day after day, watering that vision of loveliness, and caring for it as one would a beautiful wisteria. In my ears your voice sings constantly, unparalleled, rising and falling in soulful, heavenly strains. But you, my perfect Esperanza, are not a precious plant, and though you mean more to me than you will ever know, I do not love you for what you give me, for your voice, or your perfect form, but rather for who you are. I do not mean that hard, angry exterior you display to all the rest of the world. I mean that soft, beautiful young woman I have seen on late summer days by the ocean or on the bowling green, standing in the clear, sepia light of the sun, somehow more brilliant in appearance than even our brightest star. Nothing can compare to those visions of that unparalleled woman, forgetting herself and speaking truly, with such honesty, such breathtaking authenticity, laughing, joking, free. You are truly the most beautiful when you allow the icy veneer of that cold shield you always wear to melt away, and let others see the kindness, the humor, the intelligence, and the courage that lies beneath. That is the woman I have come to love, not what you pretend to be.'"

Murdoch paused and skipped ahead, glancing up at Esperanza to gauge her reactions. Her face remained impassive as she paced. He wondered with amusement if Louis was made delusional by his love, or if indeed there was something more that went on beneath that cold, beautiful, impenetrable exterior.

"'The only thing, truly, that makes this prison called Lubrerum in any way bearable is the memories I carry of you, and the knowledge that one day, very soon, we shall be together again and free of the convoluted hell of this deranged island. Though you may think me a fool for writing so candidly, I believe that a husband and wife should know one another's minds as intimately as they know one another's bodies, and we have failed in that so far. My love, I miss you every second of every minute of every hour of every day. Not an instant passes that you are not there, not at the edge, but at the forefront of my mind.

"'My prayers are, as always, with you and our child. Your adoring husband, Louis Firefax.'"

"I don't know what you imagine you gain by these little sessions," said Esperanza. "If you think to melt my disposition toward that insidious fool, you are wasting your time, and a great deal of mine as well. If you are trying to prove something to yourself, or Louis . . . I ask you to please do it in some manner that does not inconvenience other people. If it is your aim to torment me into second-guessing myself and my decision to end this marriage, then you are only prolonging your disappointment. My decision is final."

Murdoch stood up and placed the letter on her small cot on the floor. She stared at it for a moment, as if fighting some inner battle. Then she snatched up the paper and tore it into a dozen pieces.

"What will your reply be, my lady?" asked Murdoch without expression.

"You know it already. I have no reply, Murdoch Firefax. Now get out and don't come bothering me again with your silly love letters. I haven't time for you, or your brother."

Murdoch nodded his head and turned, slipping past the wall separating her from the rest of the cave.

"I think she's warming to him, as I predicted," said Rafael, with a grin.

"How does that verse go?" asked Murdoch. "'Faith is the substance of things hoped for, the evidence of things not seen'? Either way, your letters have kept Louis happy and motivated, and I needed him to be motivated if we were going to find a crew for the *Apostle*. I'm not much of a proselytizer myself."

"I would never have guessed that about you, brother," replied Rafael. "We are ready here. We have the few weapons you've managed to sneak out. Our bags are packed at all times. I've got a wicked limp still, but I'm quite up to my old strength. I speak for all three of us when I say we are ready to leave right now if you say the word."

"It will have to be soon, or never," replied Murdoch.

"That's rather ominous. You think all hope of escape ends if Istäni gets here before we leave? You think he means to kill us?"

"Or worse. Stay ready, not tonight, but within the next two or three days."

Once ashore, Murdoch took a long, meandering path back to Fluic Praem. In the last eight weeks he had learned every cave and rock of the island and now he knew Lubrerum intimately, better than most Lubrerites. There was a restlessness within him that he did not like, an uncomfortable sensation. He had felt a strange, foreign warmth, a fondness, when Louis teased him in their shared courtyard the day before. The image of a blond-haired child, smiling and reaching toward his older brother, flitted repeatedly through his mind. He endeavored to rid himself of it as he walked, his mind wandering back to all the insufferable things that Louis had done over the few years they had worked together for the Argonauts. The list was quite long. This very nearly had the effect he wanted, comfortable disgust and loathing rising again to its rightful place in the forefront of his mind, blotting out the unwelcome affection that had briefly disturbed him the afternoon before.

He wound his way through the gradually lightening golden streets of Fluic Praem. The city was too quiet, even for that early in the morning. A sense of foreboding and dread hung over the shuttered homes. As was his habit, he slipped in and out of shadows, moving invisibly along the southern edge of the town. His feet stopped before his mind realized why. The house where he and Louis stayed was not right. Someone had trampled the gardenias, brutally, cruelly, as if an entire troop of soldiers had stormed through the courtyard. The curtain that hung over Louis' bedchamber doorway had been torn down. Murdoch sensed men approaching, though they were nearly soundless. They had been waiting for his return.

His hands slid to one of the many knives he had arrayed under his garments. He paused, however, at the quiet threat issued by the familiar voice of Prost, the first Thrateer.

"If you want to see your brother alive, Prophet, I wouldn't try anything."

"Where is he?"

"Turn over your weapons, and come along, calm and quiet. We'll take you to him."

"Lead on, then, first cuckold of the Abbess. I haven't moved to resist you, have I?"

"Careful with your insults, Master Firefax. Follow me." Prost spoke a few earnest commands to his knights in Erlandagar, and they flanked Murdoch. With a mocking sneer on his face, he removed his weapons, turning them over one by one to the knights surrounding him. Once the Thrateer was satisfied that Murdoch had surrendered his entire extensive armory, they marched back toward the insulae of Fluic Praem.

The sun had fully risen, but there was still little movement in the streets. Word had gone quickly through the city, and people peered through their curtains or around partially closed doors as Murdoch swept past with his entourage. When they entered the towering arched hall of the great church, he strode in like a conquering hero leading his soldiers, rather than as a prisoner under guard. There was a crowd gathered inside and the ancient Tribunal were all seated on their thrones and all, miraculously, awake. But this time another figure had joined them upon the dais: the Abbess herself. She stood, regal, looking down with a solemn, sorrowful gaze at the assembled crowd.

"First Thrateer, take the Prophet near to his brother," commanded the chief of the Tribunal.

Murdoch scanned the crowd, his gaze settling at last on Louis, standing in an enclosed prisoner's dock before the elders, flanked by guards. He let Prost lead him over to stand beside his brother. Louis had his hands chained in front of him, and he bore a few new bruises on his face. He was clothed in a light blue tunic and brown breeches, and he looked beautiful, as beautiful and defiant as the old Louis, but with that strange new softness to him as well, head held proud and steady.

"What sort of trouble have you gotten yourself into, little brother?"

"Oh, just a misunderstanding. The Abbess will sort it all out, I'm sure. Won't take a minute for Her Holiness to set everything to rights."

"Silence!" ordered one of the elders tersely.

Then the chief elder began speaking ponderously in Erlandagar.

"Hold on just a moment! A man should be accused in his own language, don't you think?" Louis interrupted the proceedings.

"You are a Firefax," said the Abbess. "Is it not true, as Henry told me, that you all learn to read Erlandagar when you are children?"

"When we are children. We learn to *read* it. We don't speak it. And that was many years ago, Your Grace. If you carry on the proceedings in Latin, Spanish, Greek, French, German, Italian, Chinese, Arabic, English, or Russian I shall understand without difficulty, but not your archaic little language."

"Very well," replied the Abbess. "Elders, proceed in English."

The Ted nodded almost as one and cast ugly glances at

Louis before the elder that had begun speaking continued, "The accused is here today charged with many offenses, and grave ones. First among them, using his hands to write, as is forbidden for one of his station, lest a common man, led by the Devil, fabricate and mislead God's children. Only the Abbess, the Thrateers, the Prophet, and the elders on this council are permitted to write, as has always been the law. Furthermore, among his writings were found letters to a person not known in our city; therefore he stands accused of harboring fugitives on this holy island. He stands accused as well of conspiracy to desert Lubrerum without leave, and incitement of Lubrerites to leave with him. Hidden in his bedchamber he kept a list of people that he had enticed to leave with him. You, dear people, will be relieved to know that they have all been apprehended. Second Thrateer Spiogni, bring in your prisoners."

Spiogni marched in, leading behind him a string of Lubrerites in silver chains, their heads hanging low. Some were battered and bloodied, having apparently already been whipped or beaten to confess their crimes.

"Your Worships, I have only just begun to interrogate these prisoners," said Spiogni apologetically. "I have not yet determined who among them must be punished."

"They must all be punished," replied the Abbess. "The fact that they were included on the list found hidden in Louis Firefax's secret papers means that they heeded his temptations. They allowed evil to enter their ears and did not alert the knights of the city, or their elders, or the constables. For this they will lose the ability to hear and to speak. As it is written, 'And if thy right hand offend thee, cut it off, and cast it from thee: for it is profitable for thee that one of thy members should perish, and not that thy whole body should be cast into hell.'"

The elders nodded in assent to this, their faces grave.

"No Lubrerite leaves the holy island save on the wings of the angels," the chief elder affirmed.

"What, then, shall be done with Louis Firefax?" continued the Abbess, shifting her gaze to the pale young man in the prisoner's dock. "For, since the word was first brought to us of his faithlessness by the good and honest baker's apprentice, Cecile Freur, have I not read thoroughly every hideous, evil document seized from his hiding place? Do I not already know the extent of his crimes, and the truth of them? What more knowledge do I need to condemn him? What more knowledge do I require to sentence him? Speak now if you have additional information, do not hold your peace, my people. I could take his life for his evil, for enticing good people to follow in the ways of wickedness, but I will be merciful. I will take his hands for daring to write when he is not of a station to do so, his tongue for speaking the words of the Devil, his eyes for looking upon the sheep of this island like a cunning wolf to steal them away, and his ears as well, that the last words he will ever know will be my judgment, until the day he goes before the Lord of Lords Himself, for his final sentencing. I have spoken, and so shall it be. Unless, as I said, someone has additional evidence to bring against him that I have not already reviewed."

"I have additional evidence, my lady," said Murdoch. Everyone in the church, including Louis, turned toward him in surprise.

Murdoch stepped to the foot of the dais, casting his scornful gaze up at the Abbess. "Listen to me, people of Fluic Praem. There sits your Holy Mother, the most honored and sacred person in all Lubrerum, after myself. There she sits over you, the Whore of Babylon."

A loud collective gasp went up and Prost started forward, reaching out to restrain the Prophet. But Murdoch evaded him easily, darting forward and leaping onto the dais with a grace that belied his awkward, gangly form.

"Yes, you heard me. Your Holy Mother has lain with men out of wedlock. *Men*—I said she has lain with *men*, for she has lain with more than one. Among them, Harvey Killinger, with whom she mothered the favored Istäni Seänkea, who you have met, and given freely part of my own inheritance, under the direction of this corrupt, heinous woman. Not satisfied, this mother of harlots has had relations over the years with Thrateers, and with knights, and even with Henry Firefax himself. She even sought to seduce me. She has had intercourse in the Holy of Holies. Jezebel herself would be embarrassed by this shameless, blasphemous strumpet's actions. So, people of Lubrerum, what will you do? Will you listen to the words of a whore, who wishes you to let her butcher your own families while they still live, and leave them maimed forever in suffering and pain? Will you slaughter the family of your Prophet at the direction of this prostitute who lords over you? What sentence would she give to herself for the crimes I bring against her?"

"Enough! Blasphemer! You are not the grandson of Henry. You are not a Prophet here, but a wolf sent by the Devil in the guise of a sheep to steal, to kill, and to divide!" cried Prost. "Seize him! *Teigenc si!*"

The guards, as if one, all piled on Murdoch, who, taking one of his opponent's swords, killed six guards and four knights before he was overwhelmed. As they struggled to contain his older brother by force of numbers, Louis looked up and saw the Abbess standing regally, her jaw set. But, ever so faintly, he saw her lower lip quiver, and then Louis knew that Murdoch spoke the truth, and more than that, that the Abbess Seänkea was infatuated with his brother.

"This son of Lucifer does not deserve a trial! Kill him! Kill him now!" shrieked the first Thrateer, almost manic with rage at the insult to his Abbess.

"Hold! Hold, I say!" shouted the Abbess in a voice like rolling thunder, a voice that froze everyone in the hall. For a long moment no one even seemed to breathe, waiting for the judgment of the offended holy woman. Finally she spoke, and to Louis' discerning ear, the tremor in her voice was unmistakable. "The Prophet should be placed in our most secure cell, with guards posted night and day. I must pray upon his punishment, for truly he has done a great wrong here today, a wrong that you have all borne witness to. Imprison the others as well, to await the carrying out of their sentences."

The guards led Murdoch in chains back along the still-solemn streets. Rumors of what had transpired before the Ted were already spreading and shutters and doors began opening. There were calls of disgust from the children in their court-yards and their parents, and even a few poorly aimed rotten vegetables tossed at him as he passed. Murdoch still bore his usual haughty, knowing smile.

Prost, marching beside him, raised his spear threateningly. "I'll wipe that bloody grin off your face if you don't wipe it off yourself."

"Try it. I'll cut your liver out and eat it while you watch," replied Murdoch.

"You may as well leave off your high airs, Murdoch. You'll be lucky if you even have a face when the Abbess is done with you."

Several hours later Murdoch, casually draped across the cot in his cell, heard the sound of keys jingling. There were a series of six doors, all locked, that had to be passed through to reach his cell, deep beneath the city. He listened, motionless, until he heard a key turning in the last door. Perhaps, he thought, they were going to make it just that easy for him. He lifted his head, shoving his hat back. The door stood wide, and just on the other side was the Abbess, dressed in her long robes, only her eyes visible through her veil. Behind her were dozens of soldiers, crammed into the narrow confines of the hall.

"Come to release the most holy member of your society?" asked Murdoch, not bothering to stand, watching the reactions of the soldiers, who all looked down when he spoke.

"I've told you before, Murdoch, you are only as powerful as I let you be," replied the Abbess, her voice soft enough to be barely audible to the guards behind her. "The people revere you, they honor you, and they fear you, but you are a stranger here. You cannot supersede the centuries of tradition, of law and order, and power that I personify. You went too far today. Much too far."

"Indeed? You arrested Henry's grandson and condemned him to mutilation like some commoner who's been caught fornicating, but *I'm* the one who went too far?"

The soldiers stared hard at their feet, not daring to look up.

"Stop looking at my guards for support. I have told them the story from the fragments of the Holy Book that you brought here, of how the Devil entered the tongues of the Prophets to lead them astray so that Ahab would fight a hopeless battle and die. I have told them that you may not be the true Prophet, Murdoch, but a devil may be speaking through you."

"And you will believe this woman, this Jezebel, above your own Prophet, the grandson of your beloved Henry?" asked Murdoch, casting a scornful glance over the hapless men.

"Stop it, Murdoch. They will not listen to you. Caught in a crux, the Lubrerites will follow their Abbess, not you."

"'The man that girdeth on his armor ought not boast as he that removes it,'" sneered Murdoch, quoting from the portion of the Bible he had given the Abbess on his arrival to Lubrerum. "So that's it, you came here to gloat about your own power versus mine?"

"No," she replied, her voice catching for a second. "No, Murdoch, I came to give you a chance to survive."

There was a disturbance behind her, someone pushing through the tightly compressed guards, and then Louis was standing before Murdoch, his wrists still in chains. In the tense silence between the two brothers, the veiled Abbess slid back down the hall, disappearing among the soldiers crowding the narrow passageway.

"You're free, Murdoch. With some constraints," said Louis. "You can come out."

"Old honey-tongued Lightfoot, at it again?" asked Murdoch, unfolding his legs and standing. "You ought to have been a politician."

"Well, brother, it's not quite . . . it's not quite what you think." Louis kept his head down as he spoke.

"What, then? Have these soldiers come to take me to my execution already?"

"No, you're free. You can go. There will be guards watching you, and you're not permitted to go outside the walls of Fluic Praem, but essentially you're free to move about the city as you did before."

Murdoch's face grew icy. "What did you do?"

"I . . . nothing really. I didn't do anything. You can go."

"Please, sir, come out of there. We need the cell for your brother now," said one of the guards nervously.

Murdoch didn't even acknowledge the terrified Lubrerite, his fierce gaze fixed on Louis. "What did you do?" he repeated.

"I . . . I made a sort of deal with the Abbess."

Murdoch waited for the full confession while the guards shifted impatiently, eager to be away from the two men who had brought so much trouble to their peaceful island. When his younger brother still did not expound, Murdoch pressed him again, words ground out through clenched teeth. "What deal, Louis?"

"I challenged the first Thrateer to a duel, Murdoch, for your life. If I win, then you are free. If I do not win, then you die."

Murdoch's thin lips tightened as he studied his brother. "It's a fight to the death."

Louis nodded. "Of course, yes. As is their custom."

"You fool. Did you think I would just let them execute me? Even now we could easily kill all these guards and escape. It would take only a few seconds."

The guards shifted and gripped their weapons tighter, recognizing the strange, fey exultancy in Murdoch's tone. Here was a dangerous man, as close to snapping as they had ever seen him. Louis stepped forward, lifting his chained hands to stay his brother.

"Not this time. There's too many of them. I made a bargain with the Abbess, and I intend to honor it, Murdoch. You would think less of me if I didn't."

"You assume it's possible for me to think less of you. If I leave the city, if I disappear, they'll kill you?"

Louis nodded.

"I should fight him."

"You can't. You can't fight for your own life here, but someone can fight for you, a champion, voluntarily. Plus, it's a joust. I've been watching them practice these last few weeks, so I understand how it's done, and, more importantly, I can sit a horse. I have to be the one. It's me or no one. Please, brother. Just . . . this one last thing."

Murdoch and Louis shared a hard stare, and Louis was not sure how much his brother read, though probably a great deal more than he wanted him to. He shuddered as the cold, scathing gaze dropped at last.

"They're sending out search parties, with those hounds of theirs, looking for someone that I have supposedly been writing to. I wonder if . . . if you get a chance, if you could find a way to ask a young priest we both know to pray for me," said Louis carefully, then, becoming suddenly more brusque, he went on, "Anyway, it's not as though I'm doing this for you, really. If I do this, the Abbess won't cut off my hands, my ears, my tongue, and whatever else she was planning to chop, probably my member. I'm just looking out for myself, brother, as always."

"Of course you are," replied Murdoch, and there was a strange catch in his voice, a catch that Louis had never heard there before.

CHAPTER 21

THE JOUST

It was pitch black as Cara wound her way through the streets of Fluic Praem, her dark eyes scanning every alley and open courtyard. Louis had described the grids of the city well, even drawing small maps and diagrams in his correspondence. She slipped from one dark shadow to another, all but invisible. There were no oil lamps in Fluic Praem, and she wondered if it was because there was no danger of outsiders nor fear of crime. She had noticed several patrols of knights, easily avoided in their straight, stereotypical marches. She did not know the rhythms of the city well enough to realize how odd these figures were in those peaceful golden avenues.

She had been prowling in circles in the southern grid where she knew her brothers' residence to be for nearly an hour but still had not identified the house where they stayed. There was a sense of some deep restiveness about the city. Even at that late hour, shutters opened and then slammed shut, figures paced in their homes, children were awake and crying. It was not the calm before a storm, but the trepidation, the soul-crushing, bone-gnawing anxious energy of an army before they launch into battle.

Even in the night she could tell that Fluic Praem was beautiful, extraordinarily beautiful. If the sun had been up, it would have been breathtaking, the gold and silver catching the light of the great star, sending lances of pure gilt light shimmering along the walls of the volcano that towered overhead. The courtyards were full of flowering and fruiting trees and plants, and the tropical smells were intoxicating. Then another scent hit her nose, the scent she had been looking for all along, an acrid whiff of tobacco, wildly out of place in that pristine city. She flattened herself against a wall, scanning the houses around her, and, at last caught sight of the tiny flicker of embers in a pipe bowl, held by a man lounging in a hammock strung between two columns under a gold-shingled roof. She paused, searching the streets, surprised to find multiple knights standing guard near the low wall of the residence.

She flattened herself to the street and slid along the ground like a serpent and then over the low courtyard wall. Perfectly silent, she slithered toward the man in the hammock, hardly daring to breathe. She was soundless, she thought proudly. In her whole life she did not think she had ever crept so quietly. She allowed herself a faint smile as she dared to hope that for the first time she would be the one to startle Murdoch. Then a harsh, gravelly voice, impossibly quiet, dashed her briefly held dreams.

"Hello, Cara."

She let out a sigh and rolled over onto her back, gazing up at her brother, dangling in his hammock above her. She was just at the edge of the mosaic floor, still lying in the grass, her dark clothes blending into the green. For a moment she wondered vaguely if, in light of the danger they had all been through, it would be customary for ordinary siblings to embrace during a meeting like this.

"Come to check on your beloved brothers?"

"It's been four days. You didn't come."

"Has Esperanza had her baby yet?"

"No. Not yet, but any moment. Why have you not come? Where is Louis?"

"Are you really going to interrogate me out here when there are eight guards posted just outside the walls of the courtyard?"

She turned her head and scanned the street. "I counted six."

"Count again."

After a brief pause she whispered, "I still get six."

"Pathetic," murmured Murdoch in disgust. "I'm going to stand up, at which point you will need to become one with me, and we will move like that into that room, just ahead and to the left. They need to see only one person walking, understand?"

Cara nodded.

As Murdoch slid his long legs over the hammock, she rose to stand directly behind him, making sure her own frame was lost in his silhouette. Then, moving with the same ungainly, awkward steps, they shuffled together into one of the few fully enclosed rooms of the house. Once inside she flattened herself against the wall, trying to increase the distance between herself and her brother.

"Where's Louis?" she asked. "Why do you have guards? Why are there hounds baying in the forest, as if on the hunt?"

"Maybe I always have guards and need to evade hounds every time I come to see you."

"Shut up, Murdoch. I need answers, not glib, sarcastic responses. We are waiting to leave. I need to know that we are all getting out of this alive, that nothing has gone wrong."

"We are not all getting out of this alive, and something has definitely gone wrong. Is that better?"

"What happened? And where the hell is Louis?"

"He's in prison."

"In prison?!"

Murdoch clamped a hand over her mouth, muffling his sister's exclamation. "God. Sometimes I think we are two birds of a kind, Cara, other times it strains credulity to believe we're even related. Conspiracy to lead Lubrerites from their homeland or something of that nature. Writing also—you aren't allowed to write here. They'll chop your hands off."

Cara's breath caught in her throat. "Tell me they didn't chop Louis' hands off."

"They haven't. Not yet, anyway."

"Why are you so casual about all this? Let's go set him free, and then we can leave, tonight. No more lazing around, smoking your pipe. We have to get out of here."

Murdoch shook his head.

"Why not?"

"You don't make the plans, Cara. If you go to break him out, it's over, we're all dead. No one asked you to come here. Go back to your safe little island. Watch out for hounds on the way back, though. They know there are trespassers lurking somewhere. They think you are on Lubrerum itself."

"They already knew there were trespassers on Lubrerum. At least, the Abbess did."

Murdoch raised his eyebrows, waiting for her explanation.

"When I went to get the Favor of God from the Holy of Holies, I . . . the Abbess caught me there. She let me go, because she could tell I was a Firefax."

"Interesting," Murdoch mused, then shrugged. "Well, that's neither here nor there now. Go back to Rafael. Everything is under control."

Cara stared at him, feeling numb, but angry, feeling as if she needed to say something that had been burning inside her for months. Perhaps this would be her last chance to say it to this strange, hideous man who had so upended and destroyed her life. She drew herself up tall. "You're wrong, you know."

"Wrong about what?"

"You think your apathy makes you stronger and better than the rest of us. You think by not caring about anyone or anything you've given yourself some preternatural power. You didn't leave Maralah all those years ago because you were angry with Robert, you left because you were starting to care about your family, and you thought that would make you weak. So you ran away. You took family, and attachment, and love out of the equation and thought it made you stronger. Then you came back all these years later to prove it, that you were beyond the ability to love, even your own family. That no matter what happened to us, you could not be induced to care. But you're wrong. Your layers of apathy make you less powerful. Imagine if you did care, how hard someone with your skills and abilities would fight for those he loved."

Murdoch chuckled. "Love is weakness, little sister, especially for a Firefax. Didn't Robert teach you that? You imagine what your victims' family and friends will experience when their loved ones are gone, because you know those feelings yourself. Sentiment impairs your judgment, it distracts you. You miss things."

"I'm not the one who's missing something, Murdoch."

"Says the girl who only counted six guards around my enclosure."

Cara clenched her teeth. She felt like a foolish child, a stupid, naive little girl, before a cruel, taunting bully. "Murdoch, I know you've been hiding something from the rest of us this whole time. You still are. What are you not telling us?"

"Nothing of vital importance," he replied, smiling half to himself, but the grin faded, for once, into a serious expression. "Cara, you're going to have to trust me this time. The half-cocked scheme you've come up with in the last thirty seconds is not going to work. Go back to Rafael, help Esperanza have her baby, and wait."

After a moment she sighed, letting the pent-up frustration wash out of her like water slipping over the lip of a dam. "When can we expect you?"

"Tomorrow night, you can expect me along with Louis, and the crew we've found for the *Apostle*."

"Why don't we just abandon the idea of the *Apostle*? We could break Louis out right now, take the cutter and get out of here. We've made modifications to it over the last few months, added more oars and oarlocks. With the experience the two of you have aboard ship, and the food stores I've saved up, we can make it to the mainland with just the cutter."

"We're not doing that. Now go. Tomorrow, after dark. Be ready."

Cara nodded, biting her lip. Murdoch aided her in walking, melded as one person again, across the mosaic tiles. Once she was in the grass and he had deposited himself in his hammock again, she began to slither back the way she had come, pausing abruptly at the sound of Murdoch's voice.

"Cara."

She turned back, almost afraid to hear what he had to say.

"Louis asked if Rafael could pray for him."

She felt a tight band constricting her throat but nodded and, finding her voice again, said, "He already does, you know. He prays for all of us, every day. But . . . I'll tell him."

The journey back to the island was much slower and more cautious. She was no longer delighted by her invisibility; instead, she was overwhelmed by concern for Louis, for Rafael, Esperanza, herself, and for the plan that had apparently fallen apart. In the distance, the howls of Lubrerum's hunting hounds punctured the air like the bloodcurdling shrieks in a nightmare. It was nearing dawn when Cara emerged from the water at last onto their islet, the high-pitched moans of the hounds still baying as the first light appeared, glowing in the east.

Rafael was waiting outside the entrance to the cave, limping as he paced. He ran to her and grabbed her shoulders in a fierce, viselike grip. "I didn't know where you were! I woke up and you were gone, Cara, gone! I've been worried sick. What's happened?"

"There's been a bit of a setback, but we're still leaving, just not yet. As you can hear, the hunt is on for us, so we haven't much time. Murdoch says he'll come, with Louis, and a crew, tonight."

"Why would they be hunting us, now? More than eight weeks we've been here and no one has come looking. Are they all right?"

"For now they are, I think. As much information as I could get out of Murdoch."

"Was Louis there?"

"No. I guess he's run afoul of their laws—he's in prison."

"In prison?!"

"Yes. But Murdoch . . . Murdoch says he has a plan."

"He always has a bloody plan. Look where that keeps getting us!"

Cara felt strangely detached. Sodden, she shivered from the breeze. She stared at Rafael's scowl, blinking back her own exhaustion. "Louis asked for you to pray for him. That's what Murdoch said, anyway. And he says we must be ready tonight."

"Pray for him about what?"

"I don't know. He's in prison, something about that, I'm sure. You're the minister, Rafael."

"You went into Fluic Praem? Do you have a letter for me?"

The siblings turned in surprise toward the cave entrance. Esperanza was standing there with a strangely soft, hopeful expression.

"No, no letter today," said Cara wearily, annoyed. "If you

need paper to shred I'm sure Rafael can spare a few pages from his Bible."

"I . . . I just wondered," replied Esperanza, suddenly imperious and cold again. She turned brusquely on her heel, calling back, "If it's not tonight, Cara, then I swear I will turn myself over to the Abbess so I can get a little rest in a real bed. Even if they chop my head off for stealing their holy water, it'll be worth it to finally get a good night's rest."

In Fluic Praem the morning dawned slowly but relentlessly. Murdoch watched it from a perch on the high wall of the arena on the outskirts of Fluic Praem. A white gleam above the eastern rim of the volcano gradually grew, at first mixing gently with the darkness to form a soft gray, and then a slight pink tinge appeared at the center of the gray. The faintest peach hue began to color the harvested fields of Lubrerum. The pink gradually overwhelmed the gray-white and the peach, then faded, leaving a washed-out blue pallor behind. Beyond the borders of the mountain walls, beyond Murdoch's line of sight, a rosy light in the east brightened until a fierce orb of colored fire appeared. Phantom rays of beauty spread, alighting upon the dewy stalks of grass and shrubs speckling the mountainside, turning them from gray shafts to long green tendrils, glittering, spangled with bright, incandescent pearls of liquid. As the light became full, Murdoch heard a late rooster lamenting the end of night and the coming of a new day.

There were fourteen Thrateers in Lubrerum, each with their own knights, and they had all set up camp around the arena the night before. Their tents dotted the green lawn; white canvas spattered with bright emblems and insignia. Through the night each of the Thrateers, save Prost, who needed rest before the battle, had kept their traditional vigil, praying for justice to be done in the coming contest. Outside their colorful yet solemn tents, a holiday atmosphere pervaded. It had been many years since an earnest joust had been fought in Lubrerum. Families were coming through the arena doors to take their seats in the golden stands or upon the lawn. The smell of the smoke from the knights' cooking fires filled the air. The babble of voices chattering grew suddenly more excited, and Murdoch watched as a troop of guards led Louis, still in chains, to the tent that had been prepared for him. Murdoch unfolded his legs and slipped down the stairs. By the tent flaps he paused as the guards blocked him for a moment, but then, at a nod from the armored knight supervising them, they stepped aside.

"He'll need a squire to help him into his armor," explained the knight.

Louis had been unchained inside the tent, though the guards still stood uncomfortably close to him. He unconsciously rubbed at his wrists, staring at the suit of armor arrayed carefully on a table. He glanced up at Murdoch for an instant, then past him as the tent flaps lifted and another guard appeared carrying a steaming silver tray. With a slight bow, the man set the tray on the table beside the armor and backed away. After a few minutes, all the guards slipped outside, leaving the two brothers alone.

"Last meal?" asked Louis ruefully.

"Only if you let Prost beat you."

"Touché, brother." Louis lifted the cover on the tray, revealing steaming fish fillets, sliced avocados, and fried plantains. Arranged around the rest of the tray were an assortment of various fruits and vegetables, a steaming cup of dark liquid, and a small bejeweled bowl with a silver spoon protruding from a thick, beaded pudding.

"Caviar?" asked Louis in a dubious voice, poking at the pudding with the spoon.

Murdoch nodded.

"Oh, joy," said Louis. "Well, you can certainly have all of that if you like. What's this?" He leaned forward, studying the murky steaming liquid in a ceramic cup. He picked it up, sniffed it, and wrinkled his nose. "It smells almost like . . . great God in heaven! It's coffee! Here I thought they had no idea how to use those plants. They're scattered all over like weeds, but I've never seen them make it into a beverage. There's goat's milk cream and cane sugar to go with it. Well, if Prost kills me, I'll die happy for having a bit of this in my stomach. Here, try some!"

Murdoch acquiesced to the request. It was indeed coffee, but different from any he had drunk before, sweet and almost buttery. It tasted familiar and comforting.

"I know you didn't care for Katerina," said Louis, as if reading Murdoch's mind. "That's what Henry told me, anyway. But you have to admit, her coffee was something special. This isn't quite like it, but there's a hint of it there." Then he laughed, musing for a moment, his eyes taking on a distant look, as if lost in pleasant memories. "Coffee in the morning, with Katerina, Henry's little ones squalling all around, Cara and Rafael bickering about something, Henry just blabbering on. Those were the days I forgot the work I did. Forgot I was a Firefax." He prodded at the fish and plantain but only ate a few bites. Finally he pushed the tray away. "Anyway, I hope you know something about how to attach this armor. I'm not entirely sure which part goes where, honestly."

The gambeson and the chain mail tunic were easy enough, as were the chain mail trousers, but when it came to the confounding array of vambraces, gauntlets, couters, greaves, and poleyns the brothers were at a loss. Even the helmet presented problems.

"Makes me wish I had paid just a little more attention to the lessons Robert taught about ancient forms of armor and weaponry. I never thought they would actually be useful. It's 1781, after all," said Louis as Murdoch was trying for the third time to buckle a gleaming, curved metal plate around his calf. "You've been very quiet this morning. Are you all right?"

Murdoch said nothing, continuing to fiddle with the leather strap.

"Don't think I blame you," Louis went on. "It was my own damn fault. I got caught, I trusted that baker's apprentice. You warned me."

"I know that," said Murdoch, straightening and glancing up for an instant, annoyance plain on his face. "When have I ever felt guilty?" he snapped, before he could stop himself. Having let that much slip, he allowed himself to go a little further. "I've done unspeakable things, things that would make the blood of ordinary men run cold, all without an ounce of remorse. Why would I care about what happens today, Louis?"

"That's what I wondered," replied Louis, with infuriating compassion. Yet as much as it infuriated Murdoch, it also soothed him. He returned to his work, concentrating all his attention on the ten long, sweating fingers before him as he manipulated the buckles and twisted the screws. All too soon he had everything attached and there was nothing left to distract him. When he started to stand, Louis dropped down on one knee beside him, placing his gloved hand firmly on Murdoch's shoulder.

"I'm sorry, Murdoch. I'm really, deeply, immensely sorry for everything. Everything, I mean it. If you need to say anything, to slap me across the face, please, go ahead. I wouldn't blame you."

"I don't need a confidant. I don't need your pity or your apologies, Louis. Christ, I didn't need you to sign up for this fight for me." Murdoch pushed Louis' hand away from his shoulder and stood.

"I know, but I was spared death for some purpose, some reason. I think this may be it. I . . . I have a favor to ask, Murdoch."

"What's that?"

"My child will be born any day, maybe any moment."

"You don't want me to watch out for your child, Louis."

"Because of Istäni? Because of what he turned out to be? But you're not the same person you were when you raised him. I've asked Rafael already, but he will need to go to seminary to fulfill his calling, and I don't want to hold him back from that. Murdoch, there's no one I trust more to watch out for my wife and my child's safety if I can't be there for them."

"I didn't think it was possible, but have you grown stupider? Did they knock you upside the head when they arrested you? Late effects of the poison?"

"Come on, Murdoch, be serious. I could die out there!"

"You're not going to die. You're a Firefax, aren't you? You're going to beat that pompous idiot and then we're all leaving this cursed place tonight. That's it."

A loud blast from the trumpets cut off their conversation, calling the combatants forth to the lists. Louis looked down at himself, in his stiff, gleaming armor with a blue cloth tunic emblazoned with a red rose hanging over it. He raised his head, staring at Murdoch with a pleading expression—a familiar, pleading expression. For an instant Murdoch was transported back to a small, pale, almost white-haired child, reaching up toward him, begging to be picked up, to be held.

"Fuck you. If you die, Louis, and you're not going to, I will make sure no harm comes to this stupid child you've decided to create with that odious excuse for a woman."

"Thank you," whispered Louis, a peaceful expression coming over his beautiful face. "Out of curiosity, why did you raise Istäni?"

Murdoch shrugged. "To see what he would become, I suppose. Why did you ask the Abbess if you could be my champion?"

"That's easy. Because you're my brother, Murdoch, and I love you."

Then Louis put on his helmet, picked up his shield, and stepped out through the tent door to the call of the trumpets beyond. Murdoch followed his brother, but the guards blocked him from going to the inner ring of the arena, instead leading him up into the stands to a box to the right of the Abbess. It appeared that every human inhabitant of Lubrerum had gathered in the arena. From the youngest toddler to the oldest crone, they sat in the stands or crowded behind the fence on the grass. He was dimly aware of nearly every conversation around him from his many years of habitual awareness, but he kept his eyes pinned on Louis, letting the conversations he could discern melt into the general, inexhaustible drone of voices—the voices of hundreds, no, thousands of people eager to see his brother's blood spilled on the sand of the lists.

The two warriors mounted their horses, each awaiting the signal of the Abbess, who sat in her chair, apparently unaffected by the excitement around her and lost in her own reflections. Eventually she straightened a little and looked down at the two men waiting below. She nodded and the two combatants maneuvered their nervous, dancing horses into their starting positions along the tilt that divided them. Then the crowd grew quieter, as Prost and Louis advanced toward each other slowly, reining their horses to an impatient walk. Their steeds were high-stepping, enormous creatures, their bloodlines supplemented every few decades with imports brought by the Firefaxes. They snorted and danced as they drew closer, their harnesses jingling and peytrals swinging. Louis rode a stout, muscular bay with feathers on his feet, while Prost was mounted on a dappled gray horse. When they were close enough to nearly touch each other, Louis' bay shied suddenly and rose a few inches off the ground on his back legs. Louis managed to calm him, rubbing his hand soothingly along the horse's already sweating neck, draped in embroidered cloths. The animal continued forward, drawing up to his opponent and then halting as the two men studied each other. They drew their swords and raised them together, locking the blades, and turning their eyes submissively to the Abbess, who nodded again. Resheathing their swords the combatants turned, kicking their horses to a fast trot back to the end of the tilt. Two young knights raced forward and handed each rider a lance. Then the combatants waited, while every eye in the arena, virtually every eye in Lubrerum, turned to Abbess Seänkea.

Her bright green eyes swept the field, the lists, the crowd, finally landing on Murdoch as she raised her hand, holding a scarlet kerchief. A faint breeze tugged at the sheer slip of fabric, on which the lives of two men hinged, as total silence descended on the arena. Never taking her eyes off Murdoch, the Abbess let the fragment of cloth drop and the trumpets sounded.

The trumpets died away, lost amid the thundering of the destriers' hooves on the turf. Louis was crouching low in his saddle, urging the bay on. Prost had kicked his horse's flanks a second later than his opponent. Murdoch noted that split-second delay. Prost had it all calculated; he was gauging his adversary before he chose where to aim, how to ride, what strategy to use. As they grew faster and faster it seemed that the lists were growing longer. There was no sound, not even a whisper, not the sound of bird or breath, only the trampling of the horses' hooves. The men brought their lances to bear. Louis, with all the cocky assurance of a beginner, aimed straight for his enemy's head, a sure downfall and almost certain death for Prost if he could hit the helmet accurately. The sharp tips of the lances gleamed in the noonday sun, flashing prongs of death. Prost aimed his lance at Louis' chest and held it straight and true, never wavering.

For a few seconds it seemed to Murdoch that they would never reach one another. The world was not ready for such a clash; somehow, they would stop short, or veer, or their lances would not hit anything at all. It was all a game, some joke on the part of the Abbess, and she would rise, signal the end, and they would all laugh at him. Of course they would laugh at him, because he was sitting there, leaning forward, grinding his teeth and holding his breath, like a fool; like a man who cared what happened that bright October day.

Having almost convinced himself that it was all a dream or a silly game, he was startled when he heard the crash of their impact and his body involuntarily jumped in his seat. Louis only managed to graze his opponent's shoulder, his lance buffeted easily aside, leaving no damage. But Prost's lance held true, though Louis' shield did slow the impact and glanced the sharp point away from his heart. Still the tip of the lance drove straight through the cloth tunic, the breastplate, and the chain mail, straight into Louis' chest. Murdoch leaned further forward, his fists clenched, cognizant of the Abbess' eyes upon him. The lance hoisted Louis bodily into the air, carrying him several yards before it tore loose and he smashed to the waiting earth below. Louis let out a cry of pain as he fell, but it was cut short by his landing, as all the breath was knocked from his body.

After the impact it took Prost a few minutes to get his

horse under control. The gray was fighting madly against his master, angry at being pulled up so sharply, maddened by the sound of metal striking metal and the impact that the blow had taken upon both him and his rider as they reeled. If there had been anywhere to bolt to, the animal would have, but the lists were enclosed and the rearing, bucking destrier only smashed into the arena wall. Finally, grudgingly, the enormous horse yielded to his master and allowed Prost to direct his movements. Prost shouted something and a knight raced out, replacing the Thrateer's shattered lance with an enormous mace. Louis was stirring by then, but slowly. He had rolled onto his stomach and was holding himself halfway up with his arms. There was blood draining from his chest, a steady flow of dark maroon streaming into the sand, and he was taking slow, gasping breaths. He looked around, seeking his own horse, but, with the rider dismounted, a knight had led the panicking bay off the field of battle.

Prost, with a cry of exultation, spun his horse and the thunder of hooves filled the air again as the animal bore down on the fallen Firefax. Louis was on his knees, and though he knew what was bearing down on him, still he moved with agonizing slowness. He turned just as the horse reached him, and threw himself from the animal's path, a hoof striking his leg. He rolled, as Prost pulled his horse up too sharply for the animal to bear, and it rose high on its haunches, front legs flailing, almost toppling over backwards. But Prost was a skilled rider and managed to readjust the horse's balance, turning him as his feet struggled to find ground. The horse wheeled at his rider's direction, and brought his front hooves straight down, just as Louis rolled onto his back. Louis cried out as the enormous hooves struck his armored chest and stomach. Instinctively the animal had risen again almost immediately, trained for years not to step on a human. But still Prost drove his weaponized steed on, digging his spurs hard into the gray's flanks. Then the arena was nothing but a senseless whirling melee of hooves, sand, blood, grunts of pain, and the screams of a panicked horse as it was made to dance upon the fallen warrior. Louis rolled frantically, but he could not escape all of the relentless blows.

Then a cry of surprise went out, not from the fighters but from the crowd, as the horse bolted. Louis was clinging to Prost's armored leg, dangling beneath the belly of the frantic destrier as it galloped around the arena, seeking an escape route, seeking to shake its clanking, clinging, bleeding attachment. Prost, thrown off at first, leaned heavily to the right, away from Louis, trying to balance the weight. The horse stumbled badly, stepping on Louis' dragging legs.

Prost hoisted his mace and brought the weapon down on Louis' helmeted head. The angle was poor, and Prost could not bring the full force of his strength upon the younger man, but it was enough, and Louis' movements became slower, as if he were dazed. Murdoch could see his brother's grasp on Prost's leg weakening. Louis, nearly battered to unconsciousness, still clung with one hand to the knight's leg; with the other arm he reached down to his belt and drew a small knife. Prost let out a cry as Louis' plunged the blade repeatedly into the knight's relatively unprotected calf, behind his greave.

The horse began bucking frantically, rhythmic, bounding leaps. Prost let out a roar and brought his mace down again, but his aim was thrown off by the wild lurching movements of his horse, and he struck another glancing blow to Louis' head, knocking his helmet askew, then striking his arm and causing Louis to drop the knife. Prost raised and swung the weapon again, but Louis had lost his death grip on the stirrup at last and rolled through the sand, away from the mounted knight. Unfortunately for Prost, he had put too much force into his final swing and the mace embedded itself in his own leg and struck the side of the horse at the same time. Already crazed, the animal screamed, reared up and fell onto its back, crushing the knight into the bloody sand of the arena. With Prost dismounted, the animal, free at last, struggled to its feet and ran trembling and bleeding around the arena before finally slowing and standing expectantly at the gate.

The two armored combatants lay in sad, broken heaps. This time Louis struggled to his feet first, though Murdoch could not be sure how. His brother was battered beyond belief. He tore his helmet the rest of the way off, setting his bloody, tangled locks free. One side of his face had become nothing more than a mass of congealing blood. Even his eye was obscured beneath mangled, swelling skin. His right arm dangled uselessly at his side. Staggering, he drew his sword with his left hand and advanced on Prost. Unexpectedly Louis reeled, toppling to his knees, but caught his balance there and forced himself up again. Prost, standing with agonizing, painful slowness, yanked his bloody mace from where it was embedded in his left leg with a moan of agony, and then, using the mace as a crutch to stay upright, drew his own sword and turned to face his advancing opponent.

It was painful to watch their slow movements, and the glancing, awkward blows they traded, arcs of blood drops spattering from their bodies as they moved, graceless, broken men, exhausted nearly to the point of death. Back and forth they hewed pointlessly at one another, until at last, Louis swung and missed, losing his grip on his sword, which hurtled through the air to land point first a few yards away.

Weaponless, Louis crouched in a defensive posture. Prost dropped his own sword and raised the mace, its head crusted with bits of chain mail, sand, flesh, and blood that spattered as he stumbled forward, gimping horribly. He swung the weapon at Louis, who managed to duck, but so clumsily that he lost his footing, leaving the opening Prost wanted. Crying out in triumph, Prost caught Louis with a raking, terrible blow across his abdomen as he fell. Prost swung the heavy weapon again, bringing it down on his enemy's back as Louis struggled vainly to escape. Louis rolled onto his back and raised his arms, shielding his face instinctively. Murdoch waited, breathless, knowing what the only possible outcome of such a battle would be. Prost lifted the mace again, but just then Louis went still, his arms slackening over his face. The Thrateer kicked Louis' arms aside, standing over him, staring down, trying to make out if he had already won and the younger man was dead.

Louis' eyes were shut tight, the blood on his face crusted with sand and grit, but he was not dead, he was grimacing in pain. He stirred and instantly Prost raised his weapon high over his head again and swung the killing blow at Louis' unprotected head. At the last possible second, Louis' eyes snapped open and he rolled out of the path of the mace, and then lunged upward, with something of his old grace and agility. He latched onto Prost's helmeted head.Prost, exhausted, reeled under the weight of his opponent. He shook Louis off, once, but in an instant the younger man was on him again, knocking him to the ground. Then, pinning the Thrateer down with his body weight, Louis thrust his left hand under the man's helmet, tearing it off and wrapping his fingers around Prost's neck. He clung on as the exhausted Prost bucked and flailed, striking him with his own mailed hands, but to no avail. Finally the first Thrateer's thrashing movements grew slower, more feeble, until at last they stopped altogether. Still Louis held on, seemingly unaware that Prost had stopped fighting. Finally he drew his hand back, staring at it strangely. He looked up at all the people around him, horror scrawled across his battered face. Then, without a sound, he toppled over in the sand beside his vanquished foe.

All Murdoch could hear were the awful gasps of the armored man lying in the sand. The armor, once silver and bright, was plastered with blood, sand, and grass. He heard something else, a fly buzzing, and he startled as it settled on an ugly, bloody gash across Louis' once-perfect face. Above him he knew that the second Thrateer was whispering in the Abbess' ear, but he could not make out the words.

Then a sound, so loud in the stillness that it made everyone wince, caused all eyes to turn from the ghastly, bloody scene of the arena to the Abbess' box. Spiogni, standing beside the Abbess, had struck his sword against his shield, sending out a ringing noise, reverberating across the silent battlefield.

"Never, in all of my years, have I seen a joust to equal this. The prisoner has shown himself strong beyond belief. But, the victor cannot be pronounced such until he has stood and made homage to our Abbess. Only then can he be declared the winner of this contest. If he cannot perform this rite, then his life is forfeit, as is that of the man he calls brother. These are, and have always been, the mandates of our jousts."

Again silence fell like a suffocating blanket. The heavy noonday sun beat down mercilessly upon Louis' still form. No one moved or spoke as minutes slipped past. Time had slowed, and with each second it seemed the balance for two lives was going up against the counterweight of archaic, chivalric codes. The people began to fidget, turning their eyes to the second Thrateer, who gazed almost longingly at the fallen men on the field. The Abbess did not move, her face unreadable. After a long time, with one darted, sorrowful glance at Murdoch, she raised her hand. The second Thrateer, for the first time in his life, hesitated before obeying his mistress. But still there was no movement from Louis, lying in an ever-growing pool of blood, steadily moving past hope of help. The Thrateer reluctantly nodded to his guards on the arena floor and they drew their swords and started forward.

Murdoch was dripping sweat, and there was something irritating and wet in his eyes. He blinked hard, noting his own guards drawing their weapons just outside his box. His mind felt dull, but it still mechanically calculated the moves he would need to make to escape. He could get out but Louis was lost, even if he could survive his injuries. Then someone let out a gasp, and Murdoch rose, unable to believe what he was seeing, his mouth gaping, eyes locked on his brother's battered form.

The pile of metal and bloody blue fabric stirred and then, with a painful thump, rolled over. There was a gentle moan, growing just a little bit louder, then more high-pitched, like the whining of a dog, then fading. The mutilated young man came up, just an inch, and then another, his hands grinding into the sand. He let himself fall once, panting, but, clenching his teeth, he pushed himself up again, drawing his knees inward, then paused, gasping, his face twisted in agony. Murdoch was not breathing. He watched as Louis jerked forward, a horrible hacking sound filling the air, all the remaining contents of his stomach heaving up, then came bile, and then nothing but ragged, tortured breathing. But Louis did not fall forward this time. There was nothing to hold on to, nothing to pull his aching, shattered body up with, and he paused briefly, resting on his knees. He sat there, his head bowed onto his chest. In that moment Murdoch's own breathing began again, the rhythm matching the labored gasps of his brother. No one spoke, no one moved, no one believed what they were watching. A twisting, wrenching agony hit Murdoch in the pit of his stomach. Louis lifted one knee, till his metal-clad foot was firmly planted in the sand and he was kneeling, facing away from Murdoch, toward the Abbess. An eternity slipped by before he gathered himself for one last surge of strength, and then, miraculously, Louis was standing, swaying and unsteady, but he was standing.

Louis lurched two steps forward, dragging one leg, and nodded his head, his hand pressed against his heart. The Abbess rose, without a word, and there was something strange in her eyes, something Murdoch could not read. Then the Abbess herself bowed, not a simple curtsy—no, the Abbess of Lubrerum dropped to her knees in the stands. All around the arena the people followed their Mother Superior's lead. The sigh that issued from the wounded young man seemed to fill the whole silent arena. Then Louis turned slowly. His face was still recognizable, though pitiably masked by blood, bruises, and lacerations. Murdoch could plainly see his piercing blue eyes as they swept over the audience and settled at last upon his older brother. Haunted, beautiful eyes in a body ruined by an unimaginable ordeal. As Murdoch stared, the stricken knight faded into the vision of a small boy, still in skirts, skin like alabaster, white-gold ringlets framing his round face and pleading blue eyes.

Murdoch thought there was sweat dripping into his own eyes. Frustrated, he wiped it away. Then his little brother raised his arms, stretching them toward him, and he heard a strangled, gasping, tormented whine and realized in shock that the sound wasn't coming from Louis but from himself.

Murdoch scrambled through the boxes and benches and vaulted over the side of the arena, pushing his way through the crowd, shoving men and women aside, leaping over the fence and into the lists just as Louis went down again, wilting like grass before a fire. There was a soft crunch as his mailed body crumpled in the sand, face down. Murdoch ran, staggering. He did not know quite what was wrong with him, but his legs barely seemed able to hold him up in the centuries that it took to reach Louis' side. He was relieved to finally drop to his knees beside the still body. A fly buzzed about them; Murdoch waved it away bitterly and turned his brother over. Two perfect blue eyes stared without comprehension from white and purpling flesh and congealed, drying blood. Murdoch pressed his ear against his little brother's armored, blood-covered chest, listening for a sound he could not find. There was still sweat dripping into his eyes, he thought. It had to be sweat; what else could it be? He heard the fly buzzing again, and then going quiet as it settled on his brother's face. Then his whole body began shaking. It was as if he had no control over himself anymore. He heaved, his breathing coming in sudden, gasping jerks, as he buried his face in Louis' unmoving chest.

The heaving stopped for an instant, and he waited, perfectly still, like the unmoving, unbreathing body beneath his head. A voice, the only voice that could have penetrated his consciousness in that moment, suddenly broke into his dazed mind. It was just a far-off gurgle at first, but slowly, words, low, strangled, gasping, slurred, and almost completely incomprehensible, formed by his ear.

"You must've . . . asked Raf to pray . . ."

The awful, agonizing sound caused Murdoch's entire body to slump and he began to gulp fresh air, to breathe again. "You idiot," he said, lifting himself up to look at his brother's face.

Louis struggled to speak. Finally he managed, "Not . . . nice, Murdoch." After a pause as Louis trembled from pain, he spoke again, his voice a little more clear, yet farther away and so quiet that Murdoch had to lean closer to hear the words. "I guess it's . . . over . . . now."

"Listen to me, Louis," said Murdoch, his frenzied gentleness giving way to an even more frenzied anger as his brother seemed to fade a little, strangely, as if he was losing his presence in the reality that Murdoch and everyone else in the arena occupied. "Listen to me! It's not over. You should be dead, do you hear me?

You should be dead, but you're not, because you're too strong. Do you understand? You are too strong to die. You have a wife, and a baby coming, you have brothers and a sister who need you. You're not going to die, Louis Firefax. Is that fucking clear?"

The cloudy blue eyes seemed to grow clear and sparked for an instant with mischief. "Big brother . . . always so bossy." He passed out for a second, and Murdoch felt the now-familiar churning pain in his gut. He shook his brother's shoulder and Louis was back.

"Don't," said Louis, frowning. "Hurts."

"I know it hurts, but you're going to be fine. Are you fucking listening to me? You're going to be just fine." He was astounded by the gentleness of his strident voice. It sounded like someone else was speaking through him. His hands were shaking, and he was terrified, but the voice was calm, determined, sure.

Louis stared up at him, face twisting in agony, and then spoke one clear word. "Home?" Then his whole body grew rigid and he trembled so violently that Murdoch leaped back, fearful that his brother was seizing. The shaking fit passed and Louis sighed.

"Little brother," said Murdoch, reflecting bitterly that he had never before said that phrase without irony. "Little brother, I can't take you home. But I will take you to the doctors. I'm . . . I'm going to pick you up, and it's going to hurt like hell."

Louis shook his head vigorously, terror in his ice-blue eyes.

"I have to, Louis. Look, the clouds are becoming jealous of your pallor, and I believe we could fill a lake with the blood you're still losing. I'll be as gentle as I can."

Then Murdoch, more tenderly than he would have lifted a newborn, slid his arms under his brother's battered form and picked him up. Despite the armor, the body of his brother felt small and light, and Louis, fading in and out of consciousness, reached his left arm impulsively up and wrapped it around his brother's neck as Murdoch carried him slowly from the battlefield.

Murdoch could feel Louis' blood seeping down his own torso. He shuddered at the droplets falling like rain as he walked, streaming down his arms and legs and dripping onto the ground below, leaving a spattered trail behind him. The crowd was beginning to come alive again and they clamored around him, chattering and obstructing him as he walked.

"Leave him be!" the Abbess shouted as the crowd surged forward to surround Murdoch and his unhappy burden. "Let him pass!"

Murdoch made for the tent where he had so recently helped Louis into his armor, ignoring the people clustered in his path.

"Blue . . . ," Louis mumbled suddenly and Murdoch cocked his head, startled. "Then everything was . . . blue . . . ," Louis continued, trailing off, then his eyes opened wider, staring past Murdoch and up at the sky, his voice strengthening slightly. "We took the blue and made it red, the red we . . . ." He shuddered uncontrollably, and relapsed into silence as Murdoch began to walk faster. "The red we . . . bathed our babies in, and in the black of bloody days, we tied a knot in inky haze. On our backs they drew the cross, we carried it through torrid vales, and then in lofty clouds of gray, we lost ourselves in burnished white." He started to say more, frowning, and stumbling over the words. "Everlasting was our fall, and all we lost we lost for all, we found forever in their . . . trying . . . no . . . no . . . we found forever in their . . . can't remember. Can't remember."

Murdoch said nothing in reply, but his face had become almost as pale as his brother's.

"What's he saying?" asked someone pushing behind Murdoch, as Louis began his recitation over again.

Murdoch did not answer, but in his growing rage he jerked his elbow back into the face of the man who had asked the question. The man gasped and withdrew, clutching his nose as it gushed blood. The people who were crowding so anxiously after the two brothers fell back and watched as Murdoch ducked into Louis' tent, leaving a stain of blood upon the entrance flaps as he passed.

Louis shuddered, but otherwise he was still, his face waxy pale, almost translucent beneath the purplish, growing welts. Murdoch laid him down gently on the cot, and then the tent flap lifted again as the Abbess entered. Murdoch was trying with little success to undo some of the straps keeping Louis in his armor. The Abbess moved him aside and several more physicians joined her, carefully removing every strap and buckle, each plate and piece of chain mail that they lifted revealing a hideous wound beneath. Picking the tiny chain links out of the cuts made Louis scream and Murdoch became frantic, pacing angrily, until someone administered something sedating to his younger brother, and Louis was finally still again.

At last all the garments had been removed and Louis Firefax lay a bloody, shivering, insensate mess beneath a thin sheet, his breathing still ragged and uneven. Murdoch stood at his head, staring down as the physicians attempted to remove splinters, bits of chain mail, fragments of cloth, and grains of sand. The wound from the lance was horrific, crushing and tearing, caving his ribs in so they moved with a strange, paradoxical motion against the rhythm of the rest of his heaving chest.

"Woman," said Murdoch, turning his cold, dark eyes to the Abbess. "Fix him."

The Abbess took Murdoch's elbow and drew him aside.

"I am not a sorcerer, Murdoch, I cannot fix this. He is too broken. I can make him comfortable."

"Make him comfortable, by all means. But also fix him."

"I cannot."

"You will. Or I'll kill you."

"He knew what might happen. He knew what he was risking, Murdoch. He risked it anyway and he won your life but lost his own. There is *nothing* I can do."

"He's not going to die."

"He may as well already be dead, Murdoch."

Murdoch stepped forward, towering over the woman, and she looked up at him with her piercing green eyes, the faintest hint of fear in their depths.

"You owe me his life."

"How do you figure that?"

"You promised Istäni that you would kill us both, using your power and your wiles, and when he returned we would be dead. He couldn't kill us, that would set everyone against him. We are Firefaxes, the children of their Prophets. But you could ensnare us, and kill us lawfully here, in this hellhole. His injuries are your fault and you will fix them. Take him to the Holy of Holies and use your breathing machine, use every medicine you possess, all the skill you have at your disposal and make him well. If you don't do that, I promise you I will kill not only you but your son as well."

"He cannot be moved to the Holy of Holies, Murdoch! Are you not listening to me? Do you want me to kill him right now? He's bleeding—he's bleeding inside, he's bleeding everywhere. Every movement only quickens the bleeding. He would die before they got him ten minutes up the side of the volcano."

"Then your blood and the blood of your son will be upon your head," snapped Murdoch and turned toward the tent entrance.

"I've called off the hunt. No guards will be following you," said the Abbess. "I've read those letters, Murdoch. If . . . if there is someone on this island that loves him, you should bring her to him. As soon as you can. Tonight. He doesn't have long."

It was still early evening when Murdoch left for the islet. The light had not yet faded into the west. The Abbess had not lied—no one followed him through the forests, and he kept a keen eye out for any sign of watchers from the rim of the volcano, but saw no movements. The Lubrerites had returned to their homes to tell the story of the joust to the few that had not attended. It was the sort of event that the islanders would talk of for decades, if not centuries.

There was a strange, unfamiliar conflict within Murdoch. He did not like the feelings that had been aroused and was trying every strategy he had to crush them. Feelings of protectiveness, of anger, of sorrow, real sorrow, and something else, behind it all. Every time he saw in his mind's eye the image of another blow striking Louis, he tried to bury it under a memory of Louis as an Argonaut; arrogant, cocky, assured, and yet stupid, so immensely stupid for all his skill. This strategy had worked before, only a few days previously. But it wasn't working anymore, and the uncomfortable, painful sensations churned relentlessly in his chest and stomach.

He paused just under the cover of the bushes along the beach and waited, watching. The sun was setting, casting her long orange beams across the ocean, turning the sea before him a warm, comforting hue, like the glow of a hearth fire. Then, in a twinkling, the sun was gone, the moment had passed, and Murdoch took the familiar swim out to the island, emerging near the cave. For once Cara was not waiting out front; no one was. In the eerie quiet, Murdoch drew a knife from his boot and entered the cave warily. The fire was going, a steaming pot of water sizzling above it, the bubbles boiling over and sloshing onto the wood below, hissing. Then he heard the first agonized moan, and it set his heart racing. The memory of Louis, limp in his arms, clasping his bloody arm around his neck, surged to the forefront of his mind. He could feel the droplets of blood coursing down his body again. He shook his head and focused on the cave before him.

Esperanza was pacing behind the wall of her makeshift chamber, followed by Cara and Rafael, trying desperately to assuage her labor pains. Cara stepped out from the enclosure as Murdoch approached, wiping sweat from her brow. She appeared relieved, for once, to see her oldest brother.

"The baby is coming. I think. To be honest I don't know. She's been like this for hours—all day, since this morning, and now into the night. I can't tell if there's something wrong. The labors I attended in Wilmington were not like this. Halsey never labored so hard. Is that . . . is that blood on your shirt?"

Just then cries of rage drove Rafael from Esperanza's chamber as well and he darted from the enclosure, trembling. "Well, you see, we can't go tonight," he said apologetically upon catching sight of Murdoch. "I don't see how we could. Have you not brought Louis and the crew?"

Murdoch did not answer them, pushing past his siblings to enter Esperanza's chamber. Esperanza drew back at first in horror. She was drenched in sweat, clearly in agony, her hair plastered about her face. But there was something changed in her usually cruel dark eyes; a softening, a look of fear, her glances darting back and forth, as if looking for an escape, like a trapped, injured animal. He approached slowly, and she calmed and let him reach out and touch her abdomen, feeling carefully around the edges of her taut womb. Then, Rafael and Cara appeared at the entrance to her chamber and she almost hurled herself at them, screaming in rage and pain.

"Go," said Murdoch softly. "I'll help her."

For hours Cara and Rafael paced the cave, listening to the

screaming and moaning, the cries of rage and pain echoing off the dark stone walls, until they became numb to the sounds. Then, as the night passed dully through the middle mark, after a final horrific, screeching cry, an almost deafening silence fell. Cara sat up, sluggish and tired, alarmed by the sudden quiet, but then she heard the faint mewling cries of a newborn.

Breathlessly the siblings entered the separate room to find Esperanza lying quiet on her makeshift bed, a blanket spread over her sweaty, bloody form, reaching out to take the wriggling, slimy bundle that Murdoch extended to her. The baby was wrapped in Murdoch's own shirt, the shirt stained with the blood of the newborn's father, though the others did not know that yet. Esperanza was crying, silent tears streaming down her face as she clutched the infant to her naked bosom.

"Louis should be here. Louis should meet our son," she said suddenly, turning her tear-filled eyes toward Murdoch. "Did he not send a letter?"

Murdoch opened his mouth to speak, then shut it again and simply shook his head. Cara could see there was something Murdoch was not telling them, again, something important, something about the blood on his shirt. There was a haunted look, an almost human expression glittering in his unreadable black eyes.

"Then . . . I know you have paper and quill. I know one of you has been writing letters for me, I can tell by the words he sends. Let me write my own letter this time."

Cara brought her the paper, quill, and ink. By the light of a dim candle, with the infant suckling for the first time at her breast, Esperanza dashed off a few lines before sinking back onto her bed again, utterly exhausted, but triumphant.

"Take that to him, Murdoch. And don't come back without him this time, do you hear me?"

Murdoch nodded and stood. He left the dirty shirt wrapped around the infant, taking a relatively clean one from

Rafael, and corked the letter into the little glass bottle that he always carried in his visits to the cave. Then, without a word, he left.

He was faster on his return trip, desperately fast, but still it was nearly dawn when he reached the tent still set up outside the arena. There were no guards around it as before; indeed, it was perfectly silent, no scurrying movements, no muttering conversations, nothing. He paused for an instant at the tent's entrance, taking a slow, deep breath to quell the trembling of his hands, and then pushed his way inside.

The tent looked empty, but there was one human form lying prone on Louis' cot, stretched out, head pressed into its elbow. But it was not Louis. The form lying in his brother's place had long dark hair falling over its shoulders, glittering with strands of silver. He stepped forward, recognizing the smooth curves of the body on the bed. He had almost reached her side when she sat up and peered around in the darkness. Instinctively he paused.

"Is that you, Murdoch?" asked a woman's voice, deep and melodious.

"Of course it's me," he hissed. "Where's my brother, Rebecca?"

The woman choked briefly at that and then said, in a voice so quiet Murdoch could barely hear her, "He's dead."

He stepped forward, taking hold of her shoulders, lifting her almost bodily off the bed, bringing her eyes close to his, their noses nearly touching. "He can't be dead. Try again. Where is my brother?"

"He's dead! I told you he was dying! I told you to go and bring back this woman that he loved so much. And here you are, alone, hours after he passed. He died around midnight. Alone. Completely alone. You left and let him die alone, after what he did for you!"

For a moment Murdoch said nothing, foul-tasting bile

rising in his throat. Then he wrapped his fingers around the Abbess' neck, squeezing and squeezing while she struggled against him, grabbing at his hands, trying to remove them, reaching vainly for his face. In five minutes it was over and he let her limp body topple back on the bed. Then Murdoch, eyes burning with quiet, dangerous rage, stalked from the tent and disappeared into the last hour of darkness that remained.

CHAPTER 22

A ROLL OF THE DICE

Cara, seated outside the cave in the morning light, heard it first. The sun had cast a dazzling, warm glow over the world, and all around her the gray-green sea shimmered and winked. She felt a strange sense of exultancy at the new life in the cave behind her, at the trial and pain she had witnessed that had led to something so immeasurably beautiful. She had slept a little while after helping Esperanza clean herself and the infant, but then morning had broken, another morning on Lubrerum, when she had hoped the day before would be their last. She was sitting there, reveling in the beautiful glow of life that had fallen upon their tiny refuge, when she heard a long, high sound, echoing from the main island, the dirgelike howl of the great hounds pursuing their prey. She sat up in alarm and scrambled to the northern side of their islet, looking toward the shore in the distance. Of the dogs there was no sign save the continued distant baying, but she could see a form in the water, an unmistakable form wearing a floppy chapeau even as he swam.

Murdoch emerged onto the beach, dripping wet. He glanced back at Lubrerum and then headed directly toward the cave, with Cara following behind. "We have to leave. Now."

"Where's Louis?" asked Esperanza, rising in alarm, clutching her tiny infant in her arms.

"Louis isn't coming."

"What do you mean?"

"I mean he's dead!" snapped Murdoch, with vicious, heartless intensity.

As Cara watched, Esperanza's expression crumpled into such devastation and disbelief, that she thought her own heart would break for the arrogant woman. For her own part, she did not react. Somehow it was logical, it made sense, of course he was dead, of course that was going to be the outcome all along. First Robert, then Henry, now Louis. How much longer before both she and Rafael were dead too, and the only Firefax left was this cruel, hateful man called Thrayder? There was something, some terrible anger and sorrow rising within her, but she fought it. She could hear the glib voice of Istäni echoing in her mind: *We shall not all sleep, but we shall all be changed.* This was always going to be how their journey ended.

"What happened?" asked Cara, finding her voice choked and trembled a little in her throat, despite her detachment.

"If I stand here and tell you the whole story we might as well wait and Louis can tell you himself in hell when we're all dead," Murdoch sneered. "There's no time. We need to leave."

"How . . . how are we going to get out of here, Murdoch?" asked Rafael, holding back his own horror and questions about his brother's death, struggling to focus on the task at hand. "Esperanza has a newborn now."

"We sail the cutter around the west side of Lubrerum to take the *Apostle*, just like we always planned. But we have to pick up my crew from shore."

Rafael mechanically began gathering the things he had staged around the cave, exactly as he had planned for weeks.

Cara watched him, sensing that her brother was horrified and saddened and . . . angry, Cara thought. Rafael was angry. She could see it in his clenched jaw, his white knuckles, the unnecessary death grip on the strap of his satchel. She could also see his grim determination. He was going to get his sister off the island, and Esperanza, and the child, if it was the last thing he did.

The baby whimpered in his mother's arms as Esperanza settled in the stern of the cutter, but he soon fell asleep again as Murdoch and Rafael pushed the small vessel into the water, putting up the sail. Cara climbed in last of all, taking one set of oars, while Rafael took another, and they set off toward the shore that echoed with the howling of the hounds. Before they even neared the island, a group of desperate Lubrerites ran from cover, diving into the water and swimming toward them. Behind the fugitives the hounds burst from the shrubbery, practically dragging their handlers into the water after their quarry. Murdoch steered the cutter toward the swimmers and they assisted the men and women over the side, one by one, nearly tipping the boat over in the process. Cara thrust oars into their hands the moment they boarded, demanding that they row as if their lives depended on it. The shore was alive with common soldiers in chainmail and green tunics, knights in gleaming plate armor, and Thrateers wearing their tall plumed helmets, waving and shouting and following the boat along the shoreline. As Murdoch steered expertly among the tall rocks, a few small fishing boats appeared in their wake, coming around the eastern side of the island.

"They are following us!" Rafael cried.

"They won't catch us with this wind," replied Murdoch, smug and confident.

"Maybe we ought to just take the cutter and go," Rafael suggested, for what seemed to him the thousandth time. "We don't need the *Apostle*. We can make do with this smaller boat, until we reach another island, or mainland, or something. Someplace civilized."

Murdoch shook his head. "We're taking the *Apostle*, or rather, *you're* taking the *Apostle*." He shifted the heading of the little cutter toward the long peninsula jutting off the island.

"What do you mean?"

Murdoch did not reply and continued steering for the outcropping of land, while all the Lubrerites in the ship watched him in terror. The little fishing vessels behind them were beginning to catch up, similarly making use of rowers. The cutter's keel scraped against the rocks in the water, nearly overturning. Murdoch yanked the tiller still harder, aiming the prow directly toward the beach.

"They're gaining on us!" cried Rafael. "Murdoch! Why are you taking us so close to the shore?"

"I'm not taking you close to shore, I'm taking you to shore," Murdoch answered, and, a second later they ran aground, the crew tumbling over each other from the sharp, jolting stop. Murdoch leaped into the water, yanking the boat a few more feet up in the sand. The cries of their pursuers and the baying of the hounds were getting much louder.

Murdoch turned to Rafael. "You need to take these men and women, and Esperanza, and commandeer the *Apostle*. It's less than an hour on foot, at a run."

"What about you?"

"I'm taking Cara with me. We'll knock out your nearest pursuers. Meet us on the north side of the island when it's over."

"When what's over?"

"The north side, Rafael. Cara, with me." Cara, bewildered, but her curiosity getting the better of her, started to follow Murdoch into the dense jungle of the peninsula.

"How do you expect me to commandeer a ship with this motley crew?" asked Rafael, incredulous. "We have one sword,

Murdoch, no other weapons. We left in such a rush, we have nothing. If we even make it to the ship, what the hell are we supposed to do?"

"Oh, I'm sorry," said Murdoch, turning to face Rafael with an amused, taunting smirk. "I thought you were a Firefax."

Rafael rankled at that and turned back to the disheveled, terrified Lubrerites, waving for them to follow him. They set off through the trees, in the opposite direction from Murdoch and Cara, who had headed toward the towering volcano. The islanders knew the way to the *Apostle* and took the lead. Rafael maintained a rear guard, brandishing their one weapon, the broadsword that Murdoch had taken from the armory in Fluic Praem a few weeks before.

Esperanza stayed near Rafael, terrified that any stumble would cause her to crush the tiny burden in her arms. She was still bleeding heavily into the sea sponges that Cara had found for her, and she was exhausted, her usual tan skin a ghostly pale. Still she raced on doggedly, trying to keep up with Rafael. They tore through dense, overgrown forest, stumbling over logs, battling through grabbing vines and tangles of brambles. No matter how fast they ran, the baying of the hounds still drew closer.

"I thought Murdoch was going to kill our pursuers," panted Esperanza.

"He probably did, but not all of them," replied Rafael. "He wouldn't want to deprive me of the opportunity to use my skills, you know."

Esperanza flashed a brief, strained grin. "You know him well, don't you?"

"I do now."

Just as Rafael said this, six Lubrerite guards in chain mail burst from the trees ahead of them, cutting them off from the rest of the party. Rafael could hear running feet behind them, and the dogs, the loud, gasping, hoarse noise of dogs straining against their collars. Rafael broke into a sprint, running directly at the soldiers blocking their path. An instant later two of the soldiers were dead, while Rafael was locked in combat with the other four.

Esperanza snatched up one of the swords from the men Rafael had killed. Holding the weapon in one hand and clutching her infant in the other, she turned as two enormous slavering hounds burst through the brush behind them. The dogs growled and tore against their collars, dragging their handlers. They had been bred, raised, and trained for hunting and killing, and now their prey stood before them, pale and anemic, smelling of blood, holding a squeaking, helpless bundle of flesh in her arm. Esperanza struggled with the heavy sword, trying to remember what few skills Cara and Rafael had managed to teach her in the last two months.

The dog handlers glanced at each other, and then they released the animals, who tore forward, snapping and growling. Esperanza, struggling to keep her child away from them, cut a wide slash across the rib cage of one hound as the other caught hold of her leg, snarling and tearing into her flesh. She managed to sever the ear of the one gnawing on her leg and it fell back, yelping in pain. Both bleeding dogs crouched low and circled her. One moved around to attack her from behind, the other distracting her from the front, where she menaced the animal with her sword. She glanced over her shoulder to see the dog behind her pouncing and swung madly, slicing the animal's throat. It dropped, flailing and dying. The other hound lunged forward while Esperanza was distracted, but it was Rafael that blocked it, cutting the animal's head clean off just before it caught hold of the arm in which Esperanza was clutching her newborn son. Esperanza and Rafael stood back to back against the remaining soldiers, swords raised.

Just as the Lubrerite soldiers attacked, Murdoch's crew of

fugitives returned through the trees, picking up weapons from the trail of fallen men that Rafael had left in his wake. They stormed the soldiers with high-pitched cries of rage. In a few moments the glade was quiet, save for the panting breaths of the fugitives.

"Well, let's not stick around for more of that, shall we?" said Rafael. "Arm yourselves, if you haven't already, and let's move!"

The Lubrerites wore the panicked expressions of people realizing that they had taken the last step in a dangerous journey, the step from which there can be no turning back. One of them, a tall, broad-shouldered woman, called out in Erlandagar and the others grimly nodded, falling in again behind her and Rafael. They ran on, their sides aching, their lungs burning, Esperanza limping badly from the dog bite, trailing blood behind her. Rafael was doing little better, his own wounded leg screaming out for rest, every step a wrench of agony, and the baying of the hounds in the distance was growing louder again.

At last they crouched, gasping in the dense jungle overgrowth that grew along the narrow peninsula lining Lubrerum's harbor, gazing down along the dock at the *Apostle*, motionless and waiting. The crew aboard, excited by the trumpets and hounds baying in the distance, paced along the deck, watching the shore. Beside her, Esperanza heard Rafael draw in a breath sharply as he scanned the sea beyond.

He pointed out toward a distant vessel and whispered, "Istäni."

She nodded, numb, exhausted, bleeding, too far gone to experience any thrill of emotion at Istäni's long-expected return. What did it matter now, if they were all going to die?

The *Penumbra*'s sails were reefed and she sat already anchored, unmoving on the glass-like ocean beyond. Esperanza could see beads of sweat rolling down Rafael's face as he studied the *Penumbra* and then the *Apostle* in rapid succession. He turned to the fugitives, crouched low around him, all staring back at him with fear and desperation in their glassy eyes.

"You all speak English?" he asked.

They nodded.

"We learned it in school," explained the tall woman who had led the escapees against the Lubrerite soldiers in the forest. "I am Sarah Stellenc. I was a schoolmaster."

"Good, then listen to me. I need you to split into two parties. One will board from fore, one from aft. There are what, twenty guards aboard the *Apostle*?"

"There's thirty men on that ship, sir," replied Stellenc. "They keep it ready to sail at any time. Though it's rare enough that it does go out."

"Thirty, that's not bad," said Rafael.

The ten Lubrerites looked at him in surprise and then at each other with alarm.

"If I may say, sir, none of us are soldiers," said one of the men.

"Nor do I expect you to be," Rafael snapped. "Now split into groups. You, since you are speaking back to me, you lead your people over the prow, and you, Stellenc, lead the party over the stern. We aim to crowd them in the middle. Esperanza, you'll stay here this time."

Esperanza glanced anxiously back at the forest, where the baying of the hounds still sounded, growing ever nearer.

"Where will you be, sir?" asked Stellenc.

"Aloft," said Rafael with a nod toward the rigging. "Give me about twenty minutes to get up there before you move."

"Someone will see you!"

"Perhaps," said Rafael, then, leaning in, he spoke quietly to Stellenc, so quietly that Esperanza could not hear what he said.

Esperanza frowned as Rafael secured his sword on his back and stowed a knife in his belt. She caught his arm just before he slipped away.

"You shouldn't, Raf. Your leg isn't up to a climb like that. How are you going to get up there without them seeing you?"

"I'm a Firefax, aren't I?" asked Rafael, winking roguishly back at her. On his face he wore the unmistakable thrill of the chase, the hunt, and the coming kill. For a moment, with his wink, his haughty assurance, he did not look like Rafael at all to his sister-in-law. He looked, for the first time, just like Murdoch, with that same wild, dark exultation in the glory of battle and death. Then he was gone, melting into the underbrush as though he had never been there.

Esperanza was never sure after how Rafael got on the ship. Later she surmised that he must have swum underwater all the way around to the larboard side and ascended there, as all the sailors were intently staring at the shore to starboard.

After clumsily attaching their own weapons to their belts, the islanders crept down through the brush, closer to the dock. Esperanza scanned the rigging, finally catching sight of Rafael. He was perched just above the main topsail, dripping wet and peering down at the deck below him.

Stellenc suddenly shoved one of the young men from the brush and he raced down to the dock. Esperanza felt her heart sinking as the youth's feet pattered along the wooden boards. He stopped, panting, and shouted up to the deck crew in Erlandagar. There was a brief exchange, and then the crew's gazes followed the young messenger's pointing finger toward Rafael. A moment later the rigging was swarming with men climbing toward Rafael, who, clenching his knife in his teeth, began climbing higher in the ropes.

The infant started sobbing in Esperanza's arms. The baying of the hounds was too close and they had been betrayed by Murdoch's band of Lubrerites. This, then, was the end of the whole terrible adventure. And in that moment all Esperanza wanted was the husband she had so thoroughly spurned and so long hated. Confident, charming, stupid, wonderful Louis. The overwhelming sense of loss washed over her again, choking her, suffocating her, as she prepared to watch Rafael die, and then to die herself. She closed her eyes, not daring to look at the traitors gathered around her in the brush, steeling herself for the end, gripping the sword she had dragged all the way to the harbor. She set her jaw. She would fight, she decided, though it did not matter; she would fight until the end, the way she was certain Louis had. Her eyes snapped open and she raised the sword, just as the Lubrerites around her erupted into horrendous, earsplitting battlecries.

The Lubrerites, rather than turning on her, burst through the brush and ran out along the wooden dock toward the *Apostle*. Whatever the young man had told the *Apostle*'s crew, he had done well, and they continued their clambering pursuit of Rafael, fearing no danger from their own fellow islanders racing toward them. They kept climbing until the two boarding parties had made it aboard and attacked the captain and first officer. In panic the crew began a frantic descent to engage the new, unexpected threat on deck.

High in the rigging, Rafael's eyes glowed with pleasure as most of his pursuers turned back, struggling to climb down without being skewered by the Lubrerite fugitives waiting below. He managed to dispatch the remaining six in the rigging, knocking one loose from the ropes to fall to his death on the deck below, another into the lagoon; the other four he put his broadsword through. Many of the crew on deck were quickly felled by the dogged determination of the escaped Lubrerites, but a small contingent managed to cluster on the quarterdeck, holding their assailants at bay with their blades. Rafael's look of pride faded as he saw the sailors swivel the stern chaser to face the fugitives on the main deck. At the same moment, hearing a disturbance, he glanced toward the jungle and saw Esperanza burst from the brush, her sword lost, running, practically dragging her bleeding leg, with two more hounds and a host of Lubrerites racing after her.

<hr>

Far away, ascending the volcano, Cara heard the distant sound of what she thought was thunder, at first, then recognized as cannon fire. She was pouring sweat as she climbed behind the indefatigable Murdoch. He had killed twenty men since they had parted ways with Rafael. To say that he had killed them easily would have been a criminal understatement; Murdoch made killing men look like child's play. She, with a sword taken from one of Murdoch's victims, barely had time to parry a few blows before he was done, and, before she could kill any of them herself, her own adversaries had fallen like wheat before her brother's blade. She was awed and terrified at once, scampering to chase after him each time he finished wiping out a group of pursuers and set off again with maddening speed. But, for the last mile, there had been no pursuers, and they were no longer following the line of the beach at all but ascending the mountain, along faint switchbacks that were nearly invisible to her, but not to Murdoch, who never wavered or slowed.

She turned back for an instant at the sound of the cannon firing again. When she whirled back to the path, Murdoch had disappeared. Gasping through burning lungs, she raced toward where she had last seen him as the ledge narrowed precipitously. Something grabbed her arm and yanked her to the side. She toppled as she reacted to the attack, raising her blade as her feet left the rock face, her body swinging wildly into nothing. But the iron grasp clung to her arm as she fell. She struck the rock face hard and then braced her trembling feet against the side of the mountain. She swung her weapon at the person holding her arm, before she saw that it was Murdoch, with his habitual mocking smile.

"If you cut my arm you'll fall to your death, you know," he said as he hoisted her onto the ledge beside him. He had vanished into a dark cave, which now stood gaping before them. "Reached your destination only to fall off the side of the mountain. You've a great deal to learn yet, Cara."

"I'm not sure I should have expected a hand to reach out of the mountain and grab me," she retorted.

"That's where you and I differ, I suppose."

"Did you hear the cannon?" she asked, looking back worriedly toward the peninsula and the inlet where the *Apostle* sat, obscured from their vision by the side of the volcano.

"Yes. You think our noble, pious brother has come to his end?"

"Of course not!" she cried, quelling the panic in her voice with difficulty, struggling to repress the urge to run back down the mountain to make sure Rafael was all right.

Murdoch disappeared again into the dark recesses of the cave, and, after a moment, she heard flint against steel and saw a flash of light. A torch in Murdoch's hand illuminated the dark walls. He gestured into the twisting cave system beyond.

"Coming?"

She nodded, swallowing her fears of what might be happening to Rafael, or what might already have happened, trying not to think that she and this human monster were the only Firefaxes left. She plunged after him, stumbling through rocky, tight crevices that threatened to squeeze the very life out of her. They pushed on, and on, and on, until she was quite lost in the convoluted maze of the endless network of caves. It felt as if they had been in the heart of the volcano forever, and all noises from outside faded away, all knowledge of the outside disappeared, all sense of time and space was lost as the air grew musty and dank.

She found her mind churning in torment again. Visions of her family flitted in her mind. Robert, dead, first of all. Then Henry, gone forever. Then Louis, dead by some unknown mechanism, after all he had been through, after how hard she had tried to save him, and now, somewhere beyond the slick walls of stone that had become her only reality, she felt certain Rafael too had died. It would just be her and her mirror left, this evil, hateful creature ahead of her. There would be no other Firefaxes, just the two of them, living out their bitter, lonely existences. As the despair rose up, threatening to suffocate her, she turned another corner, around which the light had briefly vanished, and then froze with a sharp intake of breath.

In the dim light of the torch lay dozens of barrels, filling the cavern, barrels that contained something with a sharp, acrid smell. She stared at the barrels, then down at the ground, where a thin black wick led away from them, into another cave, and another one beyond that, barely visible in the flicker of light cast by Murdoch's torch.

"What is this place?"

"Just one of a thousand such places hidden in the caves of Lubrerum, all perfectly spaced apart, all connected together by these wicks."

Cara stared, mouth open, then turned toward her brother with accusing eyes. "'Because thou hast let from thy hand a man I appointed to utter destruction, therefore thy life shall go for his life, and thy people for his people' . . . this was your plan all along? If you can't have the wealth of the island, no one can?"

"This was my plan all along," replied Murdoch simply.

"Why bring me here? So we can both die together in the rubble of Lubrerum?"

Murdoch chuckled and then handed her the torch. "I brought you here because I thought you might like to do the honors, Cara Firefax, who has never killed a man."

She held the torch away as if it would bite her. "Why would I do that? There are ten thousand people on this island."

"Closer to eight thousand, actually."

"There are medicines and technologies here that border on the supernatural. Wondrous, lifesaving tools that will never be seen again."

Murdoch shrugged. "Maybe not."

"Then why would I destroy it? My inheritance is here."

"Yes. Indeed it is. An inheritance of lunacy."

"How do you even know if this will work? You think these wicks are still intact? How many years have these been planted here? You think the powder is dry?"

"Because I've checked every single one of these caves and every wick, and every barrel, Cara. You think I've spent the last few months on this island picking my toes in the sun, learning how to weave baskets? Istäni didn't know all the secrets Grandfather confided in me. He didn't tell me only where Lubrerum was, but also how to destroy it, when the time came."

"You can't do this. Eight thousand lives. You're not God, Murdoch, to send them to judgment like this."

"That's where you're wrong, Cara. What is God, except what people make him out to be? And here, on Lubrerum, I am God. The Firefaxes are God. These people have made us their gods. We bring them the Word, and they obey it. And if you have made someone your God, and you displease that God, what, naturally, should follow?"

"You're insane."

"Am I?"

"Why would I do this?"

"Because Louis wasn't supposed to die, Cara."

She shuddered and felt the same strange cold sweat she had known nearly a year before. She could hear the drumming of that mare's hooves and the thuds of her father's dead body against the frozen earth. She shivered, clenching her fists. "What do you mean?" she asked through gritted teeth.

"He wasn't supposed to die. Their Abbess tricked him into a fight that he won, you know that? He won a battle on the island against the greatest knight among them. Defeated the man, killed him, in a feat of such courage and strength that even I have never seen the like. He was wounded, but he was on the island of Lubrerum, where they can save anyone, with their surgical skills, their ventilation box, their medicines injected directly into the bloodstream. He should have lived, Cara. He wasn't supposed to die. They killed him. This bloody cursed island with its mad cult of believers killed your Losi."

She felt tears building in her eyes, and the quiet rage, which had started to simmer behind her detached facade when Murdoch first said Louis was dead, growing again inside her, a rolling hurricane of unquenchable rage. She blinked hard and said, "You loved him too."

"Why do you say that?"

"Otherwise you would not have brought me here. You would not have cared enough to destroy Lubrerum."

"Maybe I did . . . love him, as you say. But it doesn't matter now. He's dead, and there's nothing left but this. You, me, this torch, and heaven or hell waiting for the arrival of eight thousand murderous fanatics."

"Did you kill Henry?"

Murdoch looked at her with a strange, incredulous stare. "What a stupid question. It's as if, for all your pretenses at familial devotion, you don't know any of your brothers at all. The sooner you finish this, the sooner we can go and make sure the last person that you love in all the world is still alive."

She shook her head, trying to quell the smoldering rage that continued to grow within her. "I'm not going to do it."

"What will you do then, Cara Firefax? Are you going to go back to the colonies, marry some man that you have no taste for, raise his children, slaughter chickens, cook, and mend for the rest of your life? Who's going to carry on the family name if not you? Who's going to reaccrue our wealth? Who's going to rebuild what Istäni destroyed? Rafael? Even if he's still alive, he has no stomach for it. Henry didn't either, though I do give him credit for trying. Louis could have done it. He was good enough, a bit thick, but so was Robert. But he's dead now. So who does that leave, girl? It leaves you, and me. What are you saving yourself for? What other future do you have? You are a killer, Cara, through and through, a cold-blooded killer like me. You were bred and raised to murder. You can't escape it, you can't run away from it, you can't continue pretending it's not true. Sooner or later you have to embrace who and what you are. Now I'm giving you this one chance to avenge your brother. This is your chance to prove your point, that a person with my skills and abilities who dares to love is more dangerous than one who cares for nothing."

"What if I don't do it?" she asked, her mouth dry, the anger and hatred rising like a choking bile in her throat. All the months caring for Louis, wanting nothing more than to save him, whatever the cost, all for naught. Her brother was gone. Another brother she would never see again, never laugh with again, never fight alongside again.

Murdoch tossed his head back and laughed, the awful, throaty croaking sound echoing off the stone walls pressing in around them. He laughed for a long time, until Cara, still clutching the torch, clamped her hands over her ears, trying unsuccessfully to keep out the evil in those horrible cackles. When at last he stopped, she lifted her hands from her ears.

"It doesn't matter what you choose, Cara. Lubrerum ends today."

She shook her head, trying to clear the echoes of Murdoch's laughter, but the sound that filled the space left behind was the ominous staccato beat of a phantom horse at a gallop, growing louder and louder.

"You were so close, Murdoch," she whispered. "So very close."

"So close to what?"

"So close to being human."

Rafael caught hold of a line and swung down from the rigging to land on the quarterdeck behind the gun crew just as Esperanza's feet started pounding along the wooden dock. In the chaos that descended on the quarterdeck, Rafael cut his way through the gunners and spun the chaser just as his fugitive band gained the quarterdeck. In the melee, someone had the foresight to cut the *Apostle*'s anchor and the ship was drifting away from the dock, away from Esperanza. He snatched the torch from a dead gunner and touched it to the wick. A second later, a deafening explosion sounded and there was nothing but blood, smoke, and screams behind Esperanza as she made a desperate leap, clutching her infant. She landed with a splash, struggling to swim while holding the newborn above the water.

"Bring her aboard!" cried Rafael, working rapidly to reload the chaser, aiming it again at the Lubrerites on the shore as they stumbled over the maimed, dismembered bodies of their fellow islanders. He fired again as the *Apostle* drifted still further out toward the end of the inlet.

The remaining crew of the *Apostle*, about fifteen in all, had surrendered when Rafael took the chaser. The fugitives rushed to lower a net that Esperanza scrambled into while her newborn infant screamed his faint, pathetic cries.

"We make for the north of the island!" cried Rafael, looking back toward their pursuers standing useless on what remained of the dock. He turned and cast his gaze out to sea. The sails of the *Penumbra* had unfurled and she was bearing toward them.

Though not sailors by trade, there was not a Lubrerite that did not know the basics of sailing; they were an island people, after all. He watched with satisfaction as they moved about the ship rapidly to carry out his orders. She handled easily enough, he thought as he took her helm, using the knowledge he had gained in their months aboard the *Mariposa*, steering her out of the small enclosed lagoon. It took well over an hour for them to round the lagoon edge and turn toward the north side of the island, and by then the *Penumbra* was well upon them.

As they rounded the lagoon, a shot rang out from the fore-chaser of the *Penumbra*, splashing water on Rafael as he steered. Istäni was aiming for her rudder, looking to disable her. Rafael scanned the shore anxiously, but there was no sign of Murdoch or Cara. Another ball from the *Penumbra* hit the rail near him and he yanked his hand back from the helm, an enormous splinter protruding from his forearm. Tearing it out, he called for more sails and, ignoring the blood, turned his attention back to the shore of Lubrerum.

Then he heard it—a sound, a distant, muffled rumble, followed by another, and another, and he turned in bewilderment toward the volcano. There were blasts of fire and rock erupting from the stone sides of the mountain. Every few dozen yards explosions rocketed forth, showers of stone, dust, fire, and smoke, creating a perfect ring of destruction. Rafael's mouth dropped open, even as his heart sank. In a few moments the base all along the northern wall of the volcano had been blown out, and the dome began to crumble. Another explosion sounded and the rim of the entire northern side of the volcano sagged. More explosions blasted forth and then the entire north wall of Lubrerum's volcano fell inward, collapsing in an overwhelming haze of dust and smoke. There were more explosions, all along the eastern and western sides of the mountain, and finally to the south as well. There were detonations along the shoreline too, the water quivering, as if someone were blasting beneath the very sand of the ocean floor. All-consuming, choking stone dust rose up as the entire volcano caved in upon itself with a rumbling that seemed to shake the very foundations of the earth. The air was so full of dust that for a moment Rafael could not breathe or see at all, gasping and choking along with everyone else. As the dust cleared a little, he could just make out the Lubrerites aboard, captured crew and fugitives alike, staring in absolute shock at the rubble that remained of the only place they had ever known.

In a few moments there was nothing left of the volcano but a heap of debris, still with faint, muffled explosions ringing out, deafening across the wide expanse of water. Rafael spun the wheel, feeling the pull of new, powerful currents, created as water seemed to rush away beneath them, streaming toward the island as if to swallow it up.

"All sails! Drop every bloody sail she's got, turn the main topsails to the wind, turn them to the damn wind!" he cried.

They turned, in a halting, agonizingly slow maneuver, making their course east and north, and Rafael set his teeth grimly, tears, rock, and grime staining his cheeks. The wind from the west cleared a bit of the debris for just an instant, and Rafael saw that the caldera of the fallen volcano was filling with water. There was nothing to see of the civilization that had lived there, of the city of gold, of anything, save a crumbled, enormous heap of stones.

"Wait! Wait!" cried Esperanza, pointing wildly toward the water. "There! Do you see them? Rafael, you have to wait!"

Rafael turned and saw through the haze of dust, two tiny forms swimming toward the ship. They were dark, familiar forms, black hair, long arms and legs, one towing the other.

"Throw them a line!" he called, hardly daring to hope that what he saw was real.

The Lubrerites, still reeling, half of them sobbing even as they worked, cast ropes into the water, and Murdoch caught hold of one of these, clinging to it as they towed him in. He handed the stupefied, shivering form of Cara up first. She had a gash across her forehead and looked dazed and distant, uncomprehending of anything happening around her. She sat on the deck in a puddle of muddy water and smiled at last when Rafael, having passed off the helm, reached her side and knelt beside her.

"You're all right, you're all right," she whispered, but her eyes stared past him.

He shuddered, remembering the way she had looked the day Robert died, and seeing the same strange expression on her face, as though she were a million miles away, wholly unreachable and untouchable. He hugged her and kissed her cheek, then began fussing over the wound on her head anxiously, blood still streaming down his own arm. Murdoch, ignoring his siblings, stalked to the quarterdeck, shoved the slobbering, sobbing Lubrerite at the helm aside, and turned the ship two points further east.

The *Penumbra* had given up her pursuit, veering toward the still-collapsing island. The bewildered crew of the *Apostle* raced to do the bidding of their new, hideous captain. Under his practiced hand the ship began to make speed, and before long they were putting distance between themselves, their former pursuers, and the shattered remnants of Lubrerum. Once Murdoch stopped belting out orders, the escapees and the former crew of the *Apostle* lay weeping together in confused, worthless heaps on the deck. Some had screamed for the ship to turn back, to look for survivors, but Murdoch savagely refused. As they watched, the *Penumbra* put down her anchor near what remained of the shore, and they could see the movement on the beach of the few who had not been in the caldera, those that had been pursuing the fugitives on the island, making their way across the beach, toward Istäni's ship in slow, huddled groups.

"What the hell happened?" demanded a voice. She wanted to answer, but the voice wasn't talking to her, and she was too far away anyway from that familiar, angry voice.

The speaker, a vague, ghostlike form, was staring past her, toward the quarterdeck, toward someone there, something there. Cara frowned. It was Raf speaking, she thought, or it sounded like him. But he was dead, so it couldn't be him. Perhaps, she reflected, she was dead too. She should be dead. She felt dead.

Of course it was Raf, she chided herself, he had been there all along, gently cleaning her forehead. She smiled at that. He didn't need to be so gentle. He didn't know that she felt nothing, nothing at all anymore. He had kept repeating over and over again, "You're fine, Cara, you're all right." so many times that even when he stopped, the phrase rolled through her mind like waves against the beach.

"How should I know? It's an island, out here in the middle of nowhere, attached to no other landform. An island like that is inherently unstable. I guess today was the day." The other voice was harsh and grating; it made her body shudder, and the hairs on her arm and neck stand up. Perhaps she was not beyond feeling after all.

"That's stupid, Murdoch. Those explosions were not some random event."

"Maybe the water hit the pyrite under the sea just so, or whatever Buffon has been postulating. The island was a volcano, after all. Anyway, I'm not particularly interested in exchanging geological theories with you right now, little brother."

"What are you particularly interested in talking about, then?"

"Not particularly interested in talking at all. Perhaps you should ask your sister if you're so keen on learning what happened to Lubrerum."

Cara's nose wrinkled. Her spectacles were gone; she hadn't realized that before. They were lost, somewhere in the caves of Lubrerum, or perhaps in the water. Gone beyond recall, like her father, like her brothers, like her, now. She was gone too, she felt that keenly. Soon she would be away forever, with all the lost things that haunted her, joined with Robert, with Henry, with Louis, with the dead Lubrerites, with that poor, dumb mare, with those lost spectacles.

"She won't say anything. She's in some sort of trance, or shock, I don't know. I can't . . . I can't get through to her."

Cara considered this stupidly. He was right; Raf was right. She was very far away from them, safely out of reach, and getting further away every second, entering that beautiful dreamlike state she had known the day Robert died. This time she would stay there, in the faraway halls of her repressed madness, where it was safe.

"Well, then, I suppose that's that," came the croaking voice of her oldest brother. "We shall just have to let some mysteries remain mysteries."

Both men fell silent after that. Beautifully, perfectly silent. Cara reveled in that quiet, melting into nonexistence as the sun sank behind the waves. Heatless fingers of light stretched out to caress their vessel, bathing the sorrowful crew of survivors in a glow of vibrant sepia. Then, at first so soft Cara wasn't sure it was real, a sound entered her battered consciousness. It rose, higher and higher, irrefutable, piercing, bursting unwelcome through the clouds of withdrawal. At last, urged by Esperanza's relentless voice in its haunted visceral ecstasy of grief, Cara Firefax wept.

> *"Tristes apprêts, pâles flambeaux,*
> *Jour plus affreux que les ténèbres*
> *Astres lugubres des tombeaux,*
> *Non, je ne verrai plus que vos clartés funèbres.*
>
> *"Toi, qui vois mon cœur éperdu,*
> *Père du jour, ô soleil, ô mon pére !*
> *Je ne veux plus d'un bien que Castor*
> *Et je renonce à la lumière.*
>
> *"Tristes apprêts, pâles flambeaux,*
> *Jour plus affreux que les ténèbres*
> *Astres lugubres des tombeaux,*
> *Non, je ne verrai plus que vos clartés funèbres."*

THE END

A Note to the Reader

Dear Reader,

Thank you from the bottom of my heart for taking the time to read *Firefax*. This is a story I wrote as an escape during dark times. For more about why I wrote this, feel free to review my substack post, found here: https://substack.com/@amvergara/p-137776286

If you enjoyed the book and have a few minutes to spare, I sincerely appreciate any ratings or reviews you are able to provide on whatever retail site you used to purchase the book, or through Amazon, Goodreads, LibraryThing, or StoryGraph. Your honest ratings and reviews help me to reach other readers who may enjoy this work.

Many thanks again for your time, and I hope you never have the misfortune of crossing paths with a Firefax.

With gratitude and in solidarity,

Amelia Maria Vergara

Acknowledgments

This book would not have been possible if not for the tireless support of my beloved soon-to-be husband, Eric. I must also acknowledge my betareader Mina, who believed in my work and gave me one of the greatest compliments a writer could ever receive. Thanks to my critique partner, PurpleEggHead who really kept me going during the darkest moments of this endeavor. Many thanks to my tireless copyeditor Eliza Dee of Clio Editing Services, and my meticulous proofreader Daniel Pugsley.

I spent countless hours researching from many sources, and would like to particularly acknowledge the works of Thomas More, Dale Taylor, Patrick O'Brian, Catherine Thrush, Robert Middlekauff, and Kenneth A. Daigler, though the numerous other resources I used would be enough to fill an entire library in themselves. Special thanks to Vulgar Language Generator for the creation of Erlandagar. There were many other people who, whether they knew it or not, were an enormous encouragement and support during the process of writing this work and provided help with publishing. Thanks to Logolane for the press logo. For typography on the cover I am indebted to Casey White. For my author portrait a huge thanks to Erika Saguran.

Finally, but most importantly, I want to say a special thank you to Ellie, my Rafael, and without a doubt my most faithful and reliable reader. My many other siblings, my weekly library writing group, and my friends were also hugely important in the process of writing this, and especially my mother who put the drive and love of reading and writing in me and my father who gave me my fanatical devotion to the outdoors and history which I know shines through these pages. Thank you all for believing in me and encouraging me to tell this story.

About the Author

(Author Portrait Courtesy of Erika Seguran)

A.M. Vergara is not an assassin, but she is one of eleven siblings and thus has a unique perspective allowing her to write a story revolving around the complexities of sibling relationships. When not writing and reading voraciously she can be found working her day job in the hospital as a physician associate or on the ambulance as a paramedic, or out in the woods, camping, hiking, foraging for edible mushrooms, searching for reptiles and amphibians, riding her mule, or playing her banjo.

www.ingramcontent.com/pod-product-compliance
Lightning Source LLC
Chambersburg PA
CBHW061300190726
48288CB00002B/286